Through
THORNS

Through
THORNS

MARK VULLIAMY

IGUANA

Published by Iguana Books
720 Bathurst Street, Suite 303
Toronto, Ontario, Canada
M5S 2R4

Publisher: Meghan Behse
Editor: Paula Chiarcos
Front cover design: Ruth Dwight, www.designplayground.ca

Issued in print and electronic formats.
ISBN 978-1-77180-503-2 (paperback)
ISBN 978-1-77180-504-9 (ebook)

This is an original print edition of *Through Thorns*.

To Teresa, Claire and Evan, my family and my foundation, with much love for your constant support.

One

2007

The main penitentiary gate opened on schedule, without any last-minute hitch. Sandra Treming and four other old cons walked out into a rainy Monday morning. All dressed in their best civvies, each clutching an identical plastic drawstring bag of personal possessions. Not talking to each other, they headed in a loose formation across the parking lot to a shuttle bus that would take them into the city. Sandra had served twenty-five years, with no time off for good behaviour nor, for that matter, time added for bad behaviour. Technically though, she was still serving a life sentence. For the rest of her life she would have to check in on a regular basis at a parole office. But today she was leaving the pen, and part of her was thinking there had to be a catch. It couldn't be this easy. At any second some screw might run out from the prison gate and drag her back inside. In a way she would welcome that. The air outside was intoxicating, but the prospect of living free, terrifying.

Halfway across the parking lot Sandra noticed a crowd clustered around the shuttle. As it was sinking in that they were media, she heard a voice to her right. "Sandra! Sandra Treming!" She turned to see a stranger rising out of a parked car and waving. Male, about the same age as her, possibly a little younger. Car, new and immaculate. Her impulse was to bolt, either to the shuttle or back into the prison; she couldn't decide which option would be safer.

"Sandra, it's me, Norbert. Norbert Cubbin." The man came forward a few paces. "Come on. I'll drive you into town. Hurry!"

A hubbub broke out over by the shuttle; alerted by Norbert's shout, the reporters and camera people had gotten a fix on their target. Norbert advanced quickly, grabbed Sandra's arm and pulled her into a run away from the baying pack. He propelled her down the passenger side of his car and sprinted around to the driver's side. Sandra lost her balance and stumbled against a panel van parked beside Norbert's vehicle. The van came to life with a series of angry honks. She pushed herself backward and Norbert opened his passenger door just in time to catch her. She flopped awkwardly onto the seat next to him. With Sandra's feet still protruding from the car, Norbert reversed out of the parking spot. She managed to pull herself in before he shifted into drive, and forward momentum closed the door. A close call. One of the more athletic reporters managed to bang on the trunk twice; the rest of the hounds barked questions from farther back.

At the parking lot exit Sandra looked up at a guard in one of the outer towers staring impassively down at the ruckus below. She was out of her cage; he was still inside his. She stuck out her tongue and waved.

Norbert didn't speak as they drove down the road coiling across the open expanse around the prison. He concentrated on negotiating sharp unbanked curves, which were there Sandra knew so no one could come or go in a hurry, or without being seen. She held her breath and tightly gripped the sides of her seat until they reached a final cordon of light standards at the outer edge of the prison grounds where the road straightened. Norbert checked his rearview mirror and grinned. Sandra looked over her shoulder and saw a convoy of media vehicles only now leaving the parking lot. They exhaled their relief in unison. Sandra let go of her seat and put both feet up on the dashboard. Norbert stepped on the gas and the car picked up speed. "I'll lose our tail before we hit the highway. Feet on the floor and fasten your seat belt."

Seat belt? Sandra brought her feet down, lifted her bum off the seat and rummaged underneath where she expected the seat belt to be. Norbert reached across in front of her, so dangerously close to her breasts she almost swatted his hand away. He took hold of something beyond her range of vision, drew it across her body and clicked it into place. It was two seat belts joined together, and as she settled back in her seat, the straps tightened against her. Confined again. Fighting a rising panic, Sandra forced herself to breathe slowly and deeply. She was beginning to feel that getting into this car was a bad idea. But she was at a loss to figure what would have been a good idea.

They drove on in silence for a while, Norbert making frequent turns such that Sandra became utterly disoriented. She hoped the media dogs were lost as well. Every few seconds Norbert checked his rearview mirror and nodded — tail successfully lost, evidently. But was her driver really Norbert Cubbin? She tried to extrapolate this well-dressed middle-aged man from the ragged boy she knew so many years ago. The connection just wasn't there. She didn't recall the younger Norbert even being able to drive. "You've changed," she said.

"Sure." Norbert turned his head to examine Sandra at length. The extended scrutiny made her uncomfortable and not only because his eyes weren't on the road. "You have too. It's been what? Twenty something years?"

"Twenty-five. But you still recognized me right away."

Norbert turned his attention back to the road. "Well, I heard you were going to be released today. Marked my calendar. No one else coming out of the gate could've been a match. Then I saw you scrunch up your mouth and grab the back of your neck. Something you always used to do when you were about to make a decision."

"I don't do that."

"Yes you do. You really haven't changed all that much. Although, I don't remember you having much in the way of muscle. If you don't mind me saying so, you're looking buff."

"I work out a lot. Helps pass the time. And people think twice about messing with you."

"I work out too. Well, I've got a gym membership but don't go as often as I should. What are the fitness facilities like in jail?"

"Totally Club Med." Norbert nodded and Sandra suppressed a laugh — same old gullible Norbert. "Pretty basic actually. But you don't need a gym to pump yourself up. There's no shortage of iron inside."

"Huh." Norbert studied Sandra again, his eyes sliding to and from the road ahead. "You almost look younger. Apart from the grey hair. Which suits you."

Sandra tucked her hair behind her ears and switched topics. "You never visited me."

Norbert shifted his weight in the driver's seat. Sandra thought he was pretending not to hear. She was casting about for something else to say when Norbert responded in an almost angry tone. "No, I didn't. I tried, Sandra, but it wasn't easy. They kept moving you around the country. And once when I did come, you were in solitary — no visitors allowed."

"I wasn't exactly a model prisoner. Early on."

Norbert took two long, controlled breaths and continued in a quiet voice. "Truth is, I didn't try too hard. The whole idea scared me. Being in jail. They could easily have locked me up too." More forced breathing. "I wasn't even sure you'd want to see me. Thought you might still be mad at me."

Instead of offering the reassurance Norbert seemed to be fishing for, Sandra nodded. She had been mad at him, mad at all her former comrades. At times in prison she thought she wanted to see some old familiar faces, but the few visitors she received either wanted to rehabilitate her or analyze her. Except on one occasion when a distant cousin implored her to accept Jesus as her lord and saviour. She instructed that cousin to go fuck himself and die.

A surge in acceleration brought Sandra back to the present. They were speeding up a freeway on-ramp to merge with heavy traffic. Sandra gasped to see so many vehicles around them. The rain was now torrential. Norbert jockeyed from lane to lane, at times passing through blasts of spray from large trucks. Sandra flinched with each blast, the road now menacing and their destination still uncertain. Her misgivings prompted a question she realized she should have asked before getting into the car: "Norbert, you know how to get to the halfway house, right?"

"Halfway house?" Norbert switched lanes. "What halfway house?"

"The halfway house the shuttle was taking us to, me and those other women. It's in town. We're supposed to stay there until we can get more permanently settled."

"So the Man lets you out of one box and puts you in another."

"Whatever. I need a place to live and I don't have a lot of money."

"Sandra, you're not going to a halfway house. I rented an apartment for you. And don't worry about money. I've got more than I know what to do with. You'll have a place to stay as long as you like. Absolutely free."

"Fuck, Norbert, what are you up to? The state has been controlling my life for twenty-five years and now you're going to start? Just take me downtown and let me out at a bus stop. I'll figure it out from there." Sandra accidentally hit a button on the door. The window rolled down; cold wind and rain buffeted her.

Norbert reached across and hit the button again. The window rolled back up. "I'm not trying to control you. I-I owe you this … at the very least."

"Fine, if you're not going to take me where I want to go, let me out right here." Indignation and rage surged. This was some imposter claiming to be Norbert, abducting her and tying her up with a seat belt. She had to take a stand now or never be free.

"I can't stop on the freeway. Against the law."

An absurd counter, given their shared history. Sandra stifled the laugh that would have undermined her credibility. "Pull off at the next exit then; I mean it."

"Okay, fine, you win. I'll let you off downtown."

Although nothing was familiar yet, Sandra could tell they were getting closer to the city. The farm acreage and remnant forest areas surrounding the prison were now yielding to tracts of suburbia. Roofs of houses poked above the cement walls bordering both sides of the freeway. Had living behind walls become the fashion now everywhere? Nothing to celebrate then, in getting out of prison. At least the routines in the joint were familiar.

From the crest of a hill she caught a glimpse down a sinuous corridor between two sets of interlocking townhouses. A paved road, no sidewalks and, abandoned at the end of a driveway, a solitary tricycle, the lone hint of human habitation. "So," she asked, "any idea where the others are these days? Louie or Phyl—"

"Phyl, that shithead — I don't know where the fuck he is and I don't want to. I hope he's rotting in the deepest pit in hell." Definitely not the Norbert of old — Mister Positive, as Sandra used to think of him. After a pause to regain his equanimity Norbert continued: "As for Louie, I dunno. Got a phone call from him once. He was pretty drunk and, you know how he gets, real ornery. He hung up on me without leaving his number. Not that I cared."

"How about Bet?"

"Yep, Bet's around. At least she's still in the phonebook. Tried calling her a couple of times. Only got an answering machine. But it was her voice, definitely her voice. Seems she's working for some kind of charity. I expect she's still doing what she's always done: scribbling on behalf of whatever cause she believes in now. Bet being Bet; same old same old."

"And you?"

"What about me?"

"Well, this car, the apartment, the money … you're rich now. How did that happen?"

"Oh I robbed a couple of banks." Norbert laughed and then abruptly turned serious. "Sorry, Sandra, that was insensitive."

"Don't worry about it. I'm not easy to wound. But seriously, what gives?"

Norbert gave vent to a deep sigh. "Basically I'm a sellout. After all the craziness back then, everybody either dead, in jail or in deep cover somewhere. Leaving me…" Norbert searched for the right word. "Stranded. For a while I drifted, totally bummed out. I really missed living with other people, friends. Like in Berkman House but, you know, more stable. So I started looking for ways to recreate that kind of connection. Even took some courses, can you believe it?"

"What kind?"

"Well, on how to set up a co-op or strata council, that sort of thing. Which led into actual work experience where my timing turned out to be pretty good. You know, there's a growing demand what with, baby boomers fed up with crash-pad chaos and big-city alienation, so I set 'em up with what they were hungry for. Real homes in an authentic community setting."

Norbert was starting to sound as if he was reciting ad copy. "So, basically you're a real estate agent." An unlikely career choice for any of the Berkman alumni. Hard to believe Norbert had changed so much since those days.

Norbert drove on without responding. After enduring a minute of sullen silence Sandra made an effort to reconnect. "Listen, I didn't mean to be rude. But if not real estate, what are we talking about?"

"I do development. Sure, real estate is a part of it. A small part. But there's so much more. In essence, I make real estate transactions worthwhile. I assemble properties — underused, old and rundown buildings — arrange financing, get rezonings approved by municipal governments, coordinate planning and design, etcetera, etcetera." His better mood restored, Norbert glanced over at Sandra. She looked back at him blankly.

"It's complicated. But the end result is new roofs over people's heads and more housing than there was before. Right in the heart of the city, not way out in the boonies with a one-hour commute, another hour back to the wife and kids. No, not for me; not for a lot of people."

Sandra just nodded. It still sounded like sales hype to her. She glanced at Norbert's left hand, splayed out on the top of the steering wheel, ring finger clearly visible. No ring on it — meaning zilch where men are concerned. "So, I take it you're not married?"

Norbert frowned. "Why do you assume I'm not married?"

"I don't know. Maybe because I think married life in the heart of the city — with kids especially — wouldn't be ideal."

"Some people do it. But you're probably right about it not being ideal. At any rate, I was married once."

"Kids?"

"Nope. Escaped that — which is mostly why I'm no longer married."

Sandra didn't probe further. Norbert clearly didn't want to talk about his domestic life, which was fine because she didn't want to talk about her prison life. They were now in very heavy traffic; their car couldn't move any faster on the freeway than it had on the prison exit road. Through a gap between buildings Sandra saw a distant bridge but lost sight of it as they crawled forward. Ten minutes later the car swung around a curve and the bridge reappeared; then they were on it and soon reached its crest. There Sandra caught her first view of the heart of the city. The city she'd previously lived in. A city she no longer recognized.

The sky had cleared in the distance and along the sunlit horizon stretched a frieze of high-rise towers gleaming bronze and silver. Sandra searched for a familiar landmark. All she could detect was the apex of a green pyramid poking out among the rectangular jumble of blocks. She wasn't sure, but thought this might be the roof of what was once a major hotel dominating the downtown skyline. "What the hell happened?" she muttered, more to herself than to Norbert.

Norbert glanced over and followed the line of her gaze. "Yeah, quite something isn't it. I take it for granted, but I guess most of those buildings weren't there before you … um, when you were last in town. What I said about me doing development, this is what I was talking about. Pretty cool, eh."

"So, you're the guy responsible for all that?" Sandra couldn't resist a poke.

"No, just a small bit of it. Lots of people are in the development industry. In fact it's the biggest wealth generator we have now. The resource sectors — logging, mining, fishing — they're pretty much depleted. And secondary industries played out as well—we don't make things anymore; much cheaper to import stuff from Asia. Instead we're building the city beautiful and inviting the world to come and check it out."

"Okay, but when you've done building your beautiful city, what then? What do the lucky residents do for work?"

"Great question." Norbert smiled. "The answer is in knowledge and information industries — high tech, media and communications, creative enterprises — all clean stuff. People with the right skills can work anywhere in the world in the comfort of their own homes. So they choose to live where the built environment ensures the highest quality of life."

"In your city beautiful."

"Exactly."

Bullshit is what Sandra wanted to reply, but she kept quiet. She didn't yet know enough about this world outside prison to muster a counter-argument to Norbert's vision of the future.

Their car was now well past the crest of the bridge. As they progressed downward, the city skyline fell from view and was soon lost behind intervening landforms, buildings and trees. Less than ten minutes later Norbert signalled and exited down a slope. The exit road curved back under the freeway. Off the road on Norbert's side, sheltered underneath the freeway overpass, Sandra saw several shabbily dressed men huddled amid a crazy assemblage of cardboard boxes, shopping carts and tarps. Another manifestation of development in the city beautiful? Not something she was bold enough to query Norbert about.

Beyond the freeway overpass, their road curved into an allée of shopping malls, along which traffic lights arrested their progress every block or so. Norbert puffed loudly every time he was compelled to stop. Sandra didn't share his impatience. She watched the passing scene in fascination. Strange cars, people, buildings — compelling to view and somehow vaguely threatening.

"Sandra." Norbert broke her trance. "Do you have any idea where this halfway house is? I might as well take you straight there so you're not wandering the streets with all your stuff."

Sandra opened the plastic bag on her lap — all her stuff — and rummaged through it. She found the pamphlet the prison gave her the previous day. Printed on the cover were the addresses and phone numbers for both the halfway house and the parole office. She held the pamphlet up in Norbert's range of vision, thumb aimed at an address. Glancing at it, he frowned and pulled over into the parking lane. He fiddled with some buttons and a tiny screen lit up in the dashboard. The screen resolved into a flashing point of light over a road map. More button pushing generated a disembodied female voice saying "Turn right at the next intersection." Seeing Sandra's furrowed brow, Norbert said, "GPS" — which failed to enlighten her.

Guided by the seductive voice, they zigzagged through a maze of streets at the fringe of the urban core. Sandra watched the bright dot inch across the screen, changing direction in sync with every corner taken by the car. She marvelled at Norbert's readiness to take directions from this unknown woman. Soon they entered a wasteland of ancient warehouses, rundown factories and badly outnumbered dilapidated houses. Norbert turned a final corner and abruptly pulled over in front of a boarded-up building. "Is this it?" Sandra asked.

"No, down there." Norbert pointed with his chin. It was still raining, but now just a drizzle. Sandra followed his gaze and saw a familiar cluster of vehicles parked about half a block ahead. The media again, presumably the same bunch as at the prison. The sight gradually blurred until a sweep of the windshield wiper restored clarity.

"Somebody must have tipped them off." Norbert stretched back, lifting himself partially off the seat. "They weren't following us after all. They came straight here."

"Got a cigarette?"

"No, sorry, Sandra, I don't smoke."

"Neither do I — except when I can get my hands on some tobacco." Actually, Sandra had never been a big smoker, but a cigarette in the joint was the price of friendship and she'd gotten used to the currency.

"So, what's the game plan? Are you ready to run the gauntlet?"

"Let's wait a while. Maybe they'll get bored and leave." Not a realistic expectation, she knew, but at least she'd have time to weigh her options.

They sat in silence for a few minutes. The thought of a cigarette had triggered in Sandra a nagging urge to smoke. Another media vehicle pulled up and parked with the others. A woman got out with a disposable tray-load of coffees, which she distributed to the waiting crew. No one was going anywhere soon.

Norbert reached over and started to massage the back of Sandra's neck. She pushed his hand away. Even with her gaze locked on the halfway house entrance, she could tell Norbert's eyes were fixed on her.

"Hey, Sandra, I'm just going to say this, okay?" Norbert evidently had been assembling a speech in his mind. "I could take you to the apartment I've rented. No obligations. I won't even come over unless you say it's okay. Stay as long as you want, at least until the heat dies down. I've paid the first month's rent already so somebody should use it. It would go to waste otherwise."

She didn't answer. A nicotine craving monopolized her attention. Norbert started the car.

"What are you doing?"

"Driving you to the door. Jump out quickly when I stop. Run to the entrance and maybe you'll catch them napping."

"No, no ... don't! You win. Take me to your damn apartment."

Norbert reversed into a U-turn. "Not my damn apartment, your damn apartment."

They retraced their route back to the main road and resumed their trajectory to the city core, passing through the business-district canyons into a zone of progressively smaller and older office buildings interspersed with residential units. Sandra sensed they were nearing their destination. Suddenly, without signalling or pulling over, Norbert stopped the car, eliciting a screech of brakes and a prolonged blare from the vehicle behind. As the blare Dopplered by on the left, Norbert eased his car over to the curb, his eyes on a rundown apartment immediately adjacent. At the roof level, four storeys up, two men on a swing stage were painting window trims. On the ground below, a pallet of sod rolls waited to be laid over the newly levelled topsoil on either side of the entry walkway.

"Is this the place?" Sandra asked.

"What? No, just need to make a phone call." Norbert reached down under his seat and extracted what looked to Sandra like a telephone operator's headset. He placed the contraption on his head and fiddled with some buttons. Sandra heard a couple of faint rings, abruptly cut off when Norbert tapped another button. He drummed his fingers on the dashboard, then abruptly spoke. "Hey, Mel, I'm looking at 1240 Beachway. Herb's got a crew touching up the paint job. Looks like some landscaping also in the works. Nothing major, though…" Norbert pressed a hand against the ear speaker on Sandra's side.

"One ringa dinga, two ringa dinga," she said, laughing. Norbert looked over at her and raised his eyebrows; the joke he couldn't hear was lost on him.

"Yeah, yeah," Norbert continued his conversation. "We jump up our bid now. We gotta land this one; we're locked into the adjacent properties … I know you know; sorry, I'm just a little anxious … Frankly, Mel, best if the offer came from you. Herb's got me pegged as bastard developer … Yeah, yeah, very funny. Anyway, Herb needs to sell, but … last time we talked he made noise about applying for heritage status … I know it's a dump, but try telling him that." Another long pause punctuated by Norbert saying "uh-huh, uh-huh" at regular intervals, and then finally, "So yeah. Tell him you've come into an inheritance or something and you're looking for an investment property; you love his building, you want to restore it to its previous glory and yadda yadda. You know the routine. Even if we close way above our original target, that's better than getting him spooked again … Yep. You're the best. Bye, Mel."

Norbert pushed another button and took the headset off. Taking a deep breath he exhaled loudly through pursed lips then frowned and massaged his temples with his fingertips. Sandra began to wonder if he had forgotten she was there. "What's up?" she prompted.

Norbert's reaction confirmed her suspicion. He stared at her blankly for a moment and then laughed. "Just doing a little business. Land assembly, always a pain in the ass. Come on, let's get you settled in."

He merged back into traffic and minutes later they were among a fringe of high-rise condominiums along the waterfront. Norbert pulled up in front of a condo tower, neither the newest nor the tallest but alarmingly luxurious from Sandra's perspective.

"Here we are." Norbert extracted the key from the ignition and, with the same hand, pressed down on the seat belt lock to free his passenger. "Grab your luggage; I'll show you to your new home."

Home? Too tired to object, Sandra tightened the drawstring on her "luggage" and followed Norbert into the building. The lobby was floored with marble tiles; etched mirror panelling on opposing walls created the illusion of spaciousness. The sight of a uniformed guard sitting behind a desk in one corner gave Sandra pause. Norbert waved at the guard and muttered to Sandra, "Concierge — keeps the riff-raff out." He shepherded Sandra into the elevator and pushed button 20; the numbers only went up to 22. He winked at her. "Not the penthouse, but I think you'll be comfortable."

"Comfortable" was an understatement. Wall-to-wall carpets, patio door leading onto a balcony with a stunning view of the outer harbour, modern kitchen with all the latest appliances (several of which Sandra couldn't see the purpose of), bedroom with a queen-size bed. Most intriguing to Sandra were the two bathrooms: one off the entry hall and one directly off the bedroom.

"What's the idea here, Norbert? Poop in one bathroom, wash your hands in the other?"

Norbert responded with a high-pitched giggle that slowly resolved into a vaguely familiar idiot grin. Sandra threw her plastic bag onto the bedroom dresser and turned, hands on hips. "Yes, yes, very nice. Am I supposed to fuck you now or later?"

Norbert's smiling face immediately contorted into an expression of dismay. "Sandra, please, this isn't about sex at all." He backpedalled from the bedroom door and she brushed by him to stare out over the harbour. "Norbert, I don't know what kind of person you remember me being, but I'm not that person anymore. I doubt I ever was. Prison changed me, and not only my face or my hair. The person I am now doesn't like owing anything to anybody. I don't tolerate bullshit."

"You never did tolerate bullshit. Something I always appreciated about you. And you don't owe me. If anything, I owe you."

"How do you figure?"

"You did time. I didn't and should have."

"So all this is like an over-the-top guilt trip? I didn't go to jail, so here, have a beautiful apartment?"

Norbert slumped against the kitchen counter. "You could say that. But it's more because…" He tilted the head of a kitchen mixer up and back down. "I like you, Sandra. I always have. Plus I genuinely want to help you. You've been punished more than you deserve. I'm going to leave you to settle in and, like I said, I promise not to come over or call unless you call me first. Which reminds me, this is for you."

She stared at the device he placed on the counter. Compact? Electric shaver? Flummoxed, she was compelled to ask, "What the hell is this?"

"Cellphone."

"A cellphone? But it's so teensy."

"The latest release, welcome to Brave New World. But you must know about cellphones, must have seen them before."

"Of course, the prison guards had them. They looked like they were talking into a shoe. Rumour was some inmates had newer models — on the QT. I didn't want to know; who was I going to call?"

Norbert pointed at a desk to the right of the patio door. "Charger's in the top drawer over there, instructions underneath; you'll figure it out. And when you call — if you decide to call — here are my coordinates." Norbert flourished a business card and placed it on the kitchen counter. He held up a set of keys. The fob had an ornate S monogram on it. "Brass gets you into the building; silver's the one for your door." He centred the keys on top of the business card. "Take care, Sandra."

Out in the hallway Norbert paused, still holding the door open. "Oh, one more thing. There's a convenience mart down the street to your left as you leave the building. You'll find lots of food in the kitchen, but just in case you need cigarettes or something. How are you set for money?"

"I'm fine. But thanks, Norbert. Thanks for … everything."

The grin reappeared. "My pleasure, Sandra." He nodded and released the door, which closed on its own.

———————

Alexander Berkman Collective

House Meeting Minutes

Sunday, October 17, 1982

Item one: Economic Redistribution

Comrade	Total grocery etc. receipts since last meeting	Share (tot receipts/5)	Owes	Owed
Louie	$15.12	100.33	$85.21	
Bet	74.89	100.33	25.44	
Norbert	197.70	100.33		97.37
Sandra	213.55	100.33		113.22
Phyl	.39	100.33	99.94	
Total	$501. 65	$501. 65	210.59	210.59

Above figures prepared and presented for collective review by Bet.

BET: Costs out of control. House needs budget — we are living beyond our means.

LOUIE: Agrees with Bet. Personal difficulty settling account until pogey arrives.

PHYL: Fundamentally opposed to theoretical basis of redistribution plan. Does not take into account value of liberated items contributed to common good, nor labour value.

BET: Plan based upon fundamental socialist principle of equality. Willing to recalculate and include shoplifted shampoo if Phyl documents market value. Notes work assignments are item 2 on agenda.

PHYL: From each according to his or her ability; to each according to his or her need is the only true formula for socialist equality. Different consumption levels must also be considered. Has been fasting for most of past two months.

BET: Observed Phyl eating pop tarts at night in front of T.V. Neo-Islamic Ramadan?

PHYL: Considers Bet's remark racist, possibly Zionist. Demands self-criticism from Bet, and apology.

NORBERT: Not asking for repayment for grocery purchases. They are a collective good. Does not like seeing conflict between comrades. Real enemy is capitalist system.

PHYL: Agrees. Property is theft.

SANDRA: Willing to go along with consensus of the majority. Wants others to pay more in future.

LOUIE: Must change diet. Chinese People's Liberation Army able to survive on handful of rice a day. Brown rice and dried beans in cupboard never utilized — why? Suggests limit of $100 per month for household groceries. Everyone to put $20 in grocery jar.

SANDRA: Does "groceries" include coffee and beer?

LOUIE: Yes, otherwise no money needed at all.

BET: Okay on budget. Still feels need to resolve redistribution issue according to past practice.

NORBERT: Propose redistribution be linked with next item on the agenda — work assignments. Collective can then address larger issue of equity.

ALL AGREE

Item 2: Work Assignments

BET: Sick and tired of the women in the collective having to do all the shit work of laundry, cooking, cleaning, etc.

PHYL: Bet's analysis unscientific and incorrect. Points out his washing the kitchen floor and doing dishes last night as but one unacknowledged example.

BET: Always knows when house meeting is scheduled — Phyl does house blitz the night before.

PHYL: Gratuitous insults unproductive. Not interested in participating in group struggle that doesn't advance the revolution. Disengaging until such time as other people's thinking on these issues has evolved sufficiently to allow meaningful dialogue.

In Phyl's absence the collective lacks a quorum. Meeting formally adjourned.

Minutes prepared by: SANDRA TREMING

#

Sitting on my bed, half under the covers, trying to decipher my scrawled notes from tonight's house meeting. I hate this fucking house sometimes. Especially our house meetings. Nothing ever gets decided and everybody hates each other afterward. I force myself to stay on task, to generate minutes that (a) bear some semblance to what went down earlier, and (b) won't come back and bite me later. I could've played the gender card, like Bet, and declared myself exempt from secretarial duties. But that would have meant giving power to one of the men, letting them impose whatever warped version of reality they might have on our collective future. No, best to exercise some control, even if it means being a drudge.

Meeting minutes are to be posted on the bulletin board in the kitchen within twenty-four hours of a meeting. That's a house rule. I'm briefly tempted to fill a page with nonsense syllables, knowing I probably wouldn't be called on it. In fact, nonsense would be the most honest summing up. Repressing this rebellious urge, I start on a fair copy of my notes, supplementing my scrawl with recalled bits not captured in the heat of the moment.

I'm reminded as I write of how brutal the meeting was, not that the aftermath was any better. Phyl closed the meeting with his tantrum and immediately left the house. He hasn't returned since. Louie and Bet are holed up in their room, only coming out to pee. Bet is still charged up. I can hear her quite clearly through the wall between our rooms. "What am I supposed to do? Recalculate everything on his say-so about a goddamn bag of shoplifted Cheezies? And that crack about me being a Zionist. Where does that reactionary asshole get off?" A low rumble, which is Louie speaking. I can't make out the words. Then Bet again. "He *is* an asshole. And you're an asshole too for not giving me support."

So it goes. Disunity even between the lovers. I strain to make sense of further bass notes through the wall. Then someone knocks at my door. "Come in," I say, doing a hurried proofread of the now complete minutes. The door displaces slightly, and Norbert sticks his head through at an awkward angle. "I'm making tea, Sandra; do you want some?" His saucer-shaped blue eyes blink at me while I weigh my response. "Ah, no, but thanks for asking."

Dear, sweet Norbert. I think he lusts after my body. No, scratch that, I know he's horny as a billy goat. And I might be tempted to caress his pink fuzzy cheeks, dishevel his choirboy hair and pull him into my bed. But he has to take the initiative, not simply broadcast a profound neediness that threatens to glue him to me permanently if contact were ever made. Besides, fucking someone you live with is a bad idea. If things go well you become half a couple and the whole dynamic of the house changes, and not for the better. More likely, though, things don't go well. You have to shut out the other person before they shut you out. Either way it hurts. And the pain won't go away as long as you're near the other person.

I flip over to a blank page in my steno pad and scrawl across the page NOTE TO SELF: NEVER SCREW A COMMUNARD.

Norbert remains clamped between door and jamb, staring at me. Has he read my mind? Or maybe — upside down and across the room — what I just wrote? Feeling a little too exposed, I shut the steno pad and cover it with my quilt. I return Norbert's stare.

"I want to apologize about last night," he finally blurts out.

A classic morning-after cliché. Somehow I manage not to laugh at Norbert's earnest utterance. "What do you mean, Norb? Come and sit down."

"About the money." Norbert edges over to the foot of my bed and squats, half of one buttock perched on the mattress. I hold my position in the centre of the bed, certain that were I to shift away he would take it as an invitation to encroach even further.

"I wasn't thinking," he says. Norbert's eyes dart all around my room before fixing on my diaphragm case. Why the hell did I leave it on top of my clock radio? "I wasn't trying to coerce you into relinquishing your right to full restitution. I just don't like hassles over money. And I didn't want people to be so hostile. Not here. Not in our collective."

"No problem, Norb, I'm not upset." I reach out and pick up my diaphragm case and drop it into my open backpack beside the bed.

Norbert's cheeks flush bright crimson. "No hard feelings?"

"No hard feelings. Go make your tea."

As Norbert closes the door behind him, Bet's voice penetrates the wall. "It's driving me fucking crazy."

I know what she means.

Two

2007

After Norbert finally left the apartment, Sandra went into the kitchen to look for something by way of a late lunch. Something easy to prepare. Not much in the fridge, but the freezer compartment was crammed with packaged meals and plastic-wrapped trays of meat. Too much time required to thaw and cook; she needed instant gratification. At last she found an item in one of the cupboards that made her smile: granola in a gallon-size glass pickle jar. A signature concoction of Norbert's from the Berkman House days. She poured herself a bowlful, splashed on some milk and topped it with a sliced banana. Bowl in hand, Sandra opened the sliding glass door and stepped onto the balcony to breathe in the fresh air. She ate standing, staring at the ships anchored in the bay. The rain had stopped but the air was still cold. It didn't matter. For the first time in twenty-five years, the outside world was wide open to her.

Sandra returned to the kitchen to rinse out her bowl and thought about exploring the neighbourhood outside, maybe checking out the convenience mart, whatever that was. She went to retrieve her jacket from the bedroom. There, she was suddenly overcome by exhaustion. She hadn't slept much the night before, in anticipation — dread almost — of impending freedom. She flopped on the bed, thinking maybe she would go out later in the evening. Instead she slept until dawn the next morning.

Groggy and disoriented, she moved slowly, sat on the edge of the bed taking stock of her new environment: plush carpet underfoot, sunlight pouring in through gaps in the curtains, Van Gogh reproduction (*Sunflowers*) on the wall and muted cries of seagulls outside. Not home perhaps, but also not jail.

Eventually she staggered out to the kitchen in search of coffee. The makings she found easily enough, but the electric coffee maker stymied her. She began opening drawers in search of its manual. She found various kitchen utensils in every drawer, save for one. The exception contained a stack of sales brochures for a condo building and a box of business cards. Cards in the name of Mel Collis; no doubt the same Mel whom Norbert had phoned en route from the prison. Sandra resumed her search for the manual and found it tucked behind the coffee maker. After a brief study session she pushed the right sequence of buttons and was rewarded by a carafe of hot brown liquid. She carried a mug of it out to the balcony along with one of the sales brochures.

On the brochure cover was a colour sketch of people walking, cycling and rollerblading along a waterfront pathway; in the background, several high-rise towers, one more sharply defined than the others. Sandra looked over the balcony railing and reconstructed in her mind the same scene from a reverse perspective. The sun was shining and people of all ages were passing by in a steady stream. Sandra noticed the young ones most. She thought of Emma, who would be in her midtwenties by now.

Sandra sipped her coffee at measured intervals, putting off as long as possible what she had to do next. The java was cold before she finished the mug. She poured the dregs into the kitchen sink and returned the sales brochure to its drawer. She retrieved the pamphlet she'd used the previous day to guide Norbert to the halfway house and dialled the number on the cover. The ringing at the other end of the line made her gut churn.

Following the last ring she was placed on hold. Music played, instrumental pop tunes so old, Sandra could hum along. Intermittently, a stern male voice ordered her to stay on the line. At last a woman said, "Corrections, good morning." Her voice sounded eerily similar to the GPS lady who gave Norbert directions to the halfway house. Sandra braced for an inquisition, but no difficult questions were posed. The woman simply told Sandra to report in person to her parole officer, next Monday at 9:00 a.m.

Almost a whole week away. Sandra wrote the address, date and time on the back of the pamphlet. Anxiety thus abated, or at least postponed.

As she hung up she was hit again by a nicotine craving. As good an excuse as any to venture out into the world. She quickly showered and dressed and was almost out the door before she remembered to grab her keys. No way could she ask the concierge to let her back in.

The convenience mart turned out to be just a grocery store, but with nothing fresh, only tons of junk food. No tobacco in sight. Sandra asked where she could buy cigarettes.

The young Asian clerk hesitated, as if puzzled by her question. "What brand do you want, madam?"

What brand? She was expecting to see the packs all on display so she could just point to one, but no dice. Perhaps buying tobacco was now like buying liquor in the old days; her order would be brought from the back of the store in a plain brown paper bag. "Um, Player's Plain?"

"Plain? What do you mean plain?"

"You know, plain — Player's cigarettes, but without a filter." Sandra looked around for other staff who might be more on the ball.

The clerk shook his head. "No. We don't have that brand."

"Well, something else without a filter tip, and not mentholated either."

"I'm sorry, madam, but all our cigarettes have filter tips."

"Really? When did that happen? I've been … out of the country. Never mind, how about tobacco and papers instead?" Rattled by how complicated this simple transaction had become, her mind went blank on brand names.

"Yes, we have those." The clerk sounded as relieved as Sandra felt. He opened a metallic shutter behind him and ta-dah! There was the tobacco cache. Sandra wondered why he hadn't opened it sooner; that would have made things so much easier. The clerk drew out a pouch of Drum and threw it on the counter along with papers and matches. When he rang up the total, Sandra was shocked by the cost. She would have to severely ration herself.

At the store exit Sandra stopped dead in her tracks. A newspaper on display showed a picture of her — years out of date, fortunately — right on the front page. Headline: *Freed Terrorist Goes Back Underground.* Below the fold a blurry photo of her legs sticking out of Norbert's car in the prison parking lot. She returned to the till and paid for the paper, folded over so it wouldn't trigger more conversation with the clerk.

On her way back to the apartment she read the whole story. Mostly ancient history or, more precisely, historical fiction, a recap of the kidnapping and ensuing deaths, no more accurate than the original media coverage. Yet again she was cast as "the mastermind behind a monstrous terrorist act that rocked the nation." An anonymous prison source summed her up as "unrepentant and unrehabilitated." The account of Sandra's release (was it only yesterday?) was equally distorted. She had, with the assistance of an unknown male accomplice, executed a well-planned evasion of publicity. The pair had left the prison premises at high speed in what was later determined to be a rented car. Attempts to identify the accomplice were fruitless, as a spokesperson at the rental agency declined to be interviewed. The story hinted darkly of an international criminal conspiracy, an allegation not substantiated in any way.

"You clever bugger, Norbert," Sandra said aloud as she finished the article. She had assumed the car was his and was briefly miffed he hadn't been straight with her. But then again, he hadn't outright lied. Curious, she was tempted to phone Norbert to get the backstory. No, too soon; she'd be giving him ideas she didn't want him to have.

For the next few days Sandra hunkered down in the apartment, gradually adjusting to its comforts — total decadence compared to her previous digs. On the second morning she joined the throng on the waterfront, shuffling along in a semi-jog until she was drenched in sweat and her lungs were burning. It didn't take long for this to happen; as Norbert observed she had muscle definition, but her endurance was crap. The following day she was able to keep at it longer and go a little bit farther, and the same for successive days thereafter. On these runs she wore a hoodie pulled over to eye level and kept her head down. She otherwise lay low in the apartment and read. Norbert had stocked the place with lots of books, mysteries and science fiction mostly, but better than nothing. She lit only one cigarette the whole time. Beset by an almost constant nicotine craving, she was determined not to smoke.

Sandra avoided returning to the convenience store where she bought the tobacco and the newspaper. Instead, she found something called a Handi-24Mart, practically identical in terms of inventory. It was a couple of blocks farther, in the opposite direction, but there wasn't much she needed to buy. Norbert had supplied her well with food, albeit mostly frozen or canned. Not being a fussy eater, she had enough on hand to last for months.

Early Saturday, on Sandra's morning run, she collided with another jogger. The stranger, a woman in her midtwenties, offered an automatic apology. Sandra stared at her. She almost asked, "Emma?" There was no reason to imagine so; she had no idea what the adult Emma would look like. Hell, she had only a blurry recollection of what baby Emma looked like.

The intensity of Sandra's gaze caused the woman to frown and shift focus to look in the distance over Sandra's shoulder. As the stranger jogged away Sandra quelled an urge to chase her down and demand to know her name. Instead, she sprinted in the opposite direction, stopping short of her previous day's distance for the first time. She didn't have the breath to continue.

Back at the apartment, Sandra powered up the phone — no less complicated than the coffee maker — and punched in Norbert's number. Ten digits — could it be long distance? He answered on the second ring. "Sandra, is everything all right?"

Not yet clued in to call display, Sandra was taken aback by Norbert's immediate recognition, but it saved a step. She went straight to the point: "I need three things. I need a job. I need to find my daughter. I need … I don't know — I need someone to talk to. Can you come over?"

Sandra closed the phone and, to keep her hands occupied, opened up the bag of Drum and began to roll cigarettes.

———————————

1982

Wind-driven rain rattles my window, waking me up. My clock radio glows brightly in the gloom: 7:40 a.m. The house is quiet. Feeling room-bound, I venture downstairs. No one else is likely to be up for hours. The first thing I see in the kitchen is a cold pot of tea on the counter — chamomile mint, Norbert's favourite. I pour what's left into a saucepan and put it on the stove to simmer. Not fresh, but hassle free. I hate cooking.

After a minute or so, I swirl the tea around in the pan and a slight hiss tells me it's ready to serve. I plunk myself down on a wooden packing crate, elbows resting on the large wire spool that serves Berkman House as a kitchen table. I have a love-hate relationship with this industrial relic. It's one heavy bugger, to begin with, and huge — at least five feet in diameter. I have no idea where it came from and how it came to be in the kitchen — rolled through the back door presumably, then flopped over on its side. At some point the top was painted red, but the underlying industrial green was hard to kill, so it's now a muddy copper. And then there are the hazards on its surface: huge hex bolts that spill the beverages of the unwary, and a six-inch hole in the centre into which things fall and can never be retrieved. But for all its faults the spool was one of the things that induced me to move into Berkman House. A dozen or so people can squeeze around its circumference to eat, drink and generally shoot the shit for hours on end. As we often did … back in the good times.

Eating, drinking and shit shooting are no longer on the program, ever since the collective determined parties and like frivolous activities were antithetical to our political agenda. Even prior to that resolution, visits to our house by friends and acquaintances had begun to fall off. Louie, the most outgoing and social person in the house, was once the principal draw. But Louie blows hot and cold, not someone you want to be around when he's in a bad mood. Bet tends to engage in constructive criticism sessions with everyone she meets. Phyl is generally truculent, especially with other males. And then there's Norbert and me. Not that either of us pissed off any past visitors, but he being so shy and me being so boring hardly triggers a stampede to our door.

Today I cherish my solitude. I sip tea and stare through the window at rain pelting down. The effect is almost hypnotic. The exterior scene begins to blur as my eyes refocus on a tiny bit of fluff on the outside of the glass. On a bright day in early summer, when the five of us were sitting at the spool drinking coffee, a little bird flew smack into the pane. The bird died, but the tuft of down still marks the point of impact. A memorial … as much to housekeeping standards in our collective as to the bird.

Morbid thoughts. The relentless splash of rain on the litter of muddy leaves generates a piss-poor view of the world. Hard to believe only a month, no, three weeks ago — the opening day of hunting season in fact — our whole household spent a day target shooting in the woods. Hunting season provides the ideal cover for revolutionary training, although none of us in our T-shirts and jeans, taking turns drilling holes through rusty tin cans with Louie's single shot .22, would ever pass as a bona fide hunter. It was the height of Native American summer. A bronze tinge to the leaves, a slight chill in the shade, but for all that one helluva gorgeous day. The last gorgeous day of the year.

I hear footsteps behind me and turn to see Phyl entering the kitchen. He's wearing a shocking-pink dressing gown; his hair, tied with a ribbon matching the gown, is knotted in a clump on top of his head. Without breaking stride, Phyl lifts the kettle off the stove, lights a burner and continues on to the sink. As he returns with a filled kettle, I break the silence: "Good morning, Phyl."

He pulls down a large box of coffee filters from the shelf, shakes it and looks in. "Phyllis," he snarls as he tosses the empty box across the counter and onto the floor.

Of course. Silly me, I should have clued in when I noticed the gown. When under stress, Phyl chooses to give full expression to the female side of his personality. A need, he says, to experience firsthand the oppression of women in Western industrialized culture. Phyl's female side is also his most ornery side, which bugs me more than a little, though I'm not about to call him on it. When he's in full Phyllis mode, a dark cloud descends and he stays silently hostile for days. Over the past few months I've learned not to provoke him when he's in one of these moods — by keeping my damn mouth shut.

When I first moved into the house, Phyl tried repeatedly to provoke me into an argument on some arcane bit of Marxist revolutionary theory. I learned from Bet that this was his way of coming on to women. Not having any grounding in political theory, I just agreed with everything he said, whereupon he quickly lost interest.

I busy myself writing and pretend not to notice as Phyl rips the last paper towel off a roll. From the top of the stove he takes a plastic cone, warped from chronic proximity to the burners, and crams the towel inside. Then he balances the cone on the rim of our glass carafe and reaches deep into the green garbage can containing our collective coffee. After some scraping, he retrieves a scoop full of grounds and dumps them into the cone, just before the kettle begins to whistle. He pours boiling water over the grounds. So far, so good. I half expected we were out of java; that would be sure to set him off. Phyl releases the bungee cord holding shut the refrigerator door, and miracle of miracles, he extracts a carton of cream from deep in the bowels of the fridge. About to pour the cream into his mug, he hesitates, cautiously sniffs…

"Goddamn!" Phyl stomps back to the sink. I hear the splatter of a lumpy liquid hitting stainless steel, then the tap running.

Phyl crosses behind me again and reaches above the cupboard for a gallon-size glass jar of powdered milk. He stirs a couple of spoonfuls into his cup and then pulls down a second jar. This one has a crude skull and crossbones drawn over the original Dill Pickles label, now very much faded. He unscrews the lid and tips it. "Jesus fuck!"

"I'm going shopping later, Phyl; I'll get coffee, filters, cream…"

For a few seconds Phyl glares at me and I regret speaking. Finally, he takes a deep breath and the tension eases. Reaching into the sugar jar with a bread knife, he stabs the white residue vigorously until a chunk breaks off. He upends the jar and the chunk plops into his cup. "Get some sugar too," he says, licking the knife.

"Sugar? There's lots of honey."

"I want sugar. White sugar."

"Okay. White sugar. No problem." I tear a page from my journal and write *white sugar.*

Phyl pours coffee into his cup, stirs it with a chopstick and swallows it in two large gulps. He sets the mug down next to the sink and presses his palms together at chest level. "Okay, now to centre myself." He turns to leave the kitchen as Bet, dressed in only her pyjama top, appears in the doorway. They simultaneously recoil a half step, turn sideways and, backs to each other, pass through the narrow opening.

Bet pours herself a mug of coffee; no ritual — she likes hers black. From the next room I hear deep, almost pained breathing as Phyl starts his asanas. Bet wanders over to the spool and drops down on the only padded chair in the house. She sits with her feet on the edge of the seat, arms hugging her knees to her chest. Between her ankles I see through to a thatch of pubic hair and the sight triggers my mother's voice in my head: "A lady always sits with her knees together." I'm no lady but no way could I ever be as unselfconscious and liberated as Bet is.

A crash and prolonged wheezing from the next room signals Phyl's fall from a shoulder stand into the plow position. Part three of his customary sequence.

"What's this?" Bet picks up the paper torn from my journal.

"A list. I'm going shopping. Do you want anything from the—"

"No. What's *this*?" Bet stabs at one item on the list.

"Sugar."

"White sugar? I thought we agreed we would only buy honey. White sugar, white death."

A high-pitched choking sound emanates from Phyl; his stomach, chest and throat now must be stretched out in a full cobra pose. I pretend not to hear anything, but Bet knows no caution.

"Yes, Phyllis, are you trying to make a point?"

Phyl leaps up and charges back into the kitchen: "The point I'm making is that if I want fucking white death I'm entitled to fucking white death! And furthermore" — he picks up the carafe — "if you

want to drink fucking coffee, you can fucking well make it yourself!"
Phyl throws the carafe, with its plastic cone and soggy paper towel
and grounds, against the wall above the stove, where it shatters.
Shards litter the stove top and adjacent counters. Phyl glares at Bet,
but she — for once — is speechless. Phyl noisily breathes through
clenched teeth a few times then turns to me; it must be the expression
on my face which causes him to wilt. "Sorry, Sandra." His voice is
now meek. "I'll clean that up — later."

Footsteps pound up the stairs, then silence. Bet stares at the
rivulets of coffee cutting through the grounds on the wall. "What is
to be done?" she whispers. "What is to be done?"

I don't respond. I don't have any clue what is to be done, and I
doubt she expects an answer from me.

Three

2007

Sandra was rolling the last of the tobacco in the pouch, when her cellphone rang for the first time. Actually not a ring but rather the opening bars of "Paint it Black." Cautiously she pressed Accept Call. It was Norbert, from outside the building. Sandra buzzed him in and a minute later he was at her door, a bag of groceries in each hand. Brushing by Sandra, he went straight to the refrigerator and began to load the crisper compartments.

"Hello, Norbert," she said to his back.

He turned and flashed his blue eyes and familiar grin at her. "Just brought you some fruit and vegetables; I know there aren't many perishables to be had in this neighbourhood."

Placing a bottle of Merlot on the kitchen counter, he noticed the pile of cigarettes. "You've been busy."

"I roll them; I don't smoke them."

"It's all right, Sandra, I was only…" Norbert picked up a cigarette and examined it. "You were always good at rolling. These look tailor-made, almost."

"Put that down, Norbert. We have urgent business to attend to." She took him by the hand and led him into the bedroom.

He came along with only the faintest show of resistance. "Are you sure?"

She unrolled him from his coat. "It's either you or one of those cigarettes."

Sandra's forwardness surprised herself as much as Norbert. She hadn't contacted him with seductive intent. But now that he was here, a lingering sexual tension, somehow surviving the long hiatus of prison, was overdue to be dispelled. Not only her years in the joint but also her first week of freedom — paradoxically, a self-imposed solitary confinement in the condo — whetted her desire.

They fumbled their way through the shedding of clothes and inhibitions. Once stripped and under the covers Norbert initiated a mechanical foreplay as if following procedures learned from a manual, Sandra's presence being incidental. She almost called a halt to the proceedings, and she would have done so had Norbert been the instigator. But it was already too late to go back to how things were between them, much simpler and less awkward to continue on through the motions.

Save for the novelty of a flesh-and-blood penis, the sex turned out to be on par with a furtive prison fuck. Norbert followed his lovemaking script for what he evidently calculated to be a sufficient length of time; for Sandra it lasted too long and not long enough. Finally, with a few spasms and theatrical moans, they were done. She was left both relieved and unsatisfied. After a minute or so of stillness Norbert propped himself up on his elbow and nuzzled her ear with his lips. "How you doing, San?" he whispered.

Sandra responded with a noncommittal "hmmm."

Retreating, Norbert raised himself up and leaned back against the headboard. "Is everything okay?"

Sandra sat up and shrugged. "I'm not going to become addicted."

"Ouch. Hoo boy. Well, you kinda took me by surprise there. This isn't how I imagined we … it might happen. Not that I necessarily expected…" Norbert swivelled to the edge of the bed and slumped over. She stared at his back, which was smooth and starkly white. His shoulders were broader than she remembered; in other respects he hadn't matured at all. Norbert's male vanity was wounded, but Sandra wasn't in a rush to make amends. He inhaled and exhaled noisily through his lips, until finally she cut in. "Norbert, don't be bummed. Everything's fine. You've just got to understand I'm more than a little out of practice. Being out of prison is one thing. Getting the prison out of me isn't going to be so easy. Impossible maybe."

Norbert turned and forced a smile. His hand cautiously circumnavigated her belly. "Would you like one of your cigarettes?"

"Fuck no, too much of a cliché. Like I told you, I'm not going to become addicted. What I'm craving now is food. I'm ravenous."

"Haven't you had breakfast?"

"No, not yet."

Norbert bounced to his feet. "Well, allow me then."

Sandra made a diplomatic yet half-hearted attempt to hold Norbert back, but he was beyond reach. She shouted after him, "Not lentil stew!"

"Yuck. Don't remind me." Norbert was already in the kitchen, out of sight. Sandra heard the refrigerator door open and a rummaging through its contents. "How does a bacon-and-cheese omelette sound?"

"Absolutely perfect." Sandra staggered into the en suite. When she got to the kitchen Norbert had already cracked eggs into a bowl and was laying bacon strips on a skillet. She unhooked an apron from the side of the refrigerator. "Frying bacon while naked is a bad idea, Norbert. Put this on."

"Coffee's about ready. Help yourself." Norbert beat the eggs, grated cheese and dropped slices of bread in the toaster while the bacon heated up. As the slices began to sizzle and curl, he started on the omelette. Sandra was amazed at this unprecedented display of efficiency. Young Norbert could never have managed more than one pot at a time. Breakfast was ready by the time Sandra poured and doctored two mugs of coffee. They ate on the balcony, bundled up in blankets as much for modesty as for warmth. It was early afternoon and the temperature was unseasonably mild.

Once they finished eating, neither spoke. Sandra had taken the lead earlier, but now she shied away from her main reason for contacting Norbert — asking for job-searching advice. Her total lack of useful skills was an embarrassment. As for opening up about Emma, what the hell had she been thinking? She felt even more vulnerable in that regard. Norbert looked at her quizzically for some time before steering the conversation — deliberately or not, it wasn't clear — onto less threatening terrain: "Gotta love this view; look at all the people on the waterfront path."

"I've been going for a run along there every day since you brought me here. It's been good. Thank you."

"You're welcome. Glad you're making good use of the amenities I helped pay for. The park, the seawall and like that."

"That you *helped* pay for — what does that mean?"

"Well, this building and the one immediately west were the first projects Mel and I did together."

"I figured something like that out already." Sandra explained about finding business cards and sales brochures in a kitchen drawer.

"Ah, I see." Norbert laughed. "Housekeeping's not one of Mel's strong suits."

"So, you didn't actually rent this apartment for me."

"No, *borrow* is what I should have said." Norbert cringed, as if expecting an explosion.

"No worries. I'd be pissed if you paid for this. I'm fine with the freebie as long as I didn't displace anyone..."

"No worries. Mel buys a unit in all our joint projects. Serves as an office and then it's empty, unless out-of-town clients or friends or family need a place to stay. Smart really, a business write-off for the short term and an excellent equity investment over the long term."

Two squawking seagulls flew low overhead, and Norbert automatically covered his head with his hands. The birds passed by without incident, and he uncovered. "Mel owns about eleven units now and I'm going to start buying some too. In our business it's like a pension plan. Mel and I were so green back when we took on this project. Fortunately, we were a tiny part of a large initiative to transform a rundown industrial waterfront. So we followed the pack and learned the ropes: City Planning Department takes the lead. After securing council approval, lots of meetings between the proponents — us developers — and eventually the stakeholders, so-called. That's when the fun really starts. Or more accurately in most cases, that's when the shit hits the fan."

Sandra wasn't much interested in the process Norbert described, and she was shocked to hear how readily he had aligned himself with local power structures. "Norbert, who exactly would these stakeholders be?"

Norbert emitted a contemptuous snort. "Pretty much every person or organization with an axe to grind. They show up just to delay or derail the proposal. Public consultations are a total goddamn pain in the ass."

"So the stakeholders are people trying to fight city hall? Nothing wrong with that. Don't you encounter at least *some* reasonable objections?"

"Depends. People demand zoning regulations be enforced against their neighbours but scream when they're on the receiving end. I don't call that reasonable. Still, I quickly learned that a guy could come out ahead at this stage, if he dangles the right carrot. Say the stakeholders are concerned about homelessness; I'd propose including social housing — in a separate building away from the waterfront of course. Or maybe we're dealing with environmentalists. Ha, environmentalists are so easy. They come roaring against every development proposal, but throw in a marsh or wetland or just green space like we did here and suddenly they're purring pussycats." Norbert laughed, stopping abruptly when he noticed Sandra didn't even smile. "Yes, well, of course a lot of other valuable benefits are put on the table as well — schools, daycare centres, public art…"

"But all that stuff costs money doesn't it? How do you come out ahead?"

"Yes, public amenities definitely add cost. And we developers, of course, whine about any extra financial burden imposed on our projects. Some of my gang are serious about that and don't want to yield an inch. If they had their way, their buildings would hog the waterfront and completely deny public access. But as you can see, that didn't happen here. Instead, there's a hundred-metre setback; even so the new condos are still classed as waterfront properties." Norbert laughed again. "And what's on the cover of every sales brochure? People strolling along the seaside with new buildings in the background. That's because buyers want parks and other goodies handy to their new homes. Believe it or not, that image alone jacks up the price by a good five percent. Of course, we don't admit that in the planning stage. Instead we say, 'As much as we'd love to include these desired features, it's just not economically feasible given the proposed FSR.'"

"FSR — what the hell is that?"

"Floor Space Ratio — how much one can build in relation to lot size. One-point-oh FSR would allow a one-storey building covering the whole of a property; or two storeys over half the property; or four storeys over a quarter — you get the idea. Take this building for example; seven-point-oh FSR was originally proposed for the site. After arm-wrestling with the city planners we were able to kick it up to a fraction over eight."

"A difference of one — whatever you call it? That hardly seems worth fighting over."

"Might not seem so, but that little difference made this building several storeys higher. One little digit and now we're talking millions of dollars in added value. Easily covers the added amenities, with a significant bonus to boot."

"The city planners were fooled? Why did they agree?"

"The planners might have dug their heels in if they were just dealing with us developers. But the stakeholders are in the picture as well. City council never wants to upset the stakeholders, because they're voters after all. Happens all the time. Remember coming here from the prison and seeing the city skyline from the bridge, how impressed you were? Well, almost all of those buildings are five or six storeys higher than would have been possible under their original zoning specs. What's more, those higher storeys command higher prices. You'll never find a penthouse on the ground floor; it's all about the view. Extra value that won't appear on the planner's spreadsheet. Voilà! A huge marginal gain for the developer."

Norbert leaned back in his chair as if seated on a throne, chin up, hands gripping the armrests. He glanced coyly sideways, checking Sandra's reaction. Sandra smiled benignly back to conceal her true feelings. In the eyes of the Berkman Collective, Norbert would have been seen as a class traitor, a tool of the ruling class. At the same time, though, his transformation from a callow youth into a man of confident authority was undeniably appealing. It was all very confusing.

Some inkling of Sandra's underlying thought processes seemed to penetrate Norbert's brain. He stood and collected the lunch plates. "Hey, enough talk about me. You called me here to help sort out your issues, not listen to me boast about my wicked business practices." He headed for the kitchen, kissing Sandra in passing.

She shouted after him. "I need a job!"

A clatter of china from the kitchen. Norbert returned to the balcony and sat down. "Yeah, so you said on the phone."

"Listen, I really appreciate what you've done for me. Setting me up here and everything. But I'm not going to be your kept woman. I need to pay my own way."

"Sandra, you're not my kept woman..."

"Shut up, Norbert. I can't sit here doing nothing. I've been here less than a week and it's already driving me mental."

"What kind of work did you have in mind? I mean, what do you have experience in?"

"Well, before jail, waitressing mostly. Total shit job. And babysitting of course. Maybe daycare would be a possibility. I like kids and—"

"No. Don't give me that look, Sandra. You would need at least a college diploma in Early Childhood Education, which, do you have? No. Also a criminal record check. A bit of an obstacle, wouldn't you say?" Norbert drummed on the balcony rail with his fingers. "Have you thought about going back to school?"

"I just got out of jail. Why would I want to be institutionalized again?"

The drumming stopped. Norbert crossed his forearms on the balcony railing and rested the side of his head against them, facing Sandra. "School is not prison."

"Yes, I know. You're not helping me here, Norbert."

"Sorry. Well, did you do any coursework in prison?"

"Oh yeah, I'm a full-on nuclear physicist now." Sandra looked over her shoulder at the cigarettes on the kitchen counter.

Norbert leaned back in his chair. "Now who's not helping? You're in an awfully deep hole, my darling, and you need to dig yourself out. No certified skills. Not much in the way of job experience. Plus a sizeable hole in your work history that might be a tad difficult to explain. You're in for a lot of fun filling out employment applications."

Sandra stared down through the balcony railings. A jogger plodded along the seawall below, intermittently being overtaken by swifter runners. "Okay, in prison I worked in the library. In fact, for the last ten years I pretty much ran that room. Did a damn fine job too, if I do say so myself. Everything I built there is probably going to shit already." She kept her gaze on the runners below. "I could get a job as a librarian … maybe."

"Brrraaahh!" Norbert emitted a bizarre buzzer sound. "Forget it, Sandra. Again, you'd need at least a college diploma. So what else have you got to offer? Can you keyboard?"

"I type pretty much okay. Nowhere near as fast as Bet, but fast enough."

"Well, that's something, but I was thinking about computers. What software have you used?"

"Software? Oh, I don't know. In the joint I typed letters for other inmates, written to relatives, lawyers or whoever. The screws read everything, so I didn't write for myself unless I felt like messing with their minds. At first we had IBM Selectrics to work on — I really liked their little typeball thingies — but then computers were brought in. Don't ask me what kind. Some volunteer tutor taught me the basics but, far as I could comprehend, a computer is a typewriter hooked up to a television. I'm not a computer whiz, but so what? There can't be that many jobs that require computer skills."

A spluttering noise from Norbert caused Sandra to look in his direction. "What?"

Norbert shook his head and sighed. "Sandra, these days you need to know computing just to clean toilets. Don't laugh; it's true … well, nearly. Next visit I'll bring you a laptop to practise on. It'll help a lot, believe me. When you get the hang of it I could always use help around the office — basic data entry, filing, answering the phone, stuff like that."

"No offence, Norbert, but you as my boss is just too close for comfort."

"No offence taken." Norbert's tone belied his words. "All the same, I've got connections in the industry. When you're ready I could find you a job, easy."

"In the development industry?"

"Yep, for sure. You'd need some skills, but brains you got — much more important."

Sandra wasn't keen to follow where the conversation was leading. She switched topics. "What about the other thing I mentioned?" *Thing* — that wasn't right. But Sandra lacked words to describe what she most longed for.

"Finding your daughter. Sorry, Sandra, this is news to me. How did this … when did this happen?"

"I was pregnant when I was arrested. It was kept out of the papers."

"But who…" Norbert stopped and looked down to his right, trying to construct a tactful finish to his question.

"Who was the father? Jesus Christ, Norbert, what difference does that make now? It wasn't you."

"I know that." Grasping the balcony rail, Norbert pulled himself to his feet. "Sorry, you just blew my mind."

"I had a baby girl. I gave her up for adoption. I more or less had to. Definitely had to. Never even got to hold her. Just a bit of dark hair sticking out of a bundled-up pink blanket, there for a second, then gone." Sandra turned away from Norbert. Tears had begun to flow.

Norbert sat back down. He shuffled his chair over tight against Sandra's and put his arm around her. She didn't shake it off. "It's okay, Sandra, it'll be okay."

"Is there any hope of finding her?"

"Who knows. But I'll look into it, I promise."

"Thank you, Norbert." Her throat was tight. "Oh God…" A deep breath and then, "I'm a mess." Sandra hurried to the bathroom. She came out several minutes later with a wad of tissues in her hand. Norbert had moved inside and was seated on the living room couch. On the coffee table, an open bottle of wine and two glasses. Sandra sat down, leaving a clear foot of couch between them.

Once Sandra settled in, Norbert shifted position several times, carefully maintaining the zone of separation. He picked up the bottle and, with raised eyebrows, extended it toward Sandra. She nodded and Norbert poured. She picked up her glass and sipped; Norbert left his on the table. After fidgeting some more Norbert at last picked up his glass and stared down into it. "Sandra, I have to tell you something. Promise you won't hate me."

"Norbert, I'm no good at predicting how I'll react to something I don't know about yet. So either shut up or spill your guts and take your chances."

Norbert sighed, grimaced and took a run at his planned narrative. "Okay, have it your way. Remember the day when all the shit came down ... how I wasn't there?"

"You mean the day we were arrested? Me, Bet and Phyl? I was glad you weren't there. I assumed you came to your senses and got gone while the getting gone was good."

"No, no, I would never have deserted my comrades; not you guys. I was coming back to the house with groceries, according to plan, when this car pulls up beside me and the driver rolls down his window. Freaked me out at first but then I figured just someone needing directions. So I goes up to the car and, bam, two big guys jump out and force me into the rear seat. Scared the piss out of me."

Sandra propped her elbow on the back of the couch, chin in hand. "What were they, cops?"

"Not the police. Private agents of some kind, hired by my parents. They'd been watching our house for days, or so they said. After they pounced, they took me to a motel room out in the 'burbs."

"Didn't you scream for help, try to escape or something?"

"No, like I said, I was pretty freaked out. I thought they would, I don't know, hurt me if I tried to get away. Then at the motel, right in front of me, they phoned the cops. Gave them our house address; said the people there were dealing drugs."

"Drugs? That's all? Nothing about the Berkman Brigade? What about John and—"

"No, just drugs and the address. No Berkman, nothing about John or anything like that. Don't know why not, because they seemed to know what was what. But they could have been bluffing, or stupid maybe."

"Sounds to me like they were pretty smart. If they reported what was really going down, for sure the cops would have followed up on the call. Would've traced who made it. So your guys came up with a pretext to get the cops interested. They figured the bust would follow, and they figured right. The cops found who they were looking for and took all the credit. End of story."

Norbert's blue eyes widened, the naïve lad of years back suddenly reappearing. "You know, I think you must be right. I never thought about that angle."

"What did they do after they made the call?"

"Well, they kept me in the motel room for what seemed like forever. Deprogramming me, they said. I was handcuffed and kept awake for days while they took turns interrogating me. At first it was all questions and, if they weren't already hip to what was happening in Berkman House, they found out quick enough. I told them everything. Didn't want to, but I got slapped once to make me cooperate. So, I caved. Next they lectured me about my attitude, my politics, my … immaturity. I tried to call them on their bullshit, but they were having none of it. So then I just agreed with everything they said and eventually they seemed satisfied. Then Mom and Dad showed up. My parents made an offer — an ultimatum, more like. If I returned to university they would pay my way — fees, apartment, car, the whole shebang. Otherwise I'd be left to my own devices. Cut off without a cent."

Sandra raised her eyebrows. "So you took the money."

"Yeah, basically. But their deprogramming didn't work. I'm pretty sure about that. Still, by this time I had nothing to go back to. You guys were already busted. So … I accepted the offer … the ultimatum. But I had minimal contact with my parents after that. Now they're both dead. Good riddance, far as I'm concerned."

"That's quite a story, Norbert. And it explains a lot. We thought Wiggie sicced the cops on us."

"Wiggie? Nah, Wiggie never would've done that." Norbert fell silent; it seemed as if he'd become totally immersed in the past.

Sandra poured herself another glass of wine and, as an afterthought, refilled Norbert's glass, bringing him back into the present. He downed half of the pour in a series of gulps. "So, you're not mad at me?"

"Why exactly am I supposed to be mad at you?"

"Because … you were all busted … because of me. And like I said before, I wasn't there to take my share of the punishment."

"Norbert, we were not busted because of you; we were busted because of your parents. And we would have been busted anyway, sooner or later. The fact that you weren't scooped up with me and the others is a good-news item. You being punished wouldn't have made things any better for the rest of us. So stop beating yourself up." Sandra drained her glass and Norbert refilled it. She refilled his glass in return and leaned back into the couch.

Norbert shifted toward Sandra until their hips touched. On contact he swung his arm around her shoulder. Sandra stiffened, then relaxed into his half embrace. Talk continued, first awkwardly, then with more animation. Highlights of Norbert's married life, highlights of Sandra's prison life (as much as she chose to reveal), people and episodes from their shared past. Once the conversation achieved liftoff Sandra didn't want it to stop. It was as if a cork had exploded from a bottle and it was a relief to let everything out.

After several hours, gaps re-emerged between their sentences. The sky outside turned indigo and the room darkened. Norbert stood and switched on the floor lamp beside the couch. He went to the kitchen and threw a frozen lasagna into the microwave. When only a few shreds of pasta remained and the wine long since down to its dregs, their store of conversation was likewise depleted. Sandra was pondering how to disengage when Norbert brought his face around and glued his lips on hers. A startling move, although not unwelcome. Warmed by kiss and caress, Sandra didn't resist when Norbert took her hand and ushered her back into bed.

1982

As I'm picking up shards of glass from the floor and sponging coffee splashes off the kitchen wall, I anticipate some protest from Bet, the usual rant about womyn (her spelling) cleaning up after men, that sort of thing, but she doesn't even seem to notice what I'm doing. Feet still drawn up on her chair, she stares out the window into the rain, as I had been doing before when alone in the kitchen. She mutters something between her knees. It sounds like "infantile leftism."

"Pardon?" I say.

Bet looks up and stares at me as if seeing me for the first time that morning. "Sandra, what are we doing?"

"Come on, Bet, it's no big deal. If we wait for Phyl to clean this up, we'll be waiting for—" I'm cut off by the agitated chopping motion of Bet's right hand.

"No, no, no, what I mean is what *are* we…" Bet makes a circular motion with her hands over her head to indicate the whole household, and then says with great emphasis, "What are we doing?"

I have no idea what she's getting at, so I don't respond.

"All around the world our revolutionary brothers and sisters have taken up arms and are waging war against imperialist and capitalist structures while we — what? What are we doing?"

I think of the didactic broadsheets we printed on our little mimeo (now busted and dumped in the lane out back), the sexist billboards we defaced and the time that Phyl shoved a cream pie in the face of some bigshot politician. None of these acts seem to stack up somehow, compared with actually shooting at people and blowing things up.

"Well, Bet, you yourself have said that objective conditions aren't ripe for a more advanced level of struggle," I reply, after extended rumination. What that means, I'm not exactly sure, but when you talk to Bet, you have to speak her language.

"I know, I've said that, but is it true? Here we are in the very belly of the beast. Surely we can do more than spray-paint slogans on walls or throw pies in people's faces."

"We have to be … pragmatic," I say.

"Pragmatic? What do you mean?" Bet's eyes drill into mine.

"Well, cautious then."

"Cautious, hah! How about scared shitless."

I take a deep breath and try to keep the tone of my voice neutral. "I'm not scared shitless, Bet." Although the truth is, I am, almost all of the time.

"I know you're not." Bet stares out the window again. "But for sure I am." She gets up and leaves the kitchen. I finish cleaning up the mess from Phyl's drama-queen stunt.

I don't see Bet for the rest of the day or, for that matter, anyone else in the household. It's almost as if everyone is licking their wounds in separate lairs. You can tell when times are bad in the collective; no one leaves their respective bedrooms. Phyl says it's impossible to build a true socialist collective in housing designed for a nuclear family; the ideal design, he claims, would be a large geodesic dome with tubular sleeping units built into the outside shell around one large common area. Maybe he's right. But I can't go along with his plan of taking down all the interior doors, including the one on the bathroom, and having us rotate bedrooms every six months. Come to think of it, he's probably still miffed we voted down his proposal to do exactly that, three house meetings ago.

It's already after 2:00 p.m. when I decide to return to my bourgeois private chamber, shut my counter-revolutionary door and crawl under my backsliding quilt with a decadent novel. En route, I browse through the bookshelves in the living room, searching for a good read. Over the years Berkman House has amassed an impressive library of books left behind by countless prior residents and crashers: romance novels, murder mysteries, science fiction and pretty much every goddamned political tract ever written. The political stuff is all heavily underlined with marginal annotations in Bet's tiny and precise handwriting. Bet is obsessive about theory. I'm not big on theory (although I'd never admit this to her or any of my housemates). I'm more curious about the theorists. If Marx came for dinner, would he give me any air time? Or would he just expect me to listen to him rambling on about dialectics? Would Engels wash the dinner dishes? What would dancing with Mao be like? Would Rosa Luxemburg laugh at my jokes? If Che Guevara ended up in my bed, would I still feel like cuddling in the morning? I can't help it. I can't be an *ist* or *ite* of anyone without having a sense of them as a person.

Having read all the fun stuff already, I poke around the anarcho-Marxian-situationist-etcetera literature in hopes of finding something semipalatable. I'm about to give up and go buy a magazine at the corner store when, as I'm flipping through the pages of something called *The Essential Works of Lenin*, the page header "What Is to Be Done?" leaps out at me. This section has been particularly darkened by underlining and annotations. I take the book upstairs to read.

As I settle into my bed I hear what sounds like a hailstorm on the roof. Bet typing in the next room. The storm persists for an unusually long time, sometimes diminishing into separate hesitant keystrokes before picking up again into another furious gust of pounding. The typing blends with the cadence of Lenin's translated prose, and I'm soon lulled to sleep.

I'm not sure what wakes me up — either a fresh onslaught of typing or the smell of onions frying in the kitchen. At any rate, I'm famished; I pull on my kimono and go downstairs to investigate. Norbert is standing at the stove stirring up a mess of bloated red lentils.

"Top of the morning, Sandra-san," he says in an altogether too cheerful tone.

"What time is it?" I'm still half asleep, but feel it has to be close to midnight.

"This needs a certain something." He stabs a long wooden spoon at my face. "What do you think?"

Obediently I lap up a couple of lentils from the end of the spoon; they're still slightly crunchy. *Cooking them for starters*, I think, but I say, "Salt."

With some show of reluctance, Norbert splashes a dollop of soy sauce into the pot and samples it again. "Yum, all right." He scoops some of the stew into two bowls and adds some brown rice from another pan. "This is for Bet and Louie. They're eating in their room. Help yourself, there's plenty."

I keep my trap shut as Norbert leaves the kitchen and heads upstairs, although I'm tempted to vent. Room service in the Berkman Collective? Things are worse than I thought.

I spoon myself some rice and lentil glop and, after a dribble more of sauce, take the bowl up to my room. As I eat, sitting on my bed, I hear voices and laughter through the wall. Then music from Louie's tape deck drowns out everything else. After a while a strong scent of marijuana wafts into my room. I'm tempted to join the party, but damned if I'm going to put my nose in without being asked. And so I wait. And wait. What seems like hours later I drift back to sleep.

I wake at dawn feeling cramped and sluggish. Dinner set in my intestines like Portland cement. A blackberry bush coiled inside my skull with one long tendril of thorns running down my spine. Poisoned by lentils and too much sleep.

I can no longer remain in bed, neither in my room, nor even in the house. High-grading my laundry pile, I stuff two weeks of dirty clothes into my backpack and, after adding all the towels on the bathroom racks, rush out the front door. Louie's van isn't parked out front, which surprises me. The van hasn't moved in over a month, and besides, it's not like Louie to rise before ten.

It's even earlier than I think. The Closed sign still glows in the laundromat window, which I know opens at 8:00 a.m. I revise my destination to George's Diner on the next corner. Not hungry, but I could do with a jolt of caffeine. Every stool along the counter is occupied by ample buttocks supporting a hunched row of coveralls and green work shirts. I claim an empty booth, heave my backpack onto the bench on one side and sit opposite. Over at the counter a clatter of china and slurping of coffee, but no one speaks except a smokey-voiced waitress straight out of the fifties, with pancake makeup, fake eyelashes and varnished beehive hairdo. "Cold enough for you, Fred? Refill, Bob? Finished with the ketchup, Mike?" A series of grunts in reply.

After a few minutes, apparently concluding that I wasn't going away without a shove, the waitress manifests herself at my booth, brandishing a stainless-steel pot. "Yes?"

I tap the rim of one of the cups already on the table. "Coffee, thanks."

She frowns at my backpack and reluctantly pours while, with her free hand, she extracts a menu from behind the napkin dispenser. "Minimum charge in the booth ... dollar twenty-five."

The men at the counter are all now looking over their shoulders at me. I study the menu.

"Brown toast," I decide — which, with the coffee, puts me a nickel over the limit.

"Toast," she shouts toward the kitchen hatch. She hustles off to refill the row of cups on the counter.

She returns with a stack of white Wonder Bread, barely warm, and sneers as she places it next to my coffee. I reach into my pocket, find five quarters to put on the table and make my exit.

The laundromat has just opened when I arrive, so I have my choice of washers. I load two machines and sit on a hard plastic chair to flip through dog-eared magazines under the harsh fluorescent lights. The articles don't hold my attention for long: makeover advice, making-out tips and meal-plan methodologies. I should have brought Lenin with me — much more stimulating company. I wander over to the bulletin board. Lost cats, rooms to rent, curbside car sales, almost every notice toothed on the bottom with a row of phone numbers, here and there a missing tooth. I'm tempted to tear off random numbers and call them on the pay phone out front. If only I'd brought a roll of dimes. Suddenly, with a clank, the room falls silent save for a faint hum from the lights.

Washing done, over to the dryers. I load everything in one machine and sit where I can watch the spinning kaleidoscope of my wardrobe. A television show I can relate to, all about my life. The display holds me in a trance until, suddenly, the colours drop and silence again returns.

Folding my warm and still slightly damp clothes, I compress them into my backpack. Now what? Energized by coffee, last night's lentils still sitting heavy in my stomach, I head away from Berkman House. I'm not ready to return. Almost everything I own is on my back; I could hitchhike out of town and across the country right now. Homeward bound. Completing the round trip started two summers ago. *Back home?* Fuck, what a depressing thought. I was pretty much a teenage runaway, taking off without letting family and friends know. Haven't been in touch since and not about to do so now. Dad's an abusive boozer and Mom's a gutless bitch. End of story.

Wandering aimlessly in the drizzle, I happen upon the hippy hostel where I stayed when I first arrived in the city. A cluster of scruffy kids outside smoking, a permanent fixture in front of this hostel. They look at me curiously, but I ignore them. I was once one of those kids, but how young they seem now — or how much I've aged in just two years.

It was during my stay at this hostel when I first met Louie and Bet. I was exploring the business district, half-heartedly looking for Help Wanted signs, when I heard shouting, occasionally punctuated by cheers. My first impulse was to turn and retreat from the commotion but, bored and curious, I went to take a gander. A small crowd — maybe two hundred people — gathered on a plaza listening to some guy hectoring them through a bullhorn. Behind the speaker a serious-looking choir held up signs proclaiming justice for somebody or other. The name meant nothing to me, nor could I make out what the speaker was saying; his words echoed off the buildings and were washed out by the intermittent eruptions of a plaza fountain. "Hey," I moved in close to a couple standing nearby. "What's this about?" The woman responded with more detail than I needed, very little of which I caught and even less of which I understood. The gist of it was they were protesting the mistreatment of a political prisoner in some far-off country.

"What good does talking about it here do?" I was genuinely puzzled.

The woman's partner laughed as if I'd made a particularly funny joke and laid his hand on my shoulder. His touch sent an unexpected charge through me; I wanted the hand to move slowly over other parts of my body. He was drop-dead gorgeous: eyes intensely bright — almost fanatical — radiating charisma along with a smoldering sensuality. As he gave me the once-over, I found myself irrationally hoping that this couple was not a couple in the coupling sense. But of course they were, a status confirmed by observing his other hand wound around his companion's waist. My lonely nights sleeping on an upper single in the hostel dormitory weren't coming to an end anytime soon.

"What good does talking do?" His voice, deep and rich, sustained the effect of his touch. "Right on — action not words." The people around us hissed at him to be quiet. The three of us moved away from the crowd to where we could chat without censure. While talking, we drifted farther from the amplified babble and the loud fountain. We introduced ourselves and when Louie and Bet found out I was staying in a hostel, they invited me home for dinner. "Home" was Berkman House. That night I sat at the cable spool for the first time and was introduced to Phyl, Eric and Sue. Dinner was macrobiotic, according to Sue, who served out bowls of millet topped with a watery legume and turnip stew. No salt. The food was awful, but the company was glorious.

Over dinner, Sue asked how long I planned to stay in the hostel. "Only until I find a cheap place to rent," I said, honestly not hinting at anything. Up to that point I hadn't contemplated living in shared accommodation. But my response brought the conversation to a sudden halt; meaningful glances were exchanged around the cable spool. Somehow, with no words spoken, Bet was delegated to escort me out of the kitchen so that she and her housemates could hold a "collective meeting." I slumped onto the living room couch, wondering what I said or did to provoke this mysterious in-camera session.

A few minutes later Bet returned to the living room. "Come," she said and led me back into the kitchen. All smiles around the cable spool while Louie formally advanced a "proposal" for my consideration: "Would you be willing to move into Willy's old room?"

I probably should've given the matter more thought, but I immediately said yes. After only one week at the hostel I was already desperate to leave it behind. And plus ... Louie's voice. I'd hear it every day (not that I expected things to go any further; occasional words from his sensuous lips would have to be enough).

Willy, I learned later, was a musician and the owner of Berkman House, which he inherited mortgage-free from his grandmother.

After fixing up the basement as a rehearsal space, he and his band mates moved in. The combination of living and working together proved too much. The band soon broke up, and there was much turnover in residency over the years since: friends randomly replaced by friends of friends and subsequently by even more distant connections. Willy remained the only constant until he suddenly departed for the Amazon Basin in hopes of finding a personal shaman. Months had since passed with no word from him. My new housemates were now convinced that Willy likely wasn't coming back and they assured me, in the unlikely event he did return, we would work it out.

A few weeks after I moved in, Louie happened upon Eric and Macrobiotic Sue eating hamburgers in a café. That night another collective meeting. Louie denounced the couple for having "Stalinist tendencies" — gorging themselves while engineering a famine for the rest of the household. This meeting was my first exposure to what Bet later explained was Constructive Criticism, and the experience gave me the shivers. I couldn't quite follow Louie's twisted logic. Besides, I'd grown fond of Eric and particularly of waifish, hollow-eyed Sue. She was soft-spoken and congenitally kind. But my primary loyalty had to be with Louie and Bet. They had, after all, sponsored my entry into Berkman House. I duly voted along with them and Phyl to evict the "macrobiotic menace." The pair packed and left the next morning, simmering anger on both sides papered over with forced smiles. The following week, Louie and Bet brought Norbert home from their Marxist study group. This time, after the now familiar vetting, I smiled with the other adjudicators when he was invited back to the spool and assigned the vacant bedroom.

"Hey babe, you checking in or what?"

The question snaps me out of my reverie in front of the hostel. I automatically snarl, "I'm not your babe, jerk."

The jerk sports a wispy Zapata moustache and a camo jacket open over a Che Guevara T-shirt. As I stalk away, he shouts out the worst possible insult he can come up with. "Feminist!"

My shoulders ache like mad from the heavy load of laundry, like carrying another person on my back. I really need to be back with my family. Which raises the question, Which family? The one I was born into or the one I chose to join. No contest really. No way could I return to live under the same roof as my father, to endure his frequent violent rages interspersed with icy distance. No way could I stomach my mother's daily striving to remain invisible. I yield to the gravitational pull of my Berkman family. For better or worse, the collective is now my home. I trudge over to the nearest bus stop, but when my bus pulls up, it's jammed tight with passengers. I don't even try to board, not wanting to be hassled about my backpack. Besides, I have to stretch my money to the end of the month. So I walk. I walk for a long time, mainly uphill. Maybe one *can* go home again, but for me it's harder to return than to leave.

Once back at Berkman House, I'm met by a great commotion in the kitchen. Norbert is cooking up the traditional pot of legumes — soybeans this time — tempered by most of the contents of the fridge. Jars of mayonnaise, pickles, peanut butter and other soup-pot rejects are piled on the counters. A hoary jumble of frozen foods fills the sink. A bowl of hot water generates steam out of the empty fridge. Half obscured by mist, Phyl chisels off massive chunks of ice from the freezer compartment.

I check the bulletin board. Sure enough, pinned to it is a 5x9 file card: HOUSE MEETING TOMORROW 6 P.M. Typed underneath — Agenda items: (1) cash flow crisis resolution (2) other business arising.

Four

2007

Emerging from sleep, but with eyes remaining shut, Sandra extended her hand across the mattress. The body she intended to caress wasn't there; Norbert was gone. Relief mingled with disappointment. She'd no doubt slept more soundly without him. She hadn't shared her bed with another person for decades. Still, the intimacy had been sweet and pleasurable, a much better connection than their first attempt.

She staggered out to the kitchen where she found the coffee maker loaded and ready to fire. She pushed the Brew button and then noticed the cigarettes on the counter. They'd been arranged into words: S call soon, love N. As she doctored her coffee, she wondered whether this cryptic message meant she was to call Norbert or he was going to call her. She decided it had to be the latter, even if that wasn't what he intended.

Sandra took her coffee out to the balcony, as she'd done every morning of her stay in the condo. But today she didn't sit down on one of the plastic patio chairs. She was restless but couldn't pinpoint why. She needed to run. She set down her coffee, donned her sweats and began jogging even before leaving the apartment. She trotted by the concierge in the lobby and, once on the seawall, increased her pace. She ran hard and fast until she reached the bridge, a new milestone for her. Even then she might have kept going, but a cramp in her belly forced a stop. Drenched in sweat, she pivoted and half jogged, half walked back to the apartment. Once inside, she peeled off her clothes and, instead of taking her usual shower, drew a bath.

A wire basket of girlie products — another of Norbert's touches — hung on the edge of the tub. On impulse, Sandra poured a package of crystals into the running water. The water foamed up nicely, stinking of lavender. She immersed herself slowly, the bath so hot her flesh reddened on contact. Once fully immersed, she tried to yield to steamy luxury, but still found herself unable to fully relax. Perhaps the problem was the unaccustomed comfort she'd fallen into. The women released with her had gone from a cell to a halfway house. Why did she deserve anything better?

After a long soak, the water around her cooled to the point of discomfort. Sandra rose from the tub and towelled off. In the bedroom, as she opened a drawer in search of something to wear, she noticed an envelope on top of the dresser. *Just in case* was scrawled in pencil on the envelope. Inside was money, a lot of money, a couple of fifties and the rest twenties. She was compelled to count … a total of five hundred dollars. Her almost subliminal anxiety flamed up into rage.

Sandra dressed in the same clothes she'd worn on the day of her prison release and repacked the drawstring plastic bag with all her belongings. She included nothing that wasn't hers. Then reluctantly, she again picked up the envelope. Norbert's money was tainted, but she had to live on something. She scratched out *Just in case* and scribbled underneath *IOU $500 SJ.*

She left the empty envelope on the kitchen counter along with the apartment key and the cellphone. She rearranged the cigarettes: N fuck you S. She hoped Norbert would find that as ambiguous as the message he left her.

As the front door of the high-rise clicked shut behind her, Sandra felt liberated. She dimly recalled something she wrote way back when: *NEVER SCREW A COMMUNARD.* She'd broken this rule yet again, albeit with a former communard. How pathetic! After so many years, her libido could still overrule her brain.

As she walked, having no plan beyond distancing herself from the apartment, Sandra began sorting out where to go. Even a cheap hotel would set her back more than she could afford for very long. The best option, she decided, was to check into the halfway house where she was supposed to be staying anyway. But she would need a cover story to explain why she hadn't gone there straight from prison. She contrived various plausible rationales and finally decided to go with a version of truth: She was scared off by the media and happened to meet a friend who offered to put her up for a few days. That was all the authorities needed to know. Why would they care anyway?

Her cover story concocted, Sandra found herself deep in the office-tower canyons she'd been driven through last Monday. It was now Sunday; the streets were almost deserted, the buildings strange and foreboding. She imagined herself monitored by thousands of watchers behind the tiers of mirrored windows above. It was a relief to finally break through into a zone of older low-rises. She felt she had to be getting closer to her destination, although she began to worry that the halfway house might be difficult to find.

Then, as she rounded a corner, something familiar appeared. It was a hostel, with a sign reading Backpackers Welcome. It took a few moments before Sandra recognized it as the hippy hostel she'd stayed in before Berkman House. Purely on impulse, she entered. Inside, the same dingy reception desk; the sour-faced guy behind it could have passed for the same man she dealt with years ago. What the hell — she checked in, choosing the dormitory option, which was cheapest. She paid in advance for a one week stay, with a surcharge for "hire" sheets, towel and locker. As he handed Sandra her receipt, threadbare sheets and a fraying towel, Sour Face pointed to a sign next to the cash register: Not Responsible for Lost or Stolen Items. "Gotta lock?" he asked.

Sandra shook her head.

"Best get one; guard against theft." On her way to buy a lock, Sandra was diverted by the smell of bacon from a diner a few doors down from the hostel. It was late in the day, and she'd been running on coffee only. She ignored the several empty booths and sat at the counter instead. She ordered scrambled eggs (always the quickest option) and bacon (sausages or ham not to be trusted in a place like this). Her first restaurant meal since before jail. But she couldn't afford to eat out like this on a regular basis. She started a shopping list on a paper napkin: milk, bread, bananas.

That first night in the dorm Sandra struggled to get to sleep. She'd hated being double-bunked in the joint; this was worse. Four women in one tiny room, three of them on a cross-country cycling trip together. Not that these others were hostile or overly loud, they were just *there* when she wanted to be alone. The cyclists talked excitedly about where they'd been and where they were going; Sandra put her pillow over her head and burrowed into her bottom bunk. Eventually, one of her roomies had to clamber up past her to reach the upper bunk. "Excuse me," she said once her head had passed beyond Sandra's view. Then it was ten o'clock, lights out, and Sandra stared at the sagging mattress above for what felt like hours. Borderline snoring emanated from all around her. Eventually Sandra managed to conk out. When she woke up, mouth encrusted by saliva, the cyclists were gone. Sandra experienced a moment of panic when she couldn't locate her plastic bag, before remembering she'd locked it up the night before.

A second wave of panic was harder to dismiss. For the past few days Sandra had more or less avoided thinking about this morning's appointment. She threw on some clothes and checked the time in the lobby; 7:50 a.m. — a little over an hour to get to the parole office. Splayed out under glass on the reception desk was a city map. She checked the address of the parole office. Not far. She could walk there in under forty minutes.

As she showered and dressed, Sandra went over her narrative — what she'd been doing since her release and, more critically, where she'd been staying. Making reference to a mysterious friend wasn't safe, she decided. Not that she felt obligated to protect Norbert, but mentioning him would probably open up an unwelcome line of questioning. Like, where this mysterious friend lived, for example. Sandra didn't know; she'd tossed Norbert's card and couldn't remember his telephone number.

At 8:55 a.m. Sandra entered a nondescript office building, its connection to the Corrections Department only indicated inside on the building directory: Day Reporting Centre – 301. Sandra rode the elevator up and its door opened immediately into a large reception area. There was no room 301, as such; the entire third floor was dedicated to the Parole Office. Sandra identified herself to the receptionist who, with an almost sincere smile, handed her a form on a clipboard and said, "Take a seat over there; fill this in." "Over there" was what looked like a school cafeteria table. Sandra sat down on a hard plastic chair and examined the form. She patted her pockets for a pen before noticing the one attached to the clipboard by a short length of metal chain. Sandra navigated swiftly through the form until, near the end, she was asked for an address. Which one to give? She opted for the hostel since she figured the Corrections people would know she hadn't checked into the halfway house.

When Sandra returned the completed form, she was startled by the receptionist shouting out, "Welcome back, stranger!" It took Sandra a couple of seconds to realize that the woman was addressing someone behind her. Turning, she saw the back of a man in a suit striding down a long corridor. In response to the greeting, the man gave a token wave over his shoulder.

The receptionist directed Sandra toward a carpeted area framed on three sides by padded vinyl chairs, fake-walnut end tables and a matching credenza. On the credenza was a stack of outdated magazines, torn and scribbled on. Sandra flipped through a magazine without absorbing its contents, her anxiety level rising. A few pointed questions would easily blow her cover story. She was sweating profusely through her grey sweat top by the time her name was called. A uniformed security guard escorted her through a maze of cubicles to one occupied by a deeply tanned man — the same man greeted by the receptionist earlier. An engraved plaque affixed to his acoustic divider identified him as Case Officer.

"Sandra Treming," she said and stuck out her hand. Instead of shaking it, Case Officer motioned to a chair across from where he sat. He told Sandra his name, which she immediately forgot, along with most of her prepared narrative. Case Officer turned out to be all broadcast with very limited reception. A typical commanding officer — ex-military or ex-cop, she decided. He went over the conditions of parole (no drugs, no leaving town without notifying this office, etc.). She did her best to appear attentive, nodding each time he paused to check her reaction. Then, finally, a question: "So, are you settling in all right, Sandra?"

Settling in? The question itself was unsettling. She assumed he meant at the halfway house, but wasn't about to ask for clarification. She played it safe: "Everything's fine."

"Good, good. What are your plans?"

"Well, looking for work, I guess." Sandra squeezed the back of her neck.

"Excellent. I'll arrange for you to meet a vocational counsellor during your next visit." He jotted something in a file, checked his watch and rose to his feet. "Let's go."

"Where are we going?"

"Back to reception. We're all done for today."

Alexander Berkman Collective

House Meeting Minutes

Thursday, October 21, 1982

Present: all members

Item one: Cash Flow Crisis Resolution

BET: Need for self-criticism. Economic redistribution plan presented at last meeting, although correct in essence, was unnecessarily divisive in practice, and therefore fundamentally incorrect. Contradictions in collective not rooted in inequity but in scarcity. Therefore not to be resolved by a stricter accounting of collective resources but by expanding the collective resources.

PHYL: Not prepared to enter wage slavery even if work available, which given current crisis of capital and ensuing high unemployment levels, extremely unlikely.

BET: In total agreement with Phyl's position.

PHYL: Expresses regret for prematurely abandoning the struggle during previous house meeting.

BET: Wage slavery, welfare, government grants, student loans all counter-productive, possibly even counter-revolutionary. Collective must advance struggle onto higher plane — revolutionary in practice and not only in theory.

NORBERT: Requests concretization of terms.

BET: Ready to concretize if comrades will commit to collective in-depth study of entire twenty-page proposal before a consensus decision is reached.

ALL AGREED

BET: (summary) Proposal before the collective is to rob a bank. Such action will accomplish two ends. 1. It will resolve the cash crisis which has divided us. 2. It will be a great leap forward in terms of revolutionary activity, and thereby galvanize ourselves and the class we represent in preparation for the greater struggle to come. The plan prepared by Louie and myself over the last few days covers issues such as location, timing, weaponry, and other tactical points. All of these elements open to revision. The main objective is not.

NORBERT: Cautiously supportive of thrust of presentation. Perhaps premature though?

BET: In what way?

NORBERT: Remembers collective agreeing some months ago that objective conditions not ripe for armed action.

BET: Objective conditions now ripe.

NORBERT: How have objective conditions changed?

LOUIE: We're broke.

NORBERT: Need to hear input from other collective members.

PHYL: Plan right on. Smash the state. Venceremos!

SANDRA: Anything better than always fighting each other — even jail.

BET: Correct planning and group discipline will minimize risk. If all in favour then practice drills begin tomorrow (Friday) morning.

NORBERT: In light of enthusiasm of collective, withdraws earlier reservations. Wishes to have heartfelt solidarity with group consensus a matter of record.

BET: Any remaining objections?

None recorded. Consensus achieved and meeting formally adjourned. Minutes prepared by: LOUIE

#

Goddamn it, I love Berkman House. I love my communards. I even love grouchy old Phyl, who, as soon as Bet declares the meeting adjourned, leaps across the kitchen to the refrigerator and flings open the freezer door to display a full bottle of Polish vodka in a pristine frost-free environment. He holds the door open for an unnaturally long time, until at last Bet responds with appropriate appreciation: "Oh wow, now we can use the freezer again. Who did—" She turns to him. "Did you do that, Phyl?"

Phyl bobs his head up and down, simultaneously splashing a couple of fingers of vodka into our mostly empty coffee mugs.

"Wow, great." She sounds almost sincere. Peace is restored in the Berkman Collective. All of us grin idiotically at each other across the wire spool.

"Comrades!" Phyl lifts his mug over his head, spilling some of the vodka, which he catches with his free hand and laps from his palm.

"With this, the sweat of workers groaning under the oppression of a revolution betrayed, we drink to a new beginning."

Everyone cheers. "Power to the people!" Louie yells, and we all cheer again.

Bet taps her cup against everyone else's. "Long live the dictatorship of the proletariat!" More cheering followed by a unanimous ingestion of vodka. Norbert blows air through his cheeks, grimaces and swings his cup upward again. "A people united can never be defeated!"

Cheers and thumping on the spool. Then my comrades look at me expectantly and I feel a momentary twinge of panic. "Eat the rich," I blurt out. After a second's hesitation my suspect contribution is accepted with more cheers and thumping.

Phyl swallows what remains of his vodka and throws his mug down the hole in the middle of the wire spool. Louie shouts, "Smash the state — smash china!" and follows suit. Not to be outdone, I toss in my mug, as does Norbert. It looks like Bet is about to object but she overrules herself, rolling her cup gently over to the hole until it drops in. If she hopes it won't break she's in for a disappointment; it shatters on its predecessors.

Phyl upends the bottle to his lips; the vodka boils up inside and some dribbles down his chin onto his pristine Talking Heads T-shirt. He passes the bottle to Louie and sprints into the next room. By the time the bottle reaches me for the second time, it's clear the vodka won't complete another circuit. I polish it off as, through the doorway, the Clash start up at full volume. The music is a giant hand taking hold of the collective. It drags us out of the kitchen into the living room, pulls us into its spasmodic rhythms, makes us jump up and down until our chests heave and our clothes are plastered to our bodies with sweat. A short pause between cuts. We pant in extreme poses until the music asserts control again.

We spin with the record, amplify each other's movements, resonate in sync with the speakers. We are components of a grand system, an electrified protoplasmic mass now squirming together, now careening off each other like bumper cars at the midway. As we dance toward exhaustion, we link up more and longer, gradually sinking toward the floor. There we wriggle and roll over each other, finally resolving into one large collective hug as the music stops.

Louie is on the bottom. His laughter is infectious; it vibrates us all into fits of giggling. With tears in our eyes we roll apart, each claiming a private section of carpet. Gradually our laughing subsides, then after a minute of silence Norbert giggles, which sets us all off again.

Somehow, lying on his back, Louie finds the makings and rolls a joint. Phyl tosses over a lighter and we all smoke up, including Bet, who usually doesn't partake.

Then I lose consciousness for a while.

I wake up with a cushion under my head and a blanket over me, Phyl snoring on the couch and everyone else gone. I suddenly remember the house meeting, which spurs me to rise and move. I mount the stairs with difficulty; the treads keep tilting from one side to the other. When I reach my room it spins around my head and topples me onto my bed. The room still refuses to stabilize but eventually it fades into blackness.

I oscillate from a state of confused dreaming into a consciousness not much more coherent. Dim recollections of drowning, of fighting off mad stranglers. Surfacing, I become aware of the bed covers twisted around my upper body and neck, my feet exposed and freezing. The bedside lamp is still on and the clock faintly reads 1:27, which makes no sense at all since the room is bright as, well, day. I struggle to locate myself in time and space, remember the vodka, the dancing, the joint, the house meeting ... Oh Christ, the house meeting. I shake the jumbled images and memories in my mind into a semblance of reasonable order and marshal them into review. After a period of analysis I have to accept that the bank robbery discussion wasn't part of any dream sequence and therefore must have been an actual event. The memory remains fragmented and surreal but no less horrific.

I sit up and pull on a pair of socks, which warm my feet but do nothing for the rest of my body, ravaged by the excesses of the night before. Rob a bank ... hip hip hooray ... dance 'til you drop ... yeah, yeah, yeah. Seriously? Rob a bank? Not that I should be worried exactly; the Alexander Berkman Collective has always been short of follow-through. Like our namesake we lack the finishing touch. Alexander (a.k.a. Sasha) Berkman was an anarchist who tried to assassinate Andrew Carnegie's right-hand man, Henry Clay Frick (why he didn't attempt to knock off numero uno, I don't know; maybe he was fond of libraries). The idea was to inspire the working class to rise up and make the revolution. This was a long time ago, of course. Sasha shot Frick three times and stabbed him in the leg before getting the crap beat out of him by members of said working class. Backward elements, according to Louie. Frick survived. Sasha was sent up for a long stretch in the joint.

Voices downstairs and the smell of something cooking. Something sweet and caramelly. Maybe my housemates have had time to sleep it off and reconsider. Maybe things are back to normal. Well, not normal in the normal sense, but … best go and investigate.

The kitchen is a hive of activity, none of it very encouraging from my new-found perspective. Louie has the house armoury spread out on the wire spool: the old .22 rifle and his new pride and joy, which I've learned is a Winchester 700. Besides the firearms, a couple of hunting knives in sheathes. Bet is on her hands and knees with magic markers and a large sheet of white poster board, drawing out a floor plan that doesn't look like her dream house. Armed with a utility knife, Norbert is meticulously cutting off the heads of wooden matches. Oddest thing of all, Phyl is cooking something in the electric frying pan.

"Well, at last. Where did you put that pistol, Sandra?" Do I detect a slight accusatory tone in Louie's voice or am I being paranoid?

"Is there any coffee?" Not an attempt at evasion, I'm just not fully awake yet. Norbert jumps up from his matches and pours me a cup, doctoring it according to my preferences.

"Ta," I say to Norbert and then, at the thick goo that Phyl is so carefully stirring, "So, what's cooking?"

"This…" Phyl squints at his concoction. "This is a delicious, revolutionary, magic potion of invisibility. I think we're ready for those match heads." Norbert obediently scoops up a double handful of his handiwork and dumps it in the frying pan; a sulfuric stench fills the kitchen. Phyl folds in the match heads with some difficulty, the mixture becoming hard to stir.

"Chef's surprise." Phyl unplugs the cord.

"Finished," says Bet at almost the same moment and hands the card up to Louie. On it, the unmistakable floor plan of a bank — teller wickets and the vault neatly drawn in and labelled. Which bank, I have no idea.

"All right, now that Sandra is with us, I guess we can review the plan. Can we have some focus, comrades?"

Comrade Phyl is washing up at the sink; he dries his hands on his jeans and sits down at the cable spool on one of the tea crates.

"Is anyone taking minutes?" asks Comrade Bet.

"I will." Comrade Norbert takes down the house log, a steno pad hanging on a hook near the telephone.

"Item one," Louie says and pins up Bet's artwork on the bulletin board. "Our target. Located at the corner of 41st and Main, an ideal location from the point of view of escape routes and security arrangements. At exactly 14:55 tomorrow..." Louie addresses the room in his most formal and businesslike tone. Chairman Louie-mode I call it. Fearless Leader, Supreme Commander, Great Helmsman, et cetera. I listen carefully, repelled and at the same time fascinated. One thing for certain, Louie and Bet have done their homework. Every detail has been carefully thought through. With one exception: "As soon as I get up to the service counter, Phyl will shoot out the security camera with the Winchester and keep me covered. I'll draw the pistol and order one of the bank workers to open the vault. At that point I—"

"No!" I speak on impulse and not with any intention of subverting Louie's presentation, or maybe I do have that intention, but either way the effect is like I crapped on the table.

"What do you mean — no?" Louie adopts a tone of puzzlement to hide his indignation.

I'm stumped. What I want to say is "That pistol is mine; you can't use my gun." But I know that won't wash. My comrades would be all over me with accusations of bourgeois tendencies — property is theft, yadda yadda. I find a serviceable thread. "How come only the men get to use the weapons? Don't you think that women are capable of bearing arms? Don't you trust us?"

"Listen, I trust you. It's simply a matter of training and experience. Besides, you have a very important job to do. We're counting on you to create a diversion. As soon as you hear Phyl shooting, I want you to throw a smoke bomb in the building across the street — here." Louie's forefinger finds the place on Bet's chart.

"Smoke bomb?"

"Smoke bomb." Phyl reaches over, picks up the electric frying pan and waves it in my direction.

I'm not about to be derailed. "Aren't we simply reinforcing gender stereotypes? I mean, aren't most bank robbers men? If our collective walks into that bank and all the men are carrying guns and all the women are unarmed, what kind of message are the masses left with? How do we differ in that case from any typical gang of terrorist bandits?" There's nothing like a string of rhetorical questions to fluster the opposition.

"Well," Norbert pipes up, "we're different because we rob banks to advance the revolution."

"Fine. You men go tear down the capitalist system; we women will stay home and cook and clean the commune — right Bet?"

I can tell Bet is torn. She isn't prepared to side with me, but I've hit her at her weakest point. After a brief internal struggle, sisterly solidarity prevails — sort of. "I think Sandra has a point," she says without much conviction.

"You got my solidarity, babe," Phyl adds, whether in support of me or Bet isn't clear.

Norbert ups the ante. "I offer you my rifle, the .22."

Louie drums his fingers on the spool. "Right, I apologize for my unconscious sexism. I propose that Bet goes to the counter with the handgun. It's only fair. After all, this entire project was her idea and she should be in the vanguard of its implementation."

My throat locks against a sob reflex and I feel my chin trembling uncontrollably, but I don't burst into tears. I can't trust myself to speak so I stare at Louie, who has artfully — and I'm sure deliberately — skewered what I hoped to achieve, the paralysis of never-ending debate. Yes, he capitulated to my argument but he completely buggered my hidden agenda, and he knows it. For sure he knows it. I can tell by the little smirk on the edges of his fat lips. I can read it in his eyes which betray his not-quite-perfect poker face.

A few seconds more of having to endure Louie's ill-concealed triumph and I'll lose control, weep, yell at my communards, denounce them all along with their stupid scheme to rob a bank. A loud knock at the front door saves me.

"Oh shit, the cops." Phyl picks up several pairs of black nylon stockings (where did those come from?) with eye holes cut in them. "Fire drill, everybody." Phyl stuffs the nylon masks into his hip pocket.

It *is* like a fire drill. As I watch, the kitchen is cleared of all incriminating evidence in seconds. Louie runs upstairs with both rifles and the hunting knife. Bet slides the bank floor plan into the narrow space between the gas stove and the kitchen counter. Norbert shoves the house log down his pants and sweeps the wire spool clear of headless matchsticks, dumping them into the garbage pail. Phyl picks up the frying pan and then, reconsidering, puts it back on the counter. He extracts last night's lentil stew from the fridge and pours some in the frying pan to disguise his concoction.

One person doesn't take part in the drill — me. I stand paralyzed in the eye of a hurricane as the knocking at the front door becomes more and more insistent. I've never been in trouble with the law, never been arrested, never — back when I had a car — even got a speeding ticket. But I've heard stories. Any second now the door will be kicked in and a gang of large male strangers will flash some papers, bark questions, paw through our personal effects and break everything they touch while searching the house. And their search will be fruitful; they'll find our guns, our broken printing press, pamphlets, Phyl's baby marijuana plants, even extract the bank plan from its hiding place. We'll all be handcuffed, roughed up and beaten in places the bruises don't show, and taken downtown. There, in some windowless chamber, I'll be cavity-searched and otherwise humiliated by a bull-dyke matron. I'll be thrown in with the hookers, punks and other lumpen trash and have to fight for my place to sleep. I—

"Answer the door, Sandra." Phyl is combing his hair; no one else is present. I walk through the house and approach the front door with extreme caution. My side pressed against the back of the door, I turn the handle gingerly and ease it open, only my face peeking around it.

"Well, about time." Dorian Twisp — Louie's brother from another mother, as Phyl calls him. An apt description, but only as far as a shared physical appearance. In all other respects Dorian and Louie couldn't be more unalike. Dorian is ordinary. Beyond ordinary, in fact, having elevated ordinariness to the level of art. He's so ordinary that he is as fascinating to us Berkmanites as some sideshow freak. He works for a living, although none of us knows what his job is, nor cares to ask. We do know, though, that he's generous with his disposable income; his generosity many times having fuelled our hospitality. And he's a charmer, his charm deriving mainly from his unfailing interest in whatever and whoever he meets. At the present moment, however, I'm not charmed; I could cheerfully strangle him.

"Come on in, Dorian." I shout "Dorian" so that the whole household can hear.

"What's going on? How come you took so long to answer the door? I knew you were home. I could hear you all stomping around inside."

"Um, yeah, we thought you were Jehovahs."

"Hey, Dorian, how you doing, buddy?" Louie sashays downstairs wearing a classic set of checkered pyjamas. I've never seen him in pyjamas before.

Norbert comes around the corner from the music room. "Hiya, Dorian."

Then Phyl. "How ya doing, man."

And lastly Bet. "Dorian! What a surprise; come on in."

It's a bit much. Almost as if we haven't seen Dorian for years, rather than days. Understandably Dorian looks a little confused — a long wait on the front porch and then the red-carpet treatment. We gravitate to the kitchen in an awkward cluster, all of us — except for Dorian — giggling and speaking over each other's inanities. I pour a cup of coffee and hand it to our visitor, ignoring his "No thanks, Sandra." Suddenly all the babbling stops, as if on cue, and a painful silence descends.

"We…" Bet begins.

Louie also starts to speak. "What…"

Louie and Bet glance at each other. Louie continues, "What brings you to these parts, stranger?" Chairman Louie has abdicated in favour of good-ol'-boy Louie.

"I was wondering if any of you folks would be into going to a bar for a few brewskies."

"Thanks, but no thanks, man. I'm kinda bagged." Louie lifts the lapels of his PJs to substantiate his claim.

"Hey, buddy, come on. A couple of beers. Shoot some pool. Maybe even get lucky." Dorian tosses a just-kidding, ha-ha wink in Bet's direction. She responds with a wan smile that doesn't seem too forced. Somehow Dorian possesses immunity from what would normally trigger a rant against sexism.

Louie is visibly tempted by the raise in ante but he manfully sticks to the straight and true. "Another time. Hafta be up early tomorrow. Gotta see some people about a job."

"Okay, okay, I won't twist your arm. How 'bout the rest of you party animals? Phyl?"

"Gee, I'm right in the middle of cooking dinner. I—"

"Norbert?"

Norbert makes a helpless little gesture to indicate a reluctant negative. Bet breaks in before Dorian can continue his poll. "I think we're all pretty hungry, and since Phyl has almost finished cooking, we'll stay here and eat and then, who knows, maybe join you later."

"Well all right, what's for dinner?"

"It's sort of a lentil stew." Phyl takes the cover off the frying pan and gives the contents a token stir.

Normally this would be a safe response; Dorian is strictly meat and potatoes. But for some perverse reason he snatches the stir spoon, digs into the goo and helps himself to a large dollop. To his credit he controls his gag reflex, but barely. He pounces on the cup of coffee I poured him and half swallows, half gargles it down. Then he backs up against the wall and regards us suspiciously, as if waiting for someone to crack a smile. No one does. At last Dorian speaks. "You guys seriously eat this stuff?"

"It's an acquired taste," says Bet. "Are you sure you won't stay for dinner?"

"No, no, thanks. I'm out of here. Maybe see you guys later?"

"Say, pal," Louie suddenly breaks in, "could you lend me a ten spot 'til next week. I'm completely tapped out."

"Only if you use it to buy real food." Dorian pulls out his wallet and extracts two five-dollar bills. "No offence, Phyl, but that's a pretty weird goulash." Dorian hands over the money and makes a quick exit without saying goodbye.

As soon as the front door closes behind him, Bet bursts into raucous laughter. I've never heard her laugh so freely before and I'm completely taken aback.

"What's in that stuff, Phyl? Apart from the match heads." I seem to be the only one concerned.

"Four parts white sugar, six parts saltpetre…"

"So much for getting lucky!" Bet explodes into even greater guffaws in which the rest of my communards join. After a few seconds of trying to remain straight-faced, I let myself crack. It isn't real merriment but a badly needed release of tension.

"Right," says Bet, suddenly serious. "Back to our review." She retrieves the floor plan from its hiding place and tacks it back up on the bulletin board.

"Hang on. I've got to bottle this before it sets." Phyl starts to pour the contents of the frying pan into an empty mayonnaise jar and then suddenly stops. "Oh no," he says, picking up Dorian's wallet from the counter beside the sink. He runs out of the kitchen heading for the front door. We hear him call "Dorian!" a few times before returning. "Missed him."

"Damn," says Louie, but he doesn't sound very unhappy. "Bet, you do the review with our comrades — I better return this. We don't need him coming back." He takes the wallet from Phyl's hand.

"Louie…" Bet begins, her voice full of menace.

"Bet…" Louie replies, mimicking her tone. "Look, someone has to return the wallet and I know the plan backward and forward. Back in half an hour — max — promise."

Phyl, Norbert and I focus our attention on various neutral inanimate objects, bracing ourselves for the inevitable nuclear blast from Bet. It doesn't ignite. Louie backs out of the kitchen; we hear him running upstairs and then down again less than a minute later. He flies through the kitchen and out the back door, pyjamas now replaced by jeans and a fringed leather jacket.

After the door clicks shut behind Louie there's a period of charged silence. Then, powered by some reserve tank of energy, Bet recommences the review. "Okay, this is very important." But her enthusiasm wanes after a few bullet points, as she calls them. Her manner becomes abstracted, as if no one else is in the room. Well, no one else but me, that is. She addresses everything she says in my direction, although she avoids making eye contact. She focuses on my role in the overall plan, repeating key points several times as if I'm some kind of simpleton.

It isn't very complicated. All I have to do is wait for the signal, throw a smoke bomb through an open window and then yell "Fire!" This is the diversion. What value there would be in creating a diversion directly across the street from the scene of the crime, I haven't the foggiest. I'm not the one who plans these things. I just follow orders.

Eventually Bet is satisfied that I savvy her instructions and we wrap up the review session. No one comments on the fact that forty-five minutes have gone by since Louie's departure. Norbert prepares a vegetable stir-fry and reheats what's left of yesterday's lentil stew. No match heads but not much of an improvement taste-wise. We eat dinner. I wash the dishes and Phyl sort of dries them. We huddle around the kitchen spool, drink some beer and try not to look at the clock.

At eleven, when Louie has been gone for three hours, Phyl turns on the television set in the living room. The collective reconvenes around him and we watch *Casablanca*, the colourized version. Phyl keeps saying how much better Bogie looks in black and white.

One o'clock. No Louie. Norbert and Phyl snoring together on the couch. Bet pacing to the front window every few minutes. I turn off the television set and climb upstairs to bed.

At 1:30 a.m. the telephone rings.

Five

2007

Sandra stood in front of a low-rise apartment building, double-checking its address against a page she'd torn from a phonebook. Like the neighbourhood around it, the building had been at one time fashionable but now was sadly rundown: shrubbery out front choked by weeds, walkway pavers cracked, paint peeling from wooden siding and gutters. The general lack of maintenance suggested the area was on the cusp of becoming upscale again. Literally upscale, soon to be dominated by high-rise towers like the one she'd stayed in the week before. After old relics like this building were bulldozed, of course.

The front door was slightly recessed into the building to form a kind of sheltered landing, where Sandra paused. To her right a panel of buttons, each with an apartment number and, in some cases, a name scrawled adjacent. There was no name written next to 409. Sandra took a deep breath and pushed the button. No response.

After pushing the button three times, and then waiting for a full minute, Sandra gave up. As she turned to go, a woman carrying two plastic bags of groceries stepped onto the landing. "Who are you visiting?" she asked in a tone ambiguously curious and suspicious.

Sandra was reluctant to speak the name but felt it necessary to prove her legitimacy. "Bet … in 409. No one's answering. She must have stepped out. I'll come back another time."

"Bethany? Oh, she's home all right. She's always home." The woman switched her grocery bags to one hand and yanked open the door. "Those buttons don't work. Not that she would answer even if they did." She let the door swing shut behind her.

Startled by what she'd witnessed — twenty-five years of conditioning had led her to believe that no door was ever left unlocked — Sandra followed the woman inside. She was greeted in the lobby by stained carpeting, dusty spackled walls and a pervasive stench of rotting cabbage, stale cigarettes and mothballs. A pile of ad flyers and newspaper inserts lay on the floor beneath a row of mailboxes. Opposite the mailboxes was an elevator door; Sandra pushed the Up button and waited, again doubting her mission. Had she any reason to expect to be welcomed? How likely was it that the Bet she knew so long ago actually lived in this building?

The elevator was as unresponsive as the call panel outside. Sandra was about to give up for a second time when a man barged out from a door next to the elevator. Ignoring Sandra's presence, the man crossed to the mailboxes. Enlightened by his example, Sandra caught the door before it closed and ascended the staircase beyond.

Upon reaching the fourth floor Sandra wasn't out of breath; her morning runs were paying off. To her left, the elevator door was propped open by a glider chair, which rocked back and forth every few seconds as the door attempted to close. The elevator cab was half full of boxes and other bits of furniture. A scowling young man appeared holding a standing lamp in one hand and an electric bass guitar in the other. "Moving?" Sandra asked. Ignoring her, the young man dropped his load in the cab and stalked away.

The direction arrow to apartments 406 to 410 pointed to the right. She paused at 409 before knocking; obstacles had perhaps been put in her way for a reason. She looked back toward the elevator. The scowling bassist, almost fully eclipsed by a huge amplifier, was navigating his way around the glider chair. Sandra knocked on the door and heard movement from the other side, then silence. Undeterred, she knocked again.

After the fourth knock, Sandra heard a click and became aware that she was being scrutinized through a fisheye lens. Then the door opened on a chain and through a narrow gap an invisible person said tonelessly, "What do you want?" The voice, to her surprise, was male.

"I came to see Bet."

"Who is it, Thomas?" — from the background, a woman's voice. "Tell them the prayer session is tomorrow."

"It's Sandra, Bet; Sandra Treming."

The door immediately shut in Sandra's face. She was on the verge of giving up when the door opened wide, revealing a man in his midtwenties. She recognized him from pre-prison days — but it couldn't be. He hadn't aged; if anything he was younger than the man she remembered. Gawkier and doughier also. Once she recovered her composure Sandra knew this was not the John Edwards who had changed her life and the lives of her Berkman House communards forever. Still, the resemblance was uncanny.

The young man took her hand and drew her through the doorway. She remembered now that Bet had had a baby. She'd learned that in prison but assumed at the time that Louie was the father. Sandra stayed rooted to the spot inside the door until a voice from down the corridor demanded, "Thomas, what are you doing?"

Thomas didn't answer the question; instead, indicating with a gesture that Sandra was to follow, he led her past four closed doors. They emerged into an open area that was a combined sitting room and kitchen. Despite it being near midday, the curtains were closed and the room gloomy. Bet sat behind a manual typewriter, her face illuminated by a desk lamp, the only source of light in the room. Her hair was grey, her features gaunter than Sandra recalled, but the same dark intense eyes bored into her as they often had in Berkman days. On the wall above Bet's head was a large wooden cross; the walls were otherwise bare and, in the darkness, seemingly grey.

"What do you want?" Bet didn't smile and her hands stayed on the keyboard. On the side of the typewriter facing Sandra was a black gummy stain where a sticker had been removed. She remembered the words on that sticker, from the closing sentence of *The Communist Manifesto*: Nothing to lose but our chains … a world to win. One time Sandra had asked her which horses would place and show, but Bet didn't get the joke. She rarely got any of Sandra's jokes.

Sandra moved a stack of loose paper to one side and, uninvited, sat down on a couch. "Sorry for dropping in like this, Bet. I tried phoning — several times — but no one answered. I left a message."

"The telephone is not for our personal use. I listened to your message but had no reason to respond to it. Why are you here?"

"I came to visit you, Bet. To see how you're doing and let you know I'm out of prison."

"I know you are out of prison, Sandra, but are you truly repentant?"

"I'm sorry for what I did, yes. I'm sorry for what we all did."

Bet's expression became even sharper. From behind Sandra, still hovering at the near end of the entry hall, Thomas asked, "Would you like some tea?"

Bet switched her gaze to Thomas for a few seconds before forcing her face into an unconvincing smile. "Yes, Sandra, would you care for some tea? Thomas and I never take caffeine. But we have an herbal blend that is very cleansing."

"Sure, that sounds great," Sandra said. She watched Thomas sidle behind a counter that defined the kitchen area. He filled a kettle and put it on to boil. Sandra turned back to again receive Bet's judgmental stare. Sandra gestured at the typewriter. "You still have the Olivetti."

Bet placed both hands protectively over the machine. "Yes. It is the tool I work with. Thomas is very industrious as well." She waved one hand at the surrounding room. "Our labour provides all this — shelter, food, everything we need. We lead a very simple life, Thomas and I."

"Your writing sells?" Even as the words escaped, Sandra regretted saying them.

"I do not sell what I write. I write in the service of God." Bet paused as if she expected some kind of response. Sandra had none to give, so Bet continued on. "I should not have suggested that the typewriter provides for us. It is the Lord who provides through His church, the Absolute Church of Christ. Thomas and I have found Jesus; we have been saved."

Sandra struggled to formulate a response. "That must've been a major change in your life," she ventured.

"Not really. I have become more enlightened and more disciplined. But my core values remain what they were. It took a long time but I found the true path at last. And I have renounced the errors of my past — my sins — although you probably would reject that concept."

A shrill whistle saved Sandra from having to reply. Thomas turned off the kettle and filled a teapot.

"We are a simple people. As much as possible we reject commerce and the state, all the distractions of the material world. We focus on the better world to come. Nothing has changed for me in that regard."

Sandra wanted to ask who the "we" were that Bet was referring to but was afraid of where that question might lead. Instead she asked, "Do you still see anyone from the old days? Norbert? Phyl? Louie?" Sandra didn't really expect this new Bet would have kept in touch with any of the old crowd but was curious as to how she might respond.

Bet surprised her. "Only Louie; I visit him every week. I am trying to bring him to the light, but he is very resistant. Nevertheless, I will keep at him until the very end."

"What end? What do you mean?"

"Louie has terminal cancer. He is in a hospice. Not surprising, really; he led a very unhealthy life both in body and in spirit. But he can be saved. Once I convince him to pray with me, he will be saved. Thank you, Thomas."

Thomas had served tea to both women, not in the mug Sandra expected but in an ornate china cup on a saucer. Sandra took a sip, watched closely by Thomas and Bet. The tea tasted like diluted soap. With a forced smile Sandra said, "Tastes very … healthy."

"It is good for you," Bet agreed. Thomas rubbed his nose, looking vaguely disappointed.

Sandra put the cup and saucer down on the floor between her feet. "Bet, what hospice is Louie in? I'd like to visit him."

Bet folded her arms across her chest. "Sandra, are you ready to open your heart to Jesus?"

Sandra returned Bet's gaze with interest, but didn't say anything.

"I thought not. I don't want you to visit Louie. You would undermine the progress I've made."

Sandra recognized this was the Berkman Collective Bet speaking; there was no point arguing. She rose to her feet, angry but determined to remain composed. "I have to be on my way. Thanks for the visit." Her first step knocked over the teacup; it was still almost full and its contents splashed over the wall-to-wall carpet.

Bet cut off any apology Sandra might have made. "Don't worry about that. We will clean up your mess." Thomas was already pulling out a bucket and sponge from under the sink. "You are welcome to visit again. Our prayer sessions are on Thursdays at eight a.m. and three p.m. Please come. It will put you on the right path."

"I'll think about it." Sandra stepped around Thomas, who was on hands and knees vigorously sponging the carpet. No one escorted her back to the door. The elevator was now free; no sign of Bass Man or any of his stuff. Once outside, Sandra breathed in the fresh evening air and craved a cigarette. She decided to walk back to the hostel to save bus fare.

Less than half a block down the street she heard running footsteps from behind. She pulled out the hostel keychain and made a fist around the fob, the key protruding between her first and second fingers. Thus prepared to gouge out an eye, she turned to face her attacker.

1982

Bet answers the phone fast enough to clip off the first ring. As I descend the stairs, putting on my kimono, I hear "Louie?" followed by silence. When I reach the kitchen Bet has the telephone pressed to her ear, and a faint electronic muttering emits from the handset.

"Is it Louie?" I'm vaguely aware of Norbert and Phyl coming down the stairs behind me. Bet shakes her head in a vigorous negative.

"Then who—"

Bet sticks a finger in her free ear and pointedly turns her back. The three of us onlookers wait, impatiently watching Bet's hunched shoulders. Finally: "Okay, will do. Call you later," and Bet hangs up. She remains with her back toward us, her forehead resting on the wall over the phone. Behind her, a brief conference of glances. Wordlessly, Phyl is elected spokesperson: "Bet, what's up? Who was that?"

Bet turns and looks at us as if she hasn't noticed our presence until this moment.

"Bet?"

"That was Dorian. Louie's in jail." Bet speaks in an overly matter-of-fact tone.

"Dorian? Is he sure? I mean, did he see it happen or something?"

"No, he didn't see it happen. He knows because Louie phoned him and told him. His one phone call."

"But why would he call Dorian? Why not here?" Indignation in Phyl's tone.

"Louie phoned Dorian to warn him because he was arrested under Dorian's name."

"What for? What did Louie do?"

"Jaywalking." Bet heads into the kitchen and sits down at the cable spool. The rest of us trail after her.

"Bet, Bet, Bet."

"Phyl, Phyl, Phyl." The effort required to maintain civility is clearly audible.

"Look, Bet, maybe I'm not the brightest crayon in the box, but I'm not falling for this one. People don't get thrown in jail for jaywalking. Dorian's putting us on."

"You're right; people don't get thrown in jail for jaywalking, unless—"

"Unless they have a criminal record — but Louie's clean."

"Oh yes, Louie's clean all right, but he was busted as Dorian."

The whole scenario is becoming abundantly clear — clear, that is, to everyone but Norbert. "That's what I don't get." His blue eyes blink at everyone in turn. "Why would he say he was Dorian?"

"Norb, think." Phyl's tone is unnecessarily harsh, but Norbert doesn't take offence. "Louie gets stopped for jaywalking. Cop writes a ticket. Does Louie give his right name? Course not. He has Dorian's wallet and ID in his pocket. Louie gives Dorian's name. Cop gives him a ticket, with a little sermon. Cop splits; Louie rips up the ticket."

"That's not a nice thing to do to Dorian."

"No, Norb, not a nice thing to do. So, as soon as the cops leave, Louie would lickety-split find Dorian and tell him to phone the cops to report a stolen wallet. No fuss, no muss."

"Wow, that's really clever!"

"Yeah, Louie is a real clever cat."

"So what went wrong?"

"Well, maybe Louie gets a little too lippy — I mean, why the hell not? Or maybe the pigs are feeling ornery. They do a warrant check. Louie's not worried; after all, he's Dorian Twisp, the straightest man in the world. But seems our friend Dorian has a little secret. What's Dorian's secret, Bet?"

"Three outstanding warrants — cocaine."

"Possession?"

"And trafficking."

"Shit."

"Dorian is a little pissed off — more than a little, actually." Bet appears to have recovered from the initial shock of the phone call. "He told me to get a lawyer and arrange to identify Louie down at the police station. But he wants me to wait until morning so he has time to go into hiding."

"So much for the bank job — goddam." Phyl opens the refrigerator door and fishes around without finding what he's looking for. A beer, I'm guessing.

"What do you mean?"

"Norb, when we go down and say, 'Hey, Mr. Policeman, that's not really Dorian Twisp, ha, ha, that's Louie Del Grande, ho, ho — please let him go,' what do you suppose they're going to do? Let him go? Forget it. They're going to throw the book at him — impersonation, fraud, mindfucking a police officer, God knows what else." Phyl finds the blue Curaçao that's been in a cupboard for at least two years and pours himself a glass. This is an act of desperation, even for Phyl. "Face it, for a while the spotlight's going to be on all of us, not just Louie. We can't even think about littering, much less a bank job. We've gotta be clean, clean, clean." He sips the blue liquid and immediately spits in the sink. "Yuck. This crap is worse than I remember. I bet they'll tap our phone."

"So we're going to do what Dorian told us to do?" Good old Norbert at last catches up.

Phyl shrugs. Bet says, "I don't see that we have much choice."

Something about her casual resignation really irks me. I want to say, *Goddamn it, we're talking about the man you supposedly love. Are you wimps going to roll over and play dead to get Dorian off the hook?* But I don't say that. What I do say is even more surprising — to me at least: "Sure we have a choice. We don't have to march to Dorian's commands. We can take direct action."

"Direct action" is one of Phyl's stock phrases. I know that'll get him, and I know that any notion of obeying commands will get a rise from Bet. Sure enough …

"Sandra, if there were any viable alternative, I would of course—"

"There *is* a viable alternative. Think about it. As far as the authorities are concerned they've got their man. No need to tell them they don't. We just need to act before Louie's true identity is known."

"Wait. What about fingerprints?"

"What about fingerprints, Norb? Sure, they have Louie's now, but not his name. Dorian's prints they won't have yet from back east. They might not even check for a match. In their eyes Louie has pretty much confessed already. We just have to get to him before he recants. Let's go for it. Tomorrow morning at the courthouse. We have the arms; we have the organization."

"Are you seriously suggesting that we go down and free Louie by force?" Norbert looks around the kitchen for support. None is forthcoming.

"Exactly right. Look, we're already committed to armed struggle. Isn't liberating political prisoners as revolutionary an act — if not more so — than robbing a bank?" I speak with great emotion, but at the same time feel curiously detached from my words. I'm aware of part of me thinking, *This is madness. A few hours ago the idea of robbing a bank freaked me right out. Now I've not only signed on, I'm trying to lead my communards to take even greater risks.* But the rational voice in my head is overruled by another saying, *Louie, sweetheart, you arrogant prick, I've got my gun and I'm keeping it — because I'm prepared to use it. Who really loves you, babe?*

For once the Berkmanites are speechless. Both Bet and Phyl sit staring down at the wire-spool top. Then, once again, Norbert rides to the rescue. "Right on, Sandra; let's do it!"

So if we take a vote, the result will be at least a tie. But the collective has long since abandoned majority rule in favour of a consensus mode of decision-making. Consensus for us means that if someone feels strongly about something, about which no one else feels strongly against, that something wins out every time.

Usually, Bet and Louie have the strong feelings, or occasionally Phyl. Now I'm in the driver's seat. Even without Norbert's support I could probably get my way. With Norbert on board it's pretty much a done deal.

"Well…" Phyl begins, then sighs and looks across the wire cable at Bet, who is busy ripping a paper matchbook into increasingly smaller bits.

"Listen." I increase the pressure a notch. "If we cop out now we might as well dissolve the Berkman Collective and go sell life insurance or something. If Louie's cover is blown then we have to put the bank job on hold. For how long? Once it's on the back burner then we're going to keep putting it off and putting it off. If we're not prepared to act on our convictions now, then we'll never be prepared."

Sometimes my own eloquence amazes me.

I can tell that neither Phyl nor Bet is completely onside. Sure, they'll eventually agree to my proposal — with some show of militant enthusiasm even — but will they be sincere? I doubt it. Most likely they'll go along with me only because neither thinks of a way to say no while retaining a correcter-than-thou self-image.

I stop talking. No one else starts. With a sudden loud *clank* the refrigerator motor shuts off. An intense silence fills the room.

Phyl clears his throat. "What's your plan?"

Plan? We're moving forward faster than I'd expected. "I don't think we should be bound to a plan as such. We need to be flexible, ready for all contingencies."

"But—"

"The *concept*, however, will be essentially the same as for the bank — with a few modifications since, obviously, Louie's no longer with us. Norbert and I'll enter the courtroom. As soon as they bring Louie in, Norbert will leave and signal Bet. Bet will create a diversion with the smoke bomb…"

"Where?" Phyl asks the question; Bet maintains her silence.

"Wherever. In the women's can — or better yet, into the ventilation system. Meantime I'll make sure that Louie sees me. As soon as I see smoke or the alarm goes off, I'll pull out the gun and put the courtroom down flat on its face. Then Louie and I'll split, mingling with the crowd evacuating the building."

"What about me?"

"Same as before, Phyl, you're the driver. As soon as Norbert and Bet finish their assignments they'll join you in the van. When that happens, fire it up, because Louie and I will be right behind."

"And if you're not?"

"Wait five minutes, then take off. But don't worry, we'll be there."

Phyl gargles his Curaçao before swallowing it and refills his glass. He ingests another generous gulp and says, "So, it's like an option B. I'm in."

Three to one. After a couple of seconds Bet realizes that all eyes are on her. She smiles. "Me too," she says, "and thank you, Sandra."

Bet's endorsement of option B ends the meeting. We decide to go to bed early to get lots of sleep before the big day. Lots of sleep … Ha — fat chance. My adrenalin level is sky high; I play and replay my mental tapes of the meeting. *Thank you, Sandra.* For what? What the hell was she getting at?

2:17 a.m. I remember the exact time because I check my clock radio when someone knocks at my bedroom door.

"Hello?" I try to sound sleepier than I am.

Norbert eases through my door and into my room. "Hiya," he says, as he walks over to the foot of my bed and sits down. This time both buttocks make contact.

"Hi, Norbert."

"I can't sleep. I was on my way to the washroom and I thought I saw your light on. Figured you couldn't sleep either."

"My light wasn't on."

"Oh."

"Must have been the street light. No problem, I wasn't asleep yet."

"Yeah, quite the meeting, wasn't it?" Norbert now seems poised for flight.

"Yes, it was."

"Sandra, I wanted to tell you that I thought you…" He breathes in. "I thought you were magnificent."

"Thank you, Norbert."

"Well." He shrugs. His eyes, which have been flitting all over my room, settle for an instant on my clock radio. "Gee, it's really late."

I can't argue with that.

"But I don't feel tired somehow. How about you, Sandra? Are you tired?"

"Actually, I'm pretty tired."

"Oh. You want me to leave?"

"No, that's not what I meant. I'm just—"

"Sandra." Norbert looks at me intently. "What I'm asking is…" He shifts his gaze away, blushing.

He appears so miserable, so tense and vulnerable at that moment, I want to take him into my arms, pull his little whipcord body against mine and loosen him up somehow. But God, the complications. I reach out and place my right hand over one of his, and before he can get the wrong idea, I say, "Norbert, this isn't a good time."

He slides his hand out from under and places it over mine but makes no other movement. He sits there so mournfully, halfway down my bed, I almost relent.

Before I can yield he says, "You're right, this is not a good time. We can't afford to get emotionally involved. We must be disciplined and think only of the days of struggle ahead."

"We can talk about it later, if you'd like."

"Yes, maybe later." He rises quickly to his feet. "Your strength is an inspiration to us all." He bends forward and kisses me dryly, high on one cheekbone.

My strength? In total disbelief I watch Norbert retreat to the door. Before he exits, he turns. All the tension has mysteriously disappeared from his body. "Whatever happens tomorrow, Sandra, remember always that I love you."

He quickly shuts the door behind him. A few minutes later, I hear the toilet flush. Then silence.

I turn on my bedroom light.

Six

2007

Somehow sensing danger, Thomas halted just out of reach. Breathing heavily, he fixed his gaze on Sandra's fist and the shaft of the key protruding between her knuckles.

"What's up?" Sandra asked.

"I apologize for my mother." Thomas gasped. "She lacks charity sometimes."

Sandra casually put the keychain back in her pocket. "It's all right. She's always been that way. You seem to make up for it, though."

Beads of sweat appeared on his forehead as Thomas slowly recovered his breath. Sandra waited until his wind and perhaps his courage would allow him to say more. "I need your help," he said at last.

Uncertain where this conversation was heading, Sandra replied cautiously, "Not sure I can help you, Thomas, but exactly what are you asking for?"

Thomas's lips rehearsed what he was about to say before the words came out. "I need to find a job."

"I thought you had a job. Your mother said—"

"I mean a real job. A paying job. Not the stuff my mother makes me do for the church."

"Why? Doesn't your church provide you with everything you need?"

Thomas ignored or missed the sarcasm in her voice. "Everything my mother needs, yes, but not everything that I need. I want to have my own place. Is that sinful? I'd still come over every day and take care of her."

"So you're looking for a job and somewhere else to live?"

Thomas nodded.

Sandra laughed and then quickly controlled herself. Thomas seemed on the verge of tears. "Sorry, Thomas, I'm not laughing at you. It's just that I was visiting your mom to ask her pretty much the same thing. I'm staying in a hostel and looking for work."

"You didn't say anything about that when you talked to her."

"And if I had, would she have helped me?"

"If you were a believer she would have tried. In our church it is our duty to take care of one another."

"Well, that's the problem, isn't it? I'm not a believer. Nothing personal, but I've a hard time believing in anything, even in return for a job and a roof over my head." Sandra turned to go.

Thomas stopped her with his next question: "Aren't you afraid you'll go to hell when you die?"

"I've already done time in hell, so yeah, of course I'm afraid. But if you're a believer only to escape punishment then you don't really believe. You're just fooling yourself and everybody else."

Thomas's lips started working again. He blurted, "You're starting to sound like Mother."

Sandra laughed again and this time Thomas surprised her by joining in. She felt a surge of affection for this man-child. He and Emma would be about the same age, she realized suddenly. Warmed by this thought, she reached out and touched his arm. "I'm sorry I can't help you, Thomas, I really am. But I wish you all the best."

"Thank you," said Thomas. "Ocean View Hospice. That's where your friend is. You should visit him. Please don't go on a Friday. You might run into Mother and … you know…"

"I know. I won't get you into trouble. Promise. And thanks for the tip."

Thomas smiled weakly and nodded. "I have to be getting back. Told Mother I was going down to our storage locker for a dry mop." He turned and jogged away into the night.

1982

Once Norbert leaves my room, thankfully without kicking up a fuss, I slump back down on my mattress. My mind immediately turns to the guy I would want to have in my bed with me. The guy who's in a holding cell somewhere, probably as sleepless as me. I can't stop thinking about a day not that long ago. The day everything changed between Louie and me.

I remember being crammed in Louie's van on a highway leading north from the city, all of us half asleep in the pre-dawn gloom. All except for Louie at the wheel. Bet riding shotgun, of course. Phyl crouching in the space between, facing the windshield, arms embracing the headrests of both front seats. Norbert and I sitting on the opposite rear wheel wells, facing each other over the clutter of boxes, tools, spare van parts and empty spray-paint cans. An initial sequence of stops and starts yields to gradual acceleration as we break loose on an open road. I keep falling off my perch as Louie takes every curve at speed. Eventually I slide down on the floor where ridges of cold metal press into my butt. I pull a flattened cardboard box under me and stretch out, my feet on the spare tire and my head propped up on a case of beer.

I close my eyes but can't mute the pervasive whine of the transmission and the clockwork *thump thump thump* of tires measuring out sections of concrete roadbed. Nor can I blot out the stench of mildew, machine oil and sweat. Worst of all is the kinetic sensation of hurtling through space at unimaginable speed, like falling down an elevator shaft toward infinity. The horror of it forces my eyes open. I discover Phyl and Norbert lying on either side of me staring wide-eyed at the ceiling. Bet swivels in her seat, smiles at the three of us and says something I can't hear over the noise of the van.

I pull myself to a sitting position and cup my hand behind my ear.

"You look like ... *thump* ... in a can."

"What?"

"Sardines!" Bet yells.

"Oh." I look beyond Bet out the windshield. Louie is passing a Honda Civic on a blind curve. I bed down with my fellow sardines.

A few minutes later the van slows slightly then throws me painfully on my right side as Louie swivels off the highway onto a dirt road. The ride becomes truly unbearable, especially for the sardines. We roll helplessly against one another, bucked up and down as the van bounces over pothole after pothole. My stomach begins to shudder and I taste bile in the back of my throat. I fight for control by focusing on the small section of treetops and sky visible through the portholes in the rear doors. I don't puke, only because my stomach is empty; I've not had breakfast. The shaking and pounding seems to last forever, but after a low-gear surge across a final wicked pothole and another lurching hard right, the van settles to a full stop. Louie turns off the engine and stillness wraps us in a sweet caress.

I'm more than ready to stagger out with the rest of my communards at the abandoned gravel pit. All doors burst open simultaneously and we fan out into the bushes with one common purpose. After an extended peeing session, the collective reconvenes. We breathe in the crisp mountain air. It's still relatively early in the morning. The sun has just begun to burn the dew off the scrub alder invading the margins of the gravel pit. The shadow of a large fir wedges across the open area in front of us, reaching almost to the giant bite in the hillside a hundred yards or so away. Norbert hauls out a box of empty tin cans from the back of the van and runs down to the far end of the pit. He sets some cans in a row on the ground and hangs the rest on the branches of a dead alder. From under the driver's seat Louie extracts his .22 in two parts, connects them together and feeds a small shell into the breech.

While Norbert decorates the tree I open my backpack and munch on a slice of bread and an apple, followed by gulps of water to settle my stomach. Once Norbert is finished and back with us, Louie brings the rifle up to his shoulder, aims and fires. A tin can somersaults up and backward. The echo of the shot ripples like thunder through the surrounding hills. Louie reloads and holds the rifle out at arm's length from his body. "Anyone else want to try?"

My hands obediently reach out to take the gun. I'm surprised by its weight. Trying to copy Louie, I point the barrel in the direction of the biggest can and pull the trigger. The .22 jumps back against my shoulder and I flinch in pain. When I open my eyes the can is still there.

Louie takes back the gun and drops another shell into the breech. "Try doing it this way, Sandra." He steps behind me, brings the gun around and snugs it against my shoulder.

"Hold it," he says.

I hold it.

He gently pushes my head sideways over the barrel. "Now, close your left eye and look down the sights with your right. Do you see your target?"

"Yes." I also feel the warmth of his chest on my back, his breath on my ear.

"Okay, this time, don't blink. When you're ready, slowly squeeze the trigger."

I squeeze the trigger and watch in amazement as the can leaps into the air. Thunder again echoes through the hills. As the sound fades, two shots boom in reply somewhere in the distance. I stare at the rifle in my hands.

"Hunters," says Louie, releasing me.

"Yahoo, the people are armed and have taken to the High Sierras — the revolution has begun!" Phyl grabs the rifle, loads it and flops onto his belly. "Eat leaden death imperialist swine," he snarls and picks off a can of tropical punch hanging on the alder tree.

Phyl passes the rifle to Bet. She drills an oil can with the cry, "Death to monopoly capital!"

It's now Norbert's turn. "Power to the farm workers!" he yells, taking aim at a tomato-sauce can.

Much to my relief — I didn't want to be the only klutz — he misses. After some coaching from Louie, verbally this time, Norbert tries again. The can bursts in a splatter of red. Phyl whoops and pounds Norbert on the back.

And so our training in armed struggle begins. We take turns shouting slogans and slaying tin cans one by one until they're all gone. Then Louie draws a crude target on a cardboard box from the back of the van. By the time our carton of .22 shorts is empty the entire box is pretty much eliminated.

The shadow of the big fir has swung around in retreat leaving the gravel pit fully exposed to the late September sun. Our jackets and shirts are long since peeled off. Norbert and Louie are now bare chested but Phyl keeps his T-shirt on as, in his words, an affirmation of gender solidarity. His affirmation is somewhat undermined when Bet takes off her halter top, exposing her breasts. I don't follow her example; the occasional gunshots rolling over the hills make me nervous. Maybe just paranoia, but I fully expect an army of unwashed and horny hunters to march out of the woods at any moment, and I want to be fully clothed when that happens.

Our collective focus disappears along with the last of the ammunition. We drift apart. Bet retrieves a blanket and sunglasses from the van and lies down to read Fanon's *Wretched of the Earth*. Norbert trots off to collect firewood. Phyl starts a long set of tai chi forms in his own unique style, every movement subject to spastic repetition and muttered commentary until he's satisfied enough to attempt the next motion.

I'm not sure what I want to do, but I know that staying put and frying in the gravel pit isn't on the list. So I make an announcement: "I'm going for a walk."

No response.

"Anyone want to come?"

Norbert has built a small pyramid of twigs over a mound of scrunched-up newspaper to which he is applying a match. He speaks to the rising flames. "No, go ahead."

I'm a little surprised and disappointed but, oh well ... "Bet?"

Bet makes one slow sideways motion with her head, chin touching both shoulders.

"Phyl?"

Phyl shakes both his hands in front of his face like he's erasing something. He curtly says no and resumes carrying a tiger to a mountain.

I turn away to go it alone.

"Hang on a second." Louie is pulling an oily rag through the barrel of the .22. He puts both the barrel and the stock into an old pillowcase, which he slides back under the driver's seat. "I'll tag along with you, if that's okay."

"I-I don't mind." Louie has maintained a formal distance from me since our first encounter at the demonstration. We haven't spent time alone together, ever. I find him intimidating, actually; he rarely speaks to me directly, although when he speaks to others he's never at a loss for words and never evinces a shred of self-doubt. He makes me so nervous I can't talk to him and sound intelligent, so I don't even try, talking, that is.

We walk together up the road in the opposite direction to how we'd driven in until, about a hundred yards along we hear the muted roar of a stream from the bottom of a steeply wooded slope. A few steps farther and a rough trail leads through a conifer stand to the water. We slide down the trail, clutching at roots and branches to break our descent. At the bottom, a shoal of white stones defines an abrupt end to the forest. Beyond the shoal a stream tumbles down and eases into a deep green pool directly in front of us, about thirty feet across. Downstream, the pool becomes progressively shallower until finally it spills over into another boulder-strewn descent. To our left and right, thick bushes overhang the water. A gravel beach on the far side invites us across.

Louie strides over to the shallows and takes off his socks and shoes, stringing them around his neck. As he wades across at the edge of the riffle, I follow him in my sandals. The water numbs my feet and the current is unexpectedly strong. I lose balance and flail my arms outward. Louie turns and grabs the closest hand. "Thanks," I say, which is the first word spoken since we started our walk. He doesn't reply, but he doesn't let go of my hand either.

We reach the far shore linked together. He sets off downstream, gently pulling me after. I'm not reluctant but a bit agitated, unsure of Louie's intent. Bet is in my mind's eye, sunning herself in the gravel pit, and I feel I should ask Louie what's happening here. But I don't trust myself to speak and probably make a complete fool of myself.

The roar of the lower cataract builds as we round the bend in the shade of some cottonwoods. Directly ahead the stream is swallowed by a narrow canyon. At the point where the water disappears from view, the stream is diverted to one side by an enormous boulder; its mossy top in a patch of sunlight is vivid green against the gloom beyond.

Several smaller boulders are huddled together around the large one. We clamber over them up into the sunlight where we look down into a vortex of white water funnelling between sheer rock walls. The occasional breeze brings back a cooling spray of mist. I lean over with my eyes closed, the spray filling my nostrils, the roar of white water in my ears, the afternoon sun beating down on my shoulders and neck. Then Louie's arm reaches around my ribcage.

"Careful, San, you don't want to fall." His voice is barely audible over the chaos below.

"Part of me wants to fall," I whisper, more to myself than to him. I don't know if he hears me. I half turn, open my eyes and look up into his. He takes this as some kind of signal, his hand slides up against my breast and his lips swoop down onto my neck. My initial impulse is to resist; I try to steady myself, stay focused on our housemates back in the gravel pit, Bet in particular. But it's Louie and I'm just Sandra. My cortex kicks my frontal lobes into a corner and my body turns into compliant mush.

I swivel against Louie, pull off my shirt and sink down onto the moss. He loosens his arm and follows; his mouth glides down to fasten on my right nipple and his fingers undo the button of my shorts. I hump up and let him pull my shorts and panties under my buttocks, past my hips and down my legs. I'm dimly aware of one sandal falling off as my toes snag on the passing clothes. My body arches with lust but I can't relax, can't blot out my precarious position above the abyss, can't ignore the sense of total exposure under the sheer canyon walls, the riot of green and yellow foliage around us, the infinite blue dome over absolutely everything. Then Louie's mouth finds its way down across my belly and my thoughts dissolve into sensation, and for now nothing else matters.

Sometime later Louie is still and the roar of white water becomes external again. I'm left wanting more and yet I shouldn't want any more, shouldn't have let it start in the first place. A stone under the moss presses against my upper back; discomfort made painful by the weight of Louie slumped over me. I shift my shoulders and Louie raises himself up with a start. I roll over and peer down the upstream side of the boulder, looking for the sandal that dropped. It's irredeemably gone. I push away from Louie without looking at him.

"Let's go," I say. Pausing only to pick up my clothes, I half run, half limp back up to the pool we waded across. By the time Louie catches up I'm fully immersed. "Come on in, the water's great," I gasp, trying to sound sincere. Louie unzips a lopsided grin and wades in up to his knees. He angles down onto an exposed rock and splashes water on his now flaccid penis. Looking up, he sees me watching him.

"How are you doing, lover?" He reaches toward me with one hand.

I take the hand. "Fine," I say, but that's not what I think. What I think is *Holy crap, this is going to get complicated.*

"Come here, lover." Louie pulls me closer.

Acting on reflex, I splash cold water on him with my free hand. He lets go of me quickly and I sweep water up into his face with both arms. "Hey, Sandra, cut it out. Fuck." He turns his head away and closes his eyes while I continue to let him have it.

"Seriously, Sandra, I'm warning you…" He gives a tentative swipe at the water while simultaneously backing toward the shore.

"Come on, you wimp." The cold doesn't affect me anymore. I'm invincible.

"You're asking for it, bi—" Louie edits himself in the nick of time as he wades back into the pool, splashing water forward with two shovel-like hands.

The cold isn't a problem but I have to tuck my head down in order to breathe. "Buh? Buh? Come on you chickenshit, say it — bitch, bitch, bitch."

"Bitch-bitch-bitch…" The words are synchronized with showers of water scooped up by his hands. I wait until he gets in close then make a kamikaze dive for his knees. He topples over on top of me, and caught unprepared, I inhale water.

After a few seconds of struggle, during which Louie seems to be determined to keep me under water, I manage to slip around him and lift my head into the air again. Louie and I are holding each other's forearms, out of mistrust not affection. I'm choking and retching and laughing all at once. Louie is laughing.

"Hallooooh!" The cry comes from somewhere close in the woods. Louie and I, no longer laughing, sprint back to the shore and struggle with pulling clothes on over our wet bodies.

"Hallooh, is anybody there?"

"Just a minute," shouts Louie, as if we were in a room and someone was knocking at the door. Now we hear the crack and swish of movement down through the underbrush toward the stream bank.

"I'm lost." The voice is very close now. "Where am I?"

We're dressed and ready. Louie squeezes my hand and drops it. He walks over to the bushes and peers up the slope. We can see the bushes shaking now. A head appears, framed by salmonberry branches.

"Boy, am I glad to see you." The newcomer has at least a four day's growth of beard. His face, glistening with sweat, is blotched by sunburn and mosquito bites. A few tufts of brown hair protrude out from underneath a heavy woolen toque and curl around his ears. He looks about fifty years old, but could be much younger. When he steps into full view, I realize with shock that he's carrying a rifle. He strides into the clearing, passes by us and stops at the edge of the water. Then turning, he looks at us in our dripping wet clothes, and smiles. A wonderful, wide, toothy smile, which scares the hell out of me. His smile seems to suggest that he's been watching ever since our arrival at the stream and deliberately waited to make his dramatic entrance. But I'm not about to let my misgivings show, and I smile back as sincerely as I can.

"So, where the Christ are we?" The stranger directs the question to Louie.

Louie tries to explain where we are in relation to the main road, but he isn't exactly sure of his bearings. "Got a map back in my van," he says at last.

"Van?" The stranger pulls off his toque and runs his fingers in a scratch pattern through his hair.

Louie waves in the general direction of the gravel pit. "We're parked over yonder."

Over yonder? Since when does Louie talk this way? I stare at him. He's standing with his shoulders back, chest out and thumbs hooked into the belt loops at his hips. Good-ol'-boy Louie is back. I think, *I've never seen Louie afraid before.*

The stranger's hand works down from his scalp to his chin. "Either of you folks got a cigarette?"

"Got the makings." Louie pulls a baggie out of his chest pocket and hands it over.

The stranger squints at the baggie, then at Louie. He takes a pinch of the contents between his fingers and sniffs cautiously. Satisfied, he rolls a cigarette, lights it and inhales deeply. "Possible we might look at that map?"

"Reckon it's possible." Louie, still in his gunfighter stance.

The stranger hands back the tobacco. "Well, let's go."

We wade back across the stream. Louie and I barefoot; the stranger not bothering to take off his knee-high boots. By the time we reach the gravel pit, I'm limping badly. Our three communards are gathered around a fire, drinking cans of beer. Norbert is the first to notice us.

"Here they are. Where have you been? Didn't you hear us calling? We've finished eating. We couldn't wait any longer. Who's this guy?"

"This is…" Louie stops, realizing he doesn't know this guy's name. An awkward pause. The stranger misses his cue; he seems mesmerized by the beer and remnants of lunch spread on the ground.

Phyl breaks the trance. "Name's Phyl." He reaches up with his right hand.

The stranger shakes it. "Frank."

Norbert shifts up onto his heels. "I'm Norbert. This is Bet. Of course you've already met Sandra and Louie."

Phyl takes back the reins. "Ya wanna beer or something to eat?"

"Well…" Frank weighs the options.

"Of course he wants something to eat; the poor man has been lost in the woods for days." I briskly ladle beans and brown rice onto a paper plate. Saves having to make eye contact with Bet.

My action triggers a flurry of activity. Norbert offers his rock to sit on; Phyl cracks open a beer, and Bet fetches a couple of blankets from the van.

"Here," she says, looking at me intently, "you need this."

I take the blanket, suddenly aware of how cold I am. "Thanks, we went for a swim."

"Obviously." Bet walks over to Louie and wraps the other blanket around his shoulders.

Frank wolfs down his meal and sucks back his beer in no time. Phyl opens another can as Frank tosses his empty plate into the fire.

"Thanks," says Frank, taking the beer. His basic needs satisfied, he takes stock of the scene around him. He gestures toward the shards of broken bottles at the far end of the pit.

"Target shooting?"

"Uh-huh," Louie mutters.

"Good. These days you got to know how to handle a gun. With the womenfolk and all especially."

"What do you mean?" Bet, ready to pounce.

Frank is not to be distracted. "Whatcha using?" He addresses the question to Louie.

"Er, a .22," Louie says quietly.

Frank laughs — a kind of snort that results in a dribble of beer running down through the stubble on his chin. "Excuse me, but what you need is something like this." His hand fondles the barrel of his rifle, which is supported upright by his inner thigh.

"You may be right."

"I'm right all right." Once again Frank flashes his eerie smile. "You get yourself a real stopper, not a toy. Let's see that map."

Obediently, Louie goes to the van and rummages in the glove compartment. He returns with a small-scale topological map of the area. Kneeling beside Frank he unfolds the map and stabs it with his forefinger. "This is where we are."

Frank duplicates the gesture, running his finger from that point back to the main road. His finger then traces the paved road almost to the top of the sheet, before branching off to settle on another point. "That's where I'm parked," he announces.

Picking up his rifle and standing, Frank contemplates the mountain ridge to the north. He looks up at the sun, checks his watch and strokes the map with his finger again. Another glance back up at the mountain. "That don't look like much fun — shit. Excuse me."

The "excuse me" is thrown in my direction, with an added nod for Bet's benefit.

"We could give you a lift." As Louie speaks, Bet doubles over in a fit of coughing.

"Naw, I couldn't. You folks have been very generous, very generous. Thanks for the beer, the food and all — naw, I couldn't."

"Hey, no problem, man." Phyl rips open another can and passes it over the fire.

"Well, okay, twist my rubber arm." Frank gulps down the beer while staring at the mountain looming over us. "Tell you what," he says once he has drained the can, "make you a sort of business proposition. Drive me over to my truck and my rifle is yours for say, fifty bucks."

"I dunno—" Louie begins.

"Hey, why not? It's worth at least *a hundred* and fifty. A hundred bucks is pretty good cab fare." Frank smiles his broad, toothy, suggestive smile again and strokes the barrel of his rifle.

Louie looks over at Phyl who, raising his eyebrow, signals that this offer is not to be rejected. Many times the pair discussed ways and means of acquiring untraceable weaponry. Now, out of the blue, as it were...

"Okay, Frank, deal. Let's pack up." Louie stands up and rummages his pockets for the van keys. Norbert and Phyl throw the unwashed pots and dishes into a cardboard box, which Phyl carts over to the van as Norbert kicks dirt over the fire. Bet gathers up a stack of books and magazines. I look around for anything the others may have missed, but there's nothing. I pull the blanket tight around my shoulders and step through the back doors of the van. Norbert and Phyl join me.

The front passenger door opens and I expect to see Bet. Instead, I hear Louie's voice. "Have a seat, Frank," and Frank slides into shotgun position. A second or two later, Bet enters through the rear and, with more force than necessary, slams the doors shut. At almost the same moment Louie jumps behind the wheel and pops the van into reverse. Bet, caught off balance, flops to the floor. I wedge myself against the wheel well again and stare over Frank's shoulder through the windshield.

The drive back to the main road is even longer than I remember, but at last we reach the blissful smoothness of pavement. A few miles on, however, we turn onto another dirt road, if anything, worse than the first. By the time we reach Frank's truck, I'm about to puke. Louie manoeuvres the van around to face back the way we came and mercifully pulls to a halt alongside the other vehicle.

Taking out his wallet Louie extracts two twenties and a ten. Frank accepts the money gravely and says, "Hang on a minute — ammo." He opens the door and scoots out, leaving the rifle propped against the dashboard.

Louie looks over his shoulder at Bet. "Front seat?"

"Go ahead, Sandra, you look like you need it." The tone of Bet's voice is so full of sweetness, I know she's mad at Louie or me, or most likely both of us. I obediently slide into the vacant seat.

"Thanks," I hear myself say as Frank returns and taps at my window. I roll it down. "Here." He passes over a box of shells, which I relay to Louie. "And this is for you." Frank hands me a small silver pistol. I take it and stare at it blankly.

"Careful, it's loaded. I bought it for my ex, but she wouldn't even touch it. So you might as well get some use out of it."

I try to press it back upon him. "No," he insists. "You keep it. A girl's got to be able to defend herself. That there's a Smith and Wesson .32, your basic lady's gun. Get your boyfriend to show you how to use it."

"He's not my boyfriend." This is a declaration as much to Louie and Bet as to Frank.

"Well, in that case…" Frank doesn't actually lick his lips, but he might as well have. "I could…"

Whatever proposal Frank was going to make remains unheard as Louie abruptly stomps on the accelerator and we take off, no doubt showering Frank with gravel and mud.

"Louie!" Bet screams in protest as she's once more thrown onto her back.

"Sorry, Bet." Louie navigates at speed through the potholes, missing a few of them. "Security. He was trying to get contact information."

"I wouldn't have told him anything," I protest.

No one speaks for a mile or so. Bet is the first to say something. "What an asshole."

Whether she means Frank or Louie isn't immediately clear to me, but it is to Louie. "Hey, he's a working-class guy; maybe not very advanced in his thinking, but I wouldn't call him an asshole."

"Working class? Come on Louie, give me a break, he's lumpen as they come."

Louie doesn't reply. Instead he brakes and skids to a stop. He rips open the box of shells and feeds the new rifle; we all look on in worried silence. Rifle loaded, he leaps out of the van. The rest of us wait for someone else to take the initiative. Norbert is the first to move. He opens the rear doors and clambers out. Bet and Phyl follow. Cautiously, I wrench open my door and join them behind the van.

I hadn't noticed in the gloom of approaching night, but we've driven through a power line cut. Two paired cables hang from a pylon on one side of the road across to another about two hundred yards away. Louie is taking careful aim at the nearest pylon. A sudden flash and explosion from the gun — much louder than the .22. On the top of the pylon an armadillo-like insulator shatters and a bolt of lightning flares across the metal framework. It's like Hallowe'en fireworks. All of us admire the display; except for Louie. He runs past us yelling, "Let's go, let's go, let's go!" His shouts return us to the here and now. We hustle in panic back into the van.

The night flickers into daylight several more times as we bounce down the mountainside back to the highway. At first I assume that Louie's bullet has set off some kind of chain reaction; then rain hits the windshield, escalating into a torrent blurring the view between wiper sweeps. Louie maintains a speed that exceeds my ability to see the road ahead. But it's good to be in the front seat for a change; I don't envy my housemates in the back of the van.

We reach the main road and soon reconnect with civilization as we pass through a small town. All its street lights and house lights are on. I glance over at Louie. He seems to be smiling, or perhaps it's a grimace. It doesn't matter either way. While I know that things will be awkward for a while in Berkman House, for now I feel almost content.

Suddenly Louie's finger jabs against the dashboard, releasing the Rolling Stones at full volume. I start to complain along with Mick as he sings "I Can't Get No Satisfaction." One by one the rest of the Berkman family join in singing.

Seven

2007

Louie's room was empty. Not only was he not there, but nothing indicated that the hospice room was even occupied. No dresser drawers half open, no clutter on the side table, no clothes draped over the recliner next to the bed, no books or magazines anywhere. Sandra feared the worst. She backed into the corridor with the intention of returning to the reception desk to verify she had the right room. As she retreated she almost collided with a short brown woman in blue fatigues. An ID tag clipped to her lapel displayed a photograph of her looking passport severe, and a name: Gabriela Cruz.

"Beautiful flowers." Gabriela flashed a radiant smile, which completely contradicted the image on her ID. "I could put them in a vase if you like."

Feeling vaguely guilty, Sandra relinquished the bouquet. Surely Gabriela could tell that Sandra had picked the flowers from people's gardens on her way from the bus stop. "Louie Del Grande?" Sandra asked.

"He is in the sunroom, at the very end there." Gabriela pointed down the corridor. She pivoted and headed in the opposite direction, arranging the flowers in her hand as she walked back toward the reception desk. Sunroom? Sandra recalled the concealed chamber under the basement stairs in Berkman House. They called it the sunroom because Phyl had set it up as a small grow-op. Later they'd stashed their prisoner there. Louie, an unruly hospice inmate, in solitary confinement? Easy enough to picture him that way.

The hospice sunroom turned out to be a greenhouse kind of space tacked on to the side of the main building. Several potted plants, including some sizable trees pushing against the walls and scraping against a glass ceiling, made the room a jungle. Of the dozen or so large comfy chairs grouped amid the greenery, only three were occupied, and at first Sandra didn't recognize any of the people sitting in them. She went through a process of elimination. One of the occupants was almost certainly a woman. That left only two to be sorted out and they both looked wrong, too small somehow. Then the man in the far corner turned to look at her, or rather he looked in her direction, his focus far beyond the confines of the room. As before with Bet, Sandra recognized the eyes and knew this was Louie.

Louie's eyes drifted away without any sign of recognition. Sandra ambled over and plunked herself down in the comfy chair next to him, sliding it over until it butted up against his armrest. "Hey, comrade," she said, louder than she intended, "how's the revolution going?"

Louie's eyes briefly found Sandra's face. "Do I know you?"

"Yes, you do," she said. "It's me, Sandra."

"It's Sandra," Louie repeated, and once again he peered into some distance only he could see.

A long-buried memory of Louie suddenly surfaced in Sandra's mind. Louie striking a heroic pose, claw hammer in one hand and copy of Mao's little red book in the other, standing on the wire-spool table in the Berkman kitchen. The rest of the household looking on, laughing uproariously; even Bet tittering a little, after a futile effort to maintain solemnity. Early days in Berkman House, when there was still laughter. Sandra tried to connect the Louie sitting next to her with this memory of the people's colossus, but little of the physicality and nothing of the spirit remained. He was a spent force, a hollow husk. She shook herself into the present. "Bet told me you were here. Or rather, Thomas her son did. So I came to visit. Been a long time."

"Sandra." It wasn't a question. Louie now seemed to be flipping through a mental rolodex.

"Yep me, Sandra."

"Did Bet send you here to preach at me?" A bit of a crafty smile began to form on the skeletal face. Something of the old Louie starting to manifest.

"No, Bet doesn't know I'm here. Do you remember we used to live together a long time ago, you and me and Bet?"

"And that crazy selfish bastard..." Louie looked down and to his left, his voice trailing off.

"Phyl," she prompted.

"Yeah, Phyl — never liked that fucker." Louie leaned back and looked at the ceiling. "There was also that punk. What was his name? I don't remember."

Sandra laughed. "His name was Norbert. He was a punk all right. Still is."

"Sandra." Louie frowned at something far away. "Sandra." He shook his head. She was, as always, the inconsequential one.

"Louie, years ago I had a baby. A baby girl. She's all grown up now. You are her father."

"No." Louie shook his head with greater emphasis. "No — No — No..." Each no said slowly and deliberately, with long spaces between.

"It's true," Sandra pressed. "It happened that day we went for a walk, by the stream, on the rock over the waterfall..." She wanted to recapture the day for Louie, to make him remember, but the words didn't convey even to herself the images in her head. Recognizing the futility, she stopped trying; he added one last "No" — like a period after a long sentence.

They lapsed into silence. Without looking at her Louie said, "You should go now."

She waited, watching him closely. At last he turned and Sandra leaned forward and kissed him for the first time since that October afternoon long ago, now on the brink of an even deeper abyss. She pulled back to see Louie more clearly; he was still looking into the distance, and then suddenly his gaze locked on her for the first time.

"Sandra." Something had clicked. "Sandra, I'm fixing to die here. Don't try to make me want to live."

She reached over and took his hand in hers. "Louie, I'm not trying to make you do anything. I just thought you should know."

"Go away." Louie's upper lip trembled and he squeezed her hand tight.

With her free hand she gently pulled his thumb back and broke his grip. "Goodbye, Louie." Sandra rose and walked out of the sunroom into the long corridor, acutely conscious of the noise her shoes made on the parquet floor. Passing Louie's room she saw the flowers she'd brought artfully arranged in a cut-glass vase on his bedside table. Nothing else had changed.

Not willing to leave without some official sanction, she waited in the front lobby. No one was behind the reception desk. She picked up a dispenser of hand sanitizer from the counter, squeezed some into her palm and rubbed her hands together. She heard approaching footsteps from the corridor, the sound growing steadily louder. After an exceedingly long interval, Gabriela emerged. "You are still here," she said.

"I was just leaving."

"I hope you will come again. Your visit has done him a world of good."

"I think I made him mad."

"Perhaps that is what he needed. He was drifting away from us but now he just asked for something to read." Gabriela frowned at the bookshelf against the wall near the exit. "What do you suggest? *Reader's Digest … National Geographic…*"

"*Cosmo.*" She couldn't resist.

"Really?"

"No, not a magazine." Sandra scanned the bookshelf. It was three tiers high and evidently stocked with the discards of past residents and visitors. A half dozen pristine bibles included. Slim pickings. From the bottom shelf she pulled up a dog-eared copy of Charles Dickens's *Hard Times.* "Here, this will cheer him up."

Gabriela took the book reluctantly, as if she thought Sandra was joking. Sandra *was* joking, in part, but still it was the best read she could see on the bookshelf.

"I have to be going. Goodbye, Gabriela. Do I sign out or something?"

Gabriela treated Sandra once more to her brilliant smile. "Of course not. This is a home, not a prison. You can come and go as you please. You will visit again?"

"I will. And I'll bring something for Louie to read." Sandra almost meant it.

1982

"Name?" The court clerk doesn't even look up when we enquire about "our friend." I almost say *Louie Del Grande* and blow it right there, but Norbert has the presence of mind to say, "Dorian Twisp."

The clerk shuffles through a clipboard of papers. "Courtroom Five."

We find Courtroom Five one floor above. The corridor is full of people waiting for the day's business to begin. Most seem to be family members and friends of those appearing in court: Some pace back and forth in front of the door; some lean against the wall chewing at their fingernails; at least three people are crying and being consoled in a huddle of loved ones. In contrast, the policemen elbowing their ways through the crowd and the clustered lawyers, expensively suited and with bulky briefcases, seem totally at ease, to the point of boredom. Their equanimity shouldn't surprise me, but it does. I half expected all the court officials to be on guard against the threat of our attack. I imagine metal detectors in the walls screaming out the presence of the .32 hidden in my purse.

My purse is brand new, or at least never used. I found it buried in the back of my closet. My mother gave it to me years ago, back when we were still on speaking terms. Why I kept it I don't know — maybe in anticipation of an occasion like this.

Along with the purse, I'm wearing running shoes, a floral dress and rhinestone glasses from when I was a kid, before I got contacts. My hair is up in curlers wrapped in a scarf, Russian peasant-woman style. I feel like a drag queen, an obvious phony, although my communards are confident that I can pass scrutiny as a typical working-class woman. And so far, so good. At least, so far no one has given me a second glance.

At nine o'clock sharp an overweight man in a rumpled brown uniform unlocks the courtroom door. Norbert and I file in with the relatives and friends and find seats on the aisle, right behind an odd couple: a bald man in a tweed coat sitting beside a shaggy-haired biker in a leather jacket. The courtroom is smaller than I imagined, its lighting subdued, all sounds muffled. Just like church. The pews quickly fill with the anxious relatives and friends. My newly-shaved legs itch terribly.

My attention is drawn to a man already installed in the sanctuary area up front. He lolls in a padded swivel chair as if in his own living room, wearing his five-hundred-dollar suit with the poise of a department-store mannequin — no undisciplined wrinkles — as comfortable as I would be in blue denim. His hair is ample, Kennedy-coiffed and immaculate. His tanned face is movie-star handsome. I loathe him at first sight.

"Who's that prick?" I ask, not really expecting an answer.

Norbert shrugs.

Mr. Tweed Coat stage whispers over his shoulder. "John Edwards, Crown counsel."

"I wasn't asking for an introduction," I snap back.

Tweed Coat turns to make a full appraisal of me and Norbert. "Careful. Mr. Edwards is the prosecutor. You don't want to be on his bad side. He runs the show in here."

"No way, that's the judge's job," says Norbert.

Tweed Coat treats Norbert to a condescending smile and abruptly twists away. Fortunately, John Edwards doesn't hear any of this exchange. He's busy lecturing to a pimple-faced geek in a three-piece corduroy suit seated close by in the pews. The discourse is about Aboriginal art prints, which Edwards refers to as "collectables." I detest him even more.

The courtroom hubbub is instantly quieted when the man in the rumpled uniform appears from around a corner behind the vacant bench. "Order. All Rise." He sounds like he's been sucking on helium balloons. We all rise.

"The Honourable Justice Whosit presiding." (I don't catch the name.)

Judge Whosit enters stage right and takes his seat stage centre. "Please be seated."

Waiting out the echoing cascade of butts landing on hard wooden benches, the judge angles his leather chair slightly to the left. He winks — actually winks — at the prosecutor.

Unbelievable! The bourgeois justice system, as Bet calls it, really is corrupt. I'm sickened by how clearly the prosecutor is in cahoots with the defence counsels and the judge.

"Okay, let's get going." The judge nods at his helium-throated flunky, who takes his designated seat close to and below the bench.

Moments later, four men are brought into the dock. The third one is Louie. I turn to nudge Norbert, but he's already on his feet heading for the exit. Louie blinks at the judge and the prosecuting attorney, but doesn't look toward the audience. Then I notice problem number one: He's in handcuffs.

The first prisoner is a shaggy teenager, busted for auto theft and drunk driving. Charges read. He pleads not guilty. Trial date and bail terms set.

At last Louie scans the crowd. I catch his eye and make a furtive little wave with my fingers in front of my face. He frowns and looks away. Problem number two: Louie doesn't recognize me in my glasses, curlers and babushka.

The second prisoner sports a black eye and a swollen lip. Drunk and disorderly. Trial date set. He's freed on his own recognizance.

The court clerk squeaks out, "Dorian Twisp. Jaywalking, resisting arrest." The judge raises both eyebrows and looks quizzically at the prosecutor.

"Come on Bet; what the hell's the delay," I whisper to myself.

The prosecutor shuffles through some papers and clears his throat. "Your Honour, this is a somewhat unusual case."

"Jesus, Bet, before he gives it all away." I don't want Louie to reveal his true identity.

"Your Honour, according to information we have received from Winnipeg, Manitoba, the prisoner is wanted there on serious charges." The prosecutor pauses to put on his glasses, which are rimless at the top. "To wit, possession of a narcotic or controlled substance for the purpose of trafficking. Other drug-related offenses listed as well."

The judge swivels his chair around to face the dock. He examines Louie as if he were a virus under a microscope. "Well, young man, do you have legal counsel?"

"I don't want a lawyer."

This is blasphemy in the temple of law and the judge is having none of it. "I think you should reconsider. I'm prepared to appoint a public defender to represent you."

I fumble with the clasp on my purse. Diversion or no diversion I have to make my move fast, before Louie spills the beans.

Unexpectedly, it's Louie who stops me in my tracks. "Don't bother, Your Honour, I plead guilty."

Guilty? What the fuck is Louie trying to prove?

The judge is only slightly less taken aback. "Young man, are you aware of the possible consequences of your plea?"

Louie shrugs.

"I don't believe you are." The judge shifts his gaze toward the prosecutor. It seems to be an appeal for help.

The prosecutor adroitly picks up his cue. "Your Honour, I'd be willing to move on to other cases and allow my learned friend time to reason with the accused. We can return to Mr. Twisp later this morning."

"My learned friend" turns out to be the corduroy-clad geek who earlier received an art lesson from the prosecutor. The geek duly rises from the front row and is admitted through the barrier into the sanctum. He crosses over to the dock and whispers to Louie, who shakes his head in angry negation.

"Who's next?" asks the judge.

The court clerk shuffles some papers and finds his place. "Your Honour, this is—Jesus Christ!" A surprise introduction that has nothing to do with the fourth prisoner in the dock, and everything to do with the thick greasy smoke billowing out of the ventilation ducts. I leap to my feet with my hand in my purse and force my way to the aisle. Once there I'm buffeted by the current of panicked relatives and friends scrambling for the rear exits. I duck my head and charge toward the bench. Just before I reach the barrier a firm hand clamps on my wrist. I turn and see a police badge. I look up, way up, at the officer wearing it. Problem number three.

"Let me go," I demand. Dimly, out of the corner of my eye, I see Louie and the other prisoners being herded out of the courtroom. A heavy door closes behind them. Already it's difficult to see anything around me. Whatever's in that concoction of Phyl's, it works like a son of a bitch. Must be the lentils.

"Just come with me quietly, ma'am." The cop opens the barrier gate and pulls me through. I make a last-ditch effort to reach Louie and actually pull my captor a few steps toward the dock before he regains his balance.

"No, no, this way." He tightens his grip and hauls me in the opposite direction.

What to do? He's holding my wrist a few inches above where my fingers clamp the .32 in my purse, so I can't shoot the prick even if I had the moxie to do so. I let the gun fall to the bottom of the purse as I'm dragged out of the courtroom through the same door the judge entered by.

Now both Louie and I are firmly in the clutches of the law, the Berkman gang busted before mission accomplished. I wonder briefly if our remaining communards might attempt a rescue operation. Probably not, I conclude. Too gutless.

"Keep going down this hallway and out the door at the end. It leads into a parkade. You'll be all right from there."

It takes a few seconds to sink in. I'm not under arrest. He's letting me go. My opportunity to plug the pig full of lead, but it seems a little churlish now to do so. A wise non-move too, for at that moment the door behind us reopens and the prosecutor appears out of a cloud of smoke. "Is there anybody still in there?" the policeman asks.

"I … don't … know," the prosecutor manages between fits of coughing.

The policeman puts a handkerchief to his nose and heads back into the smoke, leaving the two of us alone. The prosecutor puts down his briefcase as if to follow the officer but immediately picks it up again and begins walking toward the exit.

"You goddamn coward," I mutter and hurry in pursuit.

I'm right behind him, a few steps into the parkade. No one else in sight; most people must have evacuated the building at street level. The prosecutor extracts a set of keys from his pocket. He angles over to a late-model sedan parked about fifty feet away. As if he's connected by a leash, I'm pulled along after him, thinking, *No way will this insufferable jerk get away so easy.*

He still hasn't noticed me when he reaches his car. He unlocks the door and throws his briefcase behind the driver's seat. Sensing my presence, he's startled by my proximity. At that moment, the plan that was brewing somewhere beneath the limen of consciousness comes to the surface of my mind in crystal intent. I draw the pistol from my purse.

Keeping the gun low and close to me, I say in a shaky voice: "Give me the keys, Edwards. Then get in."

The prosecutor complies, but with no visible sign of fear. I'm vaguely disappointed but waste no time in circling the car and unlocking the passenger door.

"Okay, drive," I say, sliding into the front seat. I hand him back the keys. He glances at me and lets his eyes slide down to take in the gun I'm now holding in both hands. Weighing the odds and evidently deciding against taking a risk, he turns on the motor.

"Don't drive too fast or too slow. Whatever happens, *do not stop* or you'll be very sorry." Honest to God, that's what I say. Too much television I guess.

As we roll down the spiral route out of the parkade, I glance back at the exit door and catch sight of the policeman who "rescued" me as he staggers out, half carrying, half dragging the judge. My view is cut off as we round the first turn.

The man at the parkade gate waves us through but, halfway into the street, the prosecutor suddenly brakes. A cop only twenty feet ahead of us is directing traffic away from the fire trucks converging at the front of the courthouse. Is this when I have to shoot someone — my hostage, the cop, or perhaps both? This question gives rise to an awareness suppressed by the chaos in the courthouse: I could never aim at another human being and pull the trigger. Plus a shot would only serve to draw fire from men whose empathy has been trained out of them.

I'm about to throw the pistol out the window and exit the car with my hands up — but then the cop blows his whistle and gesticulates furiously for us to turn right and get the hell moving. So I keep hold of the gun and jab the prosecutor on the hip with it. He turns right and gets the hell moving.

A couple of blocks later, Edwards speaks to me for the first time. "What's this all about?"

"Just keep driving and shut up."

We drive in silence for a while. Suddenly, my body is taken over by an uncontrollable trembling and tears begin to roll down my cheeks. Edwards reaches into his jacket pocket.

"Keep your damn hands on the wheel!"

He freezes for a second, then slowly extracts a package of tissues, which he drops on the console between our seats.

I ignore the offering. "Turn right, here," I say as we approach a quiet-looking side street. Half a block on, I tell him, "Pull over." He complies and looks at me, questioning. Still no sign of fear in his eyes and I hate him for his coolness, his calm command of the situation. I have the power. I hold the gun. And I'm weeping, goddamn it.

"Put it in park." He does. I lift my legs and squat sideways on my seat. "Now, facedown on the floor over here." With the gun as a pointer I indicate the space below the glove compartment. "Slowly."

He squeezes around the steering wheel and clambers over the console into a yoga child's pose in front of the passenger seat; I extend my legs and hump over behind the wheel. "Don't move," I say. "Try anything stupid and I'll blow your fucking pecker off." Whew, tough broad; if only my voice wasn't so quavery. With one hand, I pull a tissue free of the package and blow my nose, keeping the gun pointed at him with the other. I drop the tissue and jerk the gearshift lever into D. We're off and rolling again. Nothing to it.

Five minutes later I pull up in the alley behind Berkman House.

"We're here," I say.

My prisoner raises his head to look and I club him on the back of his skull as hard as I can with the butt of the gun. He drops like a dead man. I wasn't thinking about the heaviness of the gun; I just don't want him to know where we are.

But if he's dead? I reach around his neck and, after a few anxious seconds, find a pulse. After scanning the alley for possible witnesses, I get out of the car and run to the passenger-side door. When I open it, the man's head and shoulders flop out. I can neither fully extract him nor get the door closed. I look around again; we're still alone. I hurry into the house.

"Where the fuck were you?" Phyl's greeting as I step into the kitchen. My communards are sitting in their customary positions around the cable spool. The atmosphere is heavy with the simmering odour of defeat.

"Help me bring him in from the car," I say, dropping my purse on the table.

"Louie?" Bet is out the back door before I can head her off. Norbert and Phyl aren't far behind.

"No, wait! It's not Louie. They took him away too fast," I say, pursuing the others. I catch up just as the sight of a torso protruding from the car stops my housemates in their tracks. Three pairs of eyes focus in my direction.

"I took a hostage," I explain.

Phyl leans over to examine the face of the unconscious man. "Who the fuck?"

"The prosecutor."

"Jesus Christ, Sandra, are you out of your fucking gourd? What are we—"

"Don't start, Phyl, okay? We've got to get him inside, and fast."

"Hold on, maybe we should just get that door closed and wait for dark."

"Sure, you can go out every five minutes and club him under again. Phyl, it's eleven o'clock in the morning."

"What if someone sees?" Phyl looks to Bet for support but she seems to be hypnotized by the prosecutor's tie.

"No one's around. Besides, no one's going to notice if we just act casual." I deliberately invoke one of Phyl's prime maxims, which he claims is the secret of his shoplifting success. While others might surreptitiously sneak a pound of ground round under their duffle coats, Phyl is more likely to waltz out of the butcher store with a side of beef, like he was off to make a delivery or something.

Norbert gets us unstuck. "Come on Phyl. Seize the time. Wiggie's blinds are drawn. I think he's out collecting bottles." Wiggie's a total recluse and, thanks to a fortuitous placement of garages and evergreens, the only neighbour with a clear view of our backyard.

"Other arm, Phyl," says Norbert. The two guys drag the prosecutor clear of the car. As they do so, a wallet tumbles out from an inside pocket of his suit.

"Any dough in there?" asks Phyl, a little too eagerly in my opinion.

"Naw, just credit cards and shit." Norbert relinquishes the wallet to Bet's outstretched hand. The guys squat on opposite sides of the unconscious man and lift him more or less upright. Bet and I each elevate a leg and the five of us move as one unit toward the house.

"Basement door," says Norbert, as we draw close. He's already breathing heavy from unaccustomed exercise.

"Now what?" demands Phyl, once we're inside.

"Sunroom." I'm relieved that Bet speaks instead of me.

The sunroom is actually the windowless space under the concrete front stairs, lit by a track of six 150-watt grow lamps, which shine down on several trays of marijuana seedlings. Phyl's plantation.

Phyl isn't into trafficking, since he regards it as immoral and capitalistic. But his personal appetite for weed is prodigious; besides, he isn't above sharing. So the plantation keeps him — and us — well stocked.

There's no door leading into the sunroom. Phyl, being very security conscious, devised a removable panel — cunningly disguised — for access. Even the most astute observer would only see a solid continuation of the shiplap wall, with a metal vent up close to the ceiling and a light switch off to one side. The sunroom is the logical place to stash our hostage. Except for one factor — six trays of newly sprouted marijuana plants.

"Flush 'em," orders Phyl.

None of us dare move. We all know something has to be done, but hearing "flush 'em" from Phyl's lips is like hearing him propose infanticide.

"Come on, what are you waiting for? We gotta flush 'em." Phyl picks up the tray closest to him. Feeling absolutely guilt-ridden, I pick up the next two trays. Together we remove all the seedlings and set them on the floor outside the sunroom.

The prosecutor is still unconscious when we drag him into his new digs and wrestle the panel over the floor moulding and back into place. Phyl pops out the fake vent and pushes a giant slide bolt up into its lock position. Our hostage now safely stowed, we cart the seedlings into the basement bathroom.

"What about the car?" Norbert asks as the first plants swirl down the toilet.

"Shit. Give me the keys. I'll ditch it." Clearly, Phyl's heart isn't in the flushing party, and just as clearly his directive regarding the plants was only a ploy to regain some power in the new dynamic.

"You don't have a driver's license. What if the cops pull you over?" Bet sounds honestly concerned.

Phyl smiles for the first time since my return. "Like I'm gonna floor it through every red light I see? Give me a break, Bet. I'm not a moron."

I hand over the keys and he leaves. We flush another bowlful of baby plants. The water boils up chocolate brown, the green herbs swirl counterclockwise in the bouillon, then the whole soup gradually clears before disappearing in a sudden gulp. As we sit on the edge of the bathtub waiting for the tank to refill, a loud crash from upstairs shakes the house.

"Oh no; oh shit." Norbert dumps an entire tray of weed into the toilet and pulls the handle. The load rotates weakly, and then the murky water begins to rise and spill over the edges. Norbert jumps back and turns to look at me. "What are we going to do?"

"Norbert, relax, they can't have found us yet. Stay here. I'll go check." I try to sound confident, but the noise has unnerved me as well. Perhaps Phyl walked into a trap, and now they're coming to get the rest of us. I briefly visualize shooting it out with whoever has invaded, and immediately recoil from the thought. Resistance is moot anyway; my gun is in my purse and my purse is up on the kitchen table.

"Not with a bang but a whimper," I say to myself as I mount the stairs. I find Phyl rummaging under the kitchen sink. He retrieves a bottle of window cleaner and squirts some onto a dishrag. "Fingerprints," he mutters, by way of explanation, as he rushes out the open door, slamming it shut behind him. I return downstairs where Norbert is mopping up water and soggy bits of peat moss from the floor. The water in the toilet bowl is clear again.

"That was Phyl," I say. "Back for cleaning supplies."

Norbert looks confused.

"Oh yeah," says Bet. "Fingerprints."

Eight

2007

Sandra knew something was wrong as soon as she arrived for her second appointment at the reporting centre. No smile greeted her this time. Instead, the receptionist seized her phone, stabbed a button and said, "She's here." A few seconds later Sandra's case officer strode into the reception area, scowling.

"Give me one good reason I shouldn't have you apprehended," Case Officer barked.

"Sorry?" Sandra played contrite to mask the indignation she felt.

"I contacted the halfway house. You weren't there. In fact, they have no record of you checking in. So, where the hell have you been?"

"I'm staying at a hostel downtown." She kept her voice neutral. Perhaps, if she didn't push any buttons, she could weather this storm.

"You're required to keep this office informed of your place of residence at all times. Why didn't you tell us about this move?"

"I did, I—"

"You're lying. I took careful notes from our meeting. You didn't say anything about where you were staying."

Sandra pointed to the receptionist. "I wrote the address on the registration form she gave me."

Keeping his eyes on Sandra, Case Officer extended one arm over the reception counter and snapped his fingers. The receptionist spun around on castors and pulled open a drawer. After a bit of rummaging she placed a file folder into the man's outstretched hand.

Case Officer patted his chest and pulled a pair of reading glasses from his breast pocket. He opened the file and scanned the first page, then glared up at Sandra. "The *onus* is on you" — he spoke with great deliberation — "to ensure that I know where to contact you when necessary."

"I'm sorry," Sandra repeated, with a glance toward the inscrutable face of the receptionist. "It won't happen again."

"Have you found a job yet?" Case Officer was still perusing her file.

"No, I was expecting to see the vocational counsellor today."

"There, you see? That's just it." Case Officer handed the file back to the receptionist without looking in her direction. "As I was unable to reach you to confirm the appointment, I cancelled. I'm not about to waste the time of our advisors. We'll talk in my office."

Head bowed, Sandra followed the man down the long corridor. She had to trot to keep up. They passed through a cubicle farm and into an office on the other side. A room with a view; apparently Case Officer's star was in the ascendant. He sat behind his new desk and pointed at the chair in front of it. Sandra sat. He pointed to the door. She reached over and pushed it shut. He swivelled ninety degrees to face the window. She waited.

"Don't ever try to make a fool of me," Case Officer said to the window.

"I'm very sorry, sir. I didn't mean any disrespect." Sandra's prison conditioning spoke for her.

"Not as sorry as you'll be if you keep giving me attitude. From now on I want you to call in every day to confirm your whereabouts." He spun back in his chair to face Sandra and caught her in the act of frowning. "Is that a problem?"

"It is a bit," Sandra admitted. "I'm running low on funds, and residents of the hostel have to use a pay phone."

"You can use the phone at the halfway house for free. Do what you were supposed to do and move in there."

"I will, but I'm paid up at the hostel until Saturday."

"Again with the attitude." He rotated back to the window. "Your failure to plan ahead is *your* problem, not mine."

"Yes, sir, I'm sorry."

He tilted back. "Yes, sir, I'm sorry," he echoed, shaking his head.

"I'll move to the halfway house. I'll check out of the hostel tomorrow morning. Maybe they'll give me some money back and—"

"No." He swivelled back from the window and pulled his chair toward the desk. "Stay where you are until Saturday. Call me every second day, starting tomorrow. Here's my card."

Sandra took the card, looked at both sides and said, "Thank-you, Mr. Weychuk, sir."

"I'm a reasonable man, Sandra. Just don't pull any fast ones on me. I can't help you unless you take responsibility for rehabilitating yourself. Stay on the rails and you'll be reintegrated into society in no time." He gestured at the door and Sandra started to rise. But Weychuk wasn't finished. "Stay on the rails, Sandra. Phone me tomorrow and I'll set you up with the vocational counsellor."

"I will, Mr. Weychuk. Thank-you."

"You're welcome. Now scoot."

Sandra scooted, conscious of an itching in her armpits and something crawling even deeper under her skin. Having to tiptoe around power ate at her soul. She had her fill of that in prison. With every "sorry" and "yes, sir" that passed her lips, poison entered the opposite way.

Sandra walked a few blocks before she found what she was looking for — a bar that looked as cruddy as she felt. *Stay on the rails* echoed in her brain; she ordered a double scotch.

She'd barely started on her drink when she heard someone say, "Bartender, another for the lady." She appraised the man planting himself on the stool to her right: a little younger than her, a few pounds past pudgy and a habitual leer trying to pass as an engaging smile.

"Thank you," she said, shuddering, the words taking her right back to the reporting centre.

The man nodded and ordered a beer for himself. "Fred's the name," he said, as the beer was pulled and set before him with a scotch placed next to the glass Sandra was working on.

"Hello, Fred, I'm Wilma." The first name that came to her mind.

Fred emitted a booming laugh. "Fred and Wilma! This has to be fate. What do you do for a living, Wilma?"

"I work for the government." She felt a nudge against her thigh and glanced down. Fred had extended his leg awkwardly so that his knee made contact. She didn't pull away. Fred was repellent, but part of her thought perhaps crud could drive out crud. *Stay on the rails.* She forced herself to smile and downed the remains of her first scotch in one gulp.

"Another coincidence!" Fred lifted his glass and clinked it against her full one on the counter.

Taking her cue, Sandra picked up the second scotch and swirled the ice cubes around. She took a dainty sip. "You work for the government too?"

"Yup. Here, let me show you." Fred pulled out a billfold and flipped it open to reveal a police shield.

Sandra's heart pounded and her stomach lurched. Was she busted? What for this time? She blinked at Fred, breathing deep. His smile broadened. "Yessir, you're in safe hands with me, darling."

Sandra climbed down from her stool, one hand gripping the counter for balance, the other hand scooping up her scotch. She briefly contemplated spilling the drink on Fred's head, but waste not, want not. Instead she chugalugged and then slammed the empty glass down on the counter. "Thanks for the drink, Fred. Gotta go meet my husband now."

Just before the bar door closed behind her she heard, "Fuck you, bitch."

After the gloom of the bar, the glare outside was disorienting. The booze didn't help. Crud cannot drive out crud; crud can only add to crud.

It was a long walk back to the hostel; by the time Sandra got there she was almost sober but very tired. Although it was only late afternoon, she went straight to bed and immediately fell asleep. She awoke some time later with no idea what time it was. The room was dark and various snoring patterns emanated from the bunks around her, which had all been empty when she crashed.

The room was hot and stuffy. Her head ached and her mouth felt almost glued shut. She lay in her bunk, feeling too wretched to get back to sleep, too exhausted to get up. Hours passed until dawn began to define the window panes. Finally she heard a distant stirring from the direction of the common room where the hostel laid a free "breakfast" — weak coffee and stale muffins. She sat up and, after a spasm of pain and nausea passed, pulled on a pair of jeans and a sweatshirt and padded down to the common room. The large urn was still perking but the liquid in the glass tube over the spigot looked sufficiently brown. After she filled a Styrofoam cup, its bottom was still visible. Sandra stirred in a heaping teaspoon of whitener and two packages of sugar and took her cup over to the one relatively comfortable chair in the room. She swallowed half of the weak coffee in one gulp, placed the cup on the end table next to her chair and closed her eyes.

Someone shouted her name. Sandra woke up. Before she could call out in reply the hostel manager crashed into the common room, very red in the face. He jabbed a finger in her direction, shouting, "Sandra Treming, you leave here today."

"I'm paid up until Saturday." Sandra slouched back in her chair.

"Not Saturday, today you go."

Sandra picked up her coffee and took a sip; it was cold. Her display of nonchalance infuriated the manager. "Now! No time for drinking coffee. Get packing!"

"What's the hurry?"

"No criminals here. You leave now."

"I'm not a criminal." The situation was becoming clearer.

"The police were here looking for you."

Fucking Weychuk! Sandra rose to her feet and advanced toward the manager until her coffee cup was almost touching his chest. Her hand was trembling. "Give me my money back and I'll check out."

The manager backed away. "No refunds."

"Okay, fine." Heading for the door, she brushed by the manager and crumpled the cup against his belly. The remaining coffee splashed over his shirt, pants and shoes. "Oops, sorry about that," she said, only sorry that the cup wasn't full and the coffee wasn't boiling hot.

She braced, expecting the manager to hit her; instead he scurried over to the far wall. Sandra returned to her room and packed in less than a minute.

1982

It's an odd experience to watch the news when you know more about a news item than the anchorman reporting it. Once Phyl is back from his mission (after parking the prosecutor's car on a busy street and returning by bus, transferring three times to throw off a possible tail) we turn on the television. The broadcast briefly mentions vandalism at the courthouse, resulting in "emergency evacuation of the premises, but no prisoners escaping." In fact, more air time is given to the heroic policeman who rescued a judge overcome by smoke. That's all. Not even the lead item, but number three or four in the lineup.

The evening news is slightly more gratifying. The story moves up to top spot. A graphic of the scales of justice on a background of smoke projects over the anchorman's left shoulder. The focus is now on "the strange disappearance of the Crown prosecutor, reported to have driven from the scene accompanied by an unidentified female." Ah, fame. Made the six o'clock news at last.

Between newscasts we talk. The others have more or less accepted the hostage taking as an irreversible fact. What choice do they have? But now they're looking to me for a detailed master plan of the sort Bet would deliver, with typed copies for each member of the collective. Unfortunately for them, I'm not Bet. I don't have a grand strategy in mind, merely a vague notion of trading our hostage for Louie and immunity from prosecution.

Bet is uncharacteristically silent until well into the third news broadcast. I half expect a scathing critique of my adventurist action. Instead she sits next to me, puts her arm around my neck, and at one point, rests her head on my shoulder. The closest thing to a hug she has ever given me. At last she clears her throat. "Our only guarantee of ongoing freedom will be passage to another country, preferably a post-revolutionary workers' state in the third world. This should be our demand. Along with the release of Louie of course." Sensible enough, but if I'd known that my action in the parkade would lead me to a socialist paradise, I wouldn't have done what I did.

Phyl jumps in. "Not just Louie. We demand freedom for all political prisoners."

"How do you define political prisoners, Phyl?" Norbert wants to know.

"Empty the fucking prisons." Phyl glares at us across the cable spool.

"What about money? We planned a bank heist in order to continue our revolutionary program. Even working in a third-world context, we still need money." Bet, being pragmatic.

The framing of demands is abruptly cut off by a loud crash in the kitchen. This time the collective is all present and accounted for and we have every reason to be scared witless.

It isn't the police.

It's Dorian.

Dorian is a little bit drunk. More than a little actually. He's totally pissed and totally pissed off. We learn that, after his call the night before, made from a phone booth of course, he found a cordon sanitaire of police vehicles around his apartment building and all the lights on in his suite. Not stopping to enquire, he strolled by the scene and kept on walking until the first bar opened in the morning.

"Where's that shithead?" Dorian isn't in the mood for banter.

"Which shithead?" Phyl asks.

"*Louie*. The shithead who gave the Man my address."

"Louie's still in jail. Coffee?" Not waiting on a response, Bet starts pouring.

"Jail — good. I hope he rots in there. Why did he give them my address?"

Norbert leans forward. "Louie would never rat out a friend—"

"He was carrying *your* fucking wallet," Phyl says. "They must've got your address from *your* driver's license. Dickhead."

"Ha! Phyl, you're so naïve. Never carry ID with your right address. Never ever. No, that fuckhead told them."

Phyl doesn't respond, but I can tell that being out-paranoided by Dorian really rankles. Phyl doesn't even carry a wallet for chrissakes.

"Maybe when they asked for his address he figured they were testing him, so he told them what he thought would be on your ID." Norbert testifying in support of Louie.

Dorian shakes his head, and rightly so. Louie wouldn't volunteer information to the Man without a good reason. Most likely he was putting the heat on Dorian to keep it away from Berkman House.

"So, how come you didn't bail him out?" Dorian asks, as if our inaction somehow undermines Norbert's argument.

"Well—" Phyl begins.

"There was a fire," says Bet.

"So, when are you going back — tomorrow?"

"First thing tomorrow." Phyl involuntarily looks toward the door leading down to the basement.

"Do they know who he is? I mean, do they still think that Louie is me?"

The four of us shrug in unison.

"Maybe he hasn't let on. Maybe they still think they've got me. All my money is in my apartment. Maybe they didn't find it. Do you think it's safe for me to go back?"

Again a chorus of shrugs.

"If they think they've got me, then they won't be looking for me. But they're probably watching my apartment. What am I going to do?"

"I don't know, Dorian, what are you going to do?" Bet poses the question in an offhand way while the rest of us feign indifference. I think I hear a faint pounding from the basement.

"I don't know what I'm going to do. I was going to leave town, but all my money…" Dorian finally takes a seat at the cable-spool table. "I won't get anywhere without money."

Silence descends. Dorian notices the coffee Bet poured for him and picks it up as he waits for some response. We outwait him. Finally he gives up. "I've got nowhere to go. You guys are my only hope. Can I crash here for a while? Just until things blow over?"

Dorian shows no sign of hearing the pounding in the basement, now obvious to everyone else in the room. "It's only fair." Dorian slams his coffee mug down; some of the liquid sloshes over the cable spool surface. "I wouldn't be in this jam if Louie hadn't screwed me — what the fuck's that noise?"

"Nothing," says Norbert. "Probably the plumbing."

"Dorian," I say, "I think it's time we levelled with you." Ignoring the dirty looks of my communards, I pre-empt Norbert's feeble diversion. "We didn't bail out Louie because we intend to spring him. We started the fire at the courthouse. And what you hear downstairs is the Crown prosecutor who I ... whom we're holding as a hostage."

Dorian utters a weird half laugh, which dies quickly when no one else joins in. "You're serious?"

Phyl and Bet both begin speaking at once, then stop, deferring to each other. I jump into the gap. "Absolutely serious." Then, to Phyl and Bet, "We have to take him in. If we don't, he has nowhere to go, except to the police."

"Can we trust him if he stays?" Phyl asks.

"Can we trust him if he goes?" I reply.

"Not to change the subject or anything, but maybe our guest downstairs needs attention." Norbert looks around the room as if conducting a poll, but no one picks up on his suggestion. "Um, shouldn't we take him some food and water?"

"Holy shit, you weirdos are serious." Dorian collapses back into his chair.

"We are very serious about social change. We are a revolutionary organization — small in numbers perhaps, but also the vanguard of a huge popular uprising that will sweep capitalism and imperialism and all forms of people exploiting people from the face of the planet." Bet speaking, of course. She's back in the ideological saddle, and I'm happy to let her take the lead.

"But this is a democracy we live in, not some banana republic. You want change?" Dorian grasps at an appropriate cliché. "Use ballots, not bullets."

"Changing the faces of the rulers don't do shit." Phyl gets into the act. "If voting could change the system, it would be illegal."

Dorian shifts his chair to one side to give Norbert access to the refrigerator. After some rummaging Norbert locates a yogurt container of leftover lentil stew. He pours its contents into a saucepan and fires up a burner. Dorian persists in his argument. "Anyway, who's exploited? I don't feel exploited — any more than necessary I mean; Norbert, do you feel exploited?"

Norbert doesn't seem to hear the question; his mind is fully immersed in the stew he's stirring.

"Dorian." Bet repositions herself directly opposite him at the cable spool. Reaching out, she covers Dorian's hands with hers. "We all like you very much, but you must understand. The material prosperity that you enjoy comes at the expense of others who are more directly exposed to the forces of exploitation. That's true for all of us here, but most particularly for you."

"Me?"

"Yes, you, because of your, uh, chosen profession."

"What do you mean?" Dorian pulls his hands back, but Bet holds on tight, even though Dorian's retreat presses her ribcage hard against the rim of the spool.

"Dorian, the peasant who grows the cocaine you import once used his land to grow food for his family. But no longer — thanks to the appetites of degenerate North Americans. Have you never noticed that all our bourgeois vices — sugar, coffee, tobacco, cocaine — are supplied from the third world? Do you think that's just a coincidence?"

"Bet, that's history. I don't deal coke no more."

"You don't? Good. That's a start." Bet draws Dorian's hands toward her until they're again midway across the spool top. "Dorian, there's so much we could teach you. Ask questions if you like, but if you're going to stay here, you must accept the actions we are taking."

Dorian's eyes drop a fraction. Is it my imagination or is his gaze now locked on her breasts? "Okay," he whispers.

"All done," Norbert announces as he turns off the stove and pours the slop from the saucepan into a bowl.

Phyl distributes tea towels to everyone. He wraps his around the lower half of his face, Hollywood-bandit style, and motions the rest of us to do likewise. I comply so as not to be different, though in my case it doesn't make sense. After all, the prisoner has already seen my face.

The five of us troop downstairs. The pounding, which stopped for a while, suddenly renews, as if our prisoner hears us coming. Phyl hits the light switch beside the wall panel leading to the sunroom, and the pounding immediately stops.

"Ready?" Phyl pops off the vent cover and releases the slide bolt.

"Ready." I raise my .32 and cock it. Out of the corner of my eye, I see Dorian take two steps back.

Phyl tilts the wall panel slightly back and, with a sudden effort, lifts it out of place and sets it to one side. Bright light floods the dim basement, followed seconds later by the stench of body odour.

Slightly hunched over, the prosecutor stands at the back of the sunroom, both hands clamped over his eyes. The courtroom cockiness has disappeared. His suit is rumpled and a four-o'clock shadow stains his haggard cheeks. He spreads his fingers, blinks a couple of times and covers up again.

"We've brought you some food, if you're hungry." Norbert places the bowl of lentil stew at the prosecutor's feet.

Still shading his eyes, the prosecutor glances down at the bowl and squints up at us. "You expect me to eat that swill?"

His eyes growing accustomed to the light, he examines each of us in turn. When he takes in the .32 and me holding it, his nose twitches. I'm sure he can see right through my mask. But he isn't looking at me; instead something behind me has seized his attention.

"Cover up, dummy!" At the same time as me, Phyl notices the prosecutor's reaction. I glance over my shoulder and see Dorian's tea towel has slipped down to his neck. Dorian slowly lifts the towel back up over his nose, steadily returning the prosecutor's gaze.

"Who are you?" The prosecutor speaks in a hoarse whisper.

"We're the people's court, bringing you and your kind to justice." A line Phyl must have been waiting a long time to use.

"Would you like a glass of water or something?" asks Norbert.

The mumbled reply sounds something like a negative. Phyl begins to put the wall back into place.

"Wait!"

Phyl stops and peers around the wall at the prosecutor.

"I'd like to use your washroom, if I may."

A reasonable enough request, but it takes us off guard for some reason. Phyl looks at Bet, who deflects the unspoken question over to me.

I shrug and tilt the .32 upward.

"No funny business," Phyl says.

I giggle. I can't help myself.

Bet glances at me reproachfully. "Wait a minute." She taps Norbert on the shoulder. "Comrade, make sure the washroom is secure. No razors, nail files, that sort of thing."

Norbert heads for the washroom at the far end of the basement. Moments later he comes back and declares, "It's clean."

I giggle again; I'm so damn tired. "Here," I say, passing the pistol over to Phyl.

"Come on, come on." Phyl propels the prosecutor over to the washroom.

"Would you like to take a shower?" Norbert asks as the prosecutor reaches the door. "I can get you a change of clothes."

"No, thank you very much; I don't plan on staying long." The prosecutor pulls the washroom door shut behind him.

Phyl reopens the door. "No funny business," he repeats.

We all watch the prosecutor's back as he stands over the toilet. We wait a long time. Finally, a slight tinkle, a pause and then a full roaring flood splashes into the bowl. After what seems like at least a full minute, the sound tapers off into a few post-climactic spurts. He hitches up his fly, turns to face us and bows.

Phyl motions him toward the sunroom.

"Perhaps I'll take a shower after all." He speaks as he would to the staff of an exclusive hotel. Norbert hustles upstairs and comes back with a threadbare terrycloth bathrobe and a pair of white drawstring karate pants.

"Here." Norbert hands the robe and pants to the prisoner. "There's a towel, soap and shampoo next to the shower."

"May I please close the door?" The prosecutor directs the question to Phyl.

"Let him," says Bet.

Phyl chews on his bottom lip. "Okay, but—"

"No funny business, I understand. You've made the point abundantly clear." The prosecutor strips off his jacket. I catch a glimpse of a dress shirt heavily soaked around both armpits, and then the door closes, blocking my view.

Nine

2007

Sandra listened to what seemed like hours of insipid music, broken at regular intervals by a stern male voice telling her, *Do not hang up; your call will be answered faster if you stay on the line.* At the point of almost forgetting who she was on hold for, she heard a series of clicks followed by silence, and finally: "Weychuk here."

"It's Sandra Treming. You told me to call. I left the hostel. I'm moving into the halfway house today."

Faint rustling sounds. Weychuk seemed to be preoccupied with something other than the phone call. "Where are you now?"

"At a pay phone near the halfway house. It's closed until four."

Another extended pause. "Right. Good. You've made the correct decision."

"The vocational counsellor?" Sandra overruled an impulse to tell Weychuk to fuck himself.

"Working on it. Anything else?"

"No, I'll call again the day after tomorrow."

"No, call me first thing tomorrow from the halfway house. Free calling from there, remember. If I'm not in, leave a message. Daily calls from now on. Don't forget."

"Okay, fine. Tomorrow." Sandra slammed the handset down on its cradle. A young man bumped her shoulder in his haste to take over the phone and Sandra held back from slapping him on the side of his head. The pay phone was in a convenience store and the shuttered shelves behind the counter caught Sandra's attention. On impulse she ordered a pack of Rothmans. With one practised motion and no questions asked, the clerk opened a shutter and tossed a pack on the counter. Sandra paid and, once outside, lit up. She took two deep drags then dropped the cigarette on the sidewalk and crushed it with her foot. As she did so, the young man who had been in a rush for the phone came out of the store. Sandra thrust the cigarettes at his face. "You want these?"

He stopped and stared at the Rothmans pack, then at her, mystified.

Sandra flipped back the lid to show that it was almost full. "Be my guest. I don't like the taste."

He hesitated for a half second before tearing the package from her hand. "Thanks," he said, in a tone that suggested he was struggling to figure out the catch. Sandra watched him get into his car and drive off. *Better him than me* — poison to a deserving recipient.

It was now 11:00 a.m. Five hours until the halfway house opened. Still feeling like crap, Sandra wandered around the neighbourhood until she found a small park — a play structure, water fountain and two benches. From one of the benches a young Asian woman watched a blond toddler doing repeated slides through a yellow plastic tube. On the other bench someone had left a copy of the previous day's paper. Sandra planted herself on the vacant bench, wrapped the plastic bag handles tight around her left wrist and picked up the newspaper.

She read the paper cover to cover, including the classified ads, occasionally asking passersby for the time. After a while, traffic through the park subsided and she reckoned she might as well wait nearer to the halfway house. She drank deeply from the fountain and returned to the convenience store to buy a packaged burrito. Sitting on the halfway-house steps, she ate her late lunch slowly. Eventually a man arrived and unlocked the door. Sandra rose to her feet to follow him in. He blocked the entrance with his body as he withdrew the key from the lock. "We open at four." He pulled the door shut and locked it from the inside. Sandra peered through the glass down a dark corridor. The man turned into the first door on the right and disappeared from view. Sandra sat back down on the steps.

Soon a small crowd assembled around her. Almost everyone had the same style of luggage as Sandra — plastic bags of varying dimensions. Some had three or more. One exception was a twitchy fellow who arrived dragging a large rolling suitcase with a broken castor. The noise it made grinding over concrete set Sandra's teeth on edge. Among the last arrivals was what Sandra thought was a woman. Her face was painted like Raggedy-Ann: a large blotch of rouge on both cheeks, a rash in lieu of freckles across her face. Despite the warmth of the day the woman wore several coats, the inner ones hanging down to her ankles. A fur-lined hood from a winter parka was pulled down past her eye level. She piloted two heavily laden shopping carts, pushing one and pulling the other.

After cart lady arrived, Sandra became progressively more agitated; it had to be well past four thirty. "This is bullshit," she said, rising to her feet. She walked up to the door and someone shouted, "Don't knock!" She turned and faced a crowd of anxious faces. Rolling-suitcase man explained, "If you knock he'll make us wait longer." Sandra nodded and was about to sit down again when the door behind her opened. She stepped aside and let the others enter first. Unsure of the check-in procedure she didn't want to hold up the process.

Sandra followed the tide through the door and was about to speak to the man inside when he looked past her and yelled, "You can't bring that in here, Angela! You know better." Sandra turned to see the woman with the shopping carts labouring to hoist one of them up the steps. Without argument Angela reversed direction and let gravity pull the cart and her back down to the sidewalk.

The man at the door winked at Sandra and made a circular motion with his finger at his temple. "Geez, every day — she is so stupid."

"Oh, come on, let her in."

"She can come in. The carts have to stay outside."

Sandra looked around her. "You've got lots of room."

"There wouldn't be if everybody brought carts in." He let the door close. "No carts in the building. That's the rule."

Sandra rolled her eyes. "Who the hell are you?" the man demanded.

She introduced herself. The man's demeanour changed immediately, but not for the better. "So, you decided to show up at last. What happened? You get lost?"

Sandra didn't like the way he was baring his teeth, so she simply nodded.

"Had a place for you next door, but it's gone now. Can't hold a vacancy forever, princess."

"So, you got no room for me?" Sandra was almost hopeful.

"Always room, princess. But only in the women's dorm here in the shelter. You sort things out with your case officer and you're back on the waiting list for the hotel."

"The hotel?"

He smiled his ugly smile again. "Next door — the place where cons go after conditional release. The ones that show up on time that is."

"This isn't the halfway house?"

"No, that's next door." The man spoke as if to a three-year-old. "This is the homeless shelter. Our agency runs both."

"May I use your phone to call my case officer?"

"In the morning." He pointed at a clock on the wall and treated Sandra to an oily, thin-lipped smile. "It's gone five; Corrections is closed now. Allow me to show you to your room, princess."

Sandra shifted her bag to the other hand and followed the man, thinking about ways she could correct that smile. Most of them would have required a knife. Her escort stopped at a door halfway down the corridor. "This is you. Bunk 14. Your locker left of the bed — same number."

Sandra entered the room. It was reminiscent of the hostel dormitory, except bigger, smellier and with at least five times as many bunks. Almost all the bunks were empty; the lone exception was occupied by someone already snoring heavily.

Sandra turned toward the man, who was still standing outside the door. "Where is everybody?"

He shrugged. "Probably in the common room chowing down. If you're quick you can get something to eat. Sweet dreams, princess."

He bowed mockingly and went back to his office; Sandra ventured farther down the corridor. The common room was at the very end. Standing room only — people eating sandwiches and fruit, and drinking from disposable cups. A table on the far side bore several platters, a soup tureen on a burner and a coffee urn. The tureen was empty and there wasn't much left on the platters except for crumbs. Sandra managed to salvage some muffin pieces and poured coffee dregs into a used cup.

The coffee had no impact on her exhaustion. Yesterday's booze-up had caught up with her. Sandra returned to the dorm and found her bunk. She placed her plastic bag in locker 14 and latched it shut. Before she could set the lock, the door flopped open on the hinge side; the screws were all stripped. Sandra marched down to the office and found the manager at his computer, clicking the mouse in an odd sort of rhythm. "Yes?" he said, glancing up over the computer.

"My locker's broken."

"I'll put in a work order." He flinched at something on the screen.

Sandra waited for more, but he ignored her. Finally she asked, "Is there another locker I could use?"

The manager leaned forward, sliding the mouse in circles around the mouse pad, and spoke to the screen: "Nope."

Sandra weighed her options. Either kick up a fuss or go quietly back to the dorm. She couldn't see a clear win either way and was dog-tired besides. She returned to her bunk, looped the handles of the plastic bag several times around her arm and crawled under the covers.

In spite of the strange environment, she conked out almost immediately and slept soundly. Too soundly. She came to with her head in a fog and had a hard time sorting out where she was. The dorm had been pretty much full the night before; now only two other late sleepers were passed out in their bunks. She felt a tingling in her right hand and unwound the bag handles. She noticed two things simultaneously: the bag felt light and some of her clothes were on the floor beside the bunk. The fog vanished and she felt sick to her stomach. She sat up and checked the bag. A hole had been cut in the bottom, probably with a razor. Nothing much had been taken; just all her money.

Over two hundred dollars remained — had remained — of Norbert's five hundred. She was seriously screwed. Fired up by adrenalin, Sandra marched up to the office. It was empty. She entered anyway, phoned Weychuk and was immediately placed on hold. Obnoxious music tested her endurance as she sat at the desk with the handset pressed to her ear, waiting. On the computer various geometric shapes tumbled down from the top of the screen to land in a kind of box. Every so often the shapes formed a horizontal line which immediately vanished.

Sandra was almost hypnotized by the cascade and vanishings on the screen when the receptionist at the day report centre suddenly broke into the Muzak. "Mr. Weychuck is busy with a client at the moment. Do you wish to leave a message?"

"Yes, it's Sandra Treming calling. Tell him I'll call again tomorrow." The shelter manager appeared at the office door. "And tell Weychuk I was robbed last night," Sandra said into a dead phone.

"What the hell are you doing in my office?" the manager exploded after a few seconds. Then what she said seemed to register. "You were robbed?"

"Yes, someone cut into my bag and took my money. All of it."

The manager switched back into huffy mode. "Don't ever go into my office again without permission." Then quieter again, "I'll call the police for you."

"No, no police."

The manager was visibly relieved. Sandra advanced toward him at the door. He retreated as she brushed by.

"Closing in five minutes," he said to her back. "Grab your stuff and get out of here." She stopped in her tracks and turned, thinking she was being kicked out of yet another joint. Her manner seemed to scare him a little. "Until four o'clock. Then you can come back in."

Sandra shrugged and went to retrieve her remaining possessions: an improvised bath kit in a Ziplock bag and a change of clothes. Before leaving she checked the food situation in the common room. Miraculously a couple of bananas were left in a bowl. She pocketed them. Arms wrapped around the remnants of her bag and its contents, she pushed through the exit door and onto the street.

Angela was there with her shopping-cart train. "Here, Angela," Sandra said, placing the bananas on one of her carts. She was hungry but now realized she had no appetite for anything provided by the shelter. Angela frowned and moved the bananas to the other cart. "Yellow food goes here," she said.

As Sandra walked away she heard muttering behind her. "Robbers, bunch of robbers."

Sandra stopped. "How did you know?"

Angela shuffled closer and fingered the bag where it had been cut. "Bad people in there. You have to watch your stuff. Always watch your stuff. The lady lets me take my stuff inside and keeps it safe for me. Not the man. He don't care. When he's in I stay outside. Much safer. Here." It took a few seconds to register. Angela had pulled out a large plastic bag from one of her carts and was holding it out to her. "Here," Angela repeated. "You give me bananas; I give you this."

Sandra hesitated before accepting the exchange. Who knew where the bag had been or what had been in it? But already she was tired of carrying what now felt like a newborn baby in her arms. "Thank you, Angela." Sandra dropped her bundle into the new bag.

"You want to go for coffee?" Angela muttered, looking down at the ground.

"Go for coffee?" Sandra was taken aback. "Sorry, I don't have any money and—"

"Come on, I show you." Angela tugged and pushed her carts into motion and guided them expertly along the sidewalk. Sandra grasped the rear cart to help with the steering, but with a flash of anger, Angela shouted, "No!" Sandra let go immediately and ambled along in the wake of the convoy. They progressed slowly for two blocks and then rounded a corner where a lineup had formed along a stretch of storefronts. At its near end, just inside one of the storefronts, a couple of elderly ladies doled out hot drinks from large urns, along with tired-looking donuts. Angela looked troubled. "Too many people," she said.

"You get coffee; I'll guard your stuff," Sandra offered.

"No!" Angela pulled both carts snug against her hips.

"Okay. You wait here; I'll get coffees for both of us." Sandra walked down to the end of the line and shuffled along with the herd.

Minutes later she was handed a cup of coffee with a donut balanced on top. "Could I have a second cup for a friend?" she asked.

The woman behind the urns looked at Sandra suspiciously. "She's with Angela," said the man behind Sandra in the line. Breaking into a smile, the woman poured half a cup of coffee and then topped it up with hot chocolate. "Angela likes mocha," she said, handing Sandra the second cup capped with an extra-large donut.

Sandra took the coffees and donuts back outside and gave Angela her combo. Angela took a sip and then dug into the lead cart to extract a battered thermos. Coffee poured into the thermos, disposable cup and donut entered into the other cart's inventory, the convoy started rolling again. Angela led the way to the park where, the previous day, Sandra had read the paper. As they approached the playground, two young women summoned their children, lifted them into strollers and rolled them away. Angela and Sandra sat on their vacated bench.

After coffee the rest of the morning was dedicated to dumpster diving. Angela did the diving while Sandra lifted the heavy lids. Angela found a few items to add to her treasury: an old radio (sans plug), a balding Barbie and a winter coat in surprisingly good condition. In spite of the heat of the day, Angela put the coat on over the layers she already wore. They had lunch together in the basement of a church where Angela was allowed to bring her carts inside. Lunch was milk and a sandwich, the bread almost as stale as the sermon they had to sit through first. They supplemented the meagre lunch with the remains of chicken souvlaki found in the trash behind a restaurant nearby. "Tasty food … tasty," Angela assured Sandra, coaxing her out of her initial reticence. After sampling some, Sandra had to concede Angela was right. They rested and digested for a while back in the park. Afterward they wandered some more, Angela constantly alert for discarded items she could file in her carts. They had dinner in another church basement; this time the meal hot, the sermon longer.

After dinner they went back to the shelter. Angela assured Sandra that the nice lady would be on shift that day, but for once she was wrong. Mister Tetris was at the door, and he gave Angela the hairy eyeball as they approached. Angela didn't even try to haul her carts up the steps but rolled on by. Sandra paused and the man gave her the once-over. He raised an eyebrow. "You coming in?"

Sandra looked toward Angela, who was already halfway down the block. "I'll be right back," she said. Then she hurried after Angela as the man shouted after her, "Door closes at eight!"

When she caught up, Sandra asked Angela where she was going. No response. Angela was completely focused on guiding her cart convoy along the sidewalk. She gave no indication she wanted company, but neither did she tell Sandra to go away. So Sandra tagged along, sensing that Angela must know of somewhere safer than the shelter to spend the night. After a few blocks Angela turned right and continued along a stretch where there was no sidewalk. She aligned the two carts ahead of her, leaned into the rear one and with extreme effort pushed both along the shoulder of the road. Every few steps the lead cart would veer off to one side or the other and Angela would stop and realign the carts again. Sandra now knew not to help her. She contented herself with frequent shoulder checks, shouting "Car!" whenever one approached. Angela's pace slowed at these warnings but otherwise Sandra wasn't sure if her presence was noticed.

A divided highway crossed over the road ahead. When they reached the nearest of the twin overpasses Angela stopped and pushed her carts, one at a time, entirely off the asphalt. Sandra was puzzled; she could see no sanctuary, only an impenetrable tangle of brambles to their right. Then Angela picked up the end of a rope protruding from the brambles. She yarded on the rope like a sailor weighing an anchor, struggling back along the roadway, and as she did so a passage magically opened through the thorns. She tied the rope end to a jagged piece of rebar sticking out of the ground and returned to her carts. There she paused, breathing heavily as she looked directly at Sandra for the first time since they passed by the shelter. Then one word: "Don't." Sandra obediently stood back and watched Angela wrestle the first cart through the opening in the thicket. When Angela returned to retrieve the second cart, Sandra followed her into an open wasteland of mud, concrete rubble and accumulated litter from passing vehicles. Nothing grew here in the permanent shade of the overpasses. Dominating the bleak terrain was an enormous cable spool, much larger than the one used for a table in Berkman House, its lower rim half buried in the ground. Sandra looked up at a power line overhead, running along the highway median. Evidently, after the wire was strung, the empty spool was abandoned here.

The upper end of Angela's rope was cinched around the neck of the spool. While Sandra checked out their new surroundings, Angela struggled to untie the knot. In a belated act of rendering assistance, Sandra hauled back on the rope to give her companion some slack to work with. For once Sandra's help was not refused. The knot loosened, Angela signalled Sandra to let go of the rope, and the opening in the brambles closed like a jailhouse door.

The cell they were in was now guarded on three sides by natural barbed wire. The fourth side was formed by the bridge footings of the two overpasses, in between which, an almost sheer wall of concrete lock-blocks barred access to the highway median. Their refuge was secure, and as difficult to get in as to get out, unless one knew Angela's trick.

Up at the base of one of the overpasses was a section of relatively dry and level ground. Here, laid out flat on the ground, was what appeared to be a cardboard box for a large appliance. Angela handed Sandra a tattered blanket and motioned that she was to bed down on one side of the cardboard. Sandra reluctantly accepted the blanket. Angela unfolded a second blanket before she took off one of her several coats and rolled it up into a pillow. She lay down for a few seconds, then popped up suddenly and rummaged through her carts to find a length of string. She looped the string through the carts and tied both ends to her wrist. Then she re-inserted herself under the blanket and in a matter of seconds started to snore. Sandra followed suit, at least as far as lying down. Sleep didn't come as easy for her. The sun had not yet set. Traffic roared overhead. A urine smell emanated from the earth, and the contours of the ground didn't correspond to those of Sandra's body. But mostly what kept her awake was an insistent question: *Where the fuck do I go from here?*

1982

"One million dollars in US funds."

The prosecutor safely back in confinement, washed and fed (although he ate only half his lentils, grumbling the whole while), we gather back in the kitchen to discuss the terms of his ransom.

"Why US funds, Phyl? I mean, isn't that unCanadian?"

"Canadian dollars just don't cut it, Norb, internationally speaking."

Bet nods. "Nationalism is a bourgeois concept. The working class knows no borders."

During this exchange we continue to rummage through a stack of old magazines. Blunt-end scissors and a bottle of white paste are on the spool. Dorian doesn't participate. He sits on his chair staring at the floor, his arms folded across his chest.

"Got it!" Norbert proudly lifts up his magazine with an advertisement for a lottery — $1,000,000 — printed in the right font size.

Phyl watches the page being transferred from Norbert to Bet. "But where's the U and the S?"

"Here." Bet snips out two letters and pastes the clippings onto a sheet of typing paper. "Now, *Free all political prisoners*. We're going to have to define our terms."

"Why not free *all* prisoners?" Phyl insists on inclusivity.

"Because no way do I want to spring rapists and child molesters, that's why."

"Or white-collar criminals." My personal pet peeve.

"What about murderers?" asks Norbert.

"Depends on who they killed." Phyl is unwilling to concede any ground. Norbert suddenly throws his magazine across the table.

All of us are amazed.

"Look guys, this is getting us nowhere. It's Louie who's important to us — right? So let's say something like *We demand the release of all political prisoners — Louie Del Grande and others to be named in a future communiqué.*"

"All prisoners are political prisoners," says Phyl. "Just remember that."

Norbert, Bet and I nod, disinclined to argue the point. Progress for God's sake. We rifle frantically through our magazines to find the necessary words.

"Next," says Bet. "Safe passage for the Berkman Brigade to … where? Sweden? Cuba?"

"Brazil." Dorian breaks his silence with a hopeful suggestion, which we ignore.

"San Judeo." Norbert advances a counterproposal.

San Judeo is a small Caribbean island in the news a lot lately. After years of military rule it has recently elected a socialist government. The US president expressed deep concern regarding the loss of freedom for the "Santa Judeans."

"Sounds good." I recall news footage of golden beaches and waving palm trees. San Judeo is the kind of socialist paradise I can picture myself living in.

The vote carries unanimously — with one abstention. Not that Dorian's vote would count anyway.

We set to work scissoring up our magazines and soon have what we need for our communiqué. Bet assembles the words and pastes them into place. She holds the finished product up for our inspection then stuffs it into an envelope and takes off her gloves. "We need to talk about discipline."

Phyl groans and then quickly recovers. "Comrade, your thinking is correct." With immediate self-criticism through gritted teeth, he sidesteps automatic censure.

"I know this isn't a popular topic. But we've been sloppy, comrades. We need guard shifts and emergency procedures and a protocol regarding interactions with the hostage."

"What do you propose?" asks Norbert. We all know that Bet never opens a discussion with a blank agenda.

"Seven prime directives for the duration of the present crisis." Bet counts out on her fingers: "One: Constant vigilance. Someone on guard at all times. Rotating watches of four hours each. Two: Security. Doors locked at all times. No one leaves the house without authorization from the collective, and no one leaves alone."

In principle I have no issue with the second directive, but I do have an operational concern. I wasn't given a house key upon moving in. Up to now no problem — the door has never been locked. I query this point and, of course, Bet is way ahead of me. "I have a master key for front and back doors. I'll cut copies for you, Phyl and Norbert."

Bet attempts unsuccessfully to make eye contact with Dorian but, in spite of the fact he has been pointedly left off the key distribution list, he keeps his focus locked on the floor between his knees. She continues with her directives: "Three: Constant monitoring of television newscasts. Four" — Bet looks toward Phyl — "No drugs or alcohol."

It's Phyl's turn not to react; perhaps he's stopped listening. Norbert, however, is quick to take offence. "Bet, why are you addressing the comrade who took the initiative to dispose of our marijuana supply? Thanks to his direct action, we have no drugs or alcohol in the house inventory."

With uncharacteristic grace, Bet keeps herself in check. "It is not my intention to single out one comrade with any of these directives. I apologize if I gave that impression. Yes, Phyl's action with respect to the intoxicants previously in our basement was an inspirational example for the entire collective. Five" — Bet gathers momentum again — "Everyone sleeps on the main floor with weapons close at hand. Six: No unnecessary communication with the hostage. Seven: Masks to be worn when in contact with the hostage."

"Why?" Norbert again. "We'll be in San Judeo before he can ID us. Besides, he's already seen Sandra — and Dorian too." A new Norbert is emerging from the delicate chrysalis of the former Norbert. A harder and more assertive entity. I'm a bit repelled by his metamorphosis, and at the same time strangely aroused. I file my reaction away for private review later.

We argue about masks for a while, before Bet leads us to some sort of resolution by declaring that the wearing of masks could be left to individual preference, rather than being a collective obligation. "I believe in being cautious," she says, "but six is a better number of prime directives. Easier to remember." I nod, along with rest of the collective, but feel that the easiest number of directives to remember would be zero.

Phyl is the first to jump to another issue. "We oughta board up the windows, in case those bastards use tear gas."

"No. Too obvious. It would be like giving them our address." Bet's gaze drifts over to the kitchen window, taking all eyes with it. I'm not alone in imagining the sudden shattering impact of tear-gas shells on the glass pane.

"This is why we sleep on the main floor; if we're attacked, the comrade on guard duty wakes up everyone to mount a defence." All eyes snap back from the window as Bet's voice rises several decibels. "Tomorrow we'll seal off the stairway to the second floor. We can't be caught napping."

Norbert springs to his feet. "Fine. That's settled. I'll take the first guard shift."

Bet looks startled and a tad upset. I suspect she has more items on her list of disciplinary notes, but she doesn't pursue the matter. Instead she rises from the table as well. "Take the Winchester, Norbert. I'll relieve you at" — She checks the kitchen wall clock, which is unreliable at best — "oh four ten. Then Phyl at oh eight ten and — Sandra … are you okay?"

"I'm fine, I got up a little too quickly." I sink back to my seat and lean on the table, breathing heavily. Over twenty-four hours without sleep has caught up to me.

That's the last I remember from day one of the hostage taking. I miss the late news and the first media speculation that a kidnapping took place. I even miss, in terms of conscious awareness, being taken upstairs to bed by my communards in much the same manner as, hours before, the prosecutor was carried into the sunroom.

Ten

2007

Sandra had noticed the bookstore when making the rounds with Angela, but didn't — couldn't — stop to take in the window display. But now, after three arduous nights under the viaduct, Angela had suddenly repossessed her blanket to let Sandra know her company was no longer welcome. Sandra spent a long cold night huddled against the bridge footing until it was light enough to be on her way. As soon as she pulled on the rope to open the gate Angela started yelling and unravelled Sandra's hasty knot. The brambles closed before Sandra was quite clear, leaving nasty scratches on her exposed arms. She tore through to the roadway and half walked, half jogged back into the heart of the city.

After partaking of the continental breakfast served by the church ladies and wandering aimlessly about for a couple of hours, Sandra suddenly remembered the bookstore. She made a beeline to it. Since her release from prison she'd noticed several bookstores, chain outlets mostly, displaying nothing to entice her beyond the current list of boring bestsellers. This one, a used bookstore, showed its personality through its window glass. Sandra tried to make out a theme linking the books on display. She failed; what she saw was a hodgepodge of whatever the owner had bought or taken in trade: a book on Catholic saints, another on fly tying, collections of plays by Sheridan and Beckett, and barely visible in the background, a slim pamphlet, *What Is to Be Done* by V. I. Lenin. Sandra took this as a sign that she should enter the store.

The first thing she noticed was that the sales desk was at the very back of the store, down one of three aisles, almost hidden between bookshelves that went from floor to near ceiling. The ex-con in her disapproved of the lack of control that this arrangement implied. She started to browse, mainly to justify her presence in the store. The stock was in complete disarray. Sections were demarcated by hand-lettered labels tacked to the wooden shelves. These labels were faded and dog-eared and some, as indicated by empty tack holes, were missing. Their absence didn't matter, since many of the books grouped together bore little or no relation to their hypothetical section heading. Authors and titles weren't in alphabetical order or any order at all that Sandra could determine. Cardboard boxes of books, waiting to be shelved, were plunked randomly along the aisles, an obstacle course for would-be browsers.

Just for something to do, Sandra began to organize the section marked Can Lit, arranging the books in alphabet order by author and culling the misshelved, including Charlotte Brontë, Ernest Hemmingway and Saul Bellow — although she hesitated with Bellow. As she mused over *Humboldt's Gift*, a sudden squeaking noise drew her attention. The store proprietor had rolled his chair over to look down the aisle she was in. He was an older man with outsized horn-rim glasses, white hair that tufted up into points above his ears and a slightly hooked nose — like a friendly sort of owl. She flashed the owl her most winsome fake smile and kept on rearranging books as he watched.

"Are you doing what I think you're doing?" the owl asked as Sandra turned to sorting a lower shelf.

"Nothing." Sandra raised her hands, palms outward, to prove her innocence.

"Nothing? I think you're spoiling one of the joys of coming to my bookshop. The thrill of discovery, of finding buried treasure amongst the dross, without benefit of a map."

Sandra paused. The owl's face was inscrutable. "All right, I'll stop."

"No, carry on with your obsessive-compulsive behaviour, by all means. The majority of my customers seem to prefer things your way." The owl squeaked his chair and himself out of sight.

Once Sandra had finished with the Can Lit section, with about a quarter of the books removed for reshelving elsewhere, she remembered she was overdue to check in with Weychuk. Too late now to use the church ladies' phone, as she had the previous couple of days. She walked down the aisle to the back of the store and took a deep breath. "May I use your phone, please?"

The owl peered up at her impassively and leaned back. "I don't lend my phone to strangers."

"Okay, fine." Sandra turned to go. Maybe she could bum a quarter.

"Wait. What's your name?"

"Sandra ... Sandra Treming."

The proprietor extended his right hand. Sandra stared at it for a moment before she reached out and shook it.

"Pleased to meet you, Sandra Treming. My name is George Moodie. By odd coincidence my store is Moodie Books. A name which you should not assume reflects the temperament of the stock."

Sandra had seen the sign outside, so George wasn't telling her anything she didn't already know. "Moodie, as in Susanna Moodie?"

"Oh God, another Can Lit major. Yes, as in Susanna Moodie. A distant relative, or so my mother claimed. This was Mother's bookshop originally and she gave it the name. She was Moodie her whole life and in different ways."

"But you're also a Moodie?" Sandra blurted this out without thinking.

"Moodie was her maiden name and it's also my surname. I'll leave it to your sordid imagination to figure out how in the world that's possible." George turned his telephone around and pushed it toward Sandra. "As we are no longer strangers, you're most welcome to use my phone."

Sandra lifted the handset and was surprised by its weight. The phone, a black Bakelite model, would have qualified as an antique even before she went to prison. She fumbled with the rotary dial a few times before she reached the parole office and endured the customary rigmarole. After several detours she gained access to Weychuk's voicemail. She left the same message she had left twice already. "Mr. Weychuk, this is Sandra Treming. I'll call again tomorrow."

George raised his bushy eyebrows, but all he said was, "Are you hungry? Would you like a sandwich?"

"No, I'm not hu—"

George extracted a twenty-dollar bill from the till. "There's a deli down the block. Make mine egg salad on whole wheat with a decaf coffee. You can order something to drink as well, whatever this will cover."

"You barely know me."

"True, we've just met." George reached out and brushed her hand with the twenty. "But I can see only two possible outcomes here. One, I never see you and my twenty dollars again, leaving my bookshelves in complete disarray, or two, you bring me back lunch. Either way I can't lose."

Sandra left the bookstore with the twenty.

#

Sandra was tempted to take the money and run, yet another burnt bridge behind her felt like one too many. The bookstore was a homey place, and she was in sore need of a dose of homey. She returned with two sandwiches and two coffees — one decaf — on a disposable tray. Three customers were now lined up at the sales desk. Sandra waited for George to finish with the customers and then placed his lunch on the counter.

"Splendid," George said. "You'll be pleased to hear that, no doubt due to your diligence, Can Lit sales are trending upward. The young lady who just left bought a copy of *The Edible Woman*." George ostentatiously unwrapped the sandwich and took a bite. "Delicious!" he announced. "I mean the sandwich, not the book."

Sandra went back to reorganizing shelves. She turned her attention to Canadian History, which proved even more of a slog than Can Lit. She fell into a trance-like state, alphabetizing authors and relocating stray volumes. Eventually the store emptied of customers, and she again heard the squeaking of chair castors. She looked up the aisle to see George peering at her over his glasses. "Have to kick you out now I'm afraid. The store is closing. Time to go home."

Sandra nodded and picked up her jacket and bag, which she had stowed in a newly created gap in the shelves. As she headed for the door, George shouted after her, "Are you okay for a place to stay? Food to eat?"

"No worries," Sandra said, opening the door.

"Good, good — well cheerio, then, my dear."

Sandra left the bookstore at first intending to give the shelter a try again. As she approached the front door she saw Angela dragging cart number two up the steps. A woman — presumably the "nice lady" — waited patiently at the top, holding the door ajar. Neither of them noticed Sandra, who barely broke stride as she went by. She decided there was better security and better company under the viaduct, if she had it to herself.

That night it rained heavily with a fairly strong wind; the overpass proved to be an inadequate roof in such weather. Sandra spent most of the night awake and, damp through to the skin and shivering, gave up trying to sleep at first light. Some sit-ups and push-ups warmed her up and also coated her with mud. Brushing off the mud as best she could, she headed off to her now regular coffee spot and joined the lineup. She jogged in place to keep warm until the church ladies opened up. Their dishwater coffee and donut hit the spot. She lingered in the heated room until 10:00 a.m., the posted opening time for Moodie's Bookstore.

Sandra reached the bookstore just as George, newspaper under his arm, sauntered up from the opposite direction. No greeting, but he unlocked the door and held it open, wrinkling his nose as she entered. She set to work again as George ensconced himself back in his cave. Done with Can Lit, Can History and Can Geo, Sandra started on Women's Studies — a relatively small section — and had it sorted in less than an hour. Sci-Fi next, she decided, one aisle over.

As Sandra rounded the corner she saw a young man in a duffle coat in front of New Titles. He was looking up the aisle away from her, one hand on a book. Turning his head in Sandra's direction, he flinched as he caught sight of her. Smiling furtively, he released the book and rubbed his nose. Sandra recognized the signs: In Berkman House days she'd lifted a good portion of weekly groceries at the local supermarket. She had even added to the house library by liberating stock from large chain bookstores — though never, as a matter of revolutionary principle, from small independent bookstores. Feigning someone lost in a browsing trance, Sandra backpedalled out of sight, counted to ten, then leaned forward and peeked around the corner. Just in time to see a Stephen King compendium disappear into the duffle coat.

Sandra intercepted the shoplifter at the front door. As she grabbed one lapel of his duffle coat she realized the man was a head taller than her. Too late to back down. "Hand it over, pal."

He tried to break free and Sandra's prison instincts took over. She hooked her leg behind his knee and the man tottered backward. With her free hand she pushed up, thumb and fingers around his throat, tight into his carotids. As she pressed his head against the doorjamb, Stephen King fell from under the duffle coat onto the floor. "Get your hands off me, you stinky bitch," he croaked.

Stinky? Sandra loosened her grip. The man tore free and scuttled out the door. Instead of giving chase she bent down to pick up the book. When she straightened up, George was standing in front of her.

"Sandra, Sandra, Sandra … you're not guarding the crown jewels. It's just a book." He took it from her hand and sneered at the glossy photo of the author on the back cover. "Not the kind of literature worth risking one's life for."

"I'm sorry, Mr. Moodie."

"My dear, don't be sorry. He called you stinky. Did that make you angry?"

"No, it just—"

"Because you really do reek."

"Well, I…" Sandra took a deep breath. "The thing is I-I've spent the last few nights outside. I'm supposed to stay at a…" Sandra looked down at the floor, worried that she had divulged more than was prudent. When she looked up again, George was still staring at her impassively so she continued on. "I'm staying in a shelter a few blocks from here." Sandra somehow found it easy to open up to this stranger. She told him about the shelter, about losing her money and spending time with Angela under the overpass, though nothing about her criminal record or her life before jail. George remained silent when Sandra ran out of words. "I should go," she said, after an awkward pause.

"No, Sandra, first you need a bath." He walked toward the back of the store, looking over his shoulder at the halfway point to make sure she was following. "Come on. You mind the counter for a bit. Just promise not to bloody anyone who nicks a book while I'm gone. I'll be back in a jiffy." George pushed through a bead curtain in the back wall. A moment later, a young woman entered the store; Sandra recognized her from the day before as the purchaser of *The Edible Woman*. She came straight up to the counter, sniffed a bit and asked, "Do you have *A Room of One's Own*? I don't remember who it's by."

"Virginia Woolf. Aisle C on your left, second section from the front, bottom shelf."

George returned through the beads, a folded towel under one arm. "Very good," he said, nodding in the direction of the woman's back as she followed Sandra's directions.

"I reshelved it this morning. I found it in Canadian Geography."

"Surely you weren't surprised to find a Woolf in Canadian Geography? Sorry, I should be more respectful of Bloomsbury. Here." George thrust the towel into Sandra's hands. "Through the curtain, down the hall, up the stairs to your right. My apartment's at the top. Bathroom immediately inside the entrance — the door is open. You'll find everything you need and I've laid out a change of clothes. Throw what you're wearing in the hamper; I'll do laundry later."

In Sandra's mind several alarm bells were going off, but the allure of a bath overruled caution. "I've got a change of clothes."

"Do you? Where?"

Sandra retrieved her bag from the shelf where she'd stashed it and returned to the counter. George hooked a finger in the top of the bag, peered in and shuddered. "Throw those in the hamper too."

Sandra draped the towel over her shoulder and parted the curtain. Immediately she found herself in a short corridor flanked by yet more bookshelves. Multiple copies of L. Ron Hubbard's *Dianetics* to her left, various Ayn Rands to her right. She held her breath and passed through the gauntlet.

The upstairs bathroom presented Sandra with a choice between a shower and a bath. After carefully locking the door behind her, she opted for the latter. She opened the taps and, before the bath was full, stepped in and sank into luxury. The clawfoot tub allowed her to stretch out full length, an experience she hadn't had since before she went to prison.

Once the water cooled down to the point of being uncomfortable Sandra got out, towelled off and contemplated the clothes laid out for her. They were old-ladyish and smelled strongly of mothballs. Weighing her options she concluded she didn't have a choice. Now she was clean it was obvious that her clothes — all of them — stank. And she couldn't very well go buck naked back into the store. She dressed in the clothes provided and threw her entire wardrobe into the hamper.

As Sandra threaded through the bead curtain, George turned and looked at her appraisingly. "That looks not so bad. I thought you were about the same size as Mother. Sounds terribly creepy, I know, but emergency measures were called for. We'll sort out a long-range wardrobe strategy later."

"George, are you a Scientologist?"

"Speaking of creepy — no, certainly not."

"Then why…" She gestured toward the curtain.

"Oh, of course, you saw my secret repository. No, I'm not a Scientologist, nor a Randist, a — what does she call it? — an Objectivist. Far from it. However, when people come into Moodie with a box of books to sell or trade, it almost always contains a copy of *Dianetics* or *Atlas Shrugged* or something of that ilk. At one time I refused to handle such toxic stuff, but letting it get away didn't sit right with me either. So now I'll always buy or give credit, twenty-five cents each, for those books. And then they go in quarantine, out of sight, where no one can be harmed."

"Why don't you throw them out or burn them or whatever?"

"Good God, I couldn't do that to a book, no matter how objectionable. I'm not a Nazi. Now, mind the store while I put a load of laundry on."

George had just disappeared when a man carrying a large cardboard box shouldered the front door open and wormed his way through. He came straight to the counter and dropped the box with a resounding thud. "Give me thirty bucks for these."

Sandra looked at him blankly. He was tall, bearded and wore an ancient black knee-length raincoat, a caricature of a bomb-throwing anarchist — without the bomb, or so Sandra hoped. The sensible thing to do, she felt, would be to tell him to come back later. But the box being heavy and the man determined to do business, she decided to wing it. She opened the box and found it crammed with recent best-sellers, save for a dozen copies of *Dianetics* stacked in one corner.

She lifted the Hubbards out of the box. "I'll take all these for two dollars. The rest we don't need."

"What do you mean? Those hardbacks are like new. Quality literature."

"We have copies already, hardcover and paperback. Don't need more." Sandra was fairly confident this was true.

"I'll give you a deal: twenty bucks for the rest of the box."

"Ten," she said. "To save you the trouble of carting the box out of here." She opened the cash drawer.

"This is bullshit! Where's George? George is my good friend. We do a lot of business together. He's going to be very upset when I tell him about this. You'll get fired."

"Five bucks — final offer. Plus two for the Hubbards." She put seven dollars on the counter.

"Tell George that's it. I'm never bringing my business to Moodie's again, not while you're here. He snatched the money from the counter and almost broke the exit door trying to force it open the wrong way.

As soon as the anarchist solved the mystery of the door and slammed it shut behind him, George returned through the curtain. "What was all that noise?"

"I bought these from a good friend of yours." Sandra tapped on the box. "He didn't like my pricing and says he's never coming back." She lifted a stack of Hubbards out of the box. "Sorry if I cost you a valued client."

George looked at the stack and sighed. "Tall mean-looking fellow with a beard?"

"Yeah."

"And he says he's never coming back?"

"Yep."

"Oh, if only that were true. That man scares me and I pay him what he wants just to get rid of him." George tapped on the top Hubbard. "He always brings a bunch of these wretched things. He knows my weakness. Do you think he meant it? About not coming back?"

"I dunno — maybe."

"Oh, I hope so. If you see him come into the store again, come and take over the counter while I duck out. Please. I'm such a coward." He laughed and Sandra joined in, which set him off even more. Heads popped out from various points in the store — customers wondering what the joke was.

George wiped his eyes and checked his watch. "You must be hungry. Want to do the sandwich run or mind the store while I go?"

"Given what I'm wearing, I prefer that you go. No offence."

George started to say something but turned the impulse into a shrug. "Chicken salad?"

"Sure," Sandra said, not wishing to seem too choosy.

After lunch Sandra went back to reorganizing the bookshelves and had almost half the store done by the end of the day. At quitting time she headed for the exit. George was waiting for her at the door, a patterned drawstring bag in his hand. "Your laundry," he said, handing her the bag. "Which shelter are you heading to tonight? The one under the bridge or the one inside that's even more exposed?"

"I'll figure something out. Thanks for the laundry, George. Don't worry, I'll be fine."

"You don't have to figure something out, Sandra; you're most welcome to stay here. There's room in my modest accommodation upstairs. No rain, mud or thievery, I'm afraid, but there's a bathroom, kitchen and comfortable bed. You should be able to handle—"

"George," she said, louder than she intended, "I'm not going to fu—have sex with you."

George stepped back to make way for the last customer leaving the store, giving a stiff little nod as the man ducked by. Enough of a hiatus for Sandra to wish she could erase what she'd just said.

George's face transitioned from a proprietary smile to something more ambiguous. He continued nodding, now focused on Sandra, and she waited for some sign that things were still okay. The wait extended until it became uncomfortable. *Another bridge burned*, she thought, turning to go. George forestalled her leaving. "That is a happy coincidence, Sandra; I don't want to fuck you either. That isn't … the way that I am … inclined."

"Oh. I'm … so sorry for what I said. I'm not used to—"

"Shut up, Sandra. All you need to say is, thank you, George, I would be delighted to accept your kind invitation."

Sandra took a deep breath. "Thank you, George. I'd be delighted to accept your kind invitation."

1982

"Never mind who this is — listen. I'm not going to repeat myself again," Norbert presses the pay phone receiver tight against his larynx and speaks in a Donald Duck voice. "This is the Alexander Berkman Brigade. We have the Crown prosecutor. He's safe and will be released unharmed when our demands are met. These demands are outlined in a communiqué, which you'll find taped under the bench at the northwest corner of the monkey house. That's right, at the zoo. No, I can't put him on the phone. What do you mean proof?"

I yank on Norbert's arm.

"Just check it out." Norbert's mouth chases after the handset until I twist it out of his hand and hang up.

A squirrel runs up to our feet. I open the bag of peanuts we bought to blend in with the zoo environment and empty it on the ground. More squirrels charge at us from all directions.

"Maybe I should phone another radio station. I don't think they believed me." Norbert takes the empty peanut bag out of my hand and drops it into a litter bin.

"Too risky. I'm sure they just wanted to keep you on the phone. Let's head back." We follow a shabby peacock up the path leading from the zoo to the bus loop.

It's too early in the morning. My mind is swathed in cobwebs and I can't quite sort out where yesterday ended and today began. Two episodes of semi-lucidity bridged by nonstop chaotic dreaming. Falling dreams again. The planet tilting and throwing me into space. I wake up before my alarm is set to go off and immediately volunteer to accompany Norbert on a sortie to plant the communiqué. We have to get the whole operation done, phone the media and return by 9:30 a.m. That's when Louie is due to be back in court again. The confusion over Dorian/Louie's identity will soon be cleared up. And once the communiqué is broadcast, it will only be a short time before matters come to a head.

Suddenly, Norbert wraps his arms around me and smothers me with wet kisses. I'm about to knee him in the crotch when, turning my head away, I see a police car drifting by.

"Sorry, comrade," Norbert says when the car is out of sight. "I didn't want the pigs to see our faces."

"Fast thinking, comrade." I wipe my lips on my sleeve. Norbert grins like a crazed fool.

A radio-news car, from the same station Norbert telephoned, passes us at the bus stop. A few minutes later it returns at a much faster speed.

After a ridiculously long wait, the bus arrives. Once aboard, I cling to a stanchion, silently urging the driver to speed up. The bus wheels seem to be caught in molasses. But we make it back to Berkman House well before our deadline.

Bet and Phyl have been busy during our absence. Eight plastic milk crates, holding our entire collection of LPs, block access to the upper-floor staircase. All our bedding has been brought down from upstairs and is neatly laid out on the living room carpet, with several changes of clothing folded and stacked on top. Our entire arsenal — the Winchester, the .22 and my .32 — is arranged against the wall below the picture window, on the street side of the house. "Anybody home?" Norbert yells.

"In the basement!" A shout from below us.

We trundle downstairs and find Phyl by the rear basement door. He's wearing a carpenter's apron, an electric drill in his hand.

"We're back," Norbert says, unnecessarily. "Where's Bet?"

"She's out getting keys cut." Phyl winds the power cord around the drill. "Check this out." A two-by-four spans the door widthwise, supported on each side by metal brackets screwed to the frame. Phyl assumes a proud stance by his handiwork as if he's trying to sell it to us. "Beauty, eh? Nobody's gonna bust in through this door."

While I'm impressed by Phyl's installation, I have to point out the obvious. "And if somebody wants to bust out?"

Phyl is crestfallen for a split second, but recovers. "Latches and padlocks, here and here," he says, pointing above and below the right-hand bracket. As if this was his intent all along. Maybe it was; hard to tell.

We hear someone coming in the front door and then Bet in a loud voice, "Hello, where's everybody?"

"In the basement!" The three of us shout in unison.

Bet descends the basement stairs part way. "Come and get your keys. The news is on soon."

We obey Bet's summons and follow her to the kitchen where Dorian, seated at the cable spool, is methodically playing solitaire. Bet opens a plastic bag and pulls out some hardware. "Double cylinder deadbolts," she announces. Lock and unlock with the same key, coming and going. Phyl, can you install these on the front and back doors?"

Phyl picks up a deadbolt and examines it critically. "Easy peasy" is his verdict.

Bet doles out four keys on coloured lanyards. She hands me a blue one and distributes a green lanyard to Norbert and a black one to Phyl. She retains one set, which she holds up. "Mine is red. Put your keys around your neck, like so, and keep them in your possession all times. They only work the front and back doors. Not downstairs. Always lock up behind you right away. Never leave your key in the lock. If you do, we'll know by the colour who has broken discipline. Any questions?"

As the rest of us shrug, Dorian pipes up. "What about me?"

"What about you?" Bet replies.

"Don't I get a key?"

"No, Dorian, you're not one of us." Bet speaks matter-of-factly, not bothering to soften the message. "We gave you sanctuary, but that's as far as it goes. It's in your interest to stay put, at least until this situation is resolved. In our interest too, of course — given what you know."

Bet cuts off any argument from Dorian by turning on the radio:

"...*authenticity cannot at this time be verified, pending thorough examination by forensic experts. Police have declined to confirm whether the Berkman Brigade is a known terrorist group or to comment on the possible release of Louis Del Grande. A spokesman acknowledged, however, that if the note is genuine it would be the first concrete lead in yesterday's mysterious disappearance of Crown prosecutor John Edwards...*"

"A known terrorist group, that's us." Phyl takes aim at the radio with his power drill.

"Shhhh!" Everybody at once, like an enormous steam engine.

"*...the Monkey House Manifesto reads again as follows...*"

The reading of our ransom note barely starts before it's abruptly cut off by a commercial break.

Bet switches off the radio. "Monkey House Manifesto — can you believe that?"

Dorian clears his throat, and I expect him to raise the key issue again. Instead, while flipping over cards three at a time, he speaks to the table. "What did you expect? You should have done what normal kidnappers do."

Bet, Norbert and I exchange glances, each hoping another would rise to the bait. Bet gets us off the hook; she sits down at the cable spool across from Dorian. "So, what do normal kidnappers do, Dorian?"

Dorian holds one card above the others, looking for a match.

"Red jack on black queen," Norbert prompts.

Dorian hisses and sweeps his hand across the table, messing up the card columns. He glares at Bet. "Normal kidnappers would send proof they hold the hostage. A cut-off ear or something." Dorian reassembles the deck, shuffles and deals again, as we watch.

"He's got a point," Phyl mutters.

"We're not the fucking Mafia, Phyl!"

"I don't mean cutting nothing off, Bet. But maybe, like, a photograph?" Phyl with a sensible notion for once.

I chime in. "We can use my Polaroid." This was an impulse buy at a second-hand store, for which I was mocked by my communards.

"That's it," says Norbert, "a photo of the hostage with a copy of today's paper."

We take a silent vote; thumbs up around the room. Dorian concentrates on his game of solitaire, oblivious to our decision-making process. Bet and Phyl are charged with venturing out to buy a newspaper. As they head out the door, I shout after them, "We need film too — Polaroid film. And we're out of milk."

Once the door closes behind the foraging party, I wander toward the front of the house. A queen-size bedsheet now covers the living room window. I slip behind the sheet to look outside. Wiggie is walking by, two bulging garbage bags over one shoulder, a broken hockey stick — his "pokey stick" — in his free hand. Otherwise, a whole lot of nothing visible, which for some reason unsettles me.

"What are you doing?" Norbert shrieks, and I jump, unaware he's followed me from the kitchen.

"I'm waving to the cops. What does it look like I'm doing? For chrissakes, Norbert, calm down. Looking out the window is no more suspicious than not looking out the window." Listening to myself makes me aware I also need to calm down.

Nothing to do but wait for the consequences of our action, an action for which I alone am responsible. Events now seem to be out of my hands. My communards have taken charge; my input is neither needed nor requested. The police will come when they come, they'll meet our demands or — as seems more likely — they won't meet our demands, and nothing I might do now would make a damn bit of difference either way.

A quiet voice breaks into my thoughts. "Do you think anyone checked on the hostage?"

Somehow my snarl has rolled right over Norbert without fazing him at all. "How should I know?" I let the sheet fall and turn away from the window before realizing that Norbert wanted me to do exactly that.

"Best do it then." Norbert darts back into the kitchen. I sit down on the couch and listen to clattering dishes, cupboards opening and closing, and other noises I can't identify. Only Norbert can make so much racket from such a minor undertaking. Soon he reappears, wearing his mask and carrying a tray. On it is a splotchy banana, granola bars and what looks suspiciously like a slab of tofu on a bed of brown rice. Also a pitcher of water, a tin cup and a set of plastic utensils wrapped in a paper napkin.

"Cover me, Sandra." Norbert points with his elbow in the direction of our arsenal. I pick up my pistol and follow him downstairs.

As soon as the sunroom is open we see that our communards have already tended to the prisoner. On the floor beside him are the remains of a vegetable stew, the zucchini left uneaten. An apple core has been deposited in an empty paper cup. I collect the scraps and Norbert puts the tray down next to a plastic bucket. This bucket, previously kept under the bathroom sink upstairs, has been placed in the sunroom to serve as an emergency toilet. While Norbert heads over to the bathroom with the bucket, I keep my pistol pointed at the prisoner, who brings his head forward, almost making contact with the barrel. He smiles and winks at me, and I want to pull the trigger. He makes no move toward the tray. "Don't like the food?" I ask.

The prosecutor makes a face and mimes puking over the tray.

Norbert returns with the rinsed-out bucket and we lock up the chamber again. A door opens upstairs and footsteps tromp through the house. Bet and Phyl returning, I hope.

They meet us at the top of the stairs. Phyl tosses a box of Polaroid film in my direction. I attempt to field the box but muff it, almost firing my pistol in the process. Phyl grabs the gun as he and Bet edge by and descend the stairs. I clamber through the barricade to retrieve the camera from up in my bedroom and load the film on my way back to the living room.

"You know what we need?" Norbert's greeting as I return.

"No, Norbert, I don't know what we need."

"Gas masks." Spoken as if a revelation from on high.

"You're absolutely right, we need gas masks. Perhaps we should send Phyl and Bet back to the corner store."

"Don't be ridiculous. Why would the corner store carry gas masks? But we could do what they did during the First World War."

"And what was that?" I'm foolish enough to be intrigued.

"Well, during the early gas attacks, when they didn't have masks yet, the soldiers peed into their handkerchiefs and breathed through them and the urine neutralized the gas."

"So when they shoot tear gas through the window I just have to pull down my pants, squat and pee on my hankie?"

"What are you talking about?" Bet enters the room, followed by the hostage hobbled by rope tied to his ankles, propelled along by Phyl, who is carrying a wooden chair and another length of rope.

"Norbert is suggesting possible alternatives to the gas masks we don't have." I avoid going into details.

"We can piss into our handkerchiefs." Phyl places the chair in the middle of the room.

"That's exactly what Norbert said." Some workings of the male mind I'll never understand.

"Don't be gross." Bet repositions the chair closer to the sheet-covered window. "Sit there," she orders the prosecutor. Propelled by Phyl's downward push on his shoulders the prosecutor sits. Phyl ties one end of the rope to a chair leg, then winds it around the prosecutor three times, knotting it again on the other side. About eight feet of rope is left over, so Phyl finishes his macramé work with an elaborate bow.

As we set up and run the photo shoot, the prosecutor is neither resistant nor cooperative. He seems totally internalized, one spasmodic knee jerking up and down the only sign of some agitation. On our sixth try we finally have the photo we want: the prosecutor holding the paper against his chest, front page in view; Phyl and Norbert masked on each flank, rifles angled up over our hostage's head.

Phyl collects the weapons and arranges them again beneath the window. Norbert shuttles bowls of lentil stew from the kitchen to all of us in the front room. The hostage declines his share and looks on in disgust as the rest of us eat.

When finished, Bet puts down her bowl and, as I did earlier, slips behind the sheet to look out the window. Suddenly, she pulls the sheet aside, exposing the hostage and the rest of us to view from the street. Norbert shrieks and I can't blame him. It's like being stripped naked in a public place. "Relax," says Bet, "there's no one out there." She lets the sheet drop back over the window. "When the pigs come we'll tie the hostage to the chair again, where it is now, and rip the sheet down. Then they'll know we've really got him and won't dare fire."

"It won't work." The effect is startling; we've almost forgotten that our hostage can talk.

"Shut up. What do you mean?"

The prosecutor tries to rub his nose on his shoulder. It's just out of reach. He sniffs and tilts his head back, looking at the ceiling.

"What do you mean?" Bet repeats.

"May I speak, or do you want me to shut up?"

"Speak," says Bet.

"The police won't hesitate to pump this room full of teargas even if I'm in the window. My personal comfort is the least of their concerns. I'm not as important as you seem to think I am."

"Bullshit. We'd still have time to execute you, and they'd know it." Phyl comes around from behind the chair to confront the hostage. "And we'll shoot you if need be. With no hesitation at all. We're disciplined revolutionists." Phyl backpedals and drops on the couch.

"Nothing personal," Norbert inserts an addendum.

"I have no doubts about your sincerity, just as I have no doubts about the police determination. Oh, I'm sure they won't do anything rash. They'll wait until the opportunity comes, then they'll do what they have to do. If I don't survive, well, that would be viewed as an acceptable risk and a regrettable outcome. They'll call it collateral damage. The police won't be blamed. You'll be blamed. And I repeat, I'm not that significant a person."

"Shut up." From under her poncho Bet materializes a baggie of loose tobacco and begins to roll a cigarette.

"As you wish. I was about to propose a way out of your dilemma, but…" The prosecutor leans back in his chair, tilting it onto its rear legs.

The refrigerator kicks on in the kitchen.

Bet finishes rolling her cigarette, lights it and takes a couple of slow drags. "Okay…" She taps the ash over her thigh and rubs it into the denim. "Enlighten us as to your proposition."

"You still have time. Get out now while you still can and leave me here. I'll cover for you as best I can until you're clear. You can even take my car. But first, I need to—"

Our laughter cuts him off.

"Take your car? That's fucking great." Phyl jumps up again from the couch. "How far would we get now they know about us? Assuming that your wheels were still here — which ain't the case."

"What do you mean it ain't — isn't the case?"

"We ditched it. They probably found it by now."

"They? You mean the police?"

"No, the fucking navy."

"My car isn't here?"

"Read my lips, asshole." Phyl bends over the prosecutor and pronounces each word separately and with exaggerated emphasis: "Your … car … ain't … here."

The prosecutor, his lower jaw hanging open, stares back at Phyl. His face has such a classic expression of shock it has to be feigned.

"Whaddya think? We were gonna leave your car parked in our driveway for the whole fucking world to see?"

"No, I suppose not." Looking totally lost and defeated, the prosecutor lets his chair fall back onto four legs with a *thump*. This sudden change in demeanour is mystifying. I mean, up to this point he's handled being kidnapped, knocked out, locked up and threatened with death by shooting, all with relative equanimity, but the fact that we've abandoned his car somehow shatters his entire psyche. I wonder if this is a class thing or just another perplexing male thing. Perhaps both.

Norbert also picks up on the prisoner's reaction. He places a hand on the prosecutor's shoulder. "Hey, are you okay, sir?"

The hostage shakes his shoulder free and says nothing.

"News time." Bet turns on the television.

"…police experts will examine every inch of the vehicle over the next few days to find evidence that will help identify the abductors of John Edwards."

After a few seconds' delay, the screen resolves into a clip of a car bouncing over a speed bump as it's towed into a police compound. The prosecutor moans; in unison we shush him. The gate of the compound swings shut and the voice-over continues. "Witnesses reported seeing a male park the vehicle before running from the scene."

Cut to a man in the street, microphones rammed up against his face: "It kinda stuck in my mind because he was wearing these white gloves."

Cut again: a charcoal drawing of a man looking like Charlie Manson on a bad hair day.

"Police have released this artist's sketch of the suspect. If you see this man, do not approach him, but contact the police immediately…"

"I don't really look like that do I?" asks Phyl. No one dares reply.

"Earlier today the family of John Edwards made a public appeal to the kidnappers to release their captive…"

An elderly lady with blue-rinse hair appears on the screen, speaking to an unseen interviewer. Her patrician features are marred by tears. "My son has never stood for public office. He has no political aspirations. Why would they take him? We're not rich people." An awkward jump cut to a different angle — the lady speaking directly to the camera: "I beg you, please, whoever you are, don't hurt John. Let my son go."

All eyes turn toward our hostage. He sits watching the screen, displaying no emotion.

The anchorman briefly reappears: "Meanwhile, police are treating the kidnapping as the work of common criminals, not the work of politically motivated terrorists."

Cut to a silver-haired man in a police captain's uniform speaking to a wreath of microphones. "We believe the demand to free so-called political prisoners is a ploy to throw our investigation off the scent."

An energetic reporter pushes his microphone right up to the captain's lips and poses the obvious question. "What about this Del Grande, the political prisoner named in the Monkey House Manifesto? Who is he?"

The query briefly derails the police spokesman. He huddles with a phalanx of other officers behind him and then turns back to microphone. He draws himself up into a posture of gravitas. "The individual named is not now, nor ever has been, in police custody. No security organization in this country, nor any other country, has any record of this terrorist group, the so-called Berkman Brigade. We deduce, therefore, that this kidnapping is nothing more than a criminal attempt to extort a large sum of money, and as such, our department is treating it as a routine police matter."

Anchorman again: "Floods in the southern part of—"

Bet switches off the television. It's our turn to groan as the police statement sinks in. A long silence ensues. Finally, Phyl gives voice to what is on everyone's mind. "What the fuck … why are the Pigs denying they've got Louie?"

"What I think is…" Bet starts and then stubs out her cigarette, leaving us all hanging. She opens the baggie of tobacco again but makes no move to roll another cigarette.

"What?" Norbert prompts.

I glance over at the hostage, who avoids my eye. Probably not a good idea to be having this discussion in front of him, but no one else seems concerned. They're all hanging on whatever Bet might say next.

"What, Bet?" Norbert repeats.

Bet tilts her chin upward. "We should have known Louie wouldn't talk, no matter what. He'd never betray his comrades."

"Yeah, but would he let himself be sentenced in someone else's name?" Phyl poses the sixty-four-dollar question, prompting another extended silence. I try to imagine what I would do in Louie's place. My comrades are likely speculating along the same lines.

"He might." Bet's conviction seems less sure. "He would have figured out the havoc at the courthouse was us taking direct action. The smoke bomb by itself would have clued him in. If he admits his true identity now, it would lead the Man straight to Berkman House. So he's staying mum."

"But we're ready for them," Norbert says, with more confidence than I, at least, feel.

"We know that, but does Louie know that?" Bet finally opens the baggie and proceeds to roll a second cigarette.

"Shit," Norbert says as Bet lights up. He fans the smoke away with an open hand. "Wouldn't they check his fingerprints or something? They'd make the connection somehow, wouldn't they?"

No reply is forthcoming. Everyone is staring off into some private space.

"Wouldn't they?" Norbert repeats.

Eleven

2007

Sandra surfaced from the deepest sleep she'd had possibly since prior to prison. Groggy and disoriented she gradually assembled a sense of where she was and how she'd gotten there. Daylight was streaming through the cracks around an opaque window blind. She untangled herself from the bed covers and, not wanting to waste the clean laundry in her new drawstring bag, dressed in what she wore the preceding day.

George's apartment was eerily silent. In the kitchen, the clock on the stove showed 10:34. On the table was a bowl of fruit, cereal, milk and a carafe of coffee on a trivet. A note was tucked under a coffee mug: *Help yourself to breakfast and come down to the store when you're ready. P.S. Have a shower and change into clean clothes first.*

Sandra emerged downstairs a few minutes after 11:00 a.m. George waved at her from the New Arrivals section and kept at what he was doing — shelving a box of books. Several customers were browsing at scattered locations around the store. The phone on the counter rang and Sandra stared at it, remembering something ... something important.

"Answer that, please," George shouted from across the store. Sandra looked at him blankly and then reacted — too late. A dial tone.

"Never mind," George said. "If it was important they'll call back." Sandra could tell from George's expression, he minded. He restored a smile onto his face. "Are you all right, Sandra?"

"I-I forgot something important yesterday. Can I use the phone?"

"Of course, my dear. Just leave a quarter on the counter. Kidding — go ahead, you don't need to ask."

She phoned Weychuck, composing a message in her head as she did so. Unexpectedly, the receptionist put her straight through.

"Sandra Treming," Weychuck said. "I was just about to phone the shelter. You didn't report in yesterday."

"Yes, sir, I'm sorry; I wasn't able to get to a phone in time."

"You're starting to slack off on me, aren't you?"

"No sir. I was out all day, looking for work. It was after office hours when I got back — too late to call."

"Did you try to phone anyway?" Sandra hesitated, recognizing that this was a loaded question. "Don't give me any of your bullshit, Sandra."

"No, sir, I didn't try."

"I know that. I think it's time you and I talked in person. Come down to my office at nine o'clock tomorrow."

"Nine in the morning?"

"Is that a problem?"

"No, it's just, I got a job—"

"You got a job?"

"In a bookstore ... part time."

"Don't have time to discuss that now. Tomorrow at nine a.m. Don't be late."

Sandra hung up just as George joined her at the counter. "What's wrong? You're crying — never mind, none of my business." He opened a drawer, pulled out a box of Kleenex and placed it on the counter.

Sandra drew out a tissue and blew her nose. "It's nothing. It's just ... nothing."

George opened the till and proffered two twenties. "You need to expand your wardrobe. There's an elegant fashion boutique in the next block run by some nice Christian ladies. Don't be deceived by its appearance. Their entire stock is haute couture — the best in town."

"George, please don't give me money."

"Don't be ridiculous. I'm not giving you money; it's a loan." George held the bills under Sandra's nose. He showed no sign of relenting. To break the impasse Sandra took the cash. As she left the store George shouted after her, "Don't try to pay me back!"

The "elegant fashion boutique" turned out to be a rather dowdy second-hand store. It reminded Sandra of the places she'd bought her clothes from before prison. Her second-hand shopping skills quickly came back and she found several items that went together well. At the till they tallied up to almost all of George's forty dollars. For second-hand clothes the total came as a shock. Sandra didn't argue. She needed an expanded wardrobe.

When Sandra returned, George closed the store — earlier than usual — and the pair went upstairs to eat. The meal was a revelation to Sandra. She'd been so tired the night before, George just pulled sandwich fixings out of the refrigerator and let her go to it. After which she went straight to bed. Now Sandra was well rested so she watched — George refusing her offer to help — as he assembled and cooked an elaborate stovetop meal. Vegan, George informed her. "I'm not a vegetarian, much less a vegan, but I limit my consumption of meat and dairy not just for health but for environmental reasons."

Sandra understood "environmental reasons" to be the contemporary equivalent of "political reasons" which, in the Berkman days, was how the collective rationalized every unpleasant thing they did or avoided doing. She braced herself to be polite, anticipating the meal to taste like the brown rice, turnip and soybean concoctions that marked hard times in the collective. But the meal was delicious; Sandra had to concede that vegetarian cuisine had come a long way since the 1980s. Either that or her taste buds were failing.

George opened a bottle of white wine as they sat down to eat. After the ritual niceties — Sandra complimenting the cookery, George being overly modest — they occupied their mouths with food instead of conversation. Eventually the pace of eating slowed. George put down his fork and picked up his wine glass. Sandra raised hers and clinked it against his. "To literacy," he said. "To literacy," she echoed.

After a sip to seal the toast, George placed his glass delicately on the table. His expression suddenly became grave. "Sandra, I'm a bit troubled by our relationship..." *Oh-oh,* Sandra thought. "...Our business relationship. Legally and ethically you should be paid a wage for what you're doing. But that's just not possible. The bookstore hardly makes money as it is. I simply can't afford to take on an employee, even at part time." George took another sip from his glass and stared at Sandra over the rim, as if inviting her to speak.

Sandra swallowed a mouthful of wine before responding. "I understand, George; it's fine, really."

"No, it's not fine, but that's the situation. What I can do is give you a place to live and I can feed you. In fact, I'd feel much better knowing you're getting something in return for the help you're giving me. But I can't give you a job, formally speaking."

"George, I don't want to be a burden." Sandra suspected George had overheard part of her conversation with Weychuk.

"Never say that, Sandra. You're far from being a burden. I mean it. I just wanted to clear the air."

"I definitely don't want to put your business at risk."

"Things aren't that precarious. Well, they might be if I depended on this store for my living. But I'm actually a man of independent means, don't you know. I inherited this building, sans mortgage, from Mother. Her estate also included stock investments, which had done quite well. It was quite a shock when I found out. I mean a lifelong anarchist, or so I thought, but all along she had this dirty little secret. I'm not complaining really. I get a modest dividend every month, which keeps the wolf from my door." He raised his glass again. "To closet capitalism."

"I'll drink to that," Sandra said, finishing her glass. "This wine is great, George. Thanks." She set her glass on the table. "By the way, I have an interview tomorrow first thing, so I won't be in the store 'til later. I hope that's okay."

Sandra was grateful that George didn't press her for details. Instead he smirked as he refilled her glass. "Outrageous! I am going to have to dock your nonexistent salary."

They simultaneously raised their glasses and drank.

"Oh, I have a 'by the way' as well." George checked his watch. "I have a good friend coming to visit. He could be here any time. I would've asked him to join us for dinner, but I wanted to have our little talk in private." George held up a hand to forestall an objection from Sandra. "We'll do dinner together next time, assuming you like him. I'm certain you will. His name is Alexander, but his friends call him Sasha."

Sandra immediately thought of the namesake of Berkman House. "A Russian intellectual who writes treatises on anarchy?" she asked, jesting, but also fishing for a clue as to what to expect.

"No, he's a lawyer, but nice enough a fellow for all that."

A lawyer. Sandra tried but failed to respond in a positive way. She could tell by George's quizzical expression that her face had betrayed the distaste she felt. The doorbell rang. *Saved by the bell*, she thought. George wiped his mouth on a napkin and went down the hallway to the rear of the apartment, an area Sandra hadn't explored yet. George reappeared escorting his guest as he might a debutante, one hand wrapped around his elbow, steering him in. Alexander was dark-eyed and dark-haired, distinguished in bearing and about a decade younger than George; his casual but stylish dress was in high contrast to George's rumpled attire.

"Sasha, this is Sandra Treming, whom I told you about. Sandra, this is—"

"Alexander," the newcomer said, pre-empting the second half of George's introduction. "Hello, Sandra Treming." Alexander extended his hand and shook Sandra's with deliberation, making direct eye contact. His intense gaze while saying her full name was unsettling. As if he recognized the handle, yet chose not to admit his awareness.

"Hello," Sandra said, a smile frozen on her lips. She freed her hand and picked up the wine bottle. "Wine?"

"Yes, that would be kind, thank you very much."

George dragged a third chair to the table and Alexander sat down. He lifted his glass as soon as it was filled, took an experimental sip and studied Sandra intently. His examination concluded, he spoke. "George, your guest is very beautiful. There is no danger of you going straight on me, is there?"

His attempt at humour hardened the ice instead of breaking it. Sandra felt herself blush and, catching sight of George, noticed that he had gone pink as well. She rose to her feet and began to collect the dinner dishes. "I'll wash up; you two can—"

"We will pitch in with the dishes." Alexander leapt to his feet and interposed himself between Sandra and the kitchen counter. He made space amid the clutter for her stack of dishes.

"But you weren't here for supper, and George cooked, so—"

Alexander raised a hand to block her protest. "Don't be difficult, Sandra. George and I are very sensitive about stereotypes. We are men who won't sit idly by as a woman does the shit work." Over at the CD player, George released some up-tempo Latin music and then shimmied over to join Alexander, who handed him a dishtowel. There wasn't room for three at the sink, so Sandra backed away.

"Well, I'm off to bed then," she said, after a minute or so of hovering at the perimeter.

George seemed for some reason surprised. "But Sandra, the night is still young." Alexander glanced over his shoulder, but said nothing.

"Up and out first thing tomorrow," Sandra reminded George.

"Ah yes, too bad. But what can one do?" George shrugged.

Alexander spun around and, catching Sandra off-guard, kissed her on both cheeks. *Some sort of cultural thing?* she wondered. Or was there a deeper, negative meaning? She did not, could not, credit that the kiss was a show of affection.

"Well, goodnight, then, both of you." Sandra retreated to her bedroom. She heard George toss a return "goodnight" in her direction while Alexander remained ominously silent.

1982

Still smarting from the Monkey House fiasco, we send the second communiqué directly to the police, with just a two-cent stamp on it so they'd have to pay postage due. We're careful not to contaminate the envelope or its contents with anything that might identify us, going so far as to cut out individual numbers and letters for the address. This process takes the better part of an hour, after which Bet and Norbert take the communiqué downtown and mail it from the busiest mailbox they find.

For the next few days Berkman House remains on high alert, its inhabitants live in unrelenting tension, waiting for the day of reckoning, anticipating the scream of sirens, the snarl of megaphones, the pound of boots on neighbouring roofs. We wait and we wait.

From our hideout we make brief sorties each day to buy newspapers and we pour over every nuance of their coverage. We watch television and listen around the clock to the radio, eager for a special bulletin. The media attention is almost constant, but everything we hear and see is a rehash of old news.

On the third day, all hell breaks loose. Our photo of the prosecutor makes page one of all the newspapers, in one instance printed underneath a forty-eight-point banner headline: *Terrorists Make New Threats.* Phyl plasters the evening edition over his chest for our viewing convenience and announces, "Better than World War III." The politicians join the media in magnifying the significance of the abduction. The prime minister and the minister of justice hold separate news conferences to affirm their steadfast refusal to negotiate with terrorists. Emergency measures are swiftly enacted; busloads of soldiers are deployed at strategic locations around the city. In odd contrast, the police appeal for calm "so as not to imperil the ongoing investigation."

In spite of the new communiqué, the police continue to insist that Louie is not in their custody. Outside of the Berkman Collective this denial is greeted by a widespread skepticism coupled with an assumption "they" are hiding something. College students form Free Louis Del Grande committees and protest demonstrations rock the downtown. Unfettered from the normal niceties of crowd control by emergency measures now in place, the police response is immediate and savage. Police brutality sparks further protest and the escalating violence fuels bureaucratic fears of organized insurrection.

Meanwhile our wait continues and our collective discipline begins to fray, tempers flaring at small irritations. What is Louie doing?

When will he set the record straight? Will he set the record straight? What the hell is going on? On day seven, a glimmer of hope. Report of a prisoner in a court hearing shouting, "I am Louie Del Grande!" But then a clip of the prisoner in handcuffs as he's loaded into the back of a police van. He isn't Louie. Close up of a reporter on the scene in front of the courthouse. He breathlessly tells of other prisoners in the dock making the same claim. His report transitions to a voiceover of a clip from a Hollywood movie: a chorus of Roman slaves shouting, "I am Spartacus! I am Spartacus! I am Spar—"

Bet silences the gladiators with the click of a switch and flops back down on the couch between Phyl and Norbert. I'm sitting on the floor, my back against one of the couch armrests. My eyes remain locked on the now blank screen and I ignore stares from above in my peripheral vision. No one on the couch ventures to speak. Finally, I grow tired of waiting. "What?" I snarl, my upper lip trembling.

Norbert raises his hand. "We could revise our demands … say we want them to release Dorian Twisp, a.k.a. Louie Del Grande."

"No!" Bet startles us all with her shout. Having grabbed our attention she continues in a softer tone. "Not an option. What kind of example would that set for the working class? A revolutionary act in the name of liberating a drug trafficker — that's totally incorrect." Then she surprises me even more. She buries her face in her hands for almost a full minute, and when she at last looks up I see tears in her eyes. "If Louie were here, he would know what to do."

If Louie were here? Powerhouse Bet, the house ideologue, whose rigid militancy intimidated me before, now a whimpering creature needing her man to tell her what to do. But it's neither the time nor the place to say what I think. So instead I crawl over to the centre of the couch, rise to my knees and take her hands in mine. "Patience, Bet. Time is on our side. We'll figure something out."

She doesn't challenge me on this empty remark. None of them do. Dorian, who up to this point has been sitting alone in the corner on a hard chair, gets up and turns the television back on, switching the channel to a football game. No one objects. Bet shakes off my hands and abandons the couch. As I rise from the floor Dorian almost knocks me off balance in his eagerness to occupy the vacant spot. I don't bite his head off because I'm preoccupied with Bet. "Bet, where are you going?"

"Taking care of the hostage. Somebody has to." As if he were a new pet and I a neglectful child.

"Alone?"

"I can handle him. He won't to try to escape."

Bet's already en route to the kitchen, and I follow. "I'll come and cover for you."

Bet wheels around to face me. "No, Sandra, give me some space!"

"But what if he—"

"No!" I let her proceed into the kitchen. She returns minutes later with a loaded tray. I'm ready with the .32 in my hand.

"Stay here. Don't come down unless I call for help." She sweeps past. I look to the boys on the couch for backup, but they're engrossed in the game. I pivot back, but Bet is gone. From the top of the basement stairs I catch a brief glimpse of her at the bottom. I don't tail her any further.

Close to an hour later Bet remounts the stairs and brushes by me without a word. I don't speak either. I return my gun to the arsenal while Bet washes up in the kitchen. As she passes once more she mumbles, "I'm going to bed." She squeezes around the eight milk crates and goes upstairs. I glance toward the couch to confirm that everyone has witnessed this clear violation, by Bet, of Bet's fifth directive: "Everyone sleeps on the main floor with weapons close at hand." No objections voiced. A useful precedent has been set for the rest of us.

Twelve

2007

Up at first light, Sandra left by the back door, the same door Alexander entered the night before. At the bottom of two flights of wooden stairs she reached a back alley. Unfamiliar terrain, but she found her bearings soon enough and managed to arrive at the reporting centre even before it opened.

Weychuk ushered her into the chair in front of his desk. The chair was new, hard-molded plastic and stylish to look at but very uncomfortable to sit in. As she slid down into a slouch, she noticed that the entire office had had a makeover: beige wall-to-wall carpeting; Indigenous art on the walls; a cream-coloured, three-tier, lateral filing cabinet blocking the lower part of the window. Weychuk angled a legal-size form into a writing position and probed for details about where she was working, how many hours a week, where she was staying, etc. Sandra steered as close as she could to the truth, only skirting around the fact that she was not, in fact, employed. Weychuk laboriously wrote down her replies, breathing through his mouth as he did so. He was ensconced in a new and larger chair: glossy black leatherette, padded arms, chrome trim. After transcribing Sandra's response to his last question he rolled the chair back from the desk and sat upright, hands gripping the armrests. The back of the chair reached up to his neckline, and Sandra imagined him strapped in with an electrode crowning his head. *Two thousand volts ought to do it*, she thought and smiled.

"Good, good," Weychuk said, misinterpreting her smile. He rolled toward his desk again and signed the bottom of the form. "Okay, Sandra. Unless something changes in your status I need you to call me just once a week. Fridays before ten a.m. Of course call me anytime if you need something. I'm here to help you."

"Thank you, Mr. Weychuk." Weychuk jerked a thumb toward the door and Sandra scuttled out of the reporting centre.

Moodie's was soundlessly abuzz with customers roaming the aisles when Sandra returned. No sign of George, but Alexander was occupying a comfy chair to one side of the counter. He looked up from a book as she came in. "Oh, good, you're back."

This almost-friendly greeting surprised Sandra until he added, "George asked me to mind the store while he made coffee; you can take over now."

"Allow me to relieve you from the demands of commerce, Alexander." Sandra assumed a proprietorial stance behind the counter. She dealt with two customers as Alexander continued to read. She had the sense that he was pointedly ignoring her. Then suddenly, speaking to the open pages of his book, Alexander said, "I see order at last has been imposed on chaos."

"What?"

Alexander shut the book and, with it as a pointer, gestured toward the open aisles. "One can actually find what one is looking for now. And no tripping hazards underfoot. Moodie's has become an almost proper bookshop." It wasn't clear whether Alexander approved of Sandra's initiative.

"Coffee time," said George ducking through the curtain, two steaming mugs in his hand. "Oh, you're back. There's a fresh pot upstairs. Shall I fetch you a cuppa?"

"I can get my own, George, thanks," Sandra said, forestalling his exit. She needed to sort out how to warn George about a possible call from Weychuk's office to confirm her employment status. She wasn't yet ready to reveal her criminal past, especially with Alexander present. The fact that George had been explicit to Sandra about her not being an employee made it doubly tricky. Going upstairs to make coffee gave her the opportunity to prepare a script.

When she returned, an already half-empty mug in hand, George was in the middle of telling Alexander the story of her tussle with the shoplifter. Sandra winced as he reached the "stinky bitch" part, and smiled wanly as the two men chortled.

Alexander abruptly became serious. "You know, George, your main problem is where this counter is located. It should be over there, by the front door. For sure a lot of your stock drains out of the store because you aren't in a position to notice. No doubt many sales lost as well. If you were stationed by the exit your customers would feel like guilty creatures if they left without buying a book."

Sandra resented Alexander for speaking, since she had been having the same thoughts herself. She had kept her mouth shut, feeling it wasn't her place to tell George what he should do. But now the idea had been floated — even if by Alexander — she had to chime in. "Alexander is right, George. And the change would be easy enough to do."

Alexander looked at her, one eyebrow slightly raised.

George stared at his mug. "I just don't have energy for a project like that."

"But I do," Sandra said. "I'm done reshelving books; I need a new project. We could close the store on Monday and do it then."

Alexander cleared his throat. "I shall take the day off and we will make it a work party." He looked at Sandra. "Tools will be necessary; I will bring them."

"Oh, Lord have mercy." George put his mug down and looked up toward the heavens. "I should never have introduced you two. Very well, have it your way. Monday it is. I'll be here to make sure you don't trash my store." George took a final sip from his mug. "Oh, how bitter."

Sandra preferred to think he was commenting on the coffee.

———————————————

1982

Six a.m. and I'm kneeling on the floor of the bathroom staring at last night's lentils in the toilet bowl. Two periods missed and it's becoming very difficult to remain in denial. What the fuck is to be done? Can I even share the news? Maybe with Norbert. No. He'll go all weird while trying to be supportive. Phyl, of course, is out of the question. So then … Bet? Under anything approaching normal circumstances I could confide in Bet and enlist her support to help arrange an abortion, which after all, is the sensible thing to do. And even in the current state of lockdown she would of course shepherd me through the process of getting a therapeutic abortion, and the thing would be done. But the thought of opening that can of worms gives me the shakes, even though I suspect she already knows about Louie and me that day at the gravel pit. Sisterhood has its limits, after all. My body will just have to keep on doing what it insists on doing without my mind's consent.

I hear stirring upstairs where all my housemates, released from Directive Five by Bet's example, have spent the night in separate rooms. After several days crammed in close quarters, Bet isn't the only one who needs space. I quickly flush the toilet and the lentils sluggishly rotate, but the bowl doesn't completely clear. As I stand and wait for the cistern to fill, I lock eyes with my haggard gaze in the mirror. I look as shitty as I feel. As soon as the sound of running water turns to the hiss signalling the tank is almost full, I flush again. I open the door and Norbert is standing right in front of me, his smile a few kilowatts too bright.

"You're up early!" he announces, loud enough so the entire house can hear.

"Headache," I mutter and scuttle into the kitchen to rinse my mouth out with reconstituted orange juice. I know that soon there'll be a crowd in the kitchen, so I quickly prepare breakfast for the hostage: peanut butter on toast, reheated coffee and, as an afterthought, a plastic cup of OJ. Why the hell not? He's been a good boy. I load a tray and head to the basement stairs, wordlessly passing Phyl and Dorian as they mosey toward the kitchen.

I concentrate on keeping things balanced on the tray, so I'm only a step or two from the sunroom before I notice its door leaning against the wall at right angles. The room itself is wide open. "Oh shit, shit, shit," I say, too stunned at first to do anything productive, like yell at the top of my lungs for the whole household to join me in panic. Then a loud metallic crash from behind almost makes me drop the tray. I turn to see our hostage in the corner, wearing Norbert's karate pants and nothing else, seated on the throne behind Willy's drum kit, with Willy's electric guitar on his lap. Mr. Prosecutor has struck the hi-hat cymbals with a drumstick, which he places back on the snare drum.

"Ah, room service, thank you." The prosecutor plays a slow chord progression on the guitar. I recognize "Stairway to Heaven" unplugged. He returns the guitar to its place against the wall, propped up next to Willy's bass behind the amp. Rising, he comes over to lift the tray from my yielding hands. I try to formulate a question, but the words won't assemble quickly enough. The prosecutor anticipates what I want to ask. "Bet left the wall ajar last night. She seemed a little upset."

"And this morning you decided to go for a stroll?"

"I had to use the toilet. No sense waiting on you disciplined revolutionaries." Tray in hand, the prosecutor pirouettes gracefully once around. "Quite the setup you've got here. Back door bolted shut. All the windows boarded up. Low-rent soundproofing — I assume that's what all those egg cartons stapled to the walls are for. A lot of prep work for my benefit was my first thought. But then I looked under that sheet over there and, voilà, musical instruments." Our hostage retreats into the sunroom on his own accord and sits on the folding chair that Norbert recently added to the furnishings. I take hold of the sunroom door, intending to close it. Before I can do so, the hostage points a plastic fork at the instruments. "You guys in a band?"

"Those belong to a previous resident." I'm not about to ID Willy, not that he could be tracked down in Amazonia.

"Huh. Do you or any of your buddies play?"

"Nope." Truth is that Louie would often noodle around on the bass, and now and then, Phyl likes to give the drums a good workout, but the hostage doesn't need to know.

"So sad. I guess we won't be jamming together." The prosecutor keeps a straight face.

I do the same, but almost crack as I envision the prosecutor on lead guitar fronting Louie and Phyl. I shake my head to erase the image.

Amiably chewing on his toast, our captive releases a sly smile. He seems very much at home. Actually the sunroom looks pretty cozy now. I take in the whole scene: thick foam sleeping pad and pillow, down comforter, upside-down apple crate serving as a night table, along with sundry books and magazines. All the grow light bulbs lined up neatly along the far wall, save for one left in its socket where its illumination is most suited for reading in bed. I'm almost tempted to float the idea of switching rooms with him. The idea of holing up in the basement away from the rest of the household suddenly seems very appealing. I brush my mind into some kind of rationality and take hold of the sunroom door. I don't have quite enough wingspan. It moves a couple of inches at best.

John Edwards raises his eyebrows. "If you leave it open I promise I'll stay put."

I hesitate as I consider the security risk. Without a house key he'd make a lot of noise if he tried to escape. We'd be able to stop him I'm sure. Still, my communards might get pissy about me leaving the sunroom door open. But then I remember that Bet was the careless one. So, screw it. If my housemates have a problem they can move this awkward bugger themselves. I nod and turn to go.

"Hold on … take the tray; I'm done." He downs the remaining juice in one gulp, places the cup back on the tray and hands it up to me.

I notice the coffee is only half finished. I pick up the mug and hold it out to him. "You can keep this. I'll get it later."

The hostage makes a face at the mug and doesn't take it. "It's perc, isn't it?"

"It's all we've got. This ain't the Hilton."

"You don't say. Sorry, I don't mean to be an ungrateful guest. I'm just a bit of a coffee snob."

Is he being seriously apologetic or is he mocking me again? I let nothing show as I retract the mug and rebalance the tray. The prosecutor slides off the chair and onto his mat. He upends the pillow and props himself against the wall. A copy of *Steppenwolf* (one of Phyl's books) is lying open, facedown on the apple crate. Edwards picks it up and begins to read. Conversation over, it seems.

I retreat from the sunroom but I'm called back before reaching the stairs. I return to stand over him again. "What?"

"What happened to my wallet?"

"It's in a safe place." Just as likely Bet has tossed the wallet already. In fact she probably should if she hasn't. But no sense agitating the hostage.

"I could spring for some decent coffee, along with groceries for the whole household. But I'd need my wallet."

He must really hate that coffee, I think. "There's no money in it."

"Of course not. But there's something just as good as money. A bank card. Do you know anything about bank machines?"

"Sure, I use them all the time. Whenever I want to buy a new yacht."

"Okay, fine; let me explain."

A few minutes later I'm back upstairs. The entire household is assembled in the kitchen. It looks dangerously like someone might call a house meeting to order. But fortunately no one seems in the mood for conversation. The men are sipping coffee and munching on toast or cold cereal. Bet is furiously writing in a notebook, neglecting the mug by her elbow. She generally drinks her coffee lukewarm.

Over at the sink I begin washing the load on the tray, throwing in a few stray dishes that have materialized on the counter. I announce to no one in particular, "Fed the prisoner. Left the door open. Doesn't like perc coffee." No reaction from either of the men, but Bet is off like a shot downstairs. This time I know better than to follow her.

Bet comes back to the kitchen twenty minutes later, and instead of sitting back down she stands behind her chair, hands resting on the backrest. Her stance indicates she is about to deliver a speech. I expect a blast for leaving the sunroom open and prepare myself to blast back for her not closing it last night. But Bet avoids confrontation. "I have come to an agreement with the hostage. He will have the run of the basement during the day and only be locked in the sunroom overnight."

No one else questions this proposed arrangement, so I do. "What if he tries to escape?"

"The way I see it, if everyone is responsible for guarding the hostage, then no one's responsible. So, from now on, responsibility for making sure he stays put will be mine alone." Bet takes a last sip from her mug, carries it over to the sink and pours out what remains. Her lips twitch into an odd smile. "I confess I have an agenda. I am going to re-educate John. He seems ready to learn. I think I can bring him to our way of thinking."

I'm at a loss for words and it seems Phyl and Norbert are too. Dorian snorts in the direction of his playing cards, but Bet doesn't hear. She's already on her way back downstairs.

Dishes done, I hang the towel on the refrigerator door handle. My stomach has at last settled to the point that I can think about food. In fact, I'm ravenous. In the fruit basket is a half banana; on the counter a lonely bread crust in a plastic bag. I scrape out dregs of peanut butter to smear on the crust, which, to avoid having to do more dishes, I wrap around the banana, hotdog style. Closing all the kitchen cupboards left open by my communards I make a second announcement: "We need groceries. No money in the jar."

"I'll soak some soybeans." Norbert almost sounds cheerful. "We won't starve."

"Oh yummy," I say as I leave the kitchen on my way up to my bedroom. It isn't as cozy as the sunroom, but if my communards were to lock my door and bring food to me once or twice a day I'd be more or less happy. Well, maybe not happy, but not absolutely fucking miserable and right now that is as close to happy as seems possible.

#

Two days later I'm staring at the keypad of a downtown bank machine. Phyl is in the van, parked about fifty feet away with the engine running. Norbert is on point, empowered to abort the mission at the first sign of trouble.

The previous night's dinner was reminiscent of one of Macrobiotic Sue's culinary efforts. A soybean stew, not well received by the collective. As we sat around the spool masticating the resistant legumes, I felt it an opportune time to float the prosecutor's proposition. With the collective's revolutionary ardour at low ebb, consensus was surprisingly easy to achieve. Of course some immediate suspicions had to be overcome and fears allayed, but the procedure as relayed from John seemed to be straightforward and low risk. No objection which might have been raised could have stood against the prospect of a perpetual soybean diet.

I scan a sheet of paper with the prosecutor's instructions written on it. My hand trembles. I fear that as soon as I touch the keypad bank security will burst through the front door and grab me. But it's well after three in the afternoon, the bank is closed and no one is visible through its glass door. I hear Norbert's voice behind me, an octave higher than usual. "Hurry up, Sandra."

I stab at a key, cancel, stab three more times, cancel again, before successfully entering the code. A turgid mechanical wheeze from the machine and a tiny screen lights up with amber letters on black: *Amount of withdrawal.* I key in *$200*, which according to the prosecutor, is the maximum allowable. How's it possible this machine would give up that kind of dough? Sure enough, the machine hems and haws, and for the longest time nothing happens. The shaking in my hand has now infected my entire body and I'm just about to cut and run when a stack of bills slides out of a slot. I grab the cash and race Norbert to the van. He jumps in ahead of me and slips between the seats into the back. I settle into the shotgun seat.

"Let's go shopping." Phyl guns the van away from the curb.

We return to Berkman House in giddy triumph, slightly dampened by the reception we receive from Dorian. He sits alone at the wire-spool table and sullenly watches the three of us foragers relay groceries into the kitchen and stow them in the cupboards. When we're nearly finished Dorian rises and inspects the remaining boxes and bags on the counter. "No booze?"

"No booze," Norbert confirms.

Dorian sighs, fishes out an apple from one of the bags and resumes his seat at the table. Clamping the apple in his mouth he deals out his next solitaire game.

I set out our major purchase, a French press to replace the carafe shattered by Phyl weeks ago. I put the kettle on to boil. "Oh shit!" I turn off the flame.

"What?" asks Norbert.

"We forgot to buy coffee."

"Never fear, Norbert is here." He reaches into his coat, extracts a large bag of coffee from the vicinity of his armpit and holds it aloft. "Ta da! Colombian — I liberated it. John, um, the hostage, said he wanted decent coffee. Is Colombian decent? I know it is for weed, but for coffee?"

"Norbert, did you seriously lift that coffee back in the store?"

"Sure did. Wasn't about to pay what they were asking. Five bucks a pound. Give me a break."

I'm about to unload on Norbert for taking such a ridiculous risk when Bet comes into the kitchen, pistol in hand. Wordlessly, she relieves Norbert of the coffee bag and hands me the gun. She turns the burner back on and takes over coffee making. I mull over which of my communards I most feel like shooting.

Coffee back on track, Bet breaks two eggs into a fry pan and mixes white and yellow together with a fork. She drops two slices of bread into the toaster. Once omelette and toast are done, but before the filter has fully drained, she pours two coffees from the carafe. "Feeding the prisoner," she announces as she sweeps out of the kitchen.

I grab a coffee for myself ahead of my communards, who are converging on the carafe. The sight and aroma of Bet's cookery has stirred my appetite. I don't want eggs though. What I crave is meat, red meat. But it all seems like too much hassle, especially with the crowd in the kitchen. So I rummage through the cupboards for a granola bar and grab an orange from the now full fruit bowl on my way out of the kitchen. Norbert follows me but abandons the chase as we pass the television room; even he can tell I'm not in the mood for company.

Up in my room I eat my rations, drink coffee then doze for a while, remaining vaguely aware of bursts of activity around the house. I stay holed up in my cave until late in the evening, when an urgent need to pee propels me to the bathroom. I follow up with a shower. On my way back to my room I hear the television droning on downstairs. I resist a mild temptation to descend, and thankfully no one comes up to bug me. I'll cope by myself somehow, today, tomorrow, for as long as it takes for matters to come to a head.

Thirteen

2007

On Monday, as George and Sandra were pondering what to have for breakfast, Alexander showed up wearing denim overalls, a toolbox in one hand and a brown paper bag in the other. "Fuel for our labour; only two each, mind." He placed the bag on the counter and Sandra peeked in. A half dozen assorted donuts were inside.

"I didn't take you for a donut person, Alexander."

"One of many things you don't know about me. How about putting some coffee on, George?"

After coffee and donuts, the work crew tromped downstairs, George whistling the theme of the seven dwarves from Snow White. Alexander immediately set to work detaching the counter from its mooring and disassembling it into manageable parts. Sandra slid each piece to the front of the store where Alexander reassembled the counter. Sandra helped with the reconstruction as best she could, handing Alexander tools, nails and screws or whatever he asked for and holding boards while he checked levels and fastened them in place.

George sat in his rolling chair, benignly looking on as the other two laboured. "I'm helping by not getting in the way," he said. Eventually becoming restless, he found a copy of *The Communist Manifesto* and read sections of it aloud to, as he declared, "inspire the working class."

When the reassembly was complete, the counter looked like it had always been at its new location. Alexander's carpentry skills, by Sandra's reckoning, were pretty good — at least on par with Phyl's, back in the Berkman days. Competency she didn't expect from a lawyer, not that she felt a need to compliment him.

By noon, short of some finishing touches, they were done. Alexander led a tour of inspection. He pointed at the exposed floor where the counter had been. "Some paint needed here, of course." He brushed his hand against the bead curtain. "A real door here — I will find you one and hang it later this week. And look, George, room now for more bookshelves. I'll knock some up after I hang the door."

George sighed deeply as Alexander itemized the work to be done. Yet Sandra could tell he was pleased, although he pretended to be upset by his new proximity to the front window. "I'm going to be an exotic fish in an aquarium. Passersby will no doubt tap on the glass to see how I react."

"Look on the bright side," said Alexander. "Those passersby will deter anyone from robbing you at gunpoint."

"Ah yes," said George, "armed robbery of a bookstore. I'm sure the perp would be found not guilty for reason of insanity."

They broke for lunch, after which Alexander left for his office while Sandra went to buy a quart of red paint. It wasn't a bad match for the existing colour of the floor, though much glossier. Sandra proposed buying more paint to cover the whole floor, but George put his foot down. "You do that and then what? Paint the walls and ceiling? New light fixtures? Piped in Muzak? Move to a mall?"

Still energized, SanDdra washed the front windows inside and out. While doing so she studied George's eccentric window display. The book covers had faded in the sun to a bluish tinge. She cleared the window and reshelved the books inside. Then she assembled the most interesting volumes she'd run across over the past few days and arranged a new display. For each book she made up a card with a short blurb and sale price — marking each up at least twenty percent, after erasing the ridiculously undervalued price pencilled on the flyleaf.

Once finished revamping the display, Sandra was content. It was by far her most productive day at the store. The only thing she didn't get around to was talking to George about him possibly receiving a call from Weychuk's office to confirm her employment status.

———————————————

1982

The morning after the shopping expedition I'm awakened early by a strange sound, a bass drone over a faint whistle. The noise is elusively familiar but, in my groggy state, I can't quite place it. Irritated and curious, I venture downstairs to find John — I can't rightly call him "our hostage" anymore — piloting our old cylinder vacuum around the furniture in the television room. No sign of anyone else.

Intent on his labour, John doesn't notice me at first. He has a tea towel tied around his head, covering his nose and mouth. Likely one of the same towels we wore when we opened the sunroom on the first morning of his captivity. John almost runs over my foot with the vacuum nozzle before he clues in to my presence. With his heel he hits the off button and pulls the tea towel down to neck level. We both wait for the mechanical wheeze to die, but when silence is restored, nothing is said for a while.

I'm the first to give up waiting. "Company coming?"

Unexpectedly, John laughs, and I'm startled by the transformation this creates. He is, in addition to his normal good looking, almost personable somehow, which immediately puts me on guard. "You never know," he says, giving the tea towel a small tug. "Dust allergies, actually. Not even a class enemy deserves cruel and unusual punishment, don't you agree?"

I shrug. "If the class enemy cleans house, the people have no objections. That machine's been broken for months. How did you get it going?"

"I rewired the connection to the fan motor. Not that complicated. I'm surprised that none of you working-class heroes could figure it out." John lifts the tea towel back into place then slides it clear of his mouth again. He holds out a paring knife, handle pointed in my direction. "Oh, by the way, I used this to strip the wires. Sorry about that, but I couldn't find the proper tool." Towel back in place, he kicks the start button on the vacuum. I leave him to his work and return the knife to the kitchen.

My nausea isn't bad this morning, but a piece of dry toast is all I'm going to risk. As I wait for it to pop up, Bet suddenly appears. I'm startled, first because her footsteps were drowned out by the drone of the vacuum cleaner, and second because of the broad smile on her face. Bet has the loveliest of smiles but she rarely displays it.

"Good morning, comrade," she almost sings.

"Good morning, Bet," I reply. Too early in the morning for this "comrade" business. "If I'd known that hostage taking was a good way to get a maid, I'd have done it years ago."

The smile expands into a laugh, which Bet quickly clamps down on. "I have a lot of respect for John. It's good to have a man around who cleans up without having to be asked."

Fourteen

2007

"Ah, breakfast, the most important meal of the day," said George. "Next to lunch and dinner," he added, after a theatrical pause. Sandra nodded to acknowledge the quip, then dug into her poached eggs and toast. George's sense of humour was hit and miss with her, but she cherished her inclusion in his home and workplace. George imposed no social expectations and his acceptance of her in all her moods was unfailing. For the first time in her adult life she could just be herself with another person, without having to be guarded in her feelings or edit what she intended to say before she spoke.

They'd fallen into a comfortable routine. After breakfast, they would linger over a second cup of coffee and then descend not much past ten to open the bookstore. At least one of the pair would cover the store until closing. During the day, George would often find an excuse to go back upstairs "for a few minutes." Sandra didn't mind. She understood that, for George, Moodie Books was not the novelty it still was for her. She was fully at ease in the most noninstitutional environment she could imagine. The store's subdued lighting and mild mildew odour was polar opposite to the glaring fluorescence and bleached sterility of prison. She spent time searching for lost treasure hidden in the bookshelves, first editions in good condition and out-of-print books on arcane subjects, especially ones with marbled endpapers, quaint typography or engraved illustrations. These she would set aside for future window display or put in the locked Rare Books cabinet next to the counter. Sometimes she would simply watch the world go by on the street outside, gratified when people stopped to look in the window, even more so if they came in for a closer look. The shop seemed to her busier now than in the first few days she was there. She welcomed the increase in activity, especially since, for the most part, the customers were silent, whispering if they had a need to talk at all. She soon learned that bookstore clientele don't expect nor desire much in the way of customer service. If they were after a particular book they might ask; otherwise it was as if they all had Do Not Disturb signs hung from their necks.

By unspoken agreement Sandra was responsible for locking up at the end of the day while George prepared their evening meal. Then they would dine together, on occasion joined by Alexander. He had a knack for showing up as dinner was about to be served, inveigling his inclusion with a bottle of wine. Sandra was okay with Alexander's visits, although his presence often relegated her to a third wheel. The two men chatted over dinner and after about world events, concerning which Sandra had little to say as she'd been on ice for so long. Fortunately, nothing came up about her past.

Sandra avoided mentioning the impending call from Weychuk, a prospect less and less real as time passed. She was lulled into a sense of security; there was, after all, no pressing reason for Weychuk to phone unless she failed to check in on a Friday morning. When she called the Reporting Centre after the first week, she was told to leave a message. Same thing the following two Fridays. She hoped this new-found stability was to be her life from now on. She could live with that.

George and Alexander began spending more time together. Once, on a Thursday, Alexander arrived early in the day and spent the entire weekend at the store, apart from brief forays to his office. The following weekend George stayed over at Alexander's condominium. From then on George's absences became longer and more frequent, leaving Sandra with the bookstore and apartment all to herself. The aloneness upstairs was blissful — a cozy bed and no end of reading material close at hand. George would still check in on how the store was running, but typically he wouldn't appear until midday or even later.

One Monday morning, about a month into Sandra's residency, Alexander showed up again with his toolbox. He set the toolbox down in the open space by the bead curtain, went back to his car and returned with lumber, dowelling and screws. "Bookshelves!" he announced. "I'm here to make good on my promise."

"So, where's our new door?" Alexander's too effusive self-importance demanded puncturing.

"Patience, Sandra, patience — all in good time. Shelves are today's project; the door will come when it comes. The beads have served for generations; they can last a little longer."

George came through the beads just at that moment, registered what was going on and immediately forestalled work by enfolding Alexander in a long embrace.

"This project needs a kick in the butt," Sandra said. "I'm putting a kettle on."

Fifteen minutes later she headed back downstairs with three mugs on a tray, each filled according to personal condiment preference. Halfway down, she heard a male voice speaking loudly and authoritatively, in heavy contrast to the subdued muttering that occasionally breached the prevailing silence of the bookstore. At the bottom of the stairs the words "known terrorist" and "Sandra Treming" stopped her from advancing past the bead curtain.

"It's a simple enough question, Mr. Moodie." A different voice, equally loud but somewhat more benign. "We're here to verify Ms. Treming's employment status. Please cooperate with us."

"Well, the circumstances are a bit unusual…" George was floundering and barely audible. Sandra felt sick.

"Let me repeat the question." The first voice again. "Did you, with or without knowledge of her criminal past, hire Sandra Treming as a part-time employee of this store?"

A long pause during which, increasingly nauseated, Sandra could barely keep the tray from falling. At last George cleared his throat and spoke. "Ms. Treming is not a part-time employee of my store."

Sandra bolted back upstairs to the apartment and dropped the tray and mugs into the sink, none too gently. She packed all her clothes in the drawstring bag that George had given her then opened the cash drawer in the kitchen and grabbed a stack of bills. At least two days' worth of store receipts was in her hand; but no, she was not a thief. She returned the money to the drawer. From the fruit bowl in the kitchen, she picked up an apple and orange and then put them back. She was angry, angry at the fucking police state, angry at Alexander, who was no doubt relishing this visitation by the law, angry at George in particular for being such a limp dick. She would take nothing that wasn't hers.

Desperate to leave before George or the cops came up to the apartment, she ran out the back door and down the two flights of stairs to the back lane. Her mind was focused on *get away* and not much on *where to*. But no way the shelter — never the shelter — and of course not a hostel, nor any accommodation requiring payment. She needed somewhere to be alone, a place to think. Following a path of subliminal intent, she drifted to the shelter of the overpass, chancing that she would find a vacancy.

Summer was now well advanced. The blackberry thicket had grown immensely with aggressive canes reaching out in all directions. Sandra found the lower end of the rope and, pulling with all her strength against the weight of new growth, managed to partially open the secret doorway. She plowed through, clutched at and torn by vicious shoots in passing. As she cleared the thorns, the old rope broke and the brambles closed behind her into one impenetrable mass.

Inside the barrier everything appeared as before, save for the absence of Angela. But the mud underfoot had dried into the hardness of cement, and the dirty sheets of cardboard were no longer damp. She clambered up the slope to lean against the concrete foundation of the overpass. A faint vibration passed into her flesh, a tactile counterpart to the traffic noise overhead, and as she relaxed, tears began to flow. She regretted not taking the banana and orange, nor bringing water. Too late now for second thoughts.

Sandra contemplated the blackberry barrier around her. No way through without ripping herself to shreds. Another door now slammed shut, along with all other avenues of escape. She closed her eyes and retraced her steps since exiting the prison gate. Her old communards were nothing but more entanglements she didn't need or want: Norbert gluing onto her again from the get-go; Bet trading one totalitarian ideology for another; Louie about to bite the dust. Then there were her new friends, happy to make use of her but not giving support in return. She was a fool to fall into yet another honey trap. George failed her when she most needed a break; a betrayal more to be expected from Alexander, his useless friend.

She was not just friendless. Her world was full of enemies. That bastard Weychuk, relentlessly on her case, acting through his many agents; the uncaring staff at the hostel and shelter; Fred, the toad-sucking cop who tried to pick her up at the bar; the cops who came into Moodie Books to deny one little bit of sanctuary. All part of one big conspiracy to screw up her life and put her back behind bars. Why fight it? She was less free now than when locked up in the joint.

In the diminishing light of late afternoon Sandra tried desperately to think of positives. All she could come up with was Emma, the one bright spot in her life. But that was bullshit too. Emma wasn't in her life — never had been and never would be. Sandra hadn't given a thought to her when things seemed to be looking up. Now things had turned to shit, her daughter popped back into her brain. But she had to face facts; Emma wasn't a real person to connect with, just a yearning never to be satisfied.

No escape, no place to go and no point going on. So what was the alternative? Sandra visualized herself scaling the lock-block retaining wall to the highway median above. Once up there she would just have to wait for a truck, then time her leap perfectly. But that way out required more initiative than she felt able to muster.

It was hot, stifling hot, even in the shade of the overpass. Her thirst and hunger mounted but she wasn't going to leave her sanctuary even if she could. She was going to remain where she was and let nature take its course. How long could she last without food or water? A week?

As the gloom intensified inside and out, her rage subsided and was replaced by a dull lassitude. The traffic volume diminished into disconnected episodes of mounting and receding engine noise. Hunger and thirst gave rise to a massive headache, as if the blackberries around her had penetrated her skull and extended thorny tendrils through every part of her body. Fixed to the concrete wall like some tidal-pool limpet, Sandra occupied a nether region between sleep and consciousness.

1982

"Comrades, our last communiqué was ignored. We must re-examine our strategy."

Bet talking, obviously. Our first formal meeting since Louie's arrest. We've eaten our way through John's bounty with distressing speed and a transition to a diet of soybeans and lentils is again in the offing. I take minutes, having volunteered to do so over no one's objections, so I don't have to talk. Everyone is in the kitchen. To my left, Bet sits across the cable spool from Norbert; one of his legs is vibrating the table, making it hard for me to write. Dorian occupies the remaining quarter of the spool, playing solitaire as usual with now very dog-eared cards. Phyl is stretched out on the floor, his back supported by the refrigerator. John leans on one jamb of the doorway to thc living room. It seems that our hostage pretty much has the run of the house now, at least during the day; every night Bet escorts him down to the sunroom to sleep.

That morning, exiting the bathroom, I was surprised by Bet coming up from the basement, and a bit flustered, not wanting her to get wise to my condition. But she didn't seem to notice the heavy odour of puke in the air. "Just checking on the prisoner," she said. I was relieved not to be questioned, but in retrospect wondered what needed checking on downstairs so early in the morning.

The spool stops vibrating; Norbert's leg is temporarily stilled. "Should we send another communiqué, Bet?" he asks.

This gets a rise from the floor. "Damn straight we send another communiqué. We can't wait forever. We're gonna run out of food."

"Exactly, Phyl, we must take action." Bet adroitly takes up the reins. "But I think we need to consider alternatives. If they didn't respond last time why would they respond to a new communiqué?"

"Send them a body part, like I told you before." Busted, Dorian collects up the cards and shuffles. "Ya gotta show 'em you're serious."

Bet abruptly stands and goes to the cutlery drawer. She pulls out a carving knife and throws it on the table in front of Dorian. "Be my guest, Dorian. Chop away."

Dorian glances at the knife and brushes it into his discard pile. "Hey, don't try to make me part of this," he mutters as he transfers a column of cards.

The rest of us look toward John. He raises his eyebrows and smiles. Phyl hikes himself higher against the fridge. Norbert gingerly picks up the knife and returns it to the drawer. "What alternatives do you have in mind, Bet?" he asks.

"I think, and hear me out here, we need to cut our losses and move on. Remember, our primary objective was to secure Louie's release. Now, for whatever reason, Louie hasn't cooperated with this plan. We have to respect that. If we continue to draw attention to him, we will blow his cover. If we do nothing, sooner or later, we will be found and arrested, or worse." Bet pauses. I have the sense that, uncharacteristically, she's navigating through her argument without a map. "We have nothing to bargain with."

"What about the hostage?" I blurt this out forgetting my determination to keep my mouth zipped.

"We release John and go underground."

"No!" This is the unanimous response, but the fact that John joins the chorus stuns everyone else in the kitchen.

John straightens up and stands as if he was in court. "I appreciate this gesture, Bet, but your capitulation is premature. We — you — need to hold out a little longer and increase the pressure." John sounds absolutely sincere and I'm almost ready to concede that Bet's re-education efforts are taking root.

"How can we increase the pressure, John? We can't just take another hostage." The tone of Bet's voice deviates from her usual form in response to a challenge — a genuine question, not a flat dismissal.

"You say you don't want to blow Louie's cover. Why not? That's his ticket out of jail. Once his true identity is known then they have to take you seriously."

"But Louie wouldn't want—"

"Bet, I don't know Louie, but he's likely keeping his trap shut because he's not clued into your plan. How can you know what Louie would want or wouldn't want? Don't let emotions get in the way here. You have to assume leadership and force his hand."

Bet opens her mouth, but for once no words come out. She looks around the room. Up to this point it was as if John and Bet were talking to each other alone and the rest of us were spectators at a table-tennis match. Time now for all our two bits.

Phyl is in first. "Our housemaid has a point," he concedes.

"Betray Louie to the Man, no way!" The new, contrarian Norbert speaks, although not with much conviction.

Now all eyes are on me, and for several reasons this makes me very uncomfortable. I'm inclined to side with John, but it's just too weird. He's not our housemaid, he's our prisoner, the man I knocked out and dragged into the Berkman fold. That doesn't make him one of us. Or does it? I struggle to untangle mental coat hangers. "I think we can hold out a little longer," I venture at last.

Evidently I have cast the deciding vote. The release of tension in the room is almost audible. In fact there is a sound effect: Dorian's flatulent shuffle of his worn deck of cards. We have resolved to do … nothing.

#

That night a knock at my bedroom door. I expect another visit from Norbert, but Dorian's head appears in the opening.

"San, I need to talk to you; can I come in?"

A bit fearful, I just stare. Taking my silence as consent, Dorian pushes his way into the room and sits at the foot of my bed. His smile is unconvincing. "How's it going?"

I hold my place in the centre of the bed, but take care not to make physical contact. My smile is equally forced as I respond. "What do you want?"

"So, John and Bet … what's up with that?"

"What do you mean?"

"I mean, are they … you know…"

"Bet's not about to get emotionally involved with our hostage. She's too disciplined for that." Actually, Dorian's giving voice to my thoughts, but no way I'll share my misgivings with him.

"He's starting to call the shots around here. In the kitchen earlier — you saw. Don't tell me you didn't see. Isn't this guy supposed to be your prisoner?"

"He's not calling the shots. He's expressing his point of view and he's obviously a clear thinker. Bet respects that."

"I don't trust him. He's trying to pull a fast one."

"By talking Bet — talking all of us — out of letting him go free? You think he's manipulating the situation? I don't see how."

"He's up to something."

"Bet says he's coming around to see things our way. Maybe he's more progressive than we assumed."

Dorian's laugh startles me. He hasn't laughed much since he's been confined to the house. I haven't convinced him; I haven't even convinced myself. Dorian half rises as if he's about to leave. My sense of relief is premature. He settles back down again and leans toward me, staring intently. "Sandra, I want to tell you something, but you've got to promise not to tell anyone else. Especially Bet."

I mull this over before responding. I want him out of my room, but if I have any hope of sleeping tonight I need to know what's on his mind. "Okay, I promise."

"I've seen John before. He is — he was — a customer of mine. Not directly. A friend of a friend, like. But I saw him a couple of times and it's him for sure."

"And I can't tell anybody this because…"

"Bet will get pissed off. I told her I don't deal no more."

"Bet already knows you used to deal. We all know about the charges against you."

Silence. Dorian seems suddenly very interested in the pattern on my bedspread.

I nudge him to continue. "So, you were dealing up to pretty recently then?"

Dorian continues, but not in a direction I expect. "You remember how John reacted when Phyl told him we ditched his car? Like it was the end of the world? Well, maybe it was. Maybe there was stuff in his car he didn't want found. Maybe he sees you guys as a ticket out of a very tight jam."

"That's … pretty far-fetched."

"Is it? Remember how he was when you first brought him into the house? Banging on the walls — and then super passive. Like a street junkie in detox, not some big-shot lawyer or whatever."

"Or like someone kidnapped at gunpoint, knocked unconscious and locked in a dark room. But, okay, Dorian, say you're right — not that I think you are — John is a cokehead. How does that change things? Especially since you don't want me to tell anyone else. What exactly do you want?"

Dorian picks at the bedspread for a few seconds before answering. "I don't know, Sandra. I just want you to be careful, you know. Look out for number one."

"I always do." Not true, but no sense getting into a debate.

Dorian shifts a little toward me on the bed. His gaze drifts from his hand, across the bedspread, up my body to my face before wandering back down again. He looks like he's composing his thoughts to say something, something I probably don't want to hear.

"Hey, Dorian, it's getting late and I need to sleep."

"All right, fine." To my relief Dorian rises slowly to his feet. Smiling, he bends over and pats my belly.

My uterus recoils at his touch. "Goodnight, Dorian."

Dorian garnishes his smile with a wink. "Goodnight, Sandra." And with that, he exits my room.

#

Next morning I am, as usual, the first person up. I'm still mulling over last night's conversation with Dorian. Is John really to be trusted? I briefly consider going downstairs to check on him, but decide against it. What I might find or not find is worrisome. And what is Dorian up to? I remember the pat on my belly. A crude sort of come on? Or is Dorian somehow hip to my condition?

Bet enters the kitchen as I'm putting the kettle on to boil. Wordlessly, she sets a paper cone over our new carafe and measures coffee into it. It looks like about one week's supply remaining in the canister. One week until household behavioural sink sets in again and I'm not looking forward to taking John's bank card on another bank run. As the kettle starts to whistle I hear someone else coming downstairs. John enters the kitchen and lifts the kettle off the burner. As he delicately pours boiling water over the grounds I mentally replay what I thought I just heard. Maybe I heard wrong. Maybe John was coming upstairs, not down. The three of us stare at the coffee pot as the water slowly seeps through the filter. With a half inch or so remaining over the grounds, I hoist the coffee pot to the sink and, dumping the filter into the basin, start pouring out cups of coffee.

By this time Norbert and Phyl have arrived in the kitchen. Everybody grabs a mug as I pour, leaving me barely half a cup. I think about making a second pot, but that would bring on doomsday all the sooner.

We sit in silence save for the occasional too-loud sip. It isn't very long before I have grounds in my teeth, at which point it sinks in that there's a person missing from the kitchen. At almost exactly the same moment, Norbert asks, "Where's Dorian?"

Everyone looks around, which quickly confirms our inventory is one body short.

"TV room?" Phyl is off to check as soon as he poses the question. He returns with a shrug, which triggers a broader search. We fan out through the house; no Dorian.

"Check all doors and windows," orders Bet. We do another sweep and find nothing out of the ordinary. All doors locked; no windows forced; no evidence of egress anywhere. "Keys!" demands Bet, with a series of finger snaps for emphasis. Phyl, Norbert and I yank on the cords around our necks and present our keys for inspection. Bet looks momentarily puzzled. She reaches down through the neck of her sweater and comes up empty handed. "Oh, shit. I took the garbage out last night and…"

We slowly reconvene around the cable spool on which Dorian's cards remain splayed out, half faceup and half facedown. Silence prevails as we individually sort through our worst imaginings. Is it time to evacuate, to go totally underground?

The back door swings open and Dorian enters, a faintly steaming Styrofoam cup in one hand and a large paper bag in the other. He locks the door behind him, leaving the key inserted, and plops the bag on the counter. Ignoring the crowd at the table he casually drinks his coffee.

It takes a surprisingly long time for Dorian to become aware of five pairs of eyes trained on him. "What?" he asks, petulantly. As if choreographed, Phyl and Norbert each grab an arm, and Dorian drops his cup as he's hustled downstairs. John picks up the cup, disposes of it and then wipes up the coffee with a damp rag.

It takes well over an hour for the pounding from downstairs to subside.

Fifteen

2007

"Sandra! Sandra Treming!"

Sandra's mind struggled to rise from a deep pit. She'd lost track of time beneath the overpass. At some point she'd inched down the slope and onto the cardboard sheet. Just that small, gravity-assisted effort was enough to set her body trembling uncontrollably. After that she'd lain on her back racked with pain and thirst, perversely welcoming the torment. Eventually the agony became just a background state of being; she drifted in and out of consciousness, unaware of her surroundings.

"Sandra, can you hear me?" Alexander's voice. "Say something if you can."

"Fuck off." Sandra wanted to yell but what came out was barely a whisper.

"How did you get in there?"

"Leave me alone."

"Sandra, please come out. George is worried sick about you."

"Tell George he's an asshole."

"I can't make out what you're saying … I'm coming to get you."

"Go 'way."

Vaguely she heard rustling in the blackberry thicket and then, "Ow, ow, damn — this stuff is wicked!"

She was safe. Alexander couldn't get through the blackberry barricade. Sure enough, she heard retreating footsteps, a car starting up and rolling away. She closed her eyes and fell into darkness again.

Sometime later a new noise roused her, a noise that Sandra couldn't place. A short high-pitched rasping sound, culminating in a *click*, repeated over and over. Each repetition penetrated into her brain and made her headache more intense. She covered her ears and squeezed her eyes shut. Finally the noise stopped and she opened her eyes. Alexander was standing over her with an enormous pair of pruning shears in gloved hands. He placed the pruning shears on the ground and pulled a water bottle from his hip. He knelt beside her on the cardboard and applied the bottle against her mouth. Sandra shook her head from one side to the other, but a few drops fell into her mouth. They were too sweet to resist. She grabbed the water bottle, took a deep gulp and erupted in coughing.

"Easy does it. Let me help you." Alexander placed one hand behind Sandra's neck and the other around her back and lifted her into a sitting position. He waited until her coughing subsided and returned the bottle to her lips, tilting in a series of tiny sips.

After taking in water, Sandra's brain started to function again. She turned and looked at Alexander. He smiled and she slapped him across the face as hard as she could, which wasn't very hard.

He didn't respond in a way Sandra might have predicted. He didn't wince or curse. He didn't get up and leave. He just wrapped his arms about her and pulled her close. She thought about breaking his hold — although she wasn't sure she could — to hit him again. But the closeness overruled all resistance; after a second or two of rigidity, she relaxed, letting her face mash against his shirtfront. "Alexander, I'm so sorry," she whispered.

"Oh, for chrissake, Sandra, call me Sasha."

She pulled away and he let her go.

"Sasha." It took considerable mental effort for Sandra to reprogram her brain, her attitude, her feelings and to pronounce the name: "Sasha, why did you come here? I don't want to fight anymore. Not you, not George, nobody. You should have just let me…" She lay back down on the cardboard.

"I told you. George is worried sick."

"George is a prick. He fucked me over royally."

"Why do you say that?"

"I'm going back to jail because of him telling the cops I don't work in his store."

"George did not say that."

"Liar! I heard him."

Sasha frowned. "George said you weren't a part-time employee. Did you not hear what he said next?"

"No. I went back upstairs to pack before the cops did it for me."

"Ah, I get it now. Well, when George told them that you weren't a part-time employee, the cops looked very happy. Then he burst their bubble and told them you're a full-time employee. Perfect timing; you should have stuck around. I had a hard time keeping a straight face. I thought the cops might lean on him a bit and possibly they were tempted. But in the end they just said, 'Thank you, Mr. Moodie' and buggered off."

"They believed him?"

"Who knows? It doesn't really matter. They have no way of disproving what he said. Enough talk. Drink some more water … just a little bit. Now let's get you home."

Sasha helped Sandra to her feet; she was still woozy. He supported her with one hand around her waist, the other on her bicep, and together they navigated down the new passage he had carved through the thorns.

The bookstore was closed when they arrived, but George was still in his perch by the door. He leapt up and came out from behind the counter as they entered. "You found her. Oh Sandra, I'm so sorry." He reached out with both hands, palms upward, and froze in that position. Tears flowed down his cheeks. Sandra pressed through his extended arms and wrapped hers around his ribs, burying her head in his chest.

"Enough, you two. Sandra needs to take water in, not let it out." Sasha gently pried them apart and together the three climbed upstairs, George in front and Sasha behind Sandra, one reassuring hand pressed against her upper back. When they got to the top, Sandra was exhausted. George poured her a glass of water and placed it before her along with a bowl of rice pilaf. She drank the water and took a couple of bites of the pilaf. That was enough. Hungry as she was — and she was starving — she needed sleep much more. Then one of them, Sandra wasn't sure whether Sasha or George, helped her stand and guided her to her bedroom. She fell onto the bed and was asleep almost before her escort covered her with a quilt.

1982

Dorian becomes more or less tractable once we take him his deck of cards and establish a routine of three meals daily, delivered on a tray. But we're careful to have armed backup whenever we open the sunroom. Dorian has proven himself untrustworthy.

After my adventurist action at the courthouse, our security concerns focused on our hostage. When Dorian sought sanctuary from the law in Berkman House, we took it for granted he would never leave on his own volition. His recent escapade has shattered that assumption. It's now sunk in that, given the opportunity, Dorian might go to the police and cut a deal: amnesty in return for betraying us. Redoubled vigilance is called for, but our capacity for watchfulness is at the breaking point.

So we hold another house meeting — a tribunal, actually — our first meeting in weeks. Only one item on the agenda: what to do with Dorian. Bet in the chair, of course. She opens with what promises to be a long dissertation on Dorian's history in Berkman House. Stuff we already know. She's well into her narrative when John wanders into the kitchen and sits down with the rest of us at the spool table. Bet stops speaking in midsentence and frowns.

I wait for someone else to voice what I'm thinking, that John's presence at this meeting is inappropriate. But no objection is raised; it seems we're all deferring to Bet, who is suddenly intent on reviewing her meeting notes. John waits placidly in his chair. He's now looks quite scruffy, with his face framed by the sprouting of a beard and hair encroaching over his ears. I can see in him the classic

Che Guevara portrait emerging, and this thought bothers me in several contradictory ways.

Evidently interpreting our extended silence as tacit approval of his presence, John casually drops a remark to no one in particular. "You know, Dorian is a problem whether you keep him locked up or he gets away."

"You're out of order." Bet reasserts her control of the meeting but immediately undercuts herself by asking, "What do you mean, John?"

"Well, let him go, and he rats you out. Keep him here locked up, he's an extra mouth to feed, and supplies are dwindling."

The floodgates open. Everyone, it seems, has a grievance to air about the oppressive essence of Dorian: his whining, his sniping from sidelines in guise of advice, solitaire ad nauseum, hoarding funds to buy coffee for himself, breathing too loud. I don't join the chorus, but I recall Dorian's hand patting my belly and I shudder.

"Discipline, comrades, discipline." Bet's command dampens the hubbub. "Your criticisms are all valid, but the point…" Here Bet pauses, either for effect or simply to find the path forward. "The point is, what is to be done?"

Suddenly, all the air seems to leave the room, much like I want to. Instead, I remain seated and look around the table to see if anyone is about to speak. The only person who returns eye contact is John. He raises his eyebrows, smiles and, to my surprise, stands up as if to propose a toast. His movement catches the full attention of the rest of us. "I'll let you get on with your business. I'll be in the living room if you need me." With that, John exits, leaving behind another drawn-out silence.

The silence is broken by Phyl. "I say we execute him."

"Execute who? John?" Norbert whispers, looking anxiously in the direction of the living room.

"No, John's cool. Dorian's a fucking class traitor."

"Yeah, but killing him seems … a little harsh." Hard-line Norbert no longer.

"He'll screw us all if he gets the chance. This ain't a fucking tea party; it's the revolution. Let's not get sentimental." A bit of spittle launches from Phyl's mouth and lands on the table.

"Let's not be rash, either." Unexpectedly, Bet takes on Dorian's defence. "We need to analyze all options before us. Dorian will be no use to us dead."

"And what use is he alive?" Phyl leans back, folding his arms across his chest.

"Well, possibly nothing right now. But in a future standoff against the repressive forces of the state, he could be a bargaining chip."

"A bargaining chip, yeah right. Don't shoot; the coke dealer might get hurt. Where are you going, Sandra?"

I'm making a beeline for the bathroom, nauseated from morning sickness in part, but driven more by the tension around the table spool. I don't say "bathroom break," which would open me up to constructive criticism. Instead I say, "Checking on the prisoner."

"But what's your vote? Do we execute him?"

"Whatever." I'm beyond caring about Dorian, and I'm in no shape for debate. On the way to the bathroom I stick my head into the living room. John is reading. Seeing me, he tips the book back so I can see the cover: Regis Débray, *Revolution in the Revolution?*

"Assigned reading," he says. I can't tell if he's kidding or not.

I continue to the bathroom, but my nausea has subsided. Leaving the house meeting has done the trick. I take a couple of sips from the faucet, flush the toilet and brave the kitchen again. The tension has miraculously evaporated.

"It's unanimous!" Norbert's greeting as I retake my seat.

"What's unanimous?"

"We've sentenced Dorian to death." Norbert beams at me across the table. "Thanks for taking leadership, Sandra."

Leadership isn't something I like the sound of, so I'm compelled to draw the line very firmly. "I'm not going to kill him."

"No, nobody is, for now. His execution is suspended indefinitely."

I look around the table; everyone is smiling, which tells me that a typical Berkman House resolution has been achieved. A decision that each communard can endorse and one with no messy follow-up action required. Who am I to complain, even if I felt like it?

Indeed, the household mood improves over the next few days, although it's hard to pinpoint the link between cause and effect.

Perhaps it's the removal of Dorian's obsessive solitaire playing from our collective sight. Maybe it's the unprecedented cleanliness of the commune; John now vacuums every third day and has even washed all the common-area floors. Much is due no doubt to better grub; John has taken over menu planning, grocery requisitions and most of the cooking. Whatever the contributing factors, the outcome is that bickering between communards subsides to almost nothing.

One dark cloud on the horizon — the cupboards are almost empty. Norbert proposes another cash-machine run, but John advises against going back to the well. "Far too risky; you won't catch them napping a second time."

John's caution doesn't sit well with Phyl. "What's the harm in trying? We can be there and gone in seconds. After they close, same as last time."

"By now the police know that someone used my card. I expect they'll be watching the bank machine. Hey, it's not my place to tell you what you can and can't do. I'm just giving you fair warning. The account is almost certainly frozen now anyway."

Our ability to hold out over the long term is doubtful, but no one seems eager to see matters come to a head. Along with Dorian's execution, the release of yet another communiqué is on indefinite hold. We maintain a rotation of sentry duty, however, to ensure we aren't taken unawares. Anticipating an imminent showdown with the authorities, we regularly scan the streets front and back for signs of police mobilization. But apart from Wiggie on his daily rounds, and random vehicle traffic, nothing materializes. Soon our vigilance begins to sag and sentry duty devolves into taking a break from reading every fifteen minutes or so to look out the nearest window. The television is rarely on now; instead we monitor the news via radio, once in the morning and once in the evening. I'm as content as I've been in Berkman House, save for some anxiety that my communards might notice my condition. But none of them have yet — even eagle-eyed Bet. She seems very distracted these days.

I hardly ever sleep through the night now, having to get up two or three times to pee. I try to be discreet in my nocturnal sorties to the bathroom so as not to arouse household suspicions. A few days after

Dorian's incarceration, I'm woken up around 2:00 a.m. by not only a pressing bladder but also a growling stomach. I hit the bathroom and then make my way downstairs. I find Phyl snoring on the living room couch, which worries me for two reasons. First because he's supposed to be on sentry duty and second because the couch is where John sleeps, Dorian now confined to the sunroom. But I hesitate to raise a general alarm. At the present moment, eating has higher urgency.

I'm relieved as well as annoyed to find John in the kitchen, seated at the cable spool reading a newspaper and drinking from a tumbler of amber liquid. First things first. I pull what remains of a block of cheddar out of the fridge and break off a chunk. Not the red meat that I'm craving. Even if some remained I was not about to start cooking.

"Late dinner or early breakfast?"

I turn and let the fridge door close behind me. "I'm just hungry. What are you drinking?"

John pulls the newspaper aside and reveals a twenty-sixer of Crown Royal, almost a third empty.

"Where did that come from?"

"Dorian's groceries — rye whisky and this newspaper. There was also a chocolate bar but Phyl ate that. Seems that your former cadre had undeclared resources. Another good reason for him to be in the dungeon." John slides the bottle in my direction, carefully avoiding the bolts and the centre hole of the cable spool.

Mouth full of cheese, I shake my head.

"I don't blame you. I'd prefer single malt myself, but hostages can't be choosers."

"Well, obviously they can. You took that bottle for yourself without asking."

"You accuse me unjustly, Sandra. I did not appropriate this bottle for myself. Phyl decided to take — in his words — 'direct action' and he opened it. He claimed it as a justifiable reward for having to work the night shift. And then he invited me to share. How could I refuse a directive from one of my captors?"

"Okay, fine, but what stops you from making your escape? Phyl's passed out on the couch. And you're just sitting here boozing it up. Why didn't you just bust through a window?"

"An excellent question." John pours another couple of fingers of rye into his tumbler. His eyes are glassy, and it's evident that, while his usual self-control still seems intact, John is well on his way to being hammered. He gulps down half of what he's poured. "Yes, you're quite right, I should be gone. And I could have been gone, could have busted free many times already."

"So why didn't you?"

John stares at me balefully from under his eyebrows. "Fire." John takes another gulp. "I'm in the frying pan; out there's the fire. You happy band of revolutionists have cooked me good. Your guns, your double-locked doors, your little jail cell downstairs, none of that means shit. But you've totally screwed me and you don't even realize it. You don't even know *how* you did it." A second gulp empties his tumbler. "Of course you've screwed yourselves at the same time."

"What do you mean?"

"Wouldn't you like to know."

"You're full of shit, John."

John refills his glass. "Yup, just go on thinking that."

I chew on my cheese, opting not to rise to this bait. Silence turns out to be an effective way of getting more out of John.

"Dumping my car the way you did — I can't believe you guys."

"I can't believe you're still fixated on your stupid penismobile. Did you expect us to leave it parked outside?"

"Not the car, I don't give a rat's ass about the car."

This reminds me of what Dorian insinuated about stuff being in the car, stuff John wouldn't want anyone to find. I think back to my first encounter with the prosecutor. Just before I caught up with him in the courthouse parkade he unlocked the car door — the rear door. His briefcase. He tucked it in behind the driver's seat and I forgot all about it. Phyl didn't notice it either when he abandoned the car.

I look at John, who's lapsed back into brooding contemplation of his drink. "So, what's in your briefcase you didn't want to share with the world?"

This catches his attention. For a second his customary aplomb wobbles a bit. And then he forces a laugh. "You're good, you're very good. What would be your guess?"

"Money?"

"Bingo!" says John, a little too quickly. "Money, yes indeed, more money than I'd want to have to explain where it came from, not that anything really criminal was involved. Too bad you let it slip out of your hands. We could have struck a deal."

I sense that John is still playing me somehow. "Come on, John, you probably wouldn't have to explain anything. You could just say you were holding for a client. Or the money was planted by your abductors."

"Except for one little wee troublesome fact: The money was in a sealed envelope along with documents that should not have been in my possession. Documents having to do with an upcoming case where a favourable judgment is hoped for by certain parties. My briefcase in the hands of the authorities doesn't exactly advance my career. Fortunately I have offshore resources. I can still swing a deal with someone, once we get to San Judeo." John reaches for the bottle again.

"What about the cocaine?"

John doesn't pour himself another drink. Instead, after the briefest of pauses, he picks up the cap and twists it back onto the bottle, tighter than necessary. As he carefully sets the bottle back on the cable-spool top, I wait for a flat denial. Instead John says, "You really are the brains of this outfit, aren't you?"

Not what I was expecting, nor something I could concede. "Me, no. Bet's the smart one, not me."

"No way. Bet's well read, although we don't exactly share the same literary tastes. But well read doesn't mean intelligent. I'm not putting her down; I think she's rather sweet."

I stifle the urge to laugh. "*Sweet* isn't an adjective I'd use to describe Bet."

"Ah, but she is sweet. Sure, all hard edges on the surface, but underneath she's a real sweetie … once you get to know her."

"I've known Bet for over two years. How long have you known her? A couple of months, not even?"

"You're right. I'm just bullshitting you. Forget what I said. Forget everything I've said. I'm just a little drunk that's all. Can't hold my liquor."

John is now all slack-jawed and slurring his words. I don't trust this sudden transformation and I trust the silly little smirk on his face even less. I've learned everything I need or want to learn and I've long since finished the cheese. "I'm going back to bed," I say.

About twenty minutes later, I'm lying in my bed almost dropping off when I hear unsteady footsteps coming upstairs. They pass my door and then I hear the door of the room next to mine open and close. Bet's room. I wait for the resulting explosion but all stays calm, at least for a minute or so, after which I fall asleep.

When the forces of repression finally crash through our front door the following day, we're caught by surprise, yet fortuitously, we're ready for them.

Sixteen

2007

A knock on the bedroom door woke Sandra up. Before she could respond, Sasha elbowed his way into the room with a tray in his hands. He waited as she struggled into a sitting position. Then he placed the tray on her lap. "You look much better this morning."

"I don't feel better. What time is it?"

"Ten thirty. You've slept for over fourteen hours."

Sandra had a momentary panic attack. "What day is it?"

"It's Thursday. Is there a problem?"

Thursday — it didn't feel possible. The cops had arrived Monday morning and to Sandra it seemed more than three days had passed since then. "No, it's fine. I just have to call my parole officer first thing tomorrow."

"Right. You definitely can't let that go. Listen, Sandra, I'm a lawyer, as you know. I practise human rights law. I can help if you need it, though I don't have a lot of background in parole cases."

"I appreciate that, Sasha. My PO is looking to put me back in the can. Why else would he sic the cops on me? If that's his game I don't know what help you could be."

"Frankly, I don't know either. Likely you'll find out where you stand soon enough. Just do what he tells you and answer all his questions truthfully. But do not volunteer anything beyond what he asks. You'll be okay."

"I hope you're right." Sandra found Sasha's advice more unnerving than reassuring.

"So do I. Meanwhile, I'll make sure George dots the i's and crosses the t's with respect to your employment status here. They'll have a hard time faulting you for anything if you have documented employment and a fixed address."

Sandra studied the tray on her lap. One slice of toast, a small glass of orange juice and a tumbler of water. "Coffee?"

"Finish what I brought you and then we'll see. Take it slowly."

Sandra sighed and did what she was told. Taking it slowly wasn't easy; as soon as she started on the orange juice her appetite returned in force. As she ate her head started to clear. "How did you find me, Sasha?" OJ dribbled down Sandra's chin as she spoke.

Sasha sat on the one chair in the bedroom. "A little bit of deduction and quite a bit of luck. You told George you were sleeping rough the first couple of days you were at the store. You also talked about the shelter and Angela. I checked at the shelter first. You weren't there, but the woman in charge was helpful. She talked to Angela, but didn't get much out of her except something about a bridge. No bridges within walking distance; a few overpasses though. I checked them all. No Sandra to be found, at least on my initial go round. The first time I drove by your hidey-hole, I didn't even stop. It seemed unlikely — bare concrete on one side of the road and a mass of brambles on the other. How did you manage to get behind them?"

Sandra explained about Angela's rope doorway and how she'd messed up the system and locked herself in.

"Ingenious," said Sasha. "There's more to that Angela than one would expect. Anyway, after checking all the nearby overpasses I decided to go back and do a little walkabout, in case I'd missed something. Closer up it looked even more hopeless, but I called your name several times. Nada. I was about to head back to tell George my mission had failed when I heard 'fuck off' from the other side of the thorns. Music to my ears. I figured if you'd managed to get through to the other side then so could I. I gave it a go; not smart — I got these for my pains."

Sasha rolled up his sleeve and showed Sandra two nasty looking scratches. "A good shirt ruined too. So then I started to use my brain, drove to a hardware store and bought the biggest pair of loppers they had, along with the thickest gloves — opera length." Sasha pointed to his elbow and laughed. Sandra smiled.

"I hurried back to the scene, worried the whole time you might have vaulted over the brambles and made good your escape. Not really, but it was already getting dark and I needed to be able to see what I was doing. I slashed through the thorns with my trusty blade and found you — Sleeping Beauty — in your castle. Now, now … don't hit me again and stop rolling your eyes."

The Sleeping Beauty metaphor wasn't to Sandra's liking, but she laughed politely to reassure Sasha she had no violent intent.

"The rest you know. You might never have been found where you were. Not until it was too late anyway and—oh crap!"

"What?"

"I left the loppers behind. Oh well, it's not like I'm about to do any more gardening. Coffee now?"

"Yes please."

Sandra's toast, juice and water now consumed, Sasha picked up the tray and exited the room. Sandra got up to follow him, but as soon as she put weight on her feet, the room began to spin. She flopped back down, breathing deeply, arms behind her back propping her up.

"Take it easy, Sandra, there's no rush." Sasha entered with the promised coffee.

Sandra lifted her feet onto the bed and rotated back against the pillow. Once settled in she took possession of the mug. "Sasha, I very much appreciate what you did yesterday; in fact I'm grateful for everything you and George have done for me. But I don't understand why."

"Why what?"

"Well, I thought George was being a — well, I was angry when I heard him say I didn't work here. But now I know he told them I'm a full-time employee, and I realize … it was a risk, lying like that, especially after they told him about my criminal record."

"He wasn't lying. You're a full-time Moodie employee, assuming you want the job. George was going to tell you himself over dinner that day but … that plan went awry. As for your criminal history, George isn't stupid. He knew as soon as you introduced yourself —

back when you first met. He reads and he stays current. He was just too polite to let on."

"He knew all along? I wish he had let on; it could have saved us both a lot of grief."

"Yeah, well, don't underestimate George. Never underestimate George."

"Still, I don't understand why he hired me. George strikes me as someone who is a bit shy, reclusive even. How could he trust someone with my reputation?"

"Well, Sandra, that's something you'll have to ask George. Sasha repossessed Sandra's coffee mug. Do you want to rest now, or are you still hungry? A scrambled egg, perhaps?"

"Over easy. But I'll make it myself. I can't stay in bed forever."

Overruling Sasha's objection, Sandra made another effort to stand, this time very slowly and more successfully. Sasha piloted her into the kitchen. There he hovered by her side as she pulled a frying pan from the cupboard and a carton of eggs from the refrigerator. At that point she relinquished her autonomy and let Sasha take over cooking as she sank onto a kitchen chair.

After breakfast she felt much better. She successfully fended off Sasha and did the dishes. Then she insisted on going down to the store. Sasha didn't protest but he inserted himself one step ahead, looking over his shoulder as he led Sandra down the stairs.

George was standing on the store side of the bead curtain, next to Sasha's toolkit and the lumber for the shelving project. The work had not progressed at all since the police visit. George looked at his watch, theatrically. "You're late, Ms. Treming. Don't let it happen again."

1982

I'm on lookout while reading Emma Goldman's *Living My Life*. How did I miss this book before? At last, a political writer I can relate to, one who laughed freely, who loved to dance, who insisted on everyone's right to "beautiful, radiant things." I imagine sitting down to tea with her, giggling at the foibles of our comrades, enjoying the huge comfort of not having to edit anything I say. She wouldn't even criticize my relationships with men, since she herself was hardly correct in that department. In fact, she was downright goofy at times, which endears her to me.

I picked up Emma Goldman's autobiography randomly from the house library so as to divert my thoughts from last night's kitchen encounter with John. I'm still struggling with whether to report to my communards what I learned. But what exactly did I learn? And more important, what good would it do to share it with the collective? Maybe I'm mistaken about John and Bet. When I came downstairs early in the morning Phyl was still asleep on the couch. But then, taking a closer look, I realized the sleeper was not Phyl, but John. So who did I hear sneaking upstairs the night before? Perhaps Phyl going up to his room while John took over the couch? I decide to tackle John again — confront him actually — in private, once he's awake. But, as it turns out, by then the whole household is up and bustling about. And John outbustles the rest. He somehow contrives to be where I am not, and when we're in proximity, others are always present. Or am I just being paranoid?

What if I'm not mistaken about John and Bet? I'm pretty sure I heard what I heard from my bedroom last night, meaning John must have crept back downstairs before anyone else was awake. Even if I'm wrong about the nocturnal comings and goings, there's what John revealed in the kitchen. What am I supposed to make of his jibe about getting to know her "underneath," where she's a "real sweetie?" But if I blab about any of this to the collective, chances are, Bet will blow her top. And things in Berkman House have been going so well of late. Maybe discretion is the better part of whatever it's supposed to be the better part of.

Goldman soothes my mental turmoil. I become so engrossed in my reading I totally neglect sentry duty. Suddenly, heavy footsteps and strange male voices approach the house. I stand up to scan outside. Outside beats me to the punch. No knock, just the mighty crash of a size-13 boot overcoming the feeble resistance of the deadbolt. My stomach clenches like a fist. At the same time, I feel a weirdly detached annoyance, as if called to a dentist chair leaving half a magazine article unread.

I force myself toward the door to meet my fate. Three uniforms tramp by me, marching almost, before fanning out through the house. The fourth, wearing sergeant stripes, waves a blue sheet of paper under my eyes. "Search warrant," he snarls, pulling it back before I can focus on it. "We have cause to believe that you have illegal narcotics in this house."

After the initial shock I begin to pull myself together to assess the situation. Due to my inattentiveness, the police have the drop on us and our pants are down to our collective ankles. On the other hand, while these cops look nasty, as cops generally do, they also seem a little too relaxed, like they're executing some kind of drill. They're lightly armed, handguns only and those not even drawn. And drugs? They claim to be looking for drugs. It slowly sinks in that this invasion is simply routine harassment, not the massive showdown we've been anticipating. I take mental inventory: Bet is in the kitchen; Norbert is out shopping. John has my .32 and is down in the basement feeding the prisoner. Phyl is with John, on point with the Winchester. The .22 ... oh, shit. I look at the couch but all I see is the blanket I had wrapped around me as I was reading. Maybe if I ditch the gun somehow and give the boys downstairs a heads up, a total disaster can be averted.

Meantime, Sergeant Search Warrant has reached the top of the basement stairs. He hesitates, peering down into the gloom and frowning. I step forward and speak louder than necessary, in hopes that the boys in the basement will catch on. "Please be careful, *Officer.* Watch your head. Those stairs are *dangerous.*"

"Light?" He looks at me through narrowed eyes.

"On the wall to your left." And then, even louder. "You won't find any *drugs* down there, Officer. Just my *boyfriend,* doing *tai chi.* Don't frighten him, he's a *pacifist* — Sorry, I meant around the corner to your right. Behind the door." The cop emits a contemptuous sniff, finds the switch and places his foot gingerly on the top tread. I hope that John and Phyl have gotten the message and have time to ditch the guns and shut the sunroom. I amble back to the couch, sit down on the blanket and try to look relaxed with hard metal pressing into my butt.

As Sergeant Warrant disappears into the depths, screams come from the kitchen — Bet on her high horse, playing the aggrieved housewife. Her voice rises and falls, and I catch just snatches of what she's yelling: "… a free and democratic country … right do you have to invade our home … my taxes pay your salary…" Finally, a gruff voice answers, "Ma'am, shut up and wait in the next room." Then Bet appears, pushed back through the kitchen door by a burly cop. The cop points over Bet's shoulder in my direction. "Sit with your friend there. One more peep and I'll arrest you for obstruction."

Seconds later we hear Phyl coming upstairs speaking in the suckiest of voices: "It's a spiritual practice, *sir*. If everyone did tai chi or yoga or just meditated we wouldn't have a drug problem. We wouldn't need no police force. The world would be a mellower place…" Phyl appears, followed closely by Sergeant Warrant.

"Shut up and get your ass on that couch." The cop sounds more bored than aggravated and I feel my heart rate lowering and hope rising.

For the next half hour or so the cops go noisily about their business. We can hear crashing from the kitchen as cupboard contents are swept clear, and from upstairs the screech of furniture being dragged around and the thumps of objects hitting the floor. At one point, through the living room door, we see a cop suspiciously eyeing titles on the bookshelf. Are Karl Marx, Mao Tse-tung, Frantz Fanon and all of Bet's other mentors about to betray us? But no, he merely extracts one of the larger volumes and, holding it open facedown, fans through the pages before dropping it onto the floor. He follows this procedure with several other weighty tomes and then, to expedite matters, he hooks his arm around the books on each shelf, pulls them forward, and gravity does the rest. For the grand finale he tips the bookshelf away from the wall and lets it fall on the books. Browsing done, he looks over at the couch again as if wanting someone to object. I keep my face as blank as possible; I assume my communards are doing likewise.

When Library Cop wanders out of sight, I lift my butt up from the couch and push the .22 backward. Bet catches my intent and likewise lifts off her seat. Between the two of us we manage to shove the .22 down behind the couch cushions, around the wooden frame and in among the coil springs. For good measure I also relegate Emma Goldman to the lower depths. This incriminating evidence won't be easy to find, unless the cops decide to dismantle the couch. We're just settling back down on the now-comfortable blanket when Sergeant Warrant comes back into the living room. He stares at us balefully.

The crashing and banging begins to subside; Library Cop and Kitchen Cop saunter back into the living room, no longer marching. Sergeant Warrant lifts his eyebrows at each in turn as they enter.

"Nada," says Library Cop.

"Kitchen's clean," says the other.

Sergeant Warrant frowns and chews his lip. "A little too clean if you ask me," he mutters.

Feeling a bit cocky I venture a jibe. "Is cleanliness against the law, Officer?"

If looks could kill, the cop uses lethal force. "Button it. We received information that you folks deal narcotics. You got lucky this time. But we'll be back and we'll catch you, sooner or later."

Phyl pipes up. "Whoever told you that was lying. We don't sell drugs. We don't do drugs."

"Our informant has no reason to lie."

This gets us thinking. Phyl and I look quizzically at each other across the couch. Bet, in the middle, whispers, "Wiggie." I can't imagine Wiggie calling the cops but no other likely snitch comes to mind. My speculations are interrupted by Upstairs Cop wandering into view.

"Nothing doing up there," he declares.

"Let's call it then," says Sergeant Warrant.

"Wait a sec, Sarge," says the newcomer. "This couch — did anyone check it?"

Time to bluff. I stand up spritely. Taking my cue, Bet and Phyl also rise. Warrant steps forward, lifts up the blanket and contemplates the stained and threadbare cushions. He wrinkles his nose. "Naw, we're done here."

And that's it; we're free and clear. Or we would be if not for a loud crash from downstairs, followed by cries for help.

Everything immediately goes to shit. The cops rush for the basement stairs.

This is when I do a very stupid thing. I dive back onto the couch and reach down behind the cushions to grab the rifle. The damn thing gets hung up on the metal springs and I can't get it free before I'm pulled back violently and slammed down onto the carpet. My arms wrenched behind me, I'm cuffed. Turning my head sideways I see Phyl and Bet cowering at gunpoint. Then, down in the basement, the sound of a shot being fired. And then, after several seconds delay, a fusillade.

Seventeen

2007

Sandra spent the rest of the day in the store, although her productivity was at its lowest ebb ever. She just gaped at customers as they entered and left. George intercepted most of the action at the till before she could react. The few buyers she dealt with were visibly impatient by the time she finished ringing up the sale.

At the end of the work day Sasha was ready for them with takeout cartons open and steaming on the table and plates laid out with chopsticks wrapped in napkins. No fuss, no major clean-up to be done afterward, suiting Sandra just fine — the two men as well, she suspected. After dinner she ventured to act on Sasha's advice. "George, why did you hire me when you knew that I had a criminal record? I'm grateful, but ... it seems odd."

George glanced at Sasha, and then spoke very slowly and quietly. "Well ... partly, of course, because you proved to be a very capable worker and also ... because, well, a criminal record is something we have in common."

"You? What did you do?" *None of my damn business,* Sandra thought, even as the words left her mouth.

Sasha evidently concurred. "Sandra, please—"

George placed a restraining hand on his lover's arm. "It's fine, Sasha. I know all about Sandra's youthful indiscretions; it's only fair that she learns about mine. I could use a stiff drink though."

Sasha leapt up and rifled through the cupboards, eventually locating an almost-full bottle of gin. He poured out a round two-fingers high in three tumblers. George took down half of his in one gulp. He began to speak with his eyes closed, opening them once he was well launched. "When I was a young man, not yet having reached the age of majority but no longer a juvenile in the eyes of the law, I was busted in a public washroom and charged with gross indecency."

"It was entrapment," interjected Sasha. "This was back in the early sixties when being gay was a crime."

"Yes, entrapment, but also very stupid of me. I was sentenced to six months in jail and five strokes of a paddle, as it was called, thrown in for good measure. The paddle was a nasty bit of business: a heavy perforated strap about eighteen inches long and maybe three inches wide. The lashes were applied to my bare buttocks and upper thighs. Each blow drew blood."

George took another gulp of gin, emptying his glass. He reached over to the bottle and poured himself another healthy dose. "Time heals all wounds. Bullshit. I can never forget that pain. Laid me up for two months. A brief respite in hospital and then back to jail for a little more physical abuse — unsanctioned this time — along with constant humiliation. In a way I was lucky. I could have done much more jail time. Other men were sentenced to life for the same offence."

George took off his glasses and stared up at the ceiling for a while. He was fighting back tears. "I did my time; I was released. Fortunately, I had the bookstore to retreat to; fortunately, my mother stood by me, although I must have greatly disappointed her. I don't know, we never ever talked about it. Thank God for books. They became my armour, if you know what I mean. I could disappear in them; they were the medium through which I interacted with people I didn't know. Whenever I got lonely, I got drunk … and then I could face the world." George raised his tumbler to eye level and swirled the contents. Not much left in his glass. He took possession of the bottle.

After an uncomfortable pause Sasha broke the silence. "The first time I met George was in a downtown club. He was very outgoing and a brilliant talker — great company. We spent the night at my place. He left in a hurry first thing in the morning; no phone number, no address. What a prick, I thought. Then, a couple of weeks later I happened to come into the bookstore and there he was behind the counter. His sober persona was the polar opposite of the man who had charmed me off my feet back at the club. Such a contradiction — something I had to figure out. He pretended not to recognize me. But I kept coming back and gradually he thawed a little. I asked him out to see a play and when I came to pick him up he was already pickled. He was a little bit unruly that night…"

George broke in. "A little bit? We were ordered to leave the theatre."

"George behaved very badly that night, true. But after a few dates he began to relax and we were able to have fun together without him having to get plastered first." Sasha leaned over and kissed George on the cheek.

Staring into his tumbler, George didn't respond. Sasha turned his attention back to Sandra. "I came of age when things were different for gays. Still no picnic, but I never had to face what George and others of his generation faced. You have no idea how hard it was for him to stand up to the police the way he did a few days ago. But he did it; that took guts. As I said, don't underestimate George. No matter how terrified he might be of the police he would never betray a friend. And he considers you his friend."

"My friend, yes … us desperados got to stick together … screw the past," George muttered into his glass between several large gulps.

"Relocating the counter to the front of the store, that was another thing. A big step for George. For months I tried to get him to make that move. He was very attached to his hideout in the back."

"That was Mother. I inherited that arrangement from my mother."

"Well, George, I have to say, your mother was a bit … peculiar. The point is, though, that you have now come out into the light. I'm proud of you."

George pushed his chair back and rose unsteadily to his feet. He raised his glass as if to propose a toast, but inverted it instead. It was empty. "Screw the past!" he repeated, this time bellowing. He threw the glass against the floor and it shattered. Defiantly, George glared at Sasha and Sandra.

Sandra likewise stood, picked up her tumbler — which wasn't empty — and smashed it on the floor. "Fuck the police!" No rational thought involved, just a sense that George needed company at this moment and shouldn't be abandoned to solitary anger and despair.

Now it was Sasha's turn. "Well, as a lawyer, I have to—" He broke off, wilting under twin glares, and joined the other two standing. He took a deep breath. "Down with injustice!" And he lobbed his glass in a slow arc across the kitchen. The glass landed low against the wall and almost didn't break.

Sandra was about to laugh but froze when she caught sight of George's face. He took a step toward Sasha, almost falling over, and began to sob. Sasha closed the distance and held George in his arms. For a long time they stayed in that embrace, George wailing, Sasha kissing him and whispering words of comfort. At last the crying subsided. Sasha looked at Sandra over George's shoulder and mouthed, *He'll be okay.* Then, carefully and slowly, very much in the manner that he led Sandra through the thorns, Sasha guided George out of the kitchen and into his bedroom.

Tempted as she was to go to bed, Sandra couldn't leave the kitchen in a mess. What if someone forgot about the broken glasses and went barefoot to the bathroom in the middle of the night? She picked up the larger shards and deposited them in the waste bin under the sink. Footsteps from behind startled her. It was Sasha, broom and dustpan in his hands.

Wordlessly, he swept as Sandra piloted the dustpan where needed. When order was restored, she attempted some sort of apology for triggering George's breakdown. Sasha quelled her stammering by gently releasing the dustpan from her grip. "It's good for George to talk about his past. He needs to release the trauma. And he isn't able to open up with most people. But with you, since you — excuse me for saying this — since you have a shared experience, he can unburden himself. It's very hard to watch but it's for the best."

1982

We're kept inside the house for a long time while activity swirls about us. First police reinforcements arrive in large numbers, not the garden-variety cops on the drug squad, but mean-looking brutes wearing bulletproof vests and carrying heavy weaponry. More men follow the shock troops: paramedics, photographers and others whose functions are not at all clear. A silver-haired police officer appears, the one we saw many times on the television back when our hostage-taking was a hot item. Sergeant Warrant immediately straightens to attention and rattles off a report he's obviously constructed in his mind while waiting. His condensed version of events: hostage shot and killed by terrorist before rescue could be effectuated; said terrorist shot and killed while resisting arrest. A number of small arms seized. Search ongoing for more weapons, money and other evidence.

Silver Hair nods and is escorted downstairs by a posse of flunkies.

Two gurneys arrive and follow the posse down to the basement. The gurneys return, each with a shrouded figure strapped on top, and Bet loses it. She convulses with sobbing, each sob punctuated by a long wracking breath. In contrast, Phyl is silent, white and trembling. We're not allowed to talk among ourselves — not that any of us are in the mood for conversation. Eventually we're separated. Bet is led outside, unresisting, still wailing. A few minutes later, Phyl is taken out. I won't see them again until the trial.

I expect to be next out the door, but I'm left on the couch under silent guard. Why, I'm not sure. Eventually I hear an approaching rhubarb rhubarb rhubarb of voices before the posse re-emerges from the basement. Silver Hair is speaking to a new member of his entourage, a man in a lab coat. "… so the one blindfolded, tied to a chair, was definitely not Edwards?"

"Definitely not," says Lab Coat.

Silver Hair's voice begins to rise in pitch and volume. "Any idea who it was?"

Lab Coat shrugs. Silver Hair looks around at his posse. No one speaks. Silver Hair sighs and says, "Then let's get him identified. Priority one. Now then, Edwards…"

Thus prompted, Lab Coat continues. "We believe he was the other man down there. We'll have to have next of kin to confirm that though."

Silver Hair turns his attention to Sergeant Warrant. "And you shot him?"

"I'm afraid my team did, sir. He was holding a gun." Warrant looks very uncomfortable.

"Who shot the other guy?"

"Hard to say. Things happened very quickly."

"So isn't it possible Edwards overpowered one of his captors, tied him up and called for help?"

"I suppose so, sir."

Silver Hair shakes his head in disgust. As he meditates on what he's heard, men from other parts of the house and outside assemble around us in the living room. I flatten myself against the back of the couch, trying to be inconspicuous. I don't succeed. Silver Hair's gaze fixes on me. "Who the hell is this?"

Sergeant Warrant steps forward, anxious to redeem himself. "The ringleader, sir; she had a concealed weapon and attempted to use it. Fortunately, Corporal Barnes took immediate action to disarm and restrain her before she could fire."

Silver Hair smiles grimly. "I can't say I'd be sorry if Barnes had used lethal force." Comic relief — muted guffaws all around. "Well, I suppose it's for the best. Well done, Barnes, I'll make sure a commendation is coming your way. Where are the other terrorists?"

"Downtown already, sir." This from a cop who had just entered the house. "They've been kept separated."

Not ready to relinquish the stage, Warrant resumes his narrative. "I ordered this one detained here, sir. I thought you might want to have a word, she being the one who went for the gun. Also you might want to take a look at these." Warrant gestures to Library Cop, who advances with two of our books in hand.

Silver Hair reaches out as if to take the books but stops short of contact as Library Cop says, "Communist literature, sir. There's a lot more on the floor over there."

Silver Hair wipes his hand on his shirt. "This tipped you off that these were the terrorists?"

Library and Warrant exchange glances. The latter responds. "Yes, that's what did it, sir."

"Excellent police work." Silver Hair gestures toward the books still in Library Cop's hands. "Bag those and any other subversive material you find."

Silver Hair turns in my direction and raises his eyebrows. This mannerism is disturbingly reminiscent of my father when he was pissed at me, which was often. As I did back then, I imagine myself flying free and clear, out the window, up above the clouds, away from this nightmare. But I'm barely able to breathe much less fly and I'm sweating profusely.

Silver Hair barks at me. "Name?"

I hesitate, trying to sort out a way to be safely defiant. But then I hear myself saying, "Sandra … Sandra Treming."

"Well, Sandra Treming, you're in a whole shitload of trouble. But things might go better if you tell us now what you know. For starters, how many people were in this cell of yours?"

Our cell? I look up at him, mouth agape.

Silver Hair counts on his fingers. "You, the hippy, the snivelling bitch, the dead guy downstairs — who else?"

Four of us? Then I remember Norbert went to get groceries before the bust took place.

The shortest cop in the room, built like a pit bull, lunges at me as I'm trying to put my thoughts together. "Start talking, bitch, if you don't wanna get hurt…"

Silver Hair puts a restraining arm across his colleague's chest. "It would be a real good idea to cooperate with us, young lady."

With the remaining shred of my rationality I realize they're playing good cop, bad cop. I look down at the floor and keep my mouth shut, bracing myself for the release of the pit bull. But the attack doesn't come. Instead I hear Silver Hair say, "Take her out of here!"

Two ape-like cops escort me out into a night pulsating with red-and-blue lights. The street is a police parking lot; the entire block closed at both ends by yellow tape keeping the media and curious onlookers at bay. Helicopters throb overhead, but hands clamped on my arms and pushing against my shoulders keep me from looking up. As I descend the stairs, a distant roar comes from the crowd. Only one word penetrates: "Murderer!" Then I'm forced into the back of a police van and padlocked to a bench. The door slams shut, blocking noise from the crowd. The two cops sit with me in the van, one on either side. Neither speaks. I'm grateful for the silence.

Eighteen

2007

Sandra sat in the waiting area of the parole office, her nervousness mounting as minutes ticked by. Hearing nothing from Weychuk since her emergence from the blackberry thicket, she'd begun to feel out of danger. Then she received an official summons by registered mail, directing her to appear before her case officer.

Eventually her name was called and she was escorted into the restricted zone. Same long corridor, same cubicle farm, same office, same desk, but not the same person sitting behind it. Instead of Weychuk, a woman about a decade younger than Sandra looked up from an open file. The woman's expression was severe, her face, though, was oddly familiar.

"I'm supposed to see Mr. Weychuk," Sandra began.

"Mr. Weychuk is no longer at this centre. My name is Elizabeth Ferris. You may want to write that down as I don't have my business cards yet." Ferris pointed to the notebook on Sandra's lap.

The big wheel, Sandra thought as she wrote the name down. "Did Weychuk get fired?"

"Mr. Weychuk is now the supervisor at another location. But I have his files." Ferris studied the file open on her desk, turning over pages. "Yours is exceptionally detailed. He doesn't seem to have thought very highly of you. Why is that?"

"You should ask him."

"I'll do that. But I'm asking you first."

The forensic gaze from across the desk forced Sandra to deviate from Sasha's directive to not volunteer information, but she kept her account as accurate and neutral as possible. Ferris didn't interrupt; at times she looked down at the open file and otherwise straight at Sandra. Sandra felt compelled by silence to open up more than she should have. This new case officer was not someone she could easily bluff. After several minutes, including futile pauses in hopes of Ferris taking over the conversation, Sandra finally had nothing more to say.

Assured that Sandra was fully drained, Ferris nodded and flipped through pages in the file. She found what she was looking for. "But now you're employed at Moodie Books." It was a statement, not a question, and Sandra realized why Ferris was familiar. She'd bought a stack of murder mysteries at the store on at least two occasions.

Ferris closed the file and gave Sandra a peculiar half smile. "I have enough on my plate without spending time on things that don't appear to be a problem. Do you have email?"

"No, I'm planning to though," Sandra said. She'd recently resolved to convince George to get a computer for the store.

"When you do, let me know. Much easier to communicate that way. In the meantime, call in every Friday. Except for the last Friday of every month when I want to see you in my office."

Ferris led Sandra back to the reception lobby. En route, the case officer abruptly stopped and turned. "One more thing, Treming. Screw up once and you'll find me as hard to deal with as Mr. Weychuk, if not harder. Are we clear on that point?"

"Yes," Sandra said, "we are."

1982

On the way down to the police station, I'm overwhelmed in turns by anger, self-loathing and remorse. This swirl of emotions dominates my time in custody — up to the trial and beyond — blotting out most of my recall of actual events. But I recollect a series of interrogations ensuing almost immediately, merging into one long nightmare, a tedious repetition of questions met with my tedious nonresponses.

I remember being sore from rough handling at first, but have no memory of being hit, even though my refusal to cooperate angers my inquisitors. Nothing can make me talk, not because of solidarity with my communards or any remaining loyalty to the cause — whatever that was. I'm sick of the whole stupid enterprise and as unconnected to the outside world as the fetus growing within my body.

A lawyer is appointed to represent me; a man younger than me, speaking earnestly from behind a façade of professional concern. I'm no more cooperative with him than with the police. As far as I'm concerned they're all part of one oppressive mechanism grinding away on some predetermined course no matter what I say or do.

At some point the authorities become aware of my pregnancy, which triggers a great deal of consternation. The concern isn't for my wellbeing but about keeping this fact from the media. Nothing that would cast me as a sympathetic figure can be allowed.

I can only imagine how Bet's responses to interrogation differ from mine. I picture her dissertations on Marxist revolutionary theory somehow failing to raise the consciousness of her inquisitors, possibly because the rhetoric is interspersed with bouts of uncontrolled weeping. I wonder how Phyl responds. But I don't find out about that until later.

Nineteen

2007

Over the following month Sandra adjusted to her tenure as a full-time employee at Moodie Books. George's absences were now longer, often several days at a time. If he remained at the store for more than a day or two, Sasha was almost certain to drop by with fancy coffees for three. His arrival was usually the cue for George to pass the till over to Sandra and then leave with Sasha on some mysterious errand. With the two of them gone she could make improvements to the store without interference — reprice books, change the window display or keep the stock in alphabetical order. If she wasn't up to imposing order on chaos, she would find a book and read it in a comfy chair behind the counter, letting her fancy coffee get cold.

Exactly one month after becoming a full-time employee, Sandra collaborated with George and Sasha on a celebratory dinner to mark the occasion. As three friends lingered at the table after eating, satiated and not in a hurry to tackle the clean-up, Sandra took the opportunity to broach something that had nagged at her since her employment-status upgrade. "I'm worried about how much I'm costing you, George. You told me you couldn't afford an employee, remember?"

George raised his wine glass, took a sip and replaced it delicately on the table. "Things have been looking up of late, I suspect due to your efforts: organizing the inventory so customers can find things, changing the window display, buying the right stock." He took another sip of wine. "Most important is you're *not* buying titles that are going to rot on the shelves. The end effect is we now have more customers than ever before. Even your extravagant pricing seems to sit well with our clientele. People are buying more and we're prospering. Of course, prosperity in a bookstore is really just subsistence, but still. So, the difference you have made amounts to almost exactly minimum wage for you, and financially speaking, the bottom line hasn't changed. I'm happy, and I hope you are too."

George extended his glass over the table where it was met by two other glasses, but Sandra was still skeptical. "Really, George? The increase in sales covers my wages?"

"Well, I exaggerate a tad; let's just say that revenues are trending in the right direction, especially if we factor in the time that I now take off from work. Your increase in job security correlates with my freedom from labour." George abruptly turned to Sasha. "I think we should tell her now."

Sasha shrugged. "Go ahead, George. The toothpaste is already halfway out of the tube."

George turned back to Sandra. "Sasha and I have decided to live together. He sold his very posh condominium and the two of us are moving into an even posher one. Completely soulless it is, but at the same time seductively decadent."

Sandra stared open-mouthed at George, then Sasha. They both beamed back like a pair of besotted twenty-somethings and suddenly she felt very maternal. "Well, congratulations, you two. George, I'd be happy to cover the store while you move — actually for as long as it takes you guys to settle in."

"I was counting on that. And that brings me to a business proposition … I'd like you to cover the store permanently. You proved that you can do it, and so much the better if I'm not in the way."

"But, George—"

"No buts, Sandra. The store has become my albatross, a heavy load on my shoulders. I'm sick of being in the bookstore business, of being in business generally. I'm seventy-three years old; it's high time I moved out of my childhood home. So, here's the gist: I will retain ownership of the building and be a silent partner. You live in the apartment for a nominal rent and operate the store however you wish, as long as you keep the name Moodie Books. The name is the one thing I can't let go of. Whatever revenue the store earns now and in future is all yours to keep. Sasha and I will live on our combined incomes, high on the hog and in the lap of luxury, if that's anatomically possible. I'll visit at times, of course, but not too often."

George raised his glass again and the other two followed suit. For a while no one spoke. Sandra pondered the implications of the arrangement George had outlined. It made her feel a little uneasy. "I-I have to ask, what would you consider a 'nominal rent'?"

George blew air through his lips. "I don't know, Sandra; surely we can hash out all the niggling details later."

"Please, George, this whole scenario is a bit scary for me. I'm worried I might fall flat on my face."

"Very well. How about a sum roughly equivalent to one third of your current pathetic monthly wage?"

"That's ridiculous."

"Then what would you be prepared to pay?" George sounded a tad frosty.

"At least half. I'm sure I could swing half."

It took a few seconds for George to process what Sandra said; then he chuckled. "You drive a hard bargain, Ms. Treming." He placed his left hand over Sasha's right. "Fortunately for me, I have a high-powered lawyer here to look after my interests."

Smiling, Sasha extracted his hand and pinched George's ear. "I regret to have to inform you, Mr. Moodie, that Ms. Treming has previously secured my professional services. Assisting you in this matter would place me in a conflict of interest."

George threw up his hands. "I know when I've been outgunned. I'm no match for you and this shyster lawyer of yours. Very well, half your wage it is. Let's shake on it before you raise me any further." George brought his hands down and extended his right one. Sandra ignored it, instead rising and rounding the table to take George in her arms. After a full minute of hugging, George gently pushed her away and patted his brow and cheeks with a table napkin. "So, this is how people shake on a deal these days. I had no idea." George held the bottle of wine up to the light and divided what remained of its contents into the three glasses. "Seriously, Sandra, if revenues from the store don't keep up or anything else untoward happens, let me know. I'd do anything to avoid taking charge of the premises again."

"Of course," Sandra said. "Now let's open that second bottle of wine."

1982

I finally see my communards again when, for only the second time in my life, I find myself inside a courtroom. This court is much larger than the one from which I tried to spring Louie. No chances taken here that I or anyone else might disrupt the process. Armed police officers are stationed at strategic positions around the chamber. The spectator gallery is packed, not with anxious relatives and friends, but with media, and a phalanx of serious-looking suits who are here, it quickly becomes clear, to give expert testimony.

Bet and I are brought in separately and placed beside our lawyers at the defendants' table. No sign of Phyl. I assume he's mouthed off as usual and will get the book thrown at him later. Bet and I make brief eye contact before she looks away. Just as well. I'm having a hard enough time just staying upright. I can't process what's happening and, once expert testimony gets underway, I can't connect most of what's said with events I remember.

A witness is called. I don't recognize him at first: clean shaven, hair freshly trimmed and wearing a suit jacket and tie. But when he speaks I immediately place him — Frank, the hunter who gave me the .32 pistol so many months before. Now Frank has a different version of how the gun passed into my possession. While on a hunting trip he was caught unawares by a gang of desperados and stripped of his weapons. Why hadn't he reported this crime? He was afraid for his safety and that of his family. After a mild reprimand he's asked if he can identify any of the perpetrators in the court. Frank immediately points at me: "Her — she's the one who grabbed the pistol. She's the leader of the gang." Asked if he could identify anyone else from that day, Frank shrugs and says he can't be sure. "It all happened so fast."

During Frank's testimony, the .32 is introduced to the court in a plastic baggie; it remains as an important stage prop throughout the trial. At one point the gun is held aloft and declared — based on ponderous testimony given by ballistics and forensic experts — to be "the" murder weapon. That the victim was Dorian Twisp remains unstated. No mention is made either of John Edwards dying in a hail of police bullets.

After Frank is excused, a court flunky unfolds a flipchart stand to display a large and grainy photograph of a sinister figure. The ears and top half of their face is obscured by a brimmed winter hat. The face is puzzling but the hat looks vaguely familiar. I catch on when the prosecutor announces that the photo is of "a person of interest" making a cash withdrawal from John Edwards's bank account.

I was trying to stay warm in that hat, not disguising myself, having no clue there were cameras in bank machines. Yet another expert witness testifies that, based on physiological analysis, he has eighty-three percent confidence that the person in the photo is me. My lawyer leaps up to ask if this means there's a seventeen percent probability that the person in the photo is not me. The witness replies in the affirmative, and my lawyer returns in triumph to his seat. His only triumph of the trial.

Apart from such isolated moments of theatrical excess, the trial proceeds over several days at a snail's pace. Important information is given in broad distorted strokes while trivial points are examined in laborious detail. At times I attempt to follow what's being said, but mostly I just zone out through boredom.

Then a dramatic turn of events shakes me out of inattention. Philip Kaleden is called as a witness for the prosecution. Yet another arcane expert I assume. But then Phyl ambles into the courtroom and up to the witness stand. As he takes his place on stage, I see that he's undergone a fashion makeover similar to Frank, though the impact is more shocking given the years we lived under the same roof. I wonder who's responsible for sourcing his new wardrobe — solid-colour shirt with complementary jacket and tie — and what stylist has trimmed his hair and erased his beard. "Philip" is walked through the statement he's previously given to the police "for the record, Your Honour." Occasionally asked to elaborate upon certain points, he does so with gusto, directly to the jury and never once looking at either of his former housemates at the defendants' table.

Phyl mostly expounds on me and my role leading up to the kidnapping and beyond, to our eventual arrest. Not everything he says is false, but most of his testimony is exaggerated and luridly coloured. I induced my housemates to undertake a series of terrorist acts and single-handedly conceived the kidnapping plan. He and the rest of the household followed my instructions against their better judgment only because I exerted some kind of hypnotic influence on them.

At this point in Phyl's narrative, I lean forward and look down the table to check on Bet's reaction. She appears like she's in a trance, which no doubt adds credence to Phyl's outlandish claims. Phyl goes on to say that my influence wasn't total. I once commanded that the hostage be executed but the rest of the household refused to follow this order. A collective intake of breath in the court as Phyl makes this assertion, and then someone yells "Liar!" several times before I realize the person yelling is me. The judge pounds his gavel, a percussion track to my outburst. I'm levitated from my seat by two bailiffs and, on instructions from the bench, removed from the court. I don't get to hear the rest of Phyl's testimony — which is just as well.

Twenty

2007

Sandra again found Louie's room at the hospice empty. But the bed this time was stripped, with fresh linen and blankets neatly folded on top. No sign of personal effects. Sandra wasn't prepared to accept what this state of order implied, so she backed into the corridor and headed down to the sunroom. Louie wasn't there either.

For several weeks she'd intended to go back to the hospice, but somehow other things got in the way. And even when opportunities presented themselves, some part of her resisted making the effort. Now she regretted her procrastination very much.

She walked slowly back along the corridor to the exit, with the irrational hope that Louie might come out of one of the doors she passed. Near the front lobby, someone else materialized. It was the nurse, Gabriela Cruz. And she recognized Sandra.

"Oh, hello again. You must be here to pick up Mr. Del Grande's effects."

"His effects? Why would I..."

"You did not know? I am so sorry to tell you like this. Yes, he died last night. His stay here was much longer than anyone expected. He was determined to hold on to life as long as possible. But in the end his passing was peaceful."

Gabriela reached out and held Sandra's hand while speaking very gently. Not a trace of recrimination in her tone. She didn't have to recriminate. Sandra was silently berating herself for the visits not made after the first; for not bringing him something to read, as promised, for not making one last effort to reconnect.

"His effects are here behind the counter." Gabriela had steered them into the lobby without Sandra being aware of their progress. "There is not much — just this one box."

Sandra watched as Gabriela effortlessly lifted a cardboard box from the floor onto the counter, about shoulder height for her. She smiled brightly as Sandra floundered for something to say.

"Hello, I'm here to pick up Louie Del Grande's stuff." A voice from behind Sandra. She turned around and there was Thomas.

An awkward moment ensued as Thomas struggled with half recognition and Gabriela checked out the two of them to ascertain whether conflict over Louie's box was about to ensue. Sandra released the tension by sticking out her hand. "Hello, Thomas, remember me? We met at your mom's place a few weeks back."

Thomas took her fingertips between his thumb and forefinger and gave a barely perceptible shake. "Mother told me that there's a box here I'm supposed to pick up." Evidently unsure who he should deal with, he spoke to the space between Sandra and Gabriela.

Gabriela looked at Sandra as if seeking permission to hand over the box. Sandra nodded. "I'm sure Louie's things will be valued keepsakes for your mom," she said.

"No, Mother doesn't want them. She told me to take them to our church's goodwill store."

Bet's indifference irked Sandra, but there was no point in remonstrating with her son. She didn't want a dead man's possessions either. Gabriela handed the box to Thomas. He hefted it under one arm and left without saying another word.

"Well, I guess that's it then. Thank you, Gabriela, for everything." Sandra hoped that Gabriela understood that she spoke for Thomas and Bet, as much as for herself.

"Your name is Sandra, right?"

"You have a good memory."

"Not really, or I would have said something earlier. It is just that Mr. Del Grande left something for you. He wanted me to give it to you if he did not have the chance to pass it on." Gabriela reached into a drawer below the counter and pulled out a book. *Hard Times*, the same copy she'd found for Louie at the end of her previous visit.

"But that's yours. It belongs to the hospice."

"You take it. That is what Mr. Del Grande wanted. And besides, he wrote something in it for you."

Sandra opened the book and saw an inscription on the flyleaf in a shaky version of Louie's handwriting: *To Sandra San. Thanks for the cheerful read. Take good care of our baby, Sissy Jupe.* The message was a sucker punch to her gut. Her throat tightened and tears began to flow.

Gabriela handed Sandra a tissue, along with the package it came in. "Shall I make you a cup of tea?"

"No, it's okay, I'll be fine." Sandra mopped up her eyes and nose. "And I really have to be going."

Gabriela gave Sandra a hug, brief and yet very warm. "Goodbye, and thank you for visiting; do come again." Almost as if the hospice was her home and Sandra was a friend or relative.

Sandra passed through the front door back into the sunshine. Thomas was waiting outside, still holding the cardboard box. "Do you need a lift? I've got a car."

Sandra almost brushed by him with a curt "no thank you" but he looked so forlorn. Like a puppy. How could she refuse? "Sure, Thomas, anywhere near downtown will do." She followed him down the path to the hospice parking lot where he put the box in the trunk of an old Corolla. He opened the passenger door for Sandra and closed it behind her. Then he circled the car and slid into the driver's seat.

Thomas drove well enough, but carefully under the speed limit. As they progressed at a funereal pace away from the hospice, several drivers gunned by, apparently unwilling to remain in the cortege.

"So, Thomas, how long have you been driving?" Sandra asked.

"I've been driving for years, mainly for the church — visitations, meals for shut-ins, you know, like that. But this is the first car I've actually owned." Thomas patted the dashboard in a proprietary way. Sandra wondered how Thomas found the wherewithal to acquire his wheels, but didn't want to ask outright so she tried an indirect probe. "What did your mom think of you buying a car?"

Thomas scrunched up his face. "She was more upset when I got a job, but she's starting to come around. Now she has a handy chauffeur and courier. Say, do you have time for a coffee?"

Caught off guard, Sandra said, "Sure, I guess." Then, after a few seconds of reflection, she added, "Why not?" Her curiosity was piqued.

A few minutes later Thomas signalled and laboriously performed a parallel park into a space about three Corollas long. He led Sandra toward a stylish coffee shop, of the sort she learned to avoid soon after getting out of prison. She'd gone into one during her brief stay at Norbert's apartment and couldn't fathom the menu and, even more so, the prices. Thomas noticed her reluctance. He laid a guiding hand on her elbow and said, "Come on, you'll like it."

Once inside Thomas astonished Sandra by going behind the counter and slipping on an apron. She expected the two young women working there to object, but they just carried on with what they were doing.

"What kind of coffee do you like, Sandra?"

"Milk no sugar," she said, not quite understanding the options, but also not wanting to appear ignorant.

"I'll make you a latte." Again reading her expression accurately he repeated, "Come on, you'll like it."

Thomas set to work at a machine straight out of Doctor Frankenstein's laboratory, festooned with dials and spigots, emitting loud hisses and rising steam. She half expected the finishing touch to need a bolt of lightning, but no, Thomas casually presented her with what looked like a bowl of soup with more head on it than any draft beer she'd ever poured.

"Aren't you going to join me?"

"I'm not allowed to consume caffeine. Besides, I'm on shift now."

Sandra took her soup bowl to the table closest to Thomas's lab and watched him work. It was a revelation. With speed, efficiency and grace he generated beverages in a myriad of shapes and sizes to a never-ending stream of customers. Many of these he greeted by name, setting to work even before they verbalized their orders. It was as if someone had flipped a switch, turning a shy and awkward youth into a self-possessed and undeniably attractive young man. As she watched Thomas work, Sandra experienced a sense of déjà vu. It took a few seconds to make the connection: her first sight of John Edwards in the courtroom — the man who "runs the show" as she was told back then. The physical resemblance was uncanny, especially with Thomas now appearing comfortable in his own skin. But she'd hated the prosecutor right off the bat; whereas for his son she felt a surge of affection.

Sandra was also taken aback by the parade of people buying coffee, some zooming in with their own cups and zooming out again with cups filled. Others brought books, magazines and even small computers to ensconce themselves with while they sipped beverages from the store's branded mugs. What astonished her most, however, was that all these people paid more for their cup of joe than she'd willingly pay for a full café breakfast.

She took a cautious sip from the bowl. The foam was off-putting but the coffee was excellent. She saw through a valley in the foam that Thomas was smiling and became aware that she was smiling back at him. There was a break in the flow of patronage. "I knew you'd like it," he said.

"I could become addicted. How long have you worked here, Thomas?"

"A little over a month. I got this job two days after you visited our apartment."

"How did you get so good at this in such a short time?"

Thomas blushed deep pink. One of the women behind the bar laughed; she had an impressive array of tattoos visible above her neckline and below her sleeves. She crossed behind Thomas and mussed up his hair in passing. "Tommy's a natural," she said over her shoulder.

"I've served other people a lot … you know, in the church. Making other people happy makes me happy."

Sandra dipped her nose back into the foam. Interesting — Thomas whispered when he made reference to the church. Bet had reason to be concerned about her boy and his new job. Sandra finished her coffee, leaving most of the foam intact, and rose to her feet. "Thanks for the drink. I best be getting on." Thomas had signalled one of the other staff to take over his station and began removing his apron. "No, it's okay," Sandra said. "Stay here, I don't have far to go."

He quickly retied his apron as he said, "Are you sure?"

"Absolutely."

"You know where to find me."

"Yes, I do. See you around, Thomas."

1982

Phyl is sentenced to two years in minimum security and walks free within months. Bet also receives five years in minimum security and somehow retains parental rights in the joint until she's paroled. Dorian's true identity is revealed during the course of the trial. Judicial attention therefore briefly diverts to Louie, stuck in a remand centre back east, awaiting trial on Dorian's drug-trafficking charges. The discovery triggers a legal conundrum; Louie is no longer implicated in the crime for which he's being held. Neither could he be linked to the kidnapping since he was in custody when it took place. A way forward is found. With minimal fanfare, Louie is found guilty of obstruction of justice and released with time served.

I'm left as the closest thing they have to a marketable terrorist kingpin. My sullen silence before and during the trial reinforces the desired public perception. The image is packaged up so skillfully that I almost come to believe I'm the malignant person they make me out to be. The inevitable verdict washes over my numb brain: life in prison, the severest penalty that could be imposed.

My prison memories are even more disjointed than those from when I was under arrest and during the trial. One moment of relative lucidity stands out: giving birth in the prison infirmary. During labour I'm totally energized and aware of every detail — the whole sequence from the contractions starting right up to the final push. I hear someone say, "It's a girl" just before the squalling begins. But I barely get a glimpse of my baby before the cord is cut and she's swaddled. I shout out, "Emma! Her name is Emma." But they just take the bundle out of sight. And as she exits my life, the grey fog descends again.

Twenty-One

2007

Sasha knocked on the front door as Sandra was powering up the cash register and her new computer in readiness for the day's business. She unlocked the door and quickly stepped aside in retreat from a blast of cold, wet air. Autumn well-advanced; flocks of leaves were sailing over the street.

Sasha backed into the store, shaking and closing his umbrella before he crossed the threshold. "Thanks. I came early to beat the rush."

"I don't really expect a rush today." She relieved Sasha of his umbrella and helped him out of his raincoat. "Coffee?"

"Yes, please."

"Coming right up. It'll only take a minute."

Sandra fed finely ground coffee into another recent acquisition, a small espresso machine, bought at the same time as the computer.

"So, Moodie's has embraced modernity at last." There was nothing judgmental in Sasha's tone, but his remark still triggered some defensiveness on Sandra's part.

"Not really, I just got that thing to keep tabs on my competition."

"What do you mean?"

"More and more people are buying books online. Hard to compete with that. Some of them come here just to browse before going home to make a comfortable — and cheaper — purchase through their computer. Pisses me off."

"So your business is hurting?"

"I'm getting by." She handed Sasha his coffee and dragged a chair around to the front of the counter.

Sasha sat down. "Make me a list of ten must-reads and I shall buy them all from you."

"There you go, rescuing me again. Things aren't that bad. Besides, I have a plan."

Sasha took a sip of espresso and was briefly distracted. "Excellent coffee!"

"Part of my plan — an experiment, really. Buy twenty-five dollars' worth of books and you get a free cup of joe. So if you're serious about buying ten books I could get you really wired."

"Sounds like fun, but won't that cut into your margin?"

"Not if I earn customer loyalty through bribery. Not sure it'll work, but if it does then I'll expand the concept. Build a coffee bar in that empty space over there and hire a full-time barista." Sandra pointed to the back of store where the lumber to build new shelves was still stacked.

Sasha looked over at the lumber with a rueful expression. And then he laughed. "Sandra, I have to say that for a convicted terrorist you are quite the entrepreneur."

Sandra tapped Sasha's demitasse with the one she'd poured for herself. Their eyes met. It was somehow obvious that they were both thinking the same thing. Sasha was the first to put it in words: "Not to worry, Sandra, I won't tell George."

"He's sure to find out anyway. Maybe he'll develop a taste for espresso."

Sasha nodded and smiled. He seemed content just to sip his coffee and stare vacantly out the window. After an extended silence, Sandra prompted, "So?"

"So?" Sasha echoed. The light dawned. "Oh yes, the adoption registry. Well, as it happens, you don't even need to leave the store. You can use your new toy." Sasha reached over the counter and turned the computer to access the screen and keyboard. After a few quick keystrokes and sweeps with the mouse he stepped aside, yielding to Sandra. She scrolled down as Sasha spoke.

"Everything you need to know is there. Just follow the prompts. You won't need a lawyer either, much as it pains me to admit that."

"I'm not looking for legal advice. But I could use advice from a friend and you're the most sensible person I know."

"I hope 'sensible' doesn't mean boring. But fire away."

"I'm not sure I should do this."

"You don't want to get in touch with your daughter?"

"No, I do. I'm just afraid I'll be a major disappointment in her eyes."

"She might be disappointed, who knows? But I would be disappointed in her if she felt that way."

"If she's a normal human being, you mean? Finding out her mum's a convicted terrorist?"

"Sandra, put yourself in her place. If she's looking for you — and there won't be a reunion unless she is — then what would be worse: her not finding you and always wondering why or her finding you and learning about your past? At least in the latter case she should also understand that you didn't abandon her because you didn't love her. Isn't it always better to learn the truth?"

"I don't know. That's why I need your advice."

"I can't help you with this, Sandra. No one could. You'll just have to go with your gut. Sorry."

"Don't be sorry; it's okay. I'll figure it out."

"Well, is there anything else I can help you with? Any excuse to visit my favourite bookstore and its charming proprietress ... I even work pro bono, as you know. How are things with the parole office?"

"Oh, things are fine in that department. Pretty chill in fact. Now I've got the computer I just email the Big Wheel once a month. She also drops by here occasionally."

"Ferris is checking up on you?"

"No, buying books. We don't talk. She just finds what she wants, pays for it, leaves. And that's just fine."

As Sandra spoke a customer came up and placed a pamphlet on the counter. Sandra quickly scanned the store and saw that several people had come in while she and Sasha were talking. She looked down and saw Lenin's *What Is to Be Done?* — which she'd kept as a permanent part of the window display.

"I'm sorry; that's not for sale." She raised her head to look directly at the customer, and froze. Male, about the same age as her, possibly a little younger. Norbert mirrored her gaze with a peculiar half-smile on his face.

"I know. I read the label, but couldn't resist a little joke. Ha ha. How's it going, Sandra-San?"

"How did you…" But Sandra knew the answer already.

Norbert explained anyway. "Find you? It wasn't all that difficult. I just had to track down a mutual acquaintance, visit her in person because she doesn't answer or return phone calls, listen to an impromptu sermon and make a generous donation to the Absolute Church, or whatever it's called. In the end she claimed she didn't know where you were. Luckily her son was more forthcoming."

"So you met Thomas."

"Yep, sure did." Norbert snickered. "Seems that Bet picked up an interesting souvenir from our mutual past."

Ignoring Norbert's snideness, Sandra rummaged through her cash drawer. She extracted an envelope with Norbert's name on it. "I was going to mail this to you, but since you're here…"

Norbert picked up the envelope and frowned as he examined it. "What's this?"

"The five hundred dollars I owe you."

Norbert tossed the envelope back on the counter. "Sandra, you don't owe me anything. That was a gift. I'm not taking it back."

"And I'm not keeping it."

"Look, in retrospect I know I handled this badly, but I didn't want to leave you in the lurch. You'd just gotten out of jail. You were going job hunting. You needed to buy clothes, get around town and, I don't know, a lot of things. Bottom line, you needed money. You would have done the same for me if our situations were reversed."

"Okay, Norbert, thank you … but I'm set up now and don't need your money anymore. So take it back."

Norbert backed away from the counter. "I don't want it."

"Neither do I." Sandra tossed the envelope in Norbert's direction. It fluttered to the floor.

Norbert sighed. He picked up the envelope and put it back on the counter. "How about giving it to the charity of your choice?"

Sandra immediately thought of the Ocean View Hospice. The envelope stayed where Norbert left it. "I didn't come here to quibble about petty cash," he said. "I just want to stay in touch. Remain friends and..."

After a long pause, Sandra prompted, "And what, Norbert?"

"And I have a business proposition to bounce off you. A much bigger deal than five hundred bucks. Look, Sandra, I've done the research. Your store is in a strategic location; a couple of rezonings were approved near here recently. Sign of big changes to come. So, of course I'm hot to buy."

"Buy what?" Sandra snapped, anticipating the answer.

"Moodie Books. The whole building in fact."

"It's not for sale."

"Wait, just listen. As the new owner I'd be prepared to lease back the store to you for a token amount. Say a dollar a month for starters. You could upgrade at this location or, if you prefer, secure better retail space somewhere else. You'd be crazy not to jump on this offer."

"Not interested." Sandra put the envelope back in the cash drawer and folded her arms in front of her chest.

"Excuse me, if I may interject..."

Norbert swivelled toward Sasha. "Who are you?" he demanded.

Sandra leapt in to forestall a hostile escalation. "Sasha, please—" She broke off. Perhaps she had overstepped herself.

Sasha extracted a card from his breast pocket and extended it to Norbert. "As his legal representative, I will put you in touch with the owner. You can direct your proposition to him."

Sandra glared at Sasha but kept quiet. Norbert briefly examined Sasha's card before putting it in his wallet and extracting another. He handed it to Sasha. "How lucky to run into you. When would be a good time to call? Later this afternoon perhaps?"

"Tomorrow would be better. Early afternoon."

"Early afternoon tomorrow it is. I look forward to meeting ... what's his name, the owner, please?"

"Moodie, George Moodie."

"Of course, yes, Moodie. Super. See you tomorrow." On his way out, Norbert paused at the door and, ignoring Sandra, nodded back at Sasha.

As soon as the door clicked shut, Sandra hissed, "What the hell, Sasha?"

"What the hell what, Sandra?"

"Why did you have to stick your nose in? No way do I want that bastard meddling with my business."

"So did you intend to keep George in the dark?"

"Of course not. But George has to know that he'd sell to Norbert over my dead body."

"You need to stay objective. Let George make up his own mind about the future of his store. He has title to the property, not you."

"So it's fine to shut me out of a decision that affects me more than anyone else? Because you're objective and I'm not."

"Sandra, I am very mindful of your interests." Sasha examined the card still in his hand. "In fact, from a legal perspective, I would strongly advise George not to accept the deal this Mr. Cubbin has proposed. Partially because of his obligations to you, but also for other reasons. It's in neither of your interests at this time."

"Oh, fuck you, Sasha. Don't spin this like it's another rescue."

Instead of replying, Sasha reached over the counter for his coat and umbrella. He left a fresh trail of water droplets as he headed for the door, where he paused to don his coat before lunging into the storm. A blast of frigid air struck Sandra as she rotated the computer to face her again. She scrolled to the top of the Adoption Reunion page and hesitated a few seconds before closing it.

"Screw the past," she said as another customer entered. Her greeting might have driven him away, were it not warm and dry inside. Outside, the storm continued to rage.

Twenty-Two

Afterward

"Oh for chrissake, Sasha, come on in." I've finally lost patience watching him pacing back and forth on the sidewalk. He's been at it for a good couple of minutes, occasionally peering through the window, not catching sight of me in the dim interior light. Sasha smiles ruefully at my invitation. I hold the door open and he obediently enters.

I last saw him at the funeral. I visited George a few times during the final stages of his illness, but never when Sasha was present. I'm now struck by how his appearance has changed, his once uniformly dark hair now streaked with white, with deep creases in his face converging at his eyes. But still a handsome bastard; ageing definitely has a gender bias.

We held a funeral for George instead of the more fashionable celebration of life because he stipulated exactly that in a codicil to his will. Handwritten in his elegant cursive: *Mourning is optional but I insist on a funeral, not a memorial service or a damned celebration of life. If you wanted to celebrate my life you should have done so when I was still alive to party with you.* George being difficult, as usual. As it turned out, whatever one might have called it, George missed a glorious send-off: tears sweetened by fond memories and laughter.

Also in the will was a provision leaving the bookstore building to me, no strings attached. George rejected Norbert's business proposition, even before Sasha had a chance to advise him against it. Later he told me that, as a committed anarchist, he could have no truck with capitalist speculation and hoped that was okay with me. I affirmed that it was and he assured me that any decisions affecting the store and its future were entirely mine to make. Except for its name, of course.

Now Sasha is standing before the counter, so I query him about what has nagged at me since I heard about my inheritance. "Sasha, I have to ask, were you upset about the store and apartment — George just giving them to me?"

Sasha looks blank for a few seconds, making me nervous about what I might have triggered. Until he laughs. "You must be joking. I insisted on it — a used bookshop was the last thing I wanted to be saddled with."

I laugh with him, and the tension between us dissipates. "Thank you. That's a relief. So, what do you think of it now?"

Sasha commences a slow pivot, taking in the coffee bar, the newly tiled floor and lighting fixtures, the tables and comfy chairs occupied by customers with books and laptops, mugs of coffee within easy reach. He rotates 360 degrees until he faces the counter again. Besides three remaining bookcases against the wall behind me, the counter is the only unchanged feature of the store.

"Notice anything different?" I ask.

"A subtle shift," he says. "The last time I was here you were just introducing coffee as a small adjunct to the book trade. Now it looks like coffee is the mainstay and books, at best, would seem to be a sideline."

"That about sums it up. Would you like to sample some of our product? Coffee, that is."

"Do I get a free book thrown in?"

"Always, unless you start coming here every day. Then I'll have to reconsider." I emerge from behind my counter and reach out with the intent of escorting him over to the coffee bar, but he takes my arm and adroitly manoeuvers me into a massive bear hug. "This visit is long overdue, Sandra. It is good to see you again. And the store … well, if it works for you, then I approve."

"I'm glad you do, not that I'd change anything if you didn't approve." I break free. "Allow me to introduce you to Thomas, my partner and the commissar of coffee in this establishment. Thomas, this is my good friend Sasha."

Thomas says, "Hey" with only fleeting eye contact. As relaxed and affable as he's become with our regular clientele, Thomas is still apt to regress in formal situations. I order two coffees and brush away Sasha's attempt to pay. "It's on my tab."

"But you don't have to pay for coffee," says Thomas, undermining my display of generosity.

Sasha and I sit at a table close to my counter, where I can monitor customer comings and goings. Neither of us speak for a while, until Sasha nods at the surviving bookshelves. "Not carrying much stock these days?"

"No, I'm specializing at the high end and at the low end. Either good quality out-of-print books — they're in that locked cabinet — or easy stuff that people might want to read over coffee. But no current best sellers or much of anything still in print. No point really. People would just do a quick browse and buy them later online."

"What about the Rand and Hubbard collections?"

"Gone. Pulped. Thomas needed storage space." Feeling unaccountably defensive I add, "I waited until after George's funeral."

Sasha laughed. "I am sure he would have appreciated your sensitivity."

Another long silence, both of us seeming at a loss for words. Then Sasha throws out another conversational gambit. "So, any news?"

"About what?"

"I was wondering if your daughter ever got in touch."

"No, not yet. Probably she never will."

"Sorry to hear that. Family is important." Sasha leans back, physically and otherwise retreating. "Sorry, Sandra, I don't mean to be a pain."

"Then don't be." My tone surprises me as much as it does Sasha. I take a deep breath to calm myself. "To be honest, I waffled about posting on the adoption registry. I finally did it, not long ago. Not sure now that was the right thing to do, but it felt wrong to block her from connecting with me. So the door is now open. Whether she comes through it or not is entirely up to her."

As I speak, Sasha nods encouragement and keeps it up for several seconds after I stop. Silence returns, this time less comfortable than before. Sasha suddenly pushes his chair back and stands up. "Well, best be on my way."

I jump up quickly and position myself between him and the door. "We're friends, aren't we?"

Sasha leans forward slowly, tenderly kisses me on the lips and then backs off, his fingers lingering on my cheeks. "Friends, always; but I really do have to go now."

"Come visit again soon. I mean it."

"I will. And perhaps dinner together. That would be … like old times."

"Yes, old times. I'd like that."

#

I don't see her enter the store. A couple of weeks after Sasha's visit I'm looking over sales figures for the previous month. My side of the business slightly in the red, mainly due to a recent spending spree on new stock. But, fortunately, Thomas's coffee bar keeps both our heads above water. Even so, not reassuring in terms of a trend projection. Weighing the pros and cons of giving up on books altogether in favour of an exclusive focus on caffeine, I look across the floor at Thomas. That's when I notice the stylishly dressed young woman loitering between us.

She isn't our usual breed of customer, in looks or behaviour. Ignoring the books and the coffee bar at first, she stares down at the floor, up at the ceiling and then in turn at all four walls. Then, drifting across to the shelves on my left, she scoops up a book in passing. Everything seems to be of interest, save for me and the book now in her hand. Finished with her inspection she turns and ambushes me with an engaging smile.

I try unsuccessfully not to be charmed, seized by a growing irrational conviction that this is my Emma. Naturally she would first wander around the store, building up nerve before identifying herself to her birth mother. I don't want to consider more likely possibilities. This pseudo-customer must be my baby.

I almost greet her by name, but what's left of my rational mind overrules that impulse. Instead I take initiative in the standard service-industry way. "May I help you?"

She comes up to the counter, places the book on it. "I'd like to buy this."

Down the Long Table by Earle Birney, 1955 — a first edition I should have locked up. Now I'm convinced this astute customer is my daughter, even though her taste in literature seems at odds with her youth and stylish wardrobe. I have a brief impulse to offer Birney as a gift, but a petty bourgeois reflex overrules me. "Forty dollars," I say.

I expect a bit of push back, but the woman simply hikes up her shoulder bag and reaches in for her purse. "Will the owner be in today?" she asks.

My reply sticks in my throat. Suddenly short of breath and trembling, I can't trust my voice. Gripping the counter, I take a deep breath and say, "I'm the owner."

"Melanie Collis." She drops her purse back in her bag and extends her hand. I automatically take hold of it and confess my identity: "Sandra … Sandra Treming."

"Pleased to meet you. Can I just say how much I love your store? Coffee and books, what a great combo. Especially in such a pleasant, homey environment. Not soulless and antiseptic like most other bookstores — or coffee bars for that matter."

"Thank you. We do our best." I break off eye contact to reassess. Melanie — not Emma — but still, her name was probably changed by her adoptive parents. I'm reluctant to let go of my initial hope.

Undeterred by my lack of attention, Melanie continues on. "The building is quite something as well. Do you know if it's on the city's heritage registry?"

Now something about Melanie seems vaguely familiar, but I can't put my finger on it. "This old dump? I doubt it."

Melanie winces. "Well, serious TLC needed for sure. Even so, the place has good bones. I'd love a peek under that exterior vinyl siding. I bet we'd be amazed. But architecture alone doesn't create heritage value; function is also important. This store contributes to maintaining the character of the surrounding neighbourhood. It would be sad to see it go — exactly what's happening to so many retail buildings all over the city: sold, demolished and replaced with some concrete monstrosity. Or worse, a high-rise tower. Please, don't allow that to happen here."

"Don't worry. Not on my watch it won't."

"I like your attitude. Also good to see you're making improvements." Melanie points over to where Thomas is working behind his counter. "That looks like a recent project. What code upgrading was required when you put in the coffee bar?"

I look at her blankly.

"You know, when you apply for a building permit, there's always an added cost for code upgrades. Do you remember what that was in this case?"

I shrug. Melanie gazes at me intently, then raises her eyebrows and shakes her head. "Took a shortcut, eh? Don't worry. I won't tell. But you took a pretty big risk."

"For a dinky little coffee bar? Why would I throw my hard-earned bucks into a bottomless pit?"

"I wouldn't say bottomless. Let's figure it out. This building's got to be fifty years old, at least. I'm guessing not much major maintenance done since it was built." Melanie points up at the ceiling. "No fire sprinklers. Pretty sure those tiles are full of asbestos. So, clear out the asbestos, which will expose the wiring and water pipes. What better time to upgrade electrical and plumbing systems? You'd probably have to anyway. Bottom line: Over fifty years, to catch up with accumulated deferred maintenance, you're looking at close to building replacement cost. Labour and materials at two hundred dollars per square foot, times … what? Three thousand feet I'm guessing. That's six hundred grand, right? Just a rough estimate — probably on the conservative side. Something to think about next time you plan any renovations, or before city inspectors happen by and shut your business down until everything's upgraded."

"Thanks, I feel loads better now." I actually feel sick to my stomach.

Melanie reaches over the counter to touch my elbow. "No reason to panic. I can help you with this."

"What — you're going to give me six hundred grand out of the goodness of your heart?"

"Sorry, much as I might like to, no. What I propose is to use some of the equity in this building to pay for its upgrading. Not only to bring it up to current code but also to restore its heritage character."

"I wouldn't know where to begin—"

"Sure. It's a huge challenge, especially without the right experience. But this is exactly the kind of work I do. The simplest way forward would be for you to sell me the property, subject to a lease-back arrangement to you. You would continue doing business as before while I would take on all the responsibility and risks."

"You'd buy my store? You could afford that?" I struggle to wrap my mind around what Melanie is proposing. I don't want to sell, but what she described scares the crap out of me.

"Yes, I recently received an inheritance and I'm looking for an investment opportunity. This building's perfect."

"But I'm not about to sell my store…" Any lingering warmth from our initial contact has now pretty much dissipated.

"I hear you. And kudos for sticking to your guns. But really, is that in your best interest? My proposition would enable you to walk away with the full value of your property in your pocket. Plus you'd still be in business at this location. Win-win, right?"

"What's the win for you?"

"Eventually, I'll see a decent return from improvements made to the building. At the absolute worst, I'll break even. Honestly, I'm not in heritage restoration to become rich. It's more a passion of mine."

I glance over my shoulder at my three pathetic bookcases and think about my online competition. Why do I even bother? If Melanie is serious about buying me out, maybe I should seize the day.

Before I can steer the conversation in such a direction — hypothetical or otherwise — a man comes between us and slams a box of books down on the counter. I almost chew him out for his rudeness but, acting on reflex, I first scan the contents of the box. Easy enough to do — the books are packed in a single layer, spines up. Not an antiquarian-approved packing system, but ideal for a quick assessment. This guy has obviously dealt with second-hand bookstores before. Probably another of George's old suppliers. If only George were here. In the box are mostly out-of-print collectibles in fine or near-fine condition. Normally the kind of stock I'm keen to acquire, but something's not quite right. I'm leery about dealing in hot property, which is what these books look to be. To allow for closer inspection I temporize: "Give me an hour to price these. Have a coffee or browse if you like."

"No time. Usually I deal with Ivan's over on Main, but I've had it with that old fucker. So here's the deal. Thirty bucks for the box."

His response sets off alarm bells in my head. He knows something about the used-book trade, and these books are worth far more than what he's asking. I can't afford the risk. "Sorry, not interested. Take them someplace else."

I look directly in his face for the first time, bracing myself for an argument. No protest comes. The man remains frozen to the spot; his lips move but no sound comes out. Suddenly he picks up the box and crashes ass-backward against the front door.

"Hey bud, what the hell?" I yell. The man gets stuck halfway out the door and that's when I recognize him. That bastard, Phyl — wizened and balding but unmistakably Phyl. I yell out, "Asshole, come back here!" as he clears the entrance and starts to run.

I round the counter and reach the door before I realize what I'm doing. I shout over my shoulder, "Thomas, mind the store!" Thomas looks at me quizzically. "Keep your eye on my till until I'm back." He processes for a few long seconds before nodding vigorously. The chase is on.

I spot Phyl waiting at the nearest bus stop, halfway down the block. Seeing me, he picks up his box and starts to run again. I follow, confident I can catch him, burdened as he is and him never in good shape even when younger. But he surprises me, keeping a good pace with an ungainly giraffe-like lope, arms wrapped around his merchandise. The chase continues for a couple of blocks, much to the amusement of passersby. Several drivers honk their horns. I could overtake him with a sprint, but I'm saving my breath for the verbal abuse I'm eager to lay on, perhaps combined with a few good punches to his head. Small restitution for the twenty-five years he's stolen from me, the enormous hole in the middle of my life.

Phyl does a shoulder check and veers onto the road into heavy traffic. A semi-trailer truck in the near lane gears down almost to a full stop, temporarily blocking him from view. A screech of brakes and a loud thud, followed by even more horrific screeching. I start to tremble; I didn't mean to kill Phyl. The semi rolls onward and clears my field of vision. Several vehicles are halted in the farther two lanes. No sign of Phyl. Car doors open and their occupants converge beyond a minivan.

I run across to the gathering and arrive just as two men help Phyl to his feet. He's protesting, "I'm fine, I'm fine — don't call 911; no, no, don't need an ambulance." The men guide Phyl to the sidewalk, where he sinks down onto the pavement. A woman retrieves the remnants of Phyl's box, which slipped out of his hands and was crushed in the traffic. Other people arrive with books from the accident scene, stacking them into two neat piles. Rescue complete, the helpers return to their vehicles, and traffic begins to flow again, leaving Phyl and I alone together on the sidewalk.

My moment has arrived. Kick him or yell at him? I almost wish I'd brought something sharp to cut him with. Then I see Phyl is weeping. I stand over him. In the sweetest voice I can muster, I say, "Hey, Phyl."

Phyl looks up, tears streaming down his cheeks.

I take three twenties out of my wallet and hold them over his head. Rising like a fish to bait, he tries to snatch them from my hand. I pull the money out of reach. "Thirty bucks for the books, like you asked. Another thirty says don't fucking dare show your fucking face in my store again. I know some guys who, as a favour to me, would happily beat the crap out of you." Not true, but believable enough coming from an ex-con.

Phyl keeps his eyes on the money. "Give it to me, Sandra."

"Fuck you, Phyl. You owe me a hell of a lot more than sixty bucks for all the years you stole from my life." I put the twenties back in my wallet.

"I don't owe you nothing. That fuck-up at the courthouse was your idea. So was taking a hostage. None of that shit woulda happened if it weren't for you. You put yourself in the slammer."

I don't have a rebuttal for this, and it pisses me off. I kick one stack of books into the street. The second stack follows the first. Normally I would never treat books this way, but resale value has already been knocked out of most of them. Anything left in reasonable shape by the traffic was tainted by contact with Phyl. I turn back to face him, half expecting a physical attack. Instead, I see fear in his eyes.

"You crazy bitch," he whispers, backing away until he's at a safe enough distance to turn and flee.

I feel an enormous sense of release as I head back to the store. But my buoyancy deflates as I remember Melanie and her calculation of the hidden costs of bookstore ownership. She has badly shaken my sense of security. After my confrontation with Phyl, I'm not up for another round with her.

About a half block from the store I pass by a parked car. In the driver's seat a familiar figure stares down at his cellphone. *What the hell is Norbert doing here?* I don't stop to chat, and he doesn't register my presence. Just fine with me. As I continue on by, I start to put puzzle pieces together in my mind.

Inside the store, Melanie sits at a table, perusing Earle Birney while sipping a cappuccino. With her foot she pushes a chair in my direction. I sit down.

"Let's get serious," she says. "I want to buy your bookstore."

I recollect forlorn Phyl weeping on the sidewalk and then running away. I'm not about to emulate him. "Melanie, I won't sell you my business."

"I don't want your business. I'm only interested in the equity, not how you use the premises. I'm happy to make a long-term investment. Like I said before, a win-win scenario."

The last puzzle pieces click into place … Norbert driving me into town from prison. Calling someone about buying a rundown apartment building. Someone named Mel. The same Mel who owned the beachfront condo I lived in for a week.

"Mel … is that what people call you?"

Melanie pauses before responding. "Some do."

"People like Norbert?"

Melanie rubs her nose and doesn't reply.

"Okay, *Mel*, tell your buddy Norbert that my answer's the same as before. Moodie Books isn't for sale. Not to him and not to you. Go fall in love with another old building."

Melanie is hard to faze. "Sandra, we seem to have started off on the wrong foot. Yes, Norbert and I have done business together, but we're not joined at the hip. This would be my project alone. Norbert has no interest in preserving heritage, but I do. Especially when I see an opportunity like this building."

"Just how many inheritances have you come into recently?"

"What?"

"I was with Norbert when he phoned you about getting some guy to sell an old apartment building. *Tell him you've come into an inheritance and you're looking for an investment property.* I remember Norbert saying that — so different from the kid I once knew. So, Mel, did you work your magic?"

Melanie maintains her composure. "Well, he sold us the property and we made him a very rich man. And we kept part of the old building's façade on the new complex."

"How heartwarming. Tell Norbert he knows where to shove his façade."

Finally I puncture Melanie's poise. Her face reddens; rising to her feet, she almost makes it to the door before she remembers she's still holding the Birney. Waving the book in my direction she veers over to the counter and slams it down. "Changed my mind. Too old-fashioned."

I expect Melanie to continue on out the door but she stays by the counter. Thomas wanders over, tea towel in his hand, to stand by my side. Ignoring him, Melanie attempts to reconstruct her winning smile. "Okay, Sandra, you're a smart lady. I'll level with you. So, here's the deal. Norbert and I have sewn up the properties on either side of you. With you onside we can consolidate the three into one development site. No façade retention, no heritage bullshit. Huge lift in land value. You walk away with a third of the net. But if you want to play stupid and be a holdout, well, we'll redevelop what we own already and do fine — not great, but good enough." Melanie's voice suddenly increases in volume, her audience now including every customer in the store. "You, on the other hand, will be absolutely screwed. Doing business in a tiny shack stuck between two mid-rises. What a joke! If you try to sell you won't even get lot value, because our property will be stripped of any up-zoning potential. No way to build anything bigger than what's here now, if that. Yup, big-time screwed."

Melanie pauses to turn down the volume. Another attempt at a smile. "We're ready to deal, but it's a limited time offer. So, Sandra, what do you say?"

I'm close to caving at this point, but Thomas doesn't give me the chance. He places himself between Melanie and me and flaps the towel at her. "You should leave now," he says.

"Oh, fuck you," Melanie sneers at Thomas and then at her entire audience. "Fuck off all of you." As the door slams behind her, a strange sound erupts — applause from all the bibliophiles and coffee drinkers in the store. Strangely validating, but I don't play hero of the resistance and take a bow. I'm sure Melanie isn't bluffing; she and Norbert remain a real threat.

Thomas pats my back and whispers in my ear. "We'll be okay."

I nod and drape an arm around his neck. But I can't quell an underlying sense of impending confinement again, an entanglement from which I might never tear free.

End

Acknowledgements

Through Thorns jumps back and forth between imagined events of decades ago and the current era. The former scenes were mostly written at the time in which they are set, while the latter were added years later to connect the story to the here and now. As I struggled to merge past and present narratives, I benefited from the advice and encouragement of Jay Nahani, Jim Fraser, Edith Speers, Karen Wall and Rick Vulliamy, astute readers to whom I owe many thanks.

I am also grateful to Greg Ioannou, owner of Iguana Books, for so quickly accepting Through Thorns for publication. My deep appreciation as well to the rest of the Iguana team, especially the publisher, Meghan Behse, and Paula Chiarcos, a patient and rigorous editor. I hasten to add that any remaining factual errors and anachronisms in the text are solely due to my own carelessness and sometimes – in the interest of a good story – intransigence.

Many friends, and even some strangers, donated to my Indiegogo crowdfunding campaign to help cover publishing costs. Their contributions were appreciated as a vote of confidence as much as a budgetary boost. Thanks to you all, and happy reading. Also, many thanks to Beth Kallman Werner of Author Connections for her professional marketing advice.

Finally, I have to credit Al Rosa Co-op, my home for five years from the late 70s to the early 80s, as a major source of inspiration. During that period, the Co-op saw a constant turnover of twenty or so rent-paying residents (of which I was one) along with a much larger number of consorts, friends and crashers both congenial and obnoxious. All of these folks at various times squeezed in around our wire spool kitchen table, furniture which unaccountably makes an appearance in *Through Thorns*. Otherwise, there are no intentional similarities between the remembered proceedings and personalities of Al Rosa and those of Berkman House described in this book.

CPSIA information can be obtained
at www.ICGtesting.com
Printed in the USA
BVHW071949031021
618016BV00003B/13